Here to Make Friends

"*Not Here To Make Friends* is a prose ceremony—at which I was glad to accept every page. A superb third episode in a journey with drama more vivid and romance more compelling than anything you'll see on TV."
Xavier Rubetzki Noonan, *Bachelor of Hearts Podcast*

"*Not Here to Make Friends* is wonderfully funny, deeply moving, and whip-smart. Lily and Murray's sometimes heartbreaking, sometimes hilarious love story is so irresistible it will have you turning the page faster than a reality TV romance breaks up in real life. Rich with diversity and characters you genuinely care about, *Not Here to Make Friends* is a satisfying, pitch-perfect cherry on top of a perfect series."
Amy Hutton, author of *Sit, Stay, Love*

Also by Jodi McAlister

Here for the Right Reasons
Can I Steal You for a Second?

Not Here to Make Friends

A Novel

Jodi McAlister

ATRIA PAPERBACK

New York   London   Toronto   Sydney   New Delhi

ATRIA
PAPERBACK

An Imprint of Simon & Schuster, LLC
1230 Avenue of the Americas
New York, NY 10020

First Atria Paperback edition June 2024

ATRIA PAPERBACK and colophon are trademarks of Simon & Schuster, LLC

Simon & Schuster: Celebrating 100 Years of Publishing in 2024

For information about special discounts for bulk purchases, please contact Simon & Schuster Special Sales at 1-866-506-1949 or business@simonandschuster.com.

The Simon & Schuster Speakers Bureau can bring authors to your live event. For more information or to book an event, contact the Simon & Schuster Speakers Bureau at 1-866-248-3049 or visit our website at www.simonspeakers.com.

Interior design by Midland Typesetters

Manufactured in the United States of America

1 3 5 7 9 10 8 6 4 2

Library of Congress Control Number: 2024932813

ISBN: 978-1-6680-7526-5 (pbk)
ISBN: 978-1-6680-7527-2 (ebook)

For *The Bachelor/ette* Australia franchise. I have written
so much about you already, fictionally, academically,
and episodically—but if I dedicate an entire book
to you, then will you let me consult for you?

Prologue

Murray

"Okay, Brett," I said. "It's all come down to today. How are you feeling?"

Brett shifted uncomfortably on the stool in front of the green screen. "Good. I think."

"You think?" Lily said. "This is one of the last times you have to see this guy's ugly face—" she jabbed me with her elbow "—and you only *think* you feel good?"

He cracked a smile and relaxed, just a little. "Okay, I definitely feel good."

"As you should." Lily smiled sunnily at him. "You're about to ride off into the sunset with the love of your life. You should feel great."

"Exactly," I said, in my most reassuring voice. "Now, there's nothing to worry about, okay, mate? This interview is going to work just the same as all the others. Look at me and Lily, not at the camera. Remember to answer in full sentences, because the audience isn't going to hear our questions, just your answers."

I'd given him the exact same spiel every single time we'd sat down to record an interview during Season Ten of *Marry Me, Juliet*. Every single time Brett had either looked directly down the lens, given one-word answers, or both. Brett wasn't the worst Romeo that Lily and I had ever worked with, but he was certainly one of the most frustrating.

"The only special thing you need to remember is that at this point in the episode, the audience won't know who you've chosen," Lily said. "So instead of 'I've fallen in love with Mary-Ellen,' say something like 'I've fallen in love with this woman, and I can't wait to tell her.' That way we can make the fact you've picked her a big reveal."

"CJ."

"Hmmm?"

"I've fallen in love with CJ," Brett said. "Not Mary-Ellen."

"What?" Lily and I said at the same time.

Brett shrugged. "Mary-Ellen's hot, but CJ'll fit into my life better. We're more compatible."

Lily and I exchanged glances.

We were experts at this. Literal experts. We'd been working on the Romeo and Juliet shows for eight years. We could tell when two people were into each other. Usually long before they could.

But it didn't take an expert to see how Brett felt about Mary-Ellen. You could be an alien from another galaxy where they didn't have a concept of attraction and you'd be able to tell.

"Love isn't just about compatibility, mate," I said. "Take it from someone who's divorced. You can be compatible as hell and it still might fall apart."

"And take it from someone who's happily married." Lily waved the hand with her wedding ring at him. "Compatibility is great, sure, but you can be compatible with lots of people. Chemistry is rare. A real connection—that's even rarer."

"We don't want to influence you or sway you," I said.

I was lying through my teeth. Our entire story plan revolved around Brett and Mary-Ellen being soulmates. If we couldn't talk him into picking her, we were going to have to go back to square one and re-craft the whole damn season.

"But Lily and I have been with you every step of this journey. We've watched you with all the Juliets. It's obvious that what you have with Mary-Ellen is special."

"Absolutely," Lily said. "It takes a lot for two cynics like us to get invested in a love story, but we've been all-in on you and Mary-Ellen for weeks now."

Brett folded his arms defensively, his massive shoulders rippling.

"This is your decision, mate." I emphasised *your* as much as I could without getting cartoonish. "We'd never dream of standing in your way."

"But we also don't want to see you make a terrible mistake," Lily said, injecting a soothing tone into her voice. "So many people stumble at this last hurdle. They get scared. They start thinking about what's good for them on paper instead of what they actually *want*."

She leaned forward. "Going after what you want is the bravest thing you can do," she said. "So tell me, Brett: are you ready to be brave?"

"I can't believe that didn't work," I said.

"I don't understand how it didn't work," Lily said. "'Are you ready to be brave?' *always* works."

I held the production office door open for her and she walked through, dumping her folder and her tablet on our desk. At the beginning of the season, it had been two distinct desks, hers and mine, but, as usual, it hadn't taken long for it to turn into one communal mess.

She pulled out her compact, the antique silver one her husband Jeff had given her when she turned thirty, looked at herself in the mirror, and then handed it to me to hold. "It's not us, right?" she asked, reapplying her signature red lipstick, which twelve years of friendship had taught me was called *Blood of My Enemies*. "It's him."

"It's definitely him." I snapped the compact shut and handed it back to her.

"Who?" Suzette asked. She and Carrie, our two junior producers, were sitting in front of one of the monitors, going through some of yesterday's footage.

"Brett," I said. "He's picking CJ."

"No!" Carrie exclaimed.

"But they're so stilted with each other!" Suzette said. "And he and Mary-Ellen—"

She gestured towards the wall, where we'd stuck up a poster concept for the season. It was an image from Brett and Mary-Ellen's final date, where they'd gone swimming in a forest and kissed under a waterfall. The waterfall dominated the poster, but you could just see their two silhouettes behind it, locked in what we'd all agreed read as a deeply passionate embrace.

"Wait," Carrie said suddenly. "Does this mean I win the kitty?"

"No!" Lily groaned. "I had so many plans for that money!"

"Like what?" Suzette asked.

"I was going to buy Jeff a new suit. He's been wearing the same one to all our red-carpet events since I met him. It's getting embarrassing."

Lily and I had been running the kitty since we'd taken over as showrunners for the three Romeo and Juliet shows the previous year. At the beginning of every season, every producer threw some money into a communal pool. We were all primarily responsible for producing a few contestants (this year, the four of us had five contestants each). If one of your contestants won the show, then you won the kitty.

The last of my contestants had been eliminated two episodes ago, but Mary-Ellen was one of Lily's and CJ belonged to Carrie, who was now dancing around the room. "I've never won the kitty before," she said. "I'm going to take Nisha out to the fanciest dinner in the fucking world. I'm going to pay my car rego. I'm going to buy a bottle of wine that costs more than six dollars."

"Don't get too far ahead of yourself," Lily said. "It's not *that* much money."

"I don't care," Carrie said, punching the air. "I won. Pay me, bitch."

"Fine, fine." Lily took out her phone.

"When you've finished doing whatever this is—" I gestured towards Carrie "—we need to get to work. We have to go back to the beginning and work out how we're going

5

to re-edit the whole season if we don't want the audience to come away from the finale wildly disappointed."

"I'll be back in a sec," Lily said, touching me lightly on the shoulder. "I've got about a million missed calls."

I nodded. She slipped out of the room. I took a marker out of the cup on the desk and walked over to the whiteboard. "Any ideas?" I asked Suzette and Carrie.

"Could we turn Brett into the villain?" Carrie suggested.

I wrote *Brett = evil?* on the board, but I was already shaking my head. "He's too milquetoast to be a satisfying villain. He hasn't done anything offensive enough for it to land."

"What if we make CJ the villain?" Suzette said. "Like a wicked queen luring Brett away from his one true love?"

CJ = evil? I wrote on the board.

"I don't know if we have the footage to pull that off," Carrie said. "CJ's never said a bad word about anyone. The worst she's been is a bit standoffish."

"Can we do something with that?" I wrote *CJ = ice queen?* on the board. "If we can get a really soppy love confession out of her, we might be able to make that play—the ice queen finally melting."

Carrie scribbled some notes. "She's never cried in an interview. If I can get her to do it, we might be able to sell it."

"But what about Mary-Ellen?" Suzette said. "Even if we can build up CJ and Brett as a viable romance, how are we going to get people to believe that he should pick her over Mary-Ellen?"

None of us had a good answer for that.

I sent Suzette and Carrie back to their desks after a while, when it became clear we were just going around in circles, and folded my arms and stared at the whiteboard. I'd scribbled down a list of suggestions—*ME = not ready for love? ME = lust not love? ME = too similar?*—but none of them seemed quite right.

Because they *weren't* right. We couldn't spin this as the right decision for Brett, because it . . . wasn't.

I uncapped the marker again. *B = making huge mistake?* I wrote.

I could just imagine what the network would say to that. "An ambiguous ending?" Greg McDonagh—the executive VP of unscripted programming, referred to exclusively on our set as Fucking Greg—would roar. "That's not what the heartland want!"

Just the thought of Fucking Greg yelling about the heartland audience set off my chronic eye-twitch. Lily and I had been agitating for a far greater level of racially and culturally diverse casting for years now, but every time we pitched it, Fucking Greg started yelling about the heartland and calling us the woke police.

Although . . .

I glanced over at the wall, where we'd put up headshots of our potential Romeos for Season Eleven. Lily and I had deliberately selected three men of colour: Charlie Vu, a cancer scientist; Dylan Jayasinghe Mellor, an Olympic gold medallist; and Chris Gregory, a TV gardener with a cult following. They were all great candidates, but the odds of Fucking Greg throwing our briefing packet back across the desk and telling us we needed to play to the heartland and find a "boy next door"—that is, cast someone white—were high, no matter how we tried to sell it.

But what if we could absolutely, positively, one hundred per cent promise him an un-ambiguous dopamine hit of an ending?

My storytelling galaxy brain started to kick into gear.

Lily and I had purposely sabotaged a season before. It had paid off.

What if we did it again?

There was no way we could get a fairytale ending out of this Brett/CJ/Mary-Ellen fiasco, not if Brett picked CJ. So what if we steered into the skid? What if we let this ending feel awkward and wrong and weird, and used it as leverage to do a more diversely cast season, with a promise of the world's most satisfying payoff? What if—

"Murray?"

I turned. "I've just had a—"

"Murray." Lily's face was ashen, her eyes wide and wild, *Blood of My Enemies* standing out in sharp relief against her skin. "Murray—Murray—"

I took two quick steps and caught her just before her knees gave way. "What is it? What's happened?"

"Jeff," she gasped, fingers digging into my shoulders. "There was an accident. It's Jeff."

1

Murray

The fourth of my contestants left the makeshift studio we'd set up in the hotel conference room. I ticked off the name *Cecilia James*, closed my eyes, and allowed myself a quick, wistful dream about the hotel pillows.

All the cast and crew on Season Eleven of *Marry Me, Juliet* had just done two weeks of mandatory hotel quarantine before on-set filming started tonight. I'd been hoping to use the time to sleep. It had been a foolish, naïve hope—there was always another fire to put out when you were running a show, especially when you were running it on your own—but there was still something to be said about doing your job from a luxurious hotel bed.

"Who's next, Murray?" Saurav, the camera operator, asked me.

I opened my eyes. The right one immediately started twitching. I pressed two fingers into the muscle beside it. "The ringer. The supervillain. The one we don't know anything about."

9

"How did that even happen?" Indigo the gaffer adjusted one of the lights. "I thought you had this whole season mapped out. I's dotted. T's crossed. The works."

"Fucking Greg. As usual."

It hadn't been easy, talking Fucking Greg into letting me do this season, but I'd done it. I'd presented him with proposal after proposal and report after report on the audience reaction to Brett not picking Mary-Ellen, and eventually he'd cracked. "All right, fine," he'd growled. "You can have your woke season—*if* you promise me the fairytale. And it better rate its tits off, O'Connell, or you're done."

I should have expected something like this. Signing off on a million documents on our season plans and then deciding at the last minute to throw in some top-of-his-head wildcard was classic Greg.

But I hadn't expected it. Maybe because I was on my own now, doing all the work that Lily and I used to do together. Maybe because I didn't think it could get any harder than the pandemic restrictions were already making it. Or maybe it was just because I was an idiot—but I hadn't seen it coming at all.

Greg hadn't even bothered to call me. He'd done it in an email, which I'd received forty-five minutes after entering hotel quarantine. *O'Connell, I've found you the perfect villain for the latest MMJ. A real spicy meatball.*

I'd put my head between my knees to take some deep breaths before replying. *Perhaps for next season? We're all set for S11. All our cast and crew are now in quarantine, so we can't change any of our plans.*

Already sorted, Greg sent back. *Spicy meatball's been in lockdown since this morning.*

I can't just add another contestant into the mix, I replied. *Pandemic restrictions mean there are strict limits on how many people we can take into the bubble. We already had to get government permits to take this many.*

Cut one of the other girls, he wrote. *You're keeping the spicy meatball. She'll be ratings gold. Everyone will love to hate her. Make sure she stays until at least episode eight.*

He'd sent a follow-up two minutes later: *You're welcome.* 😊

The first few emails were bad enough, but it was the last one that was really responsible for the flare-up of my chronic eye-twitch. Fucking Greg.

The twitch wasn't abating, so I tried closing my right eye and pressing my fingers into the eyelid. I balanced my tablet on my knee and scrolled through it with my free hand to get to the contestant information breakdown sheet. We had these for all our contestants, and they were detailed. I could probably ghostwrite the autobiographies of the fourteen other women who would be competing for the Romeo's heart (and of twenty-four-year-old TikTok balloon artist Kristal, who'd burst into loud sobs when I'd broken it to her over Zoom that she would not, in fact, be on this season of *Marry Me, Juliet*, despite already being in quarantine, because "the network decided to go in a different direction").

I didn't even have a headshot for the spicy meatball. I hadn't had a breakdown for her at all until last night, and it was only three lines long.

Name: Lily Fireball.

Age: 25.

Occupation: Entrepreneur.

Lily.

There were two pangs in my heart, like there was whenever I came across anyone with her name. One of pain. One of guilt.

I should send a message to Thuong at some point before the madness of the First Night Party kicked off. Thuong, a successful fashion designer, was another close friend of Lily's—but more importantly, she was married to Lily's brother Michael, which meant Lily hadn't been able to disappear on her the way she'd disappeared on me. I checked in with her every month or so to see how Lily was doing.

I flicked WhatsApp open. *Any updates on our favourite drama queen?* I typed.

The last message I had from Thuong (not counting around eighty-seven baby photos) was a response to much the same question, sent a few weeks ago.

Still changing the subject every time Michael or I ask her how she's feeling, she replied now. *Still the reigning undefeated international queen of avoidance.*

I closed my eyes for a second. The fact that I was still included on the list of things Lily was avoiding was an open wound.

Every day I went to work, I was conscious of the bare desk across from mine. Every meeting I sat in, I felt the empty chair beside me. Every suggestion I made, I found myself waiting for her to "yes, and" it, to build on it, to make it better.

Tell her I miss her, I sent to Thuong.

Then I let out a long breath, tilting my head from side to side to stretch out my neck. I didn't have time to feel my feelings now. I had a job to do.

Two people's jobs, in fact. Everything was so much more difficult without her. She would have known just which buttons to press to get Fucking Greg to butt out.

A production assistant tapped at the door. This one was Tim, I thought, but there were two gangly white boys named Tim and Tom and I could never keep them straight. "Murray, Lily is here."

"Okay. Send her in."

Tim/Tom hesitated. "Um . . ."

"Tom," I said, taking a stab in the dark, "it's been a long day. We've got a long night ahead of us, and we're on a tight schedule. Just send her in."

I flicked back to the notes I'd made on the meagre contestant information breakdown. *Entrepreneur* was code for *wannabe girlboss,* which was code for *wannabe influencer.* The *Fireball* of it all supported that theory. If this Lily was not in fact descended from a long line of Fireballs, the name was clearly some kind of targeted marketing thing. She didn't seem to have any social media profiles, but that might be on purpose, to start building her brand identity from a blank slate with our glossy promo photos.

I flicked over to my list of questions. We had some standard ones that everyone answered—basics like "Why do you want to be on *Marry Me, Juliet*?"—but also some tailored to the archetype we were planning to fit the contestants into.

My best bet for this initial interview, given I knew nothing about this woman except that Fucking Greg wanted her to be the villain, was to try and plant the seeds of a classic not-here-for-the-right-reasons narrative. Eight episodes was a long time to drag one of those out, so we'd have to play a deception angle. We'd show her telling the Romeo over and over again how into him she was, while making it clear in all her other words and actions that she was just there for money and fame and brand-building.

And then, come episode eight, we'd do a big reveal. Expose the long con. The ritual humiliation of the villain was a classic reality TV trope.

"Tom!" I barked, not looking up as I scrolled down to my villain questions. "What are you waiting for? Send her in!"

"Murray, like I've told you a thousand times, that's Tim."

My head snapped up.

"Is your eye still bothering you?" Lily asked. "Are you doing any of the things you're supposed to? Taking magnesium? Cutting back on caffeine?"

I couldn't respond. My thought processes had completely short-circuited.

Lily's heels clicked against the floor as she walked across the room and settled herself on the stool in front of the green screen, crossing her ankles and hooking them around the crossbar. She was wearing the most ridiculous dress I'd ever seen: bright yellow, the colour of a daffodil, with sleeves that sat just off her shoulder. It was short at the front, secured by a wrap tie, but the back was ludicrously enormous, with a train so long that it puddled around the foot of the stool.

She took her compact out of some hidden pocket in the masses of skirts, the same one she always carried, the one Jeff had given her. She looked at herself briefly, then snapped it shut and glanced down at her train. "Could someone straighten my dress? I don't think it's being shown to its full effect."

"Everybody out."

"Murray," Saurav said quietly, "I know this is a lot, but if we don't get this now, we'll eat into the shoot time."

"Out! Everybody! Right now!"

The crew didn't make me tell them again.

One corner of Lily's mouth curled upwards. She was wearing *Blood of My Enemies,* same as always. "The First Night Party hasn't even started and you're already behind schedule?" she said. "Standards are slipping."

"Lily, what the fuck?!"

People usually started backing away from me when I used that tone of voice, but her smile just deepened. "Nice to see you too, Murray."

I wanted to scream at her.

I wanted to throw my arms around her and bury my face in her hair and crush her so hard to my chest that she'd complain that she couldn't breathe and that the cheap material of my polo shirt touching her skin was a human rights violation.

"Lily," I said, fighting to speak in a more controlled tone, "what the fuck are you doing here?"

She shrugged, one mostly bare shoulder rising and falling. Years of reading contestants' body language had taught me that a shrug was usually a passive gesture, an abdication of thought and responsibility, a physical I-don't-know-it-just-happened—but not when Lily did it.

"After how hard we fought to get this season off the ground," she said, "did you really think I would miss it?"

I stared at her.

She raised an eyebrow.

15

Blood was rushing in my ears. I could hear my own heartbeat, like there was someone with a hammer inside my head, pounding against my skull.

"Do you like the dress?" She smoothed a hand along her enormous yellow skirt. "It's one of Thuong's designs. She made it for me a few years ago and I've never had the opportunity to wear it."

"It's ridiculous."

She clutched at her heart in mock horror. "How dare you?"

"Stop," I bit out.

I was not a man who lost his composure easily. I got angry, and frustrated, and had definitely been known to lose my temper—but when push came to shove, I kept it together. No matter what was happening, I thought my way through. I solved the problem. I figured it out. I was a master at compartmentalising. No one was better at setting aside their feelings and getting the job done than I was. When I'd been going through my divorce, none of my colleagues had a single clue how raw and rough and vulnerable I was.

Except for Lily.

Lily.

Lily was *here*.

Looking at her, sitting there, with that fucking *smile* on her face, my brain stopped functioning.

And then it started racing, ricocheting between two images faster and faster, trying to reconcile them.

A year ago. The night of Jeff's funeral. After everyone had left, after even Thuong and Michael and their new baby had left, when it was just her and me.

Her agonised, broken sobs, like someone had put a hook down her throat and was yanking the sounds out of her. *Don't go, don't go. Don't leave me alone.*

I'd put my arms around her, pressing her into me, as if I could hold her together if I just held her tight enough. *I won't. I won't leave you.*

I knew her words weren't for me, but I held them close, held her close, her face warm and damp against my throat.

She'd made me leave the next morning. *I'm sorry,* she'd told me, eyes red above one of the dramatic satin dressing gowns she loved so much.

Lily, I'd replied, reaching out and clasping her hand, *you have nothing to be sorry for. I'm here for you. Always.*

She looked up at me pleadingly. *I need some time and space alone to work through this. I need to go no-contact with the world for a while, I think. Even you. Is that all right?*

Of course it is. Whatever you need.

Thank you. She'd squeezed my fingers.

Then she'd let go, and I hadn't heard a single word from her since.

Until now.

"Lily," I said, "are you all right?"

"Do I not seem all right?"

"Do you really want me to answer that question? Do you want me to sit here, think about it, say 'hmmm, yes, this all seems totally fine and normal?'"

What she was actually doing, I had no idea, but I knew exactly how I'd frame this story if I was telling it on TV. A bereaved woman cuts off her support system, completely reinvents herself, and decides to become a reality TV villain? That was the clearest, most obvious cry for help—

"This is not a cry for help, if that's what you're thinking."

God-fucking-damn it.

"I'm not here because I've lost my mind."

If she'd said that to me on any other day of our long friendship, I probably would have believed her. Lily Ong knew herself, and she did not lie.

But looking at Lily Fireball was like looking at an uncanny valley version of the real Lily. The shrewd, calculating expression in her eyes was pure Lily Ong, but it was like she was looking at me from behind a mask, a wall erected between her and me.

"I'm here because I need to be," she said, "and because *you* need me to be."

What the fuck did *that* mean?

"This season has to be a ratings draw if Fucking Greg will ever let you cast diversely again." Her tone was businesslike, as if we'd sat down for some ordinary meeting on some ordinary day. "You don't just need romance. You need conflict. You need drama. You need something to make the story go—and nothing does that like a really good villain."

"I'm aware. I've cast accordingly. That doesn't explain why you're here."

"Because no one will be as good at it as me."

She tossed her hair over her shoulder. Lily had always had beautiful hair, long and black and shiny, but the hair and makeup team had done something to it that gave it an extra lustre under the lights.

"We always planned for this season to be the greatest one ever," she said. "To do that, it needs the greatest villain ever. I understand all the right notes to hit, all the right buttons to push. No one can get the job done like I can."

I rubbed at my temple. I could barely process what she was saying.

"Lily Fireball is going to be a monster." A gleeful glint came into her eyes. "No one watching will be able to shut up about what a monster she is. And they'll tune in every week, just to hate her more. She'll be a legendary icon of loathsomeness, the kind that people will talk about for years."

Years of living off coffee, sugar, and whatever I could scavenge from craft services at two in the morning had given me an iron stomach. But hearing her say that, I felt sick.

"You got us the season we always wanted," she said. "I'm going to get us the ratings."

"And then what?"

She looked at me—not blankly, not like she didn't understand what I was saying, but with a deliberate expressionlessness. "And then *what*?"

"What happens next, in this plan of yours? Going on reality TV isn't something you can just walk back. This isn't some temp job you can dip into for six weeks then step out of again and go back to your real life."

There was an ache at the base of my skull, the sign that a massive tension headache was building. "If you do this, then this is who you are to the world, forever. Lily Fireball. Twenty-five—nice ten-year age discount you've given yourself there, by the way. Entrepreneur. Nation's biggest bitch."

"And there'll be abuse and death threats, et cetera, et cetera." She sounded as calm as if she were discussing the weather, side-stepping what I was actually saying as easily as if it was a puddle on a footpath. A year away clearly hadn't blunted her skills. "I'm well aware of the consequences. I've orchestrated some of them. Karmically, it's probably my turn—although the bonus racism and anti-Asian bullshit it'll come with will be, I acknowledge, an extra little treat just for me."

She tapped her fingernails against her knee. They were painted the same red as her lips, pristine and perfect.

She wasn't wearing her wedding ring. It was the first time I'd seen her without it since her actual wedding.

"But we both know how good I am at ruining people's lives," she said. "Now I'll just be doing it in public."

Her tone was cheerful. Of all the things in the world: cheerful.

I had a sudden flashback to that last day I'd seen her. When I'd got into my car to leave her house, the morning after the funeral, I'd caught a glimpse of myself in the rearview mirror. Lily's lipstick was smeared all over my shirt collar, like someone had tried to slit my throat.

I'd glanced back at her. Standing on her doorstep in her dressing gown, arms wrapped around herself, she'd looked so small.

Everything in me had told me to open my car door. To go back to her. To hold her a while longer.

But I'd listened to her. I always listened to her. She'd told me she wanted me to go, that she wanted time and space, and

Lily Ong had always been a woman who knew exactly what she wanted.

So I'd gone. I'd done what she asked, let her go no-contact, and waited for her to come back to me when she was ready. I waited for my best friend, my partner, the person I trusted most in the world, to take her place beside me again, where she belonged.

I'd made the wrong decision.

I wasn't going to make the same mistake again.

"No," I said.

She raised an eyebrow. "No?"

"No." I pulled out my phone. "No, we are not doing this, Lily. *You* are not doing this."

Fucking Greg answered on the second ring. "O'Connell! How did you like my surprise?"

"Hi Greg!" Lily called brightly.

I glared at her. She looked back, completely unabashed.

"Am I right, or am I right?" he said. I hated everything about the tone in his voice.

"Look, this isn't going to work, Greg," I said. "Trust me on this. I'm not sending Lily in."

"Yes, you fucking are!" he exclaimed. "She's just the spicy meatball you need, O'Connell. If you can't see that, I've got serious questions about your judgement."

I pressed two fingers into my twitching eye and searched for a line that would work. "It's not the right tone for the season. We've talked about what we're going for, what'll bring us those ratings. High romance. Real fairytale shit. Throwing such a big villain into the mix will—"

"Only make it better! Your plans are full of sugar. They need some spice to balance the nice. What fairy tale doesn't have an evil queen?"

God-fucking-damn it.

Lily folded her hands in her lap, the picture of innocence, but she couldn't fool me. Those were her words coming out of Greg's mouth.

"Fine," I said. "You want an all-time legendary villain, I'll give you one. I've cast some women we can produce into that role. But it can't be Lily."

"Who better than Lily? She knows the show inside out. Plus, isn't this season all about diversity? She's diverse! What is she again? Vietnamese? I always forget."

I knew for a fact that Fucking Greg had been through the network's Diversity and Inclusion training program seven times. It clearly wasn't enough.

I switched tack. "What about the contestants from past seasons? Lily and I have worked with every Romeo and Juliet contestant for the past nine years. They'll all know who she is the second they see her on TV. If one of them talks to the press, it'll be obvious she's a network plant."

"Already on it. The lawyers are real good at NDAs now—and we freed up some budget for hush money."

How the hell had Lily got him to do *that*?

"Greg," I said, "I think she's having a nervous—"

"Another call!" he announced. "I gave you everything else you wanted, O'Connell. You're giving me this. Do your job."

"It's—"

The line went dead.

"I'm not having a nervous breakdown," Lily said, a note of annoyance entering her voice.

"What the fuck else am I meant to think?" I snapped. "How would you read this, if you were in my shoes?"

"I know it's not exactly orthodox, and it's a bit of a surprise," she said, "but I really am here to help you."

A bit of a fucking surprise?!

There was a roaring sound in my ears. In the last part of my mind capable of any kind of thought, I noted that she hadn't actually answered the question.

"I'm looking forward to working with you again, Murray," Lily said. "I've missed you."

No matter how hard I pushed the base of my thumb into my right eye, it wouldn't stop twitching.

"Have you missed me?" she asked.

With my one good eye, I looked at her. She was still wearing the same impenetrable expression.

"What kind of a question is that?" I said.

She didn't say anything. She just raised one of her eyebrows slightly, the way she always did when she was riding a silence with a contestant, waiting for them to crack and tell her their secrets.

I didn't say anything either. She might be able to produce Fucking Greg like he was a contestant, but she wasn't going to do it to me.

"Shall we get started?" she said. "I know you have a schedule to keep, and you're going to need this interview for my intro package."

I didn't move.

"Fine. I'll interview myself."

She shifted her voice into a lower register, mimicking me. "Why did you come on *Marry Me, Juliet,* Lily Fireball?"

Then she shifted into another voice—one that had the pitch and the cadence of her own voice, but a different tone entirely. "I'm Lily Fireball, and I came on *Marry Me, Juliet* for one important reason," she purred, looking at me rather than the camera, the perfect interview eyeline. "I came here to get my man."

2

Lily

Thirteen years ago

I almost laughed when I spotted him. Of all the conference rooms in all the world, what were the odds the boy from the bar would be in this one?

I'd noticed his hair first. Both times, last night and this morning. It was spectacular: thick and dark, wavy in a way that suggested it would be curly if he cut it shorter.

Last night his hair had been spectacular, anyway. This morning, it looked like he'd rolled right off the bar floor and into the *Desert Island Castaway* crew briefing.

It didn't matter. I still had the strongest urge to tangle my fingers in it—and tug.

If I were a different kind of person—the kind that believed in fate, or destiny, or the universe, or anything besides myself—I might read him being here as a sign. Like there was some higher power trying to fling this boy and his great hair in my path.

I wasn't that person, though, so it just made me curious. What was the boy from the bar doing here?

25

He had chosen a seat about two thirds of the way back. There were a cluster of people sitting in the middle of the row, all talking to each other, but he was one seat from the end, by himself, slightly slumped down, satchel on the chair beside him.

Maybe he was new. Like me. That was the seat I would have chosen too—not too close to the front (lest you look like a kiss-ass), not too close to the back (lest you look like a troublemaker), but more committal, somehow, than sitting perfectly in the middle. More sensible, too, than trying to attach yourself to an established group—better to hang back and take the lay of the land before you made any moves.

He rifled through his satchel. I expected him to take out his phone, but instead, he pulled out a half-crushed plastic water bottle. It was mostly empty, but he downed the last of it, then exhaled and rubbed his temple.

I thought for a few moments.

Then I filled two cups at the water cooler and crossed the room. "How's your head?" I asked, offering him one.

He looked up at me. "What?"

It was a simple, blunt, almost brusque response.

I didn't mind that. I preferred it, in fact. It saved time when people got to the point.

The fact he didn't recognise me stung, though. "I was at the same bar as you last night. I was sitting in the corner, having a quiet drink, minding my own business, and you stumbled by on your way to the bathroom."

It was the director's cut of the story. I didn't need to mention that I'd been watching him long beforehand, nursing my glass of wine while I waited for the perpetually late Thuong, pretending to the world that I was scrolling through my phone—and pretending to myself that I had questions about his haircare regimen.

"Did I?" the boy from the bar asked blearily.

I offered him the water again. This time, he took it. "Thank you." His voice was croaky, and his eyes were bloodshot, the right one twitching just slightly.

It would be a mistake to take him not remembering me personally. He was clearly painfully hungover.

But that didn't mean I couldn't *remind* him. "You stopped on your way back. Stared at me for three full seconds without blinking. Then you put your hand on the table, said, 'I love your lipstick,' and walked away."

I watched him process the information.

I'd watched him do that last night too. One of his friends had been telling a story, and others at the table had jumped in right away, but he'd taken a moment before responding. Not a long moment, but long enough to make it clear that he actually listened when people talked.

His hair might have been the thing I'd noticed first, but the listening: that was why I'd kept watching.

"Shit, I'm sorry," he said. "I don't make a habit of accosting women in public. I was pretty drunk last night—it was my birthday, my mates kept buying rounds—but that's no excuse."

"Happy birthday," I said. "How old?"

"Twenty-two."

Same as me. He was probably straight out of university too. Maybe we'd even been at some of the same media careers information sessions.

Probably not, though. I would have remembered a boy with such pullable hair.

"I really am sorry," he said. "I promise it won't happen again. If you're worried about shipping off to an island for three months with someone who's going to follow you around and harass you, please don't be."

"I'm not worried."

"I'm glad to hear that, but I'm still sorry."

"It was helpful, actually." I looked him right in the eye. "I'm trying out a new shade, and I needed an honest opinion on whether or not it works. My friend told me it did, but she also hasn't told me she's been sleeping with my brother for three months, so I'm not sure how much I trust her."

Another moment. Another pause for thought.

Then the boy from the bar laughed.

"Glad I could be of assistance," he said. "For the record: assuming it's the same lipstick you're wearing today, it looks great."

A frisson went up my spine, but I didn't let it show. He hadn't earned that yet.

"Noted," I said instead, keeping my tone breezy. "It's called *Blood of My Enemies,* in case there's some lucky lady in your life you want to buy it for."

He chuckled again, but didn't take the bait.

Fair enough. It had been a clumsy attempt to figure out if he was single. I wouldn't have taken the bait either.

Instead, he moved his satchel from the seat beside him. "Want to sit?"

"Sure."

I sat, putting my handbag on the floor. The boy from the bar offered me his hand. "I'm Murray. O'Connell. Production assistant. First time on a show, in case that isn't obvious."

I shook it. "Lily. Ong. Also a production assistant. Also my first time on a show."

"Really?"

That question surprised me. "Yes, really," I said. "I don't lie unless I absolutely have to."

That was a line I tried not to cross. Most people seemed to have been born with them: lines that demarcated good and bad, right and wrong, appropriate and inappropriate. I hadn't been, not really, so I'd had to draw my own. Not lying was one of them.

Murray studied me. Even with his bloodshot eyes, he had a very intense gaze. I had the sudden feeling that, if I let him look at me long enough, he'd figure out exactly what I'd been thinking when I watched him across the bar.

"What?" I asked. "Do I look like a liar?"

"No. You just don't seem like a newbie."

It was my turn to study him. "What do I seem like?"

"You seem," he said, "like someone who knows what they're doing."

3

Murray

It should have been the most comfortable limo ride of my career. Usually, when we shot the drive out to the First Night Party, we'd have a cameraperson in the back with us. They'd take one of the seats, crammed in beside the contestants, and I'd be lying on the floor so I wasn't in shot, staring straight up at the limo roof so I didn't accidentally look up anyone's skirt.

This season, though, our pandemic-reduced personnel numbers meant we didn't have enough camera operators to have them both in the limos and on set to shoot the red-carpet entrances. The entrances were obviously more important, so we'd sent all the camera crew ahead to the Villa, and were shooting the limo rides using lipstick cameras instead.

So in some ways, yes, it was one of the more comfortable limo rides of my career. I was sitting upright.

But I was sitting next to Lily.

"Long time no see, Murray." She squeezed herself between me and one of the other Juliets and draped her enormous yellow skirt across my lap.

I gave her a look.

She looked back, unabashed, that implacable mask firmly in place.

A jolt of anger stabbed through me. She knew exactly what she was doing to me—and she was just fucking sitting there and *doing it anyway.*

Justifying her presence to the crew had been a nightmare. They'd had so many questions at the briefing that I'd had to either invent answers for or handwave away, and they were going to have more. One more thing I had to worry about, on top of the giant pile of responsibilities I was already trying to manage.

That was nothing, though, compared to the way looking at her made me feel.

How could she do this? How could she turn up here like this after a year of total silence and expect me not to completely lose my shit?

"Get that off me." I shoved the mass of her skirt off my lap. I was not a big man, and she was not a big woman, but there wasn't room for her and me and her dress and my mood in this limo, not even close.

"Where else would you like me to put it?"

That tone in her voice. That *fucking* tone in her voice.

"Lily. Move it."

"I can't just vanish it into thin air. Either it goes on your lap, or I take it off and I walk in there in heels and a G-string. I'm fine with either. Your choice."

I glared at her.

She smiled back, spreading her skirt over my lap like it was a blanket we were sharing.

We used to do that all the time on night shoots on *Desert Island Castaway*, out in the wilderness. On breaks, we'd huddle together in our giant black puffer jackets under whatever blanket or coat or tarp we could find, keeping each other warm against the bitter cold.

It had been so easy then. Just her and me and vanishingly little responsibility, under the vast blackness of the sky and the spray of the stars.

Together.

"What are you looking at?" she snapped at one of the other women.

Lily Ong, producer, rarely spoke like that to female contestants. "Sometimes men respond well to it," she'd told me once. "But if I yell at a woman, it almost always reads as bitchiness."

That was the Lily I'd huddled under a blanket with. I knew that Lily. I understood her. I trusted her. I loved her.

But Lily Fireball . . .

Lily Fireball had all my Lily's knowledge, and she was going to use it to burn down her entire life, and *she was going to make me watch.*

"Can you tell us who the Romeo is yet?" one of the other Juliets asked.

I dug my knuckles into the meat of my thigh and shoved the feelings down. There were four other contestants in this limo I was responsible for. No matter what Lily was doing, I still had to do my job.

"You'll find out soon enough," I replied.

The woman who'd asked was Amanda Mitchell, the petite blonde mechanic we'd cast basically the second her application had crossed our desk. She was Greg-bait—someone he'd look at and say, "Oh, yes, *she'll* play to the heartland audience!."

Heather Vincent, the blonde on Lily's other side, was also Greg-bait, although she'd probably just develop into a low-level mean girl. Amanda had the potential to be significantly more interesting. She had a strong narrative arc we could develop: she'd just broken up with her ex, and was trying to put herself back together.

That ex, I knew from research, was a woman, although Amanda hadn't disclosed that. I didn't blame her. The show had done terribly by its queer contestants in the past. One of the things Lily and I had on our to-do list when we took over from our old shithead boss Tony was to find a queer inter-contestant love story we could portray in a genuinely positive and romantic way. It hadn't happened yet, but I had high hopes for Amanda. There were at least two other bisexual women going into the Villa. If she happened to fall for one of them, I'd be delighted.

. . . as long as she didn't fall for Dylan Gilchrist, the tall Samoan woman she was sitting beside (who I mentally referred to as Juliet-Dylan, to distinguish her from Dylan Jayasinghe Mellor, the Romeo). If Juliet-Dylan was attracted to women, she'd kept it quiet, but she'd become friendly with Amanda at auditions, and the way they were whispering and holding hands was giving me pause. I couldn't have them falling for each other. I had other plans for Juliet-Dylan.

The last of my contestants was Cece James, a pale brunette who was biting her lip and jiggling her leg nervously. We'd cast her as a wifey—someone with the potential to go deep in the competition—because she had a strong backstory. She'd had a rough childhood in foster care, and even the worst producer in the world could spin "unloved child seeking true love" into good content.

I was concerned about how Cece was going to cope, though. She'd been very nervous during her pre-show interview. If she couldn't get her shit together, even a solid gold backstory wouldn't translate on screen. I'd intended to find a few minutes to take her aside before the limo ride and give her a pep talk.

That hadn't happened, though. For obvious reasons.

Lily elbowed me in the ribs and said something I didn't catch. I was too focused on that saccharine smile plastered across her face.

If you had asked me yesterday, *what would you give to see Lily smile again?* I would have replied, *anything.*

"I wouldn't mind if it were Chris Gregory," Amanda said. "He has kind eyes."

Beneath the cover of her enormous yellow skirt, Lily's elbow brushed mine. It wasn't an aggressive, jokey, performative nudge like before, but an inquisitive one. *Is it? Is that who you picked to be the Romeo?*

I was not prone to overt displays of emotion. I could count the number of times I had cried in the last decade on one hand (on three fingers, specifically: when I'd realised my marriage wasn't going to work out, when my ex-wife Julia and I had the formal conversation about separating, and at Jeff's funeral).

In that moment, though, there was a genuine danger that tears might come pouring from my eyes.

It was such a perfectly *Lily* gesture, that inquisitive elbow. She could nudge me just once and I would know exactly what she meant, as clearly as if she were whispering in my ear. *Is that camera angle right? Should we ask him to elaborate on that? Do you think they've got those pastries we like at craft services?*

She nudged me again and raised an eyebrow, just like the partner I'd lost a year ago would, the one I'd been hoping so desperately would come back to me. *Is the Romeo Chris Gregory? He was one of our contenders.*

"It's not Chris Gregory," I said gruffly.

I swallowed the lump in my throat. "Here's what's going to happen. Listen up. That means you, Lily."

"What is it that makes you think I'm not listening?" She rested her chin on my shoulder and batted her eyelashes at me. "I'm starting to think you don't like me."

I had a sudden, vivid flashback to the last time her face had been this close to mine.

The night of the funeral. My fingers pressed tight to the back of her head as I held her against me, trying to hold her together while she was falling apart.

Her lipstick, all over my shirt.

"In about five minutes, we're going to pull up in the driveway." I swallowed hard again and found my producer voice, the one most people obeyed without thinking. "You'll stay in the limo until I say you can get out. Say what you need

Jodi McAlister

to say to the Romeo, but make it quick. We have to film this whole thing—all the entrances, the First Night Party, and the Necklace Ceremony—while it's still dark, so we don't have time for you to take forever."

"Isn't the First Night Party usually filmed over a couple of nights?" Juliet-Dylan asked.

"Usually, yes. But we can't take you back out of the Juliet Villa once we put you in because of the bubble, so this year we have to get it all in one. Get in, get out, be memorable. The Romeo's meeting fifteen girls tonight, so if he can't remember your name, he's probably going to cut you."

A look of concern crossed Amanda's face. Juliet-Dylan squeezed her hand and then whispered something in her ear. Amanda coloured slightly.

I'm going to have to keep an eye on that, I thought, at the same time as Lily's elbow brushed against mine again. *You're keeping an eye on that, right?*

"How many is he cutting tonight?" Heather asked.

"Z will tell you that before the Necklace Ceremony," I said. "Remember: when Z comes back into the First Night Party, the party ends. Because we have to film everything tonight, the party is going to be much shorter than it would normally be, so take your chances. If you haven't taken the Romeo aside by the time the party ends, chances are you'll get cut because he won't remember you."

"Do you really think someone could forget me, Murray?" Lily said.

I made the mistake of looking at her.

She was batting her eyelashes again, an obvious Lily Fireball affectation, but that mischievous look in her eyes—that

36

was pure, distilled Lily Ong, a look that hadn't changed in thirteen years.

"Yes," I lied. "Some of the Romeos we've had have been pretty dense."

"You've been working on this show for a few seasons, right, Murray?" Amanda asked. "Do you have any tips? Apart from making him remember us?"

I reached for the easiest, most obvious things. "Just don't get too drunk. And try not to fall in the pool with your mic pack on. They're expensive."

My radio emitted a burst of static, and I tapped my earpiece, grateful for the distraction. "Your limo is just pulling into the property, Murray," said Keira, one of our assistant directors, her voice slightly distorted over the connection. "We're all good to go here. The Romeo is in position, and the cameras are waiting for the girls to enter."

"Right, we're approaching the property," I said to the five women. "One of our guys is going to open the door. Dylan G, you're out first."

"Right," Juliet-Dylan said.

My earpiece activated again. It was Carrie this time. "Murray, problem," she said. "All limos are now en route, so we're going to get into the bubble okay, but new government pandemic restrictions have just come in. They're going to have a major impact on us."

"Shit," I said. "Really?"

"Wherever you spend the night tonight is where you have to stay for the next six weeks. So we can all get into the bubble—but no one will be able to get out again."

My mind started racing.

That wouldn't be a problem for most of us. Our shoot was six weeks. All the crew had to be on set for that long anyway. Same with Romeo-Dylan.

But the Juliets?

Shit. Instead of sending them home when they got eliminated, I was going to have to keep all fifteen of them on set *for the entire shoot.*

Where the hell was I going to put them? I couldn't just keep the eliminated contestants in the Juliet Villa alongside the ones still in the game. That would be horribly confusing for the format of the show.

But it wasn't like I could snap my fingers and magically produce alternative accommodation for them either. Fuck. Shit. Fuck.

Lily's elbow pressed into mine.

I glanced at her. She raised an eyebrow. *Problem?*

"Murray?" Carrie said in my ear.

"Brief Z." As the host, Z would have to be the one to break it to the cast, and he was a natural salesperson. He might have ideas on how we could frame this as a feature, not a bug. "Give me half an hour to get my girls through intros as well, and I'll come and troubleshoot."

"Copy that. I'll keep monitoring, and I'll be boots on the ground too once my girls are through intros as well. My limo's behind yours."

Keira's voice came through a second later as the limo slowed to a stop. "All set for package number one."

Lily elbowed me again, more urgent this time. *What's happening? Tell me.*

"We're here," I said. "Get ready, Dylan."

"I'm ready," Juliet-Dylan said. "And it's 'women.'"

"What?"

Three, four, five repeated jabs of Lily's elbow, right in my ribs. *Tell me what's happening. Tell me what's happening. Tell me what's happening!*

"—adult women," Juliet-Dylan was saying. "We're all adult women."

"You're right," I said. "Sorry about that. Bad habit."

Lily was still elbowing me. *Murray, tell me what's happening!*

I pushed back, hard. *Stop.*

"You good to go?" I asked Juliet-Dylan.

"Yes."

I flicked my radio to the right channel. "Open the door."

The PA outside the limo door obeyed. Juliet-Dylan smiled at Amanda. "See you in there, Mandie."

Nicknames, I noted, in the tiny skerrick of my brain that wasn't already overflowing. They were already close enough to be using nicknames.

The long skirt of Juliet-Dylan's sequinned green dress got caught as she slid out of the limo, but Amanda deftly freed it before we had a wardrobe malfunction. The PA slammed the door closed again. "Package number one in place," Keira said in my earpiece.

That meant that Juliet-Dylan was standing still, admiring the full *Marry Me, Juliet* splendour of the set. We tried to capture this moment for all the contestants, but we only left a few of them in the final edit. When we cut it together right, it was Cinderella walking into the ball. Not everyone could be Cinderella.

"Package number one en route," Keira said. "I repeat, package number one en route."

Not quite as long a Cinderella moment as I'd hoped, but we could always put it in slow motion.

"You should have let it tear," Lily said.

I thought she was talking to me at first, but her eyes were fixed on Amanda. "What?" Amanda said, blinking in surprise.

"Her dress." Lily gestured at the limo door.

This was not the first time I'd heard Lily make an incredibly mean suggestion to a contestant. Not even close.

But this tone wasn't Lily Ong, producer. Lily Ong would suggest it in such a friendly tone you'd barely register it was mean. She'd convince you it was the right thing to do, the reasonable thing to do, just by behaving like it was.

"This is supposed to be a competition," Lily Fireball purred, every inch a predator. "We're not here to make friends."

The words were straight out of the reality TV villain's handbook.

She was doing this. She was really doing this. My best friend was going to step out of this limo and turn herself into a whole different person and there wasn't a thing I could do to stop her.

Her dress over my lap was suddenly stiflingly hot. My heart was racing, pounding in my ears.

Lily was back.

Lily was here.

Lily had snapped and now she was burning her whole life down right in front of my eyes and *I was never going to get my partner back.*

"Hi!" I heard Romeo-Dylan say, distant and distorted through my earpiece and the rushing in my mind. "Welcome! It's so nice to meet you."

"Lovely to meet you too," Juliet-Dylan said.

I forced myself to take a long, deep breath.

"All of you need to be quiet now," I managed to say. "I have to listen. We can't have any background noise pick up in the intros, or we'll have to refilm them."

"Get out of the way!" Lily said. "I want to get a look at the Romeo."

She leaned across me, practically clambering into my lap, and some dam in my brain burst. "Lily, sit down!" I barked, shoving her off. "And for the love of God, shut up!"

The look she gave me was icy, made worse by the fact that it was so familiar. "Don't you dare tell me to shut up," she said. "Don't you dare."

Don't shout at me, Murray, she'd told me firmly a few times over the years. *I'm your partner, not your subordinate. You can't boss me around. The daddy voice doesn't work on me.*

There was laughter in my earpiece. The Dylans, laughing together, a little too loud, a little too awkward, a little too forced.

"I'm sorry," I forced out. "But—just—please. I need you to be quiet."

The barest movement of her eyebrow. The smallest flair of her nostrils. The tiniest signs, the ones that no one could read but me.

"All of you," I added. "I have to think."

None of the other women—not Amanda, not Heather, not Cece—noticed their inclusion was a hasty afterthought.

The slightest quirk of her lips.

Lily noticed.

"All set for package number four," Keira said in my earpiece.

"Go. Now. Out," I said to Heather.

The limo door closed behind her. "Package number four in place," Keira said.

Lily slid over to the seat that Heather had vacated, elegant despite her complicated skirt. She leaned against the far door and swung her legs up, crossing her ankles and putting her feet on the seat, stiletto points just brushing my thigh. She was wearing gold heels with delicate straps, her toenails painted the same red as her lipstick.

"Package number four en route," Keira said in my earpiece.

Only a few minutes, then. Only a few minutes before I had to let Lily Fireball out of the limo and watch her destroy Lily Ong's life.

"Do you want to tell me what the problem is?" she asked.

I glared at her.

"Not with me." She handwaved that off as if it were a ridiculous suggestion. "Whatever came through your earpiece. The problem you have to brief Z about and go and troubleshoot when you've got us all through intros."

Us.

That word stuck in my throat. She'd said it, not me, but it felt like I could choke on it.

"Contestants don't need to know about production issues," I said shortly.

I wanted a reaction, but I didn't get one. "Well," she said lightly, "I guess I deserve that."

I looked down at her feet.

"I'm so angry with you, Lily," I said quietly.

"I know. I'm sorry."

"Are you?"

"Yes."

She uncrossed and recrossed her ankles, a simple, familiar gesture that hurt as much as if she'd driven one of her heels between my ribs. "I know how much is on your plate. I know me turning up like this is only adding to it."

"But you did it anyway."

"Yes."

"Thirteen years of friendship, and you thought a night like tonight was the right time to drop this bomb in my lap."

"Murray—"

"Because," I interrupted, looking over at her again, "you knew that if you gave me any warning—any lead time at all—I would have figured out a way to stop you."

There were different kinds of silences. Knowing when to shut up was a crucial producer skill, letting the silence draw out, extend, get uncomfortably long, until the person you were producing cracked and filled it. There, the silence was a question, and the beauty was that it could be unformed, a simple hanging question mark. Stay silent long enough, and the person you were asking would fill in the question in their mind, pinpointing their own hidden vulnerabilities for you. Sometimes, though, a silence was an answer, one that you were too proud or stubborn to speak.

Yes, Lily admitted, without saying a word. *Fine. You got me.*

"Lily," I said, "if you want me to believe that you're not having a nervous breakdown, you have to tell me why you're doing this."

There was a burst of chatter from Romeo-Dylan and Heather in my earpiece. I yanked it out, letting it dangle near my collar.

"I already told you," she replied. "You used to be much better at listening."

I pinched the bridge of my nose.

"You need me," she said. "I'm going to be the acid to cut through the sweetness. The wicked queen to Prince Charming and his Cinderellas. I'll be the bait that lures people onto the hook. By the time I'm done, people will be in love with the romance, because—"

"Because they'll hate you," I said. "Cut the bullshit. I'm not Fucking Greg."

"Murray?" I heard Keira say, tinny and distant from my dangling earpiece. "Are you there?"

"One second, Keira."

Lily straightened, swinging her feet back down and brushing imaginary dust off her dress. "Sounds like my cue."

I grabbed her hand. "Listen to me. Please."

She didn't say anything. It was a different kind of silence. Not agreement, not concession, but acquiescence. *All right. Let's see what you've got.*

I forced my frustration and my worry and my fear down. Snapping and shouting at her would get me nowhere. I had to think clearly—to choose my words carefully—if this was going to work.

"You're my best friend," I said. "You're my partner. I care about you. I love you. But most importantly, I know you."

I shifted in my seat so I could take her other hand as well. "I know you don't lie. So if you tell me you're not having a nervous breakdown, I believe you. If you tell me you couldn't stay away from the season after all the groundwork we put in—I believe that too."

"Good. Because it's the truth."

"It's not all of it."

Another silence, this one completely inscrutable.

"I *know* you, Lily. If that were all of it, you'd be in one of the other limos right now wearing this." I let go of one of her hands for a second and plucked at the neck of my black polo shirt.

"Mine would fit better."

I ignored the cheap jab. "We've been working towards this season for years. But it was only ever supposed to be the beginning. The proof of concept that would let us bring real change to the way this show is made—the way all reality TV is made. But if you do this . . ."

I was squeezing her hands so tightly my knuckles were white. "If you do this, Lily, it's the end," I said. "There's no coming back from what you're about to do to yourself."

There was no doubt in my mind that Lily would be one of the greatest reality TV villains of all time. There was no doubt either that she would be completely unfazed by all the things that usually brought villains unstuck: the online hatred, the social media abuse, the death threats. No one would be more prepared for what was to come. No one would take it less personally. If Fucking Greg's spicy meatball had been some other person with all of Lily's qualities and capabilities, I might have had to admit that he had, for once, had a good idea.

But it *was* Lily. And there was one other thing I had no doubt of.

A reality TV star could not go back to being a reality TV producer. Once you were on camera—once you were famous—there was no path back to the other side. Once everyone knew your name and your face, there was no way back to being the mastermind in the shadows.

"I *know* you," I said again. "And we've worked too hard for too many years for you to throw it all away."

For a long moment, she didn't say anything.

Then she took her hands out of mine. "You knew me, Murray."

Those words felt like a bullet in the thorax.

"You have no idea who I've been, this past year," she said. "What a mess that woman was. How lonely. How sad. How—"

She paused, taking a deep breath. "—bored," she finished. "Grief is so unbelievably boring. Did you know that? You wake up in the morning, and all that's ahead of you is another day of feeling sad, and it's so *fucking* dull."

She started gathering her ridiculous skirt up over one arm. "It sounds callous, but the boredom is almost the worst part. Sometimes I wasn't sure if I missed Jeff or if I just missed having someone to talk to. And I'm so sick of being that woman. That miserable woman, with her brain atrophying in her skull, going nowhere, doing nothing."

"You could have called me."

"Believe it or not, one conversation with you would not make up for losing my husband."

"Of course it wouldn't! But you cut me out completely, Lily. And I know you weren't saying shit to Thuong or any of your other friends either, and—"

"You were checking up on me?"

"Of course I was fucking checking up on you!"

"And here I thought she didn't keep things from me anymore," Lily muttered.

It seemed like an opening, so I took it. "I called her earlier. She's worried about you."

It was an understatement. Thuong had been almost hysterical. Michael hadn't been much better. I would have taken them up on their offer to come and get her in a heartbeat if it wouldn't have completely fucked the show's pandemic protocols.

"Thuong's always worried about me." Lily waved a hand dismissively. "All anyone is these days is worried about me."

"Including me!" I exploded. "Fuck, Lily!"

I ran my hand through my hair, tugging hard at the ends. "It doesn't have to be like this," I said. "If you need someone to talk to, you have people—even if you don't want to talk to me. And if you want to take your mind off things, you can come back to work any time you want. God knows I need you."

"No."

The word was sharp, fast, a whipcrack.

Too sharp. Too fast.

"No," she repeated, her tone more measured. "Producing is what the old Lily did, and I'm not her anymore. I can't be her anymore. I just . . ."

Her voice trailed off. She closed her eyes for a second, false eyelashes long and dark against her cheeks.

Then she opened them again. "I just need to be someone else, Murray," she said. "Can you understand that?"

"Yes."

"Thank you."

"Don't thank me yet. I haven't finished."

I took one of her hands again, gripping it tightly, as if I could keep her beside me if I just held on hard enough. "I can understand the desire to reinvent yourself. But there are a million different places you could do that. Why come back to the industry you've spent your entire career in?"

"Maybe I missed you."

"Then pick up the fucking phone!"

"And you'd answer? In all that spare time you have?"

"Of course I would answer!"

I exhaled through my nose. "I can understand wanting to reinvent yourself. Of course I can. But it doesn't have to be on *television*! It doesn't have to be as permanent and nuclear and career-ending as this will be! And it sure as hell doesn't have to be as a twenty-five-year-old aspiring girlboss who's not here to make friends!"

She paused. Contemplative, this time.

"You know what Lily Fireball is?" she said.

"You've been quite clear that she's a persona you've created specifically so everyone in the universe will hate you."

"They'll love to hate me," Lily corrected. "Because Lily Fireball is going to be so much *fun*."

"All set for package number five," Keira said from my dangling earpiece.

Lily switched seats to the other side and scooted closer to the door. That put her opposite me, our knees brushing together. "That is what I need," she said. "I just need to have some fun again. And we can have so much fun with Lily Fireball, Murray."

We.

She leaned in close. "I know what it looks like. I know why you're worried. And I love you for worrying, really, I do."

She pressed her lips to my cheek, right next to my ear. "But I know what I'm doing," she whispered. "Trust me."

I hesitated.

This was ridiculous. I shouldn't even be considering this. If it weren't for the pandemic protocols and the fact I wouldn't be able to get back into the bubble after leaving it, I would have handed the First Night Party over to Suzette and Carrie, chaos be damned, and dragged her home myself.

But—*we.* She'd said *we.* If there was still a *we* . . .

"You're sure?" I asked.

"Yes. I'm sure."

I wasn't. Not even a little.

She could spin me a thousand different stories about becoming Lily Fireball. They might all even be true.

This was Lily, though, and I *knew*—fundamentally *knew*, deep in my bones—that there was something she wasn't telling me.

We thought alike. That had been the basis of our friendship from the start: we were born schemers. We had different strengths—she had flawless dramatic instincts, I was good at big picture narrative—but it was the same skillset. We both had an innate understanding of cause and effect. I didn't know if we were both missing the same checks and balances most people had, or whether it was some kind of extra ability we had that they didn't, but we could see the strings that other people couldn't—and we didn't have any qualms about pulling them.

I understood her. She understood me.

So I knew there was no way that she would completely reinvent herself for reasons as thin as "I want to play pretend" and "I want to have fun," no matter how badly she was grieving. Not when there were an infinite number of other, better ways to play pretend and have fun. Lily Ong was better at scheming than that.

But I'd done the calculations, in my few seconds of hesitation. I could work with her, or I could work against her, but I couldn't stop her.

Either way, the show had to go on.

So I made the only choice I could. A wrong choice—a bad choice—but a choice that might let me figure out what the fuck she was doing.

A choice that might let me get my best friend back.

I put my earpiece back in. "Open the door," I said into my headset mic.

"Thank you." Lily squeezed my hand.

Just for a moment, things felt all right again.

Then the limo door opened, and she let go, and my best friend was gone. "Don't let them close the door on my train," Lily Fireball said, patting me proprietarily on the knee. "I'll murder someone if this dress gets torn."

4

Lily

Thirteen years ago

"So," I asked, leaning back in my chair, "what are you doing here? Why reality TV?"

Murray looked contemplative as he took a sip of his coffee. I was drinking a cappuccino, featuring a love heart the barista had drawn in the foam; but he'd ordered his coffee black, in the largest size they had. Was he just hungover, or did he always drink it this way?

"I care about stories," he replied.

"Interesting," I said. "Tell me more about that."

Tell me more about that was, far and away, the most successful flirting line I had in my arsenal. Boys *loved* talking about themselves, and the beauty of *tell me more about that* was that you didn't even have to give them any parameters. You just pointed them in a direction, batted your eyelashes, and made it look like you were a) listening and b) fascinated—and boom, you had them eating out of the palm of your hand.

"Do you care about things?" he asked abruptly.

I blinked. "What do you mean, do I care about things? Are you trying to figure out if you're about to spend three months stuck on an island with a sociopath?"

If he was, I probably shouldn't mention that I was fairly sure I had some tendencies in that direction. Thuong was forever extolling the values of therapy and how useful she found it and how *you should totally go, Lily, you'll find out so much about yourself,* but I'd only ever been a couple of times, out of fear that a good therapist would have between one and five conversations with me and go, *oh, no, you're completely incapable of forming normal human relationships, your shithead high school boyfriend was right actually, you're a lost cause.* (Plus, all that therapy hadn't made Thuong brave enough to fess up and tell me she was fucking my brother, so it couldn't be *that* useful.)

Murray chuckled. "No."

A curl was falling in his eye. He shook his head trying to dislodge it. "Do you have some big cause that you care about? Something that drives you? That you're passionate about?"

Now there was a question I should file away for future flirting attempts.

I rested my head in one hand, toying with my coffee spoon in the other. "I didn't take a job on *Desert Island Castaway* because I'm passionate about watching people do obstacle courses in the wilderness, if that's what you're asking."

He regarded me over the top of his enormous mug. "You don't answer questions straight, do you?"

I really hadn't been imagining it, when I'd been watching him last night in the bar.

This boy was perceptive as hell. He *listened.* He *paid attention.*

"You answered my question with another question," I said, smiling at him, "so I think we're even."

Murray smiled back. "Touché."

He took another sip of his coffee. "I don't. Have a big cause, I mean. Nothing specific. But I like the thought that I could tell a story, and it could do something. Mean something."

He brushed that errant curl out of his eye again, and I decided.

This boy was going to be mine.

He was still talking—something about a lecture he'd been to on how reality TV was trashy, but it was also watched by millions of people, which meant it had the power to deeply influence the way they thought—and part of me was still listening, but most of me was scheming.

Whether it happened in the next three months, or the next three days, or even the next three hours, I was going to have this boy. I was going to tangle my hand in that pullable hair and direct him where I wanted him to go. I was going to exploit the fact that he paid attention and make him pay all his attention to me. I was—

"So why are you here?"

I was going to take the fact that he seemed genuinely interested in what I had to say, and I was going to tell him to do a lot of things to me that I would find genuinely interesting.

"Well, I'm not noble and virtuous like you, sir."

Murray snorted. "No one has ever accused me of being either of those things."

Good. Nice boys were boring in bed.

"I like control," I said.

This was another line that always, *always* worked on boys. *Oh, do you now?* they'd say. *You gonna tie me up, princess?* Sadly, it only had short-term effectiveness (mostly, they thought it was funny that a tiny Asian girl had such top energy, and wanted to turn the tables on me and teach me my place), but you could achieve quite a lot in that short period.

Murray, though, just raised his eyebrows, the barest glint in his eye, the merest hint of mischief. "I'm not sure how much control we're going to have as PAs."

"It's a long game," I said. "First, we learn the rules. And then—"

"—we seize the means of production?"

"See!" I said brightly. "You get it."

"Of course I do. Why, though?"

"Why do I like control?"

That was a complicated question. In my few brief flirtations with therapy, it was something the therapist would always try to get to the bottom of. *Why do you think you try to control people?* they'd ask. *Why men, in particular?*

And then they'd go digging and digging and digging, trying to get me to crack and have some revelation like, "Oh my god, I must do this as a tactic to fight back against all the racist, sexist bullshit people heap on Asian women!" or, "Oh my god, I must do this because some part of me thinks I'm fundamentally unlovable and I want to feel like I'm the one pulling all the strings!"

None of them ever really accepted me shrugging and saying, "Look, I don't think it's that deep, I think I just like it."

"No, not that," Murray said, surprising me again. "I mean—

why reality TV? There are lots of things you could go and figure out how to control. Why this?"

God, this boy asked good questions.

"I like mess," I replied. "I like drama. I'm a messy bitch who lives for drama, and I like watching messy bitches who live for drama. I like it when you break something apart and there's something juicy and complicated and exciting inside and it falls all over the floor."

"Like when the *Desert Island Castaway* voting alliances splinter and reform?"

"That's one example, sure." Or the mess I was going to make of this very intriguing boy, and I was going to let him make of me.

He grinned. "I like that too. And speaking of mess—" He gestured to his upper lip.

"Oh!" I wiped the cappuccino foam away. "Got it?"

"Yes, but now your lipstick . . ."

Blood of My Enemies was a killer shade with a killer name, but it had terrible hold. I fished my black plastic compact out of my bag. "Hold this."

Murray held the compact steady as I fixed my lipstick. He had great hands: not particularly big, but strong and sure. I let my fingers brush over his as I took the compact back, and I opened my mouth to say something even the least attentive boy in the world would pay attention to—

His phone rang. "Shit, sorry, Lily," Murray said. "I've got to go. I promised my fiancée I'd take her out to one last dinner before we head out to the island, and I'm late."

5

Murray

"Am I doing okay?" Romeo-Dylan asked me. "Am I getting it right?"

"You're doing fine," I reassured him.

"Are you sure?"

"Absolutely, mate. You've got nothing to worry about."

I was about seventy per cent confident I was telling the truth. Between breaking my brain over Lily and then rushing off to figure out a solution to my new pandemic-restriction-induced Juliet accommodation crisis, I'd heard barely any of his red-carpet introductions. If there had been some kind of huge issue, someone would have told me by now, but I couldn't exactly speak authoritatively on the subject.

I wasn't about to tell him that, though. The first thing I'd learned working in reality TV was that "truth" and "lie" were points on a spectrum, not a binary.

The second thing was that this was a broad-strokes medium. True enough was good enough.

And the third thing was that people were much more likely to do what you wanted if they felt like you gave a shit about them—which usually meant making them think you had a) observed and b) approved of every single thing they did.

For once, it was genuinely true. I *did* give a shit about Romeo-Dylan. He was the perfect hero. He had a compelling backstory—the child of a white father and a Sri Lankan mother, he had lived all around the world as a kid before settling here and growing up to win an Olympic gold medal in sailing—and he might be the single most telegenic person I had ever met. He was handsome, sure, but more importantly, he was charming, eloquent, and he exhibited a level of vulnerability that was going to make all the women in the Villa and most of the viewing audience want to look after him.

I just wished *I* didn't have to look after him quite so much. The trade-off for his excellent qualities was that he needed a hell of a lot of hand-holding. I understood why—being the first ever non-white lead in this franchise came with immense pressure—but the endless reassurance was something I had neither the time nor the disposition for.

"This interview's nothing to worry about," I told him. "It's exactly the same set-up as the one we did at the hotel. Look at me, not the camera. Remember to answer in full sentences, because the audience isn't going to hear my questions, just your answers. All good?"

"Yes," Romeo-Dylan sounded a little more confident. "All good."

"We're going to run through all the Juliets, and I want you to tell me what your first impressions were."

"Okay."

"What were your first impressions of Dylan G?"

He smiled. I couldn't tell for sure whether it was genuine, but it looked genuine, and that was all that mattered. "Dylan G is absolutely stunning. She seems like a fascinating woman. I can't wait to get to know her more."

"Would you say you felt an instant spark with her? An immediate connection?"

"Yes."

"Full sentences, mate."

"Oh. Right. Sorry." He cleared his throat and shifted on the stool in front of the green screen. "I felt an instant spark with Dylan G. We had an immediate connection, and I'm excited to explore that. She seems like such a strong woman, and that's exactly what I'm looking for."

When Lily and I had done this in-the-moment interview with Brett last year (ITMs, we usually called them), it had taken ninety minutes. Trying to get him to speak in full sentences—let alone say more than one sentence—on any given topic was nearly impossible.

"I'm so honoured that someone like her would come here," Romeo-Dylan added, without any prompting. "People talk about sportspeople as heroes all the time. That word was thrown around a lot when I won my gold medal. But people like Dylan G—nurses, doctors, frontline workers, the people holding the line against the pandemic—they're the real heroes."

He smiled again, an expression that was part-bashful, part-awed, and that I could use to make him look like Prince fucking Charming. "I should be the one fighting for the chance to date Dylan G, not the other way around."

Truth might be relative, and I might have signed myself up for many hours of frustrating hand-holding, but I'd made the right call casting this man as the Romeo. It was going to be unbelievably easy to turn Dylan Jayasinghe Mellor into the nation's dream boyfriend.

"Excellent job." I gave him a thumbs up. "You're killing it."

"Are you sure? I can do it again if you want."

For fuck's sake.

"Tell me what you need me to say," he said, "and I'll say it."

That was an interesting promise. I filed it away for later. "You're doing fine, mate. Tell me what you thought of Amanda."

We ran through all the Juliets. He'd vibed with Amanda— "She put me totally at ease." Cece had fallen apart on him (I *had* to remember to give her that pep talk, I wasn't going to get anything useful out of her if she couldn't keep her shit together), and he didn't have much to say about Heather, but he talked enthusiastically about some of Suzette and Carrie's contestants—especially Kumiko the human rights lawyer, Parisa the research scientist, Naya the engineer, and Marija the philanthropist—which I made a mental note to feed back to them. We weren't running the kitty this year, so there was no cash on the line for any of us, but these were all narrative threads we could potentially develop.

"Last one," I said, steeling myself. "Tell me what you thought of Lily Fireball."

Romeo-Dylan hesitated. "Um . . ."

I let the silence unfold: partly because riding the silence was the right move to make, but mostly because, despite my ability to keep my feelings off my face, I wasn't sure I could keep them out of my voice.

"Lily Fireball seems like a force of nature," Romeo-Dylan said eventually. "Like she's not scared of anything or anyone. Like she'll go after whatever she wants, no matter the consequences."

"And that's the kind of thing you look for in a woman, right?"

"I . . . suppose?"

"Full sentences, mate."

"I'm not sure what Lily would be like as a partner," he said, "but it would certainly be an adventure."

He had no idea how cleanly he'd hit the nail on the head.

"Just a heads up, I'm not going to pick her tonight."

"Hmmm?"

"Lily Fireball. I'm not going to pick her tonight. At the Necklace Ceremony."

That wasn't a surprise. Lily's had been the only red carpet introduction I'd properly paid attention to, and she'd run a villain special on Romeo-Dylan. *I'm Lily Fireball,* she'd purred, *and I don't like your tie.*

I'd only had audio, so I couldn't see what was happening, but Romeo-Dylan had made a sharp surprised sound, and Keira had reported back to me that Lily had ripped his tie off and thrown it into the garden. *I know what I like and I know what I don't like,* she'd told him, *and if I like you, I won't let anything or anyone stand in my way.*

Even ties? he'd said.

I'll tear any article of clothing I don't like right off your body. And if you're lucky, eventually I'll tear the ones I do like off too.

Things would be so much easier if I could just let Romeo-Dylan eliminate her. If she was only on *Marry Me, Juliet* for one episode, I might be able to edit Lily Fireball out entirely.

"You can't cut her, mate," I told Romeo-Dylan. "Network's orders. She's going to be the season villain. We've got to keep her until at least Episode Eight."

He looked aghast. "That's two thirds of the season!"

"Dylan, we've discussed this. You and I both want this season to do well, and that means story is king."

"A love story!"

"Yes, but we've got to balance that with conflict," I said, hating that I was running the same line on him as Lily had on Fucking Greg. "We've got to have obstacles to overcome if we want the audience to be invested in the love story. She'll be a great obstacle."

"Okay, fine." Romeo-Dylan's thumb and middle finger started to tap together. "But how am I going to make anyone believe she and I are well-suited enough for me to keep her around?"

"You've done a great job so far. That thing you said about her being a force of nature—if we cut that together with the right music, we can frame it really positively."

He looked uncertain.

"Mate, you've got enough on your plate to worry about," I said. "You just focus on being the Romeo, all right? Leave the storytelling to me."

He let out a long breath. "Okay. Okay."

I kept my eyes on his fingers. The tapping slowed. Slowed. Stopped.

"We're about to send you out into the First Night Party," I said. "The women are going to come at you hard, and there'll be some fighting over who gets to talk to you, but that's not your problem. You just focus on having chats. Can you do that?"

"Yes," he said. "I can do that."

"Excellent. Now I've just got one last question, before you head out there."

He nodded.

"We've had news that some stricter pandemic restrictions have come in. They're not going to affect us too badly, except in one area: no one is allowed to leave the set for the next six weeks. That includes the women you eliminate."

He blinked. "Okay."

"It's not going to change how things work for you. You'll only be dealing with the women who are still in the game. But it's posed a bit of a logistical issue, accommodation-wise."

"All right."

"Our best solution is to put the eliminated women in the house at the bottom of the hill, which was going to be your Romeo Residence," I said. "We'll call it the Nunnery or the Convent or something. But that leaves you without somewhere to stay, so . . . Dylan, as a professional sailor—how do you feel about living on a boat?"

I was so busy coordinating the removal of Romeo-Dylan's things from the newly-christened Convent over to the boat on the lake that I missed the formal beginning of the First Night Party. Z had already announced Romeo-Dylan's entrance and run through most of his introductory spiel when I slipped in behind the cameras. "How's Dylan going?" I whispered to Saurav.

"He's nailing it," Saurav murmured back. "About two thirds of the women are in full swoon mode."

I nodded in acknowledgment. Romeo-Dylan might be nervous, but it was comforting to know that he could deliver me a full romantic hero performance without me having to *really* aggressively puppeteer him.

I caught sight of Cece, surreptitiously wiping sweaty fingers on the skirt of her dress. I *had* to remember to give her a pep talk. I didn't want to lose one of my wifeys to nerves this early.

"What do you like, though?" Lily called out to Romeo-Dylan across the sea of Juliets. "Blondes? Brunettes? Redheads? Fireballs?"

I was clearly in no danger of losing my villain to nerves. My eye started twitching as Romeo-Dylan's fingers started tapping again.

"I think what Lily Fireball is very subtly trying to ask," Z said, "is: what's your type, Dylan? What do you look for in a potential Juliet?"

Romeo-Dylan put his hand in his pocket. "Physically, I wouldn't say I have a type."

His eyes flickered over to me. I gave him an encouraging thumbs-up.

"But I like strong women," he finished. "Tough women. Women who like a challenge and who don't back down."

So much had gone wrong for me today, but Romeo-Dylan was going right. He was well-spoken and telegenic. The women liked him. And best of all, the man could take direction.

Instinctively, I looked at Lily. It was so deeply baked into me, that reflex: have a thought, share it with Lily.

But her gaze was fixed calculatingly on Romeo-Dylan. "Well, you're going to love me, then!" she declared. "Shall we go for a chat?"

The enormous yellow train of her dress billowed behind her, knocking over a pot plant as she towed Romeo-Dylan away. "Lily Fireball moves fast!" Z exclaimed.

"You right, mate?" Saurav asked me quietly.

"Yeah," I lied. "I'm fine."

I unclipped the water bottle from my utility belt, took a long swig, and swallowed the stone in my throat.

Lily was one of my contestants, so I had to run point on her chat with Romeo-Dylan. Our set design included several convo couches: strategically placed locations for conversations between the Romeo and the Juliets. Some were secluded to give the aura of intimacy and privacy, while others were more public, perfect for confrontations, dramatic moments and pointed exhibitionism.

Lily had towed Romeo-Dylan to the most public convo couch. It was bright white, excellent for showing off the brilliant yellow of her dress, situated on a raised deck near the pool, where she could see everyone and everyone could see her. The year away had clearly done nothing to curb her love of drama.

"Don't look so scared, darling," she said to Romeo-Dylan. "I'm not going to eat you."

He rallied, flashing his Prince Charming smile. "I'm sorry. I'm just nervous. This is the first time in my life fifteen beautiful women have turned up on my doorstep and told me they wanted to date me. It'll be the last time, too, so I don't want to mess it up."

There was a glint in her eye. *Paragraphs*, Lily Ong would have whispered. *He can speak in whole* paragraphs, *Murray!*

She reached over and loosened his tie. "I wouldn't mind messing you up a bit."

"What is it you have against my tie?" Romeo-Dylan asked, trying but not entirely succeeding to keep the apprehension out of his expression. "I already had to fish it out of the begonias once. Are you going to throw it in the pool next time?"

"I think the suit would look better without it."

Then Lily used his tie to yank his face towards hers. "And I'm used to getting what I want."

Romeo-Dylan laughed nervously. "Wow," he said, gently disentangling himself. "You are—uh—really something, Lily."

"Lily Fireball."

"What was that?"

"Lily *Fireball*. You can't forget the *Fireball*."

"Why *Fireball*?" Romeo-Dylan asked, clearly glad to have something to latch onto that didn't involve him being lightly choked.

"Because," she said, reaching out and tracing his jawline with one finger, "a fireball can burn it all down."

It took every ounce of professionalism I had not to cut the scene. Not to barge in, throw her over my shoulder, and run off into the night.

"And it'll be much better for social media searchability if you use my whole name," she said brightly, and we actually did have to stop the scene because the soundie dropped the boom mic in shock.

Thankfully for both mine and Romeo-Dylan's blood pressure, the chat didn't go too much longer. "Hi, Dylan," Juliet-Dylan said. "Can I steal you for a second?"

"Not yet," Lily snapped. "This is my time with the Romeo."

"It's been lovely to talk to you, Lily Fireball, but I need to make sure I speak to everyone tonight," Romeo-Dylan said. "I'll see you later, all right?"

Lily paused for a moment—deliberate, dramatic—then pulled his tie off. "I'm right. The suit looks better without it."

Her dress fell perfectly around her as she uncrossed her ankles and stood. The huge yellow skirts were ridiculous, but she made them look regal, a queen's robe, as she fixed Juliet-Dylan with a penetrating stare.

Juliet-Dylan stared back. "What?"

"Be careful. You don't want to make an enemy of me."

"Oh no." Juliet-Dylan rolled her eyes. "I'm terrified."

"Good," Lily replied sweetly. "You should be."

Then she turned on her heel and swept off in the direction of the rose garden.

I wanted to go after her, but Juliet-Dylan was already shaking her head and sitting down beside Romeo-Dylan. "Fucking hell," she said. "All she needs is a moustache to twirl and the cartoon villain look would be complete."

Romeo-Dylan spluttered with laughter.

It was a lovely, natural moment, but I had to stop it. "Cut. Let's do that again. Dylan G, don't swear."

"Shit. I forgot. Sorry."

"I've already forgotten about eighty times," Romeo-Dylan offered. "You're not alone."

"And I'd reconsider talking about Lily," I said.

"How?" Juliet-Dylan waved her hand in the direction Lily had gone. "How are we meant *not* to talk about whatever the fuck that was?"

"If he talks to you about another woman, he'll look petty," I said, gesturing at Romeo-Dylan. "And if your entire first conversation with him is about someone else, then—"

"—then I look like a shit-starter who's more interested in finding drama than falling in love," Juliet-Dylan finished. "Yeah. Okay. I get it."

"What should we talk about, then?" Romeo-Dylan asked.

"How about your tie?" I said. "Dylan G, you can tie a tie, right? How about you put it back on him?"

"Sure."

"Dylan JM, you've got an obvious in to talk about your charity," I said. "Tell her about Ties Out For The Boys. Philanthropy is Prince Charming shit. Milk it."

"I didn't start Ties Out to look good. I started it because—"

"Don't tell me. Tell her."

It was going to be a nice little scene, once we edited it together. We had to stop and start a few times, but the right moments were there. Her scooting towards him on the couch, the green sequins of her dress brushing against the dove grey material of his suit. Her messing up her first attempt at tying his tie, and the two of them laughing about it. Her second successful attempt, which we could make look quite sexy if we slowed the footage down and used the right music cues.

It sparked a memory, Juliet-Dylan's fingers smoothing over Romeo-Dylan's waistcoat as she tucked the tie in, but I forced it back in its box. *Just do your fucking job,* I ordered myself.

67

Heather came and interrupted the Dylans sooner than was ideal, but it didn't matter overmuch. I had what I needed.

I ran through my mental to-do list as Romeo-Dylan and Heather chatted on the convo couch. I'd sorted the accommodation problem. I had some key narrative moments in the can. Three of my contestants had had their First Night Party moments with the Romeo, and—

"How dare you?!"

"Sorry," I said to a startled Romeo-Dylan and Heather, and bolted.

Lily had bailed up three women beside the pool—Juliet-Dylan, Amanda and Cece (shit, Cece, how did I keep forgetting about her?). "How dare you?!" she exclaimed again, jabbing a finger into Juliet-Dylan's shoulder. "That was my time with the Romeo! How dare you interrupt?"

"We all want time with him," Juliet-Dylan said, standing her ground. "That's what we're all here for. You don't get to keep him all for yourself, Lily."

"It's Lily *Fireball*!"

It was absurd how slowly it happened. Too fast to stop, but so slowly I wasn't sure we'd even need to put it in slo-mo for broadcast.

Lily shoved Juliet-Dylan.

Juliet-Dylan lurched back into Amanda.

Amanda knocked into Cece.

And Cece went into the pool.

I immediately looked around for Romeo-Dylan. If I could get a shot of him hero-diving in to save her, that would be perfect nation's boyfriend material.

But he'd disappeared, so it was Amanda, instead, who

helped Cece out. "I'm so sorry," she was saying. "Your beautiful dress—your hair—"

Cece tried to answer, but her teeth were chattering, wet hair plastered to her face, goosebumps forming on her skin.

"Excuse me?" Juliet-Dylan exclaimed.

"You stole the Romeo from me." Lily's tone was infused with an infuriating level of saccharine. "If you hadn't, then what's-her-face wouldn't have ended up in the pool."

"Cece," Amanda interjected. "Her name is Cece."

Lily fixed her with one of her more terrifying gazes. "Honey, do I look like I care?"

Juliet-Dylan stepped in front of Amanda—and, oh god, I really *was* going to have to keep an eye on the two of them; Romeo-Dylan might not be here to pull a Prince Charming on Cece, but Juliet-Dylan was doing it for Amanda, right in front of my eyes. "Mandie, you take Cece to get dried off. I'll deal with this."

Lily raised an eyebrow. "Oh, will you now?"

"Come on, let's get you into some new clothes." Amanda put her arm around a shivering Cece and led her inside. One of the cameras peeled off and started following them.

I hesitated. All four women were my contestants. They were splitting into two different scenes. I needed to be present for both.

The barest movement of Lily's hand. Her eyes were still locked on Juliet-Dylan's, but her fingers flicked. *Go. I've got this.*

Despite everything, my heart leapt.

Her smile, as she looked at Juliet-Dylan, was pure villain. Predatory. Performative. Designed to strike fear into the hearts of everyone around her.

But that little gesture?

That was my partner.

I know it's not exactly orthodox, and I know it's a bit of a surprise, but I really am here to help you.

It wasn't the whole truth. I knew that. And if I just blithely went along with her plan to turn herself into Lily Fireball, I wasn't just helplessly watching her burn down her life. I'd be handing her the matches.

If I let her help me, though—could I use that, somehow? Would it give me a way to get Lily Ong back?

She flicked her fingers again. *Divide and conquer. This is under control.*

I thought about it for one more second.

Then I went.

I wasn't confident I'd made the right call—which probably contributed to me losing my patience about halfway through my ITM with Cece.

She was shaking, a combination of cold and camera-shyness. She hunched into herself on the stool in front of the green screen. When I raised my voice even slightly to her, she flinched and tried to disappear into herself.

I'd been distracted by Lily during Cece's red-carpet intro to Romeo-Dylan, but I'd paid enough attention to know it hadn't gone well. She'd babbled nervously and forgotten to tell him her name. She was doing better in the one-on-one interview setting, but that didn't mean she was doing *well*.

It was going to take me a lot of work, if I was going to get her camera-ready, and I didn't have that kind of time.

I already had one person whose hand I was going to need to constantly hold.

So I lured Cece into a trap.

"Do you think Dylan JM should let Lily Fireball stay in the Villa?" I asked her.

"No, I don't think Dylan JM should let Lily Fireball stay in the Villa," Cece replied, shoulders curled forward, fingers under her thighs. "Not after that kind of behaviour. I know she didn't mean for me to end up in the pool, but you can't go around pushing and shoving people. That's not right."

At least she'd managed to speak in full sentences this time.

"And I don't like it when women attack other women," she added. "I know we're all competing for the same man, but that kind of behaviour is toxic."

It was such a wide-eyed, earnest answer. Cece was 5'7", only a few inches shorter than me, but under the lights, bedraggled and wet with a towel around her shoulders and her hair sticking to her face, she looked very small and innocent.

I couldn't let that tug at my heartstrings, though. I rifled through my mental dossier on her. "You study criminology, don't you, Cece?"

". . . yes?" she replied, clearly surprised. "I study criminology."

"Would you say that's because you have a strong sense of justice?"

"Well, there are a lot of reasons. Justice is part of it, but—"

"Cece," I interrupted, "wouldn't you say that you have a strong sense of justice?"

She looked at me, confused.

I raised my eyebrows.

Realisation washed over her face. "Yes. I have a strong sense of justice."

"What would you say to Lily if she were here right now?"

Cece sat up straighter, drawing her shoulders back. "If Lily were here right now, I would tell her that she doesn't know who she just messed with."

Poor kid.

I waved at the camera to stop rolling. "Excellent," I told Cece. "Now let's workshop how this is going to go down."

It went exactly how I intended.

I hyped Cece up. Fed her lines. Got her in the zone.

Then I got wardrobe and hair and makeup to fuss around her for much longer than necessary. Gave it time for her adrenaline to wear off, so by the time we shot the scene, she was completely off-balance again.

She tried her best. I'd give her that.

But Lily ate her for breakfast. "Oh, honey," she said coolly, when a shaking Cece told her she didn't know who she was messing with. "I don't care."

It was an incredible economy of words. An astonishing constellation of facial expressions: the curled corner of her lips, the raised eyebrow, the amused glint in her eyes. It took a second and a half to give us the perfect grab: the one that told us Lily Fireball was a monster.

She was extraordinarily good at this, in a way that usually would have delighted me, but I had to look away. There was a dull throbbing at the base of my skull.

Lily Fireball was going to be so fucking famous.

At least I'd made sure the primary fight in the premiere was Lily vs Cece and not Lily vs Juliet-Dylan, I told myself, trying to refocus myself on what I could actually control. That worked better for my overarching season plans. And getting Cece cut would save me a lot of nursemaiding.

The First Night Party ended immediately afterwards. Suzette had called it, not me, and I clung to my annoyance over that to avoid feeling anything else. "You can't make these kinds of calls without consulting me," I growled at her. "I just needed fifteen fucking minutes, Suzette!"

"You know the timetable. We're running out of night."

She wasn't wrong. It was four in the morning, so it was still dark, but Necklace Ceremonies took forever to shoot. I instructed Tim (Tom?) to make sure the blackout curtains were properly shut in case we got any stray sunlight.

I'd wanted those fifteen minutes to shoot a scene between Romeo-Dylan and Cece. As Prince Charming, it didn't seem in-character for him *not* to spend any time with her, after the night she'd had. I wanted him to let her down easy, in the kindest, most gentlemanly way. *You've had such a rough night, Cece,* I was going to coax him into saying. *I can see that this isn't the right environment for you, and I don't want to cause you any pain.*

It would be perfect show-don't-tell characterisation, demonstrating exactly who our main players were in only a few moments of television. Romeo-Dylan was the ultimate dream boyfriend who put the needs of others ahead of his own. Lily Fireball was a monster who ate the weak (the Cece types), setting up those who could withstand her (the Juliet-Dylan types) as strong—which would in turn play into the romance plot, because that archetypal "strong woman" was who Romeo-Dylan was looking for.

It was the kind of story logic I'd usually whiteboard out, to explain how it all fit together. Automatically, I looked around for Lily, and found her standing off to the side, out of the way of the crew, reapplying her lipstick in the mirror of her compact.

She caught me looking, and winked.

My head ached. My heart ached. My whole body ached.

Why did she have to do this to me? Of all the ways for her to come back into my life, why did it have to be like this?

I made myself look away. Maybe the conversation between Romeo-Dylan and Cece would work better after he dumped her anyway. If Cece started crying and begging for a chance to stay before she was formally cut, it'd be harder for us to hold the Prince Charming line.

Do your job, Murray. Just do your fucking job. Feel your feelings later.

As the crew finished dressing the Necklace Ceremony set and Suzette and Carrie corralled the women, I took Romeo-Dylan into our war room. It was actually the Villa's multimedia room, but we'd appropriated it and installed a lock on the door so none of the contestants could sneak in.

We had a wall covered in the fifteen Juliets' headshots. I positioned Romeo-Dylan in front of it. "All right, mate. We've got to whittle it down to twelve. Who are we cutting?"

He bit his lip, thinking. "I didn't talk to either of them during the party." He indicated two of the women. "And I don't remember them particularly well from the red carpet, so . . ."

"Rani and Samantha. Okay. Who else?"

"I'm not sure. Maybe her? Or her? Or her?" He pointed to Kanda, Heather, and Jess K in quick succession.

"Can I make a suggestion?"

"Of course."

I tapped Cece's picture.

"No!" Romeo-Dylan exclaimed. "She got pushed in the pool! I'll look like an arsehole if I cut her!"

"You didn't talk to her during the party. And . . ."

I paused deliberately. I'd figured out within ten minutes of meeting him where his weak spot was, but there was an art to this, digging your thumbs into a pressure point without someone noticing you were doing it.

"I'll level with you," I said. "Cece is really struggling with the cameras. You saw how she was on the red carpet. Letting her go will be the kindest thing you can do."

Romeo-Dylan's fingers started tapping.

"If you're worried about looking like an arsehole, don't be," I said. "We can give you an earpiece. I can feed you some lines that'll have you coming out looking golden."

Romeo-Dylan sighed. "You sure I can't cut Lily Fireball?"

"Yes," I replied. "Sorry."

Romeo-Dylan delivered the lines exactly as I fed them to him. "I thought long and hard about who to give this last necklace to," he said, when only four women—Lily, Cece, Rani and Samantha—were left unchosen at the end of the Necklace Ceremony. "I told you at the beginning of tonight that I like strong women. Ballsy women. Women who aren't afraid to go for what they want."

Lily started to smirk.

"Sometimes, though," Romeo-Dylan said, "it's possible to take things too far."

"Now pause," I whispered into my headset.

He didn't really need to—I had a million other shots of him pausing that I could edit in later to ramp up the tension and the misdirect—but he did.

"Okay," I whispered. "And—"

"I like a woman who stands up for herself," he repeated. "Someone who stands up for what she believes in. Someone with a strong sense of justice. Someone who fights for what she wants."

Lily's smirk deepened. In my peripheral vision, I saw Cece's eyes light up.

"And I believe in second chances. Which is why I'd like to give this last necklace to . . . Lily Fireball."

All the blood drained out of Cece's face.

She got paler and paler as Z made an announcement about the twist we'd had foisted upon us: the imposition of the new pandemic restrictions and the fact that no one was allowed to leave the set. "Will we be paid?" she choked out.

"I'm not sure now is the most appropriate—" Z began.

"Answer me! If you don't know—"

Cece looked wildly around the room until she found me. "Murray! What's the deal? Are we getting paid? Because I've got rent, and if I'm here and I'm locked down and I'm not getting paid, then I can't afford it."

Amanda had an arm around her, but Cece was actively swaying on her feet, her eyes so wide the whites were visible the whole way around. "What if my flatmates lose their jobs too? I need to look for work! Are we getting paid? Tell me! Are we getting paid?"

"I think she's having a panic attack," Amanda said, and Cece went down.

It was horrible. Obviously.

But it was going to be killer TV.

Romeo-Dylan raced over and caught Cece before she could completely crush Amanda. Juliet-Dylan dove in and tried to help, snapping at people that she was a nurse and to get out of her way. It gave us a beautiful moment of teamwork between the Dylans as they both tried to help her, Juliet-Dylan checking her pulse, Romeo-Dylan cradling her head in his lap; a perfect contrast between the toughness of Juliet-Dylan and the fragility of Cece.

"Murray," Carrie said in my earpiece. "Insurance."

Shit. Juliet-Dylan might be a registered nurse, but she wasn't listed on our insurance policy. If something beyond nerves and low blood sugar was wrong with Cece and Juliet-Dylan gave her the wrong care, we'd be liable.

"Get the medic," I said into my headset, and reluctantly waded in to break it up.

But that ultimately gave us even better TV. Romeo-Dylan swept Cece into his arms like a princess. Trailed by the medic, the cameras, and me, he carried her out—all the way down to the Convent, the house at the bottom of the hill.

The sun was coming up, silver and pink and pale gold over the lake. The vista was incredible. In front of it, Romeo-Dylan was a silhouette, dark against the dewy green of the grass, cradling Cece against him like she was the most precious thing in the world.

The poster. This was the poster for the season, better even than Brett and Mary-Ellen under the waterfall.

In the cold sunlight of the dawn, I allowed myself a smile. It had been a long, hard, emotional, exhausting night, but this was going to be the best fucking season premiere we'd ever done.

"Nailed it," I murmured instinctively.

"What?" Saurav said.

"Nothing," I lied.

6

Lily

Twelve years ago

I really didn't want to like Julia.

In our first three months away in the wilderness together shooting *Desert Island Castaway*, I'd put together a mental picture of Murray's fiancée from the things he'd told me—his childhood sweetheart, incredibly intelligent, just starting a PhD in history—and spent a lot of time throwing mental darts at it. She was probably shy. Introverted. A gentle, nice girl next door. A librarian-type, who wore glasses and cardigans buttoned all the way up to the neck, the kind that made boys go wild fantasising about unbuttoning them to reveal the softness and the vulnerability beneath.

The more I realised how much I genuinely *liked* Murray, the more darts I threw. I had no loyalty to this cardigan girl. Just because Murray had put a ring on it (at age 22! what the fuck was he thinking?!) didn't mean he wasn't fair game.

But he was annoyingly faithful to her. Not a single one of my ploys worked. He'd spent at least sixteen hours a day with me while we were in the wilderness, eaten every meal with me, listened to all my thoughts, laughed at all my jokes, and exhibited interest in even my third- and fourth-tier stories (even I had to admit that the story of that time I modelled in Thuong's first fashion show and the heel of my stiletto snapped halfway down the runway wasn't exactly the world's most compelling narrative, but he still listened and laughed). He even masterminded a brilliant scheme that allowed us to completely ruin the life of the gaffer that kept following me around and telling me how much he liked Asian girls because they were "submissive." But then, every morning after the night shoot ended, the only person I'd ever met whose brain worked the same way as mine did would go back to his own trailer and call his fiancée.

And unfortunately, when we got back from that first stint in the wilderness and I finally met her, Julia turned out to be—*sigh*—cool.

I hadn't been entirely wrong. The woman did love cardigans. But she was also, it turned out, doing a PhD in *sex* history (objectively cool); had no problem with the fact her fiancé had become best friends with a hot girl (an extremely cool level of self-assuredness); and, contrary to the sweet, innocent, wouldn't-hurt-a-fly image I'd created of her, she had a healthy (and, alas, also cool) level of respect for schemes.

"Okay, so I need your advice," she said, sitting down opposite me. "I will pay you in alcohol."

Murray and I had just come back from shooting our second season of *Desert Island Castaway*, and we were out for drinks at the same bar I'd first spotted him in more than a year ago. Nominally, it was a group thing, but Thuong, who was the designated driver for my little crew, was once again running late, and Murray's other friends were clustered around a TV showing the football, so Julia and I were on our own.

"I think old mate already has that covered—" I nodded towards Murray, who was standing at the bar, "—but for you, I can manage a freebie. Hit me."

"I have a nemesis," Julia said. "He's in my PhD program, he works in the same field as me, and he's the worst person in the world. How do I destroy him?"

I cracked my knuckles. "Oh, honey, you have come to the right place."

I was seven points into a twelve-point plan when Murray slid into the booth. "Drinks," he announced, putting three beers down on the table and kissing Julia's temple. "What did I miss?"

"Lily's helping me destroy Elias," Julia said.

"Is my help not good enough now?" Murray looked slightly miffed.

"Some things need a woman's touch," I said.

"And I'm afraid you won't love me anymore if you understand how cutthroat I can be," Julia said. "Cheers."

We clinked our drinks. Julia spluttered as she took a sip. "What is this?"

"Oh, shit, sorry," Murray said. "I ordered on autopilot."

"There was only one pub out near where we were shooting this season," I explained, taking a sip of my own. "This was the best beer they had on tap."

"It's disgusting."

"Only at first," Murray said. "You get used to it."

Julia shook her head. "Sometimes it makes me really sad to think of you out there in the wilderness, eating and drinking absolute garbage," she said, taking his hand and pressing her lips to his knuckles. "Without anyone taking care of you."

"How sad?" he asked, looking hopeful. "Enough to make osso bucco for me?"

She laughed. "You never miss an opportunity, do you?"

"I try not to."

"Fine, fine," she said. "Because I love you, I will set aside the better part of a day so I can feed you—*and* I will even watch you ruin my masterpiece with an obscene amount of pepper and not say a word."

He grinned devilishly, and leaned in to kiss her, just once, sweetly, gently. "Love you too, darling."

I took a swig of my beer, swallowing the unwelcome flash of jealousy down. "This?" I said, gesturing to them. "All this cutesy, cuddly, lovey-dovey business? All these feelings, right in front of everybody's salads? Disgusting. Just so you're both aware."

7

Murray

The sun was almost up by the time I trudged back towards the Villa. My joints were aching. The downside of shooting perfect television like Romeo-Dylan's hero march down the hill was walking back up the hill afterwards.

I briefly considered radioing one of the PAs to swing down in a golf cart and pick me up, but discarded the idea almost immediately. I'd instructed Suzette and Carrie to send everyone to bed as soon as possible. We had a tight turnaround between the end of the First Night Party and our group date today. No one was going to be well-rested, but there was a marked difference in performance between a-bit-rested and not-at-all-rested.

I looked at my work phone. It was five to seven in the morning, and I had thirty-three unread messages.

I scrolled through them quickly. They weren't urgent, but if I didn't deal with them, they were going to snowball.

No rest for me, then.

The hotel pillows danced through my mind as I made myself coffee in the Villa kitchen. What I wouldn't give for one of those pillows right now, to put my head down and let it swallow me up for a while. To put the reins down, and let my thoughts and my emotions catch up to one another, and to have a minute to figure out what to do next.

My stomach growled. I found a muesli bar in my utility belt and took a bite, coffee in one hand as I headed for the war room. Once Tim and Tom were up, I'd have to get one of them to bring some food from craft services into the nine-thirty production meeting.

"Took you long enough."

I paused, second bite of the muesli bar halfway to my mouth, coffee mug burning my fingers.

Lily looked like a ghost, sitting there at the conference table in one of her satin dressing gowns, her own coffee cup in front of her. If it wasn't for her ringless hands, I might think that I'd time-travelled in my own life, walked from the kitchen back into a time when things were normal.

"You should be in bed, Lily."

"You should take better care of yourself. Your eye twitch is never going to go away if you keep mainlining caffeine and sugar and nothing else."

Like clockwork, my eye started twitching again.

She noticed. "Sorry."

I grunted, setting my coffee on the table and sitting. One of my knees made an ominous crunching sound as I stretched my legs out in front of me. "You should be in bed," I repeated. "We've got a long shoot today."

"Photo shoot date?"

I nodded, eating the other half of my muesli bar. The first group date was always a photo shoot. We partnered with a women's magazine and sold them the pictures for an eye-watering sum.

"Am I on the date card?"

"I haven't decided yet."

"Put me on it. And put me in a shoot with the tall one who tried to throw down with me. Girl-Dylan."

"Absolutely not."

"Why not? I set up a perfect story for you. A slam-dunk. She's the ideal rival for me. Hero to her bones, but clearly not suited to boy-Dylan. She'll be easy as hell to ricochet onto the next season of *Wherefore Art Thou Romeo.*"

I took a sip of my too-hot, too-strong coffee. "What do you mean, clearly not suited to boy-Dylan?"

"Come on, Murray, you can read the vibes better than that." Lily tapped her fingernails against her mug. "They're obviously going to end up in a 'I like you so much, and we're such good friends, but there just isn't anything romantic here' place. There's no spark."

"You saw them together for, what, thirty seconds? You're in no position to know."

"I didn't need thirty seconds. I could have told you that in three. How badly are you slipping?"

I set my coffee down a little too hard. Some splashed onto the table.

"Don't start with me, Lily," I said. "I'm still so fucking angry with you."

She paused for a moment, the deliberate pause of someone who understood exactly what she was doing.

"That's fair," she said. "I've earned that anger. I don't begrudge you it, not at all."

"How generous of you. Now you don't need to get me a Christmas present."

"But you see how well this is working, right? You see how having a chaos agent villain makes the whole thing come alive? How dynamic it makes the story? What a strong hook Lily Fireball will be? How much *fun* she is?"

I closed my fingers tight around my coffee cup and took another sip, knuckles white.

"This is going to be the best season premiere we've ever done, Murray."

In some other universe, where life followed the logic of narrative, the coffee cup exploded in my fist, sending liquid and ceramic shards everywhere.

"I'm right," she said. "You know I'm right."

"Of course I know you're right! But do you think that makes any of this go away?"

"Any of what?"

"You know perfectly well what!"

She had the good grace not to say anything.

I put the coffee cup down and smacked myself in the chest, hard, over my heart. "Do you think it changes how terrified I am, Lily?" I demanded. "How worried I am about you? How much it hurts, seeing you throw away your career? How trapped I feel, seeing you burn down your whole life right in front of me, and being forced to help you do it?"

"Murray," she said, voice even, expression composed, "I don't have a life to burn down anymore."

"Oh, great. What a comforting thing to hear you say. That really makes me feel better."

"I understand why you're worried. And the fact that you care enough to be worried—that means a lot."

"Of course I care! Do you think anything could change that? Ever?"

She paused. For a split second, I thought I saw her waver.

But then, "Thank you," she said, as calmly as if I'd passed her the salt. "But we've always trusted each other, and I need you to trust me now. I know what I'm doing."

"Why should I trust you? You didn't trust me enough to tell me you were coming. And you won't trust me enough to tell me why you're really here."

"I have told you."

"Don't bullshit me."

She took a sip of her coffee. "What's that thing you always tell junior producers? Truth is relative?"

"For fuck's sake, Lily," I groaned, burying my face in my hands. "Are you trying to make my brain melt out my ears?"

She paused again—more contemplative, this time.

"Okay, fine," she said. "You're right. I did break your trust, not telling you I was coming, and I genuinely don't want to make your life any harder. So let me prove to you that I'm here to help."

I glared at her through my fingers.

"I mean it," she said. "Give me a task. Let me take something off your plate."

I considered it, teeth gritted so hard my jaw was aching.

"All right," I said. "Back off Dylan G."

"Why, though? That doesn't make any sense, story-wise. That's not the play. The play is—"

"You want me to trust you know what you're doing? How about you trust I know what I'm doing?"

She looked at me.

I looked back.

"Fine," she said.

She stood up, stretched, and then walked over to the door. "You're wrong, though," she said. "You're making a big mistake."

"If you have so many thoughts and feelings about the storytelling strategy," I said, "why did you come back as a contestant, where you can't do anything about it?"

The smile that spread across her face was immediate, but I'd already realised my mistake. I might as well have waved a red flag at a bull.

Oh, I can't do anything about it? that smile said. *Challenge accepted.*

But, "Make sure you eat some actual food," was all she said. "You can't do your best work running on fumes."

"Listen to me," I said a few hours later in the production meeting, trying and failing to keep the frustration out of my voice. "We are setting ourselves up for a world of trouble if we put those two in a shoot together."

The theme for this year's photo shoot group date was love triangles. Eight of the twelve remaining Juliets were coming, and we needed to divide them into four pairs, so each shoot would be two women and Romeo-Dylan.

It hadn't been difficult for Suzette, Carrie and I to decide which eight Juliets to include. Pairing the women up, though, was proving to be more of a challenge.

"I see why we need to keep Lily and Dylan G apart," Suzette said. "That's obvious. But Amanda and Dylan G too?"

"You didn't notice how they were looking at each other?"

Suzette shrugged. "They just read as good friends to me."

"Which is a narrative thread we can develop down the track," Carrie said.

"We are *not* doing a Season Eight narrative."

In Season Eight, masterminded by our old boss Tony, Juliets had been cast in pairs—sisters, friends, cousins, a mother and daughter—to compete for the same Romeo. Lily and I had argued strongly against the gimmick, but we'd been overruled. The end result had torn a lot of close female relationships apart, and had been such a misogynist disaster that even Fucking Greg had been able to see it.

"I'm not suggesting a Season Eight narrative," Carrie said. "The opposite, actually. There's the potential for a beautiful friendship story with Dylan G and Amanda. We could tell a story about how romance isn't the only important relationship you can find on *Marry Me, Juliet*."

"I love that," Suzette said. "And it's only going to make the audience connect to Dylan G more, which is what we want."

I closed my eyes for a moment and exhaled through my nose.

"I think we've got some great combos here," Carrie said. "Naya and Kanda do Archie. Parisa and Kumiko do *The Graduate*. Lily and Marija do *My Best Friend's Wedding*, and Amanda and Dylan G do *Pride and Prejudice*."

"Parisa's going to hate being cast as Mrs Robinson," Suzette said. "She's already said a hundred times she doesn't want to be pigeonholed as a cougar."

"Sell it to her as getting the age difference conversation out of the way," I said, my brain making the narrative move automatically. Parisa was thirty-eight, the oldest woman in the Villa, making her seven years older than Romeo-Dylan. "Something to be addressed in Episode Two which we can then move on from."

"Copy that."

"We're making a mistake putting Amanda and Dylan G together. I'm telling you."

Carrie and Suzette both groaned.

"How about we lean into it today?" Carrie said. "*Right* into it. Let's put Amanda and Dylan G into a situation where, if there is a spark, it'll be incredibly obvious. That way, at least we know what we're dealing with."

I gave up. If I had to prove it to them, I fucking well would. "Fine."

Suzette looked at her watch. "We've got to set up for the date card reveal now, or we'll be behind schedule."

"On it," Carrie said. "Murray, go have a shower and eat something before you fall over."

She disappeared, but Suzette hung back. "What?" I said, standing up and stretching.

"Lily."

"What about her?"

"What's the deal, Murray?" Suzette said. "And don't just fob me off with the bullshit you said in the crew briefing yesterday. What the hell is going on?"

I buckled my utility belt back on. "You have exactly the same information I do."

She rolled her eyes. "Fine. Be that way."

"What do you want me to say, Suzette? We all knew the network had sent a ringer. I found out it was Lily when she turned up at pre-show interviews. What other secret information do you think I have?"

"Is she all right?"

"Your guess is as good as mine."

"Are *you* all right?"

I put my earpiece back in and checked that my radio was on.

"Murray," Suzette said gently, putting her hand on my arm, "I know how you feel about her."

I looked pointedly at her hand until she removed it.

She sighed. "If you don't want to talk to me, that's fine, but you should talk to someone. Bottling whatever the fuck is going on up will only—"

"Is it still unsolicited advice hour," I said, "or can I get back to work?"

Suzette shook her head in exasperation. "Carrie and I can cover the date card reveal, if you just want to tap back in for the actual group date. Take a nap, Murray."

I didn't. The number of texts on my work phone I needed to go through was still in the double digits.

However, I did make the short trek over to the crew trailer village, so I could have a shower and change my clothes. The water pressure in my trailer was shit, but it didn't matter. I had too many other things on my mind to care.

The part of me that was a rational human being knew Suzette was right. I should probably talk this Lily situation out with someone. Laying it all out—telling the story for someone else—might help me make sense of it.

But who, exactly, was I going to talk to?

I had friends outside of work. Sort of, anyway. I'd drifted apart from most of them—between the ridiculous hours demanded by my job and the increasing number of them getting married and having children, we didn't really see each other much—but I could probably still call one of them.

None of them had ever really understood what Lily and I were to each other, though. I'd cut ties with more than one person over the years for repeatedly saying things like, "Don't tell me you haven't nailed that girl yet."

I could call Julia. She understood. She'd listen. But this wasn't exactly the kind of thing you could talk about with your ex-wife, no matter how well you'd settled into post-divorce friendship.

I exhaled, letting the weak stream of water cascade over my head. The only person I'd ever go to with this kind of situation was Lily.

I didn't notice the bottle on the table until I was dressed, hooking my radio to my belt and threading the wire of my earpiece back up my shirt. *Good luck for the season! Thought you could use something "diverse" to drink. Greg McD*, the gift tag read.

I picked it up. It was Taiwanese whiskey.

Predictably, my eye started to twitch.

I pressed two fingers into my eyelid, sat down on my lumpy trailer bed with my head tipped forward until it stopped, popped two ibuprofen and sculled about a litre of water, and then headed over to oversee the group date.

The photo shoot was always a fiddly date to shoot. The concept was simple, but it was necessarily bitsy. Our limited crew numbers made it even more difficult: we didn't have a) anywhere near enough hair and makeup people, or b) a photographer. However, we'd cobbled together a rotational schedule that kept things moving forward and deputised Saurav, who dabbled in still photography, to do his best. "Thanks for the chance, mate," he said to me, as the crew reset from *The Graduate* to *My Best Friend's Wedding.* "I appreciate it."

"No worries."

I was paying maybe thirty per cent of my attention to him. Another twenty was on Romeo-Dylan, who'd emerged from wardrobe in black tie, looking every inch the perfect groom. He made eye contact with me, searching for affirmation. I gave him a nod and the friendliest smile I could muster.

The other fifty per cent, of course, was waiting for Lily.

I heard her before I saw her. "Why am I the bridesmaid instead of the bride?"

She stormed onto set, tail of her satiny lilac bridesmaids' dress whipping behind her, making a beeline for Romeo-Dylan. "This is completely unfair!" she said, grabbing at his lapels. "Why am I being cast as the villain?"

God, she was good. We usually had to Frankenbite a lot of our audio—take some out-of-context phrases and stitch them together to make a full sentence—but Lily could produce a perfect sound bite like it was nothing.

She looked at Romeo-Dylan and—were her eyes watering? "I know I went too far last night," she said, her voice catching. "I'm fiery. I'm passionate. All my life, people have been telling me that I'm too much. But I'm not a bad person. I swear."

93

There was not a person on the planet who could have pitched it any better.

If all she gave was one-note cartoon villain, Romeo-Dylan would look foolish for not cutting her. She needed to add dimension: a reason to keep Lily Fireball.

I had no doubt she'd pinpointed his weakness as quickly as I had. Quicker, probably. Dylan Jayasinghe Mellor was far too kind for his own good.

"Oh god, Lily, I'm sorry." Romeo-Dylan cupped her face in his hands. "Don't cry."

."Lily *Fireball*." Her bottom lip was quivering.

"Lily Fireball. I'm sorry. I'll remember next time."

"Thank you," she said, sniffing. "I appreciate it."

"Do you want a hug?"

She nodded. Romeo-Dylan wrapped his arms around her, and she buried her face in his shirt . . .

The night of the funeral.

My fingers against the back of her head, pressing her against me as she fell apart in my arms.

Blood of My Enemies, all over my shirt.

I looked away, busying myself by digging through my utility belt for another muesli bar.

"Julia Roberts might be the bridesmaid in *My Best Friend's Wedding*," Romeo-Dylan said, "but she was also the main character, okay? It's hard to be the bad guy if it's your story."

"I'm going to get that embroidered on a pillow," Lily said, smiling that watery, vulnerable smile up at him.

Behind her, Marija, who had emerged onto the set wearing a wedding dress, rolled her eyes.

"All right!" I called, my voice a little croaky. "Let's get set for our first shot."

Lily turned away from Romeo-Dylan. Completely dry-eyed, she gave Marija a little wink.

Another perfect moment I would have to put on television, the kind that would have everyone talking about Lily Fireball.

Another moment which made my stomach lurch like I was coming to the top of a rollercoaster, anticipating the drop.

Unsurprisingly, I was right about Amanda and Juliet-Dylan.

We'd put them together in a *Pride and Prejudice*-themed shoot with Romeo-Dylan. He was Mr Darcy, Juliet-Dylan was Lizzy, and Amanda was in drag as Mr Wickham (Carrie's idea: "she's our frontburner potential bicon," she'd said, "let's give ourselves some good promo shots in case she decides she wants to be out on the show"). Contestants often reacted badly when we put them in a not-conventionally-attractive costume, but Amanda threw herself into the role. "Let's have a duel, Mr Darcy!" she declared. "For Lizzy!"

I stepped in and tried to redirect the narrative, but the snowball was moving too fast down the hill. "Mandie, look at me," Juliet-Dylan instructed. "Practise on me first. Show me your intimidating glare."

Amanda looked deep into Juliet-Dylan's eyes.

And—very clearly, very obviously, in a way completely free of any nuance or subtlety—she fell head over heels in love with her.

"Touché, Murray," Suzette said to me as we wrapped up. "You were right."

"Yeah." Carrie winced. "Sorry."

If it had been Lily and I disagreeing, I would have rubbed the victory in, but there was no point. "I'm instituting a new rule," was all I said. "No putting Amanda and Dylan G on group dates together."

"This sucks," Carrie said. "This is the first time we've ever had a queer romance plot brewing that could be genuinely sweet and feel-good and not end up disgusting and exploitative. I can't believe we have to kill it."

"I know. I'm sorry. But . . ."

"Yeah, yeah, I get it." Carrie sighed. "It makes me feel dirty, though. Remind me to call my wife tonight. Tell her I love her."

Thankfully for narrative course correction, Romeo-Dylan dutifully picked Juliet-Dylan for his post-date one-on-one time. "I had such a great time with Dylan G in our *Pride and Prejudice* photo shoot today," he told me in ITMs. "What an honour, playing Mr Darcy to a Lizzy Bennet like that."

It was a good line, but I made a note to brainstorm what the next step would be. Romeo-Dylan's "she's a hero, I'm so honoured to be in her presence" awestruck thing was working well at the moment, but awe was not conducive to intimacy in the longer term.

I was going to have to sell the shift to him in a way that wouldn't make him think he was doing anything wrong, too. Wasn't *that* going to be fun.

"Great work, mate," I told him, when we finished the interview. "Well done."

"Thanks. Can I ask a favour?"

"Of course." I steeled myself for more hand-holding. Hopefully this was something I could paper over with a quick pep talk. We were going to wait for full night until we shot his one-on-one time with Juliet-Dylan, so I finally had a couple of free hours for some food and a nap.

"I want to go down to the Convent," Romeo-Dylan said. "I know I'm not supposed to have any contact with the eliminated Juliets, but I want to check on Cecilia. Make sure she's all right."

"Two steps ahead of you, mate. I've put that on the schedule for tomorrow, after your single date with Jess D. The whole you-can't-leave-even-when-you're-eliminated thing is a real twist, so we wanted to shoot some stuff with you and the Convent women for Episode Two anyway."

The expression on Romeo-Dylan's face was pained. "I . . ."

You didn't need to be as good at reading non-verbal signals as I was to understand what he was too polite to say.

"You want to go now," I said.

"I need to see for myself that she's all right."

The beautiful vision of a sandwich and some sleep shattered into a million pieces.

"All right. We've got a couple of hours. We'll make it work."

It was unfair of me to be irritated with him. His mix of compliance and eloquence was all I could ever ask for in a Romeo. His need for reassurance was completely understandable, and it wasn't his fault I no longer had a partner to split duties with.

I was still irritated, though.

I sent him off to wardrobe to get de-Darcy'd, rounded up some crew, and poured about eight litres of coffee down my throat, before I headed down to the Convent to warn the eliminated Juliets that the Romeo was on his way.

Rani and Samantha were thrilled to hear that their reality TV careers weren't quite over yet. "Is there any chance he might pick someone to bring back into the game?" Samantha asked. "We're still here, after all. It'd be silly not to give him that chance."

"Don't get your hopes up," I replied.

It was a good idea, though. I made a mental note to circle back around to it once more Juliets had been eliminated.

"Where's Cece?"

"Upstairs," Rani said. "She's been sleeping all day."

The level of jealousy that caused me was deeply unprofessional.

I had a vision for how I wanted the two scenes to play out. Once Romeo-Dylan arrived, I set him up with Rani and Samantha so he could explain to them, and thus the audience, what the new pandemic restrictions meant, and why the women in the Convent weren't allowed to leave.

With Cece, I intended for him to have the breakup conversation I'd wanted to do the night before. Instead of information, I wanted this chat to carry emotion. "We want the audience to see that you eliminated her for the kindest possible reason," I coached Romeo-Dylan. "And we want them to see that you care about her wellbeing despite there being nothing romantic between you."

"Why wouldn't I care about her wellbeing? She's still a person."

"I'm going to shoot pickup ITMs for this tomorrow, and I want you to say exactly that."

"Is that really Prince Charming shit?"

How had this man reached the age of thirty-one and remained this naïve?

"Yes," I said. "This is a broad-strokes medium. Here, men giving a shit about women they're not intending to fuck is extremely Prince Charming shit. The bar is that low."

That last sentence turned out to be a terrible mistake.

Maybe if I'd had five minutes of sleep in the last two days, I would have remembered that even though Dylan Jayasinghe Mellor was the kindest man on earth, he was also an Olympian, and thus had a huge competitive streak. You didn't put a bar in front of a man like that and expect him to simply step over it when he could leap.

Cece struggled when they sat down, stammering her way through sentences, undone by the presence of the cameras. Romeo-Dylan suggested that he take her outside for a few moments, and I agreed. Lily had always been the one who pulled good cop duty in our partnership. Romeo-Dylan's magnetic niceness had a better chance of calming Cece down than most of my methods.

I thought it had worked. When they came back in, they shot a near-perfect conversation.

But then, when we wrapped, they pitched an idea to me so utterly unhinged my brain nearly exploded.

"You want to be *fake friends*?"

"It doesn't need to be fake," Romeo-Dylan said. "I think we can be real friends."

"But for the show ... yes," Cece added. She was standing slightly behind Romeo-Dylan, trying to hide in his shadow. "He could come down here and talk to me about what's happening on the show. I could be his sounding board."

Of course *now* she could fucking speak in sentences.

"I can think of a thousand reasons why this won't work." I resisted the urge to bury my entire fist in my twitching eye. "One, where are you going to find the time, Dylan?"

He shrugged. "I'll find it."

How?! I barely managed to restrain myself from screaming.

"Okay then, two, where am *I* going to find the time? We're down to the absolute bare bones in terms of crew. We can't bring anyone new into the bubble. And now you're telling me you want to do all this extra filming? That means cameras. That means sound. That means lighting. That means me, coming down here and holding your hands. I'm good at my job, but I can't fucking time-travel."

"We could mount cameras up there," Frida, one of the camera operators, said.

I glared at her, but she'd worked with me too long and wasn't scared of me anymore. Undeterred, she outlined a perfectly sensible plan: to put mounted cameras in the living room, hang some shotgun mics, and keep them running 24/7. "Call it "Convent Cam,"" she suggested.

It was a good idea. We'd already put mounted cameras and shotgun mics in the living spaces in the Villa to cover our crew shortfall. Plus, if I had to keep the eliminated Juliets on set, I might as well make them sing for their supper. We could capture these friend chats that Romeo-Dylan and Cece wanted to do, but also some slice-of-life Convent stuff, which we could turn into bonus website or social media content.

I couldn't believe the idea hadn't already occurred to me, to be honest. It was basically the same premise as mine and Lily's first ever credit as producers: *Adjudication Station*, the *Desert Island Castaway* webshow about the group of eliminated contestants who eventually decided the winner.

But even though Convent Cam was a good idea, it would generate fucking hours and hours *and hours* of footage to scrub through. More work, to add on top of the teetering mountain I already had to tackle.

"You've got to admit you're a disaster on camera," I said to Cece, who seemed like the weakest link. "Like I said, I don't have time to come down here and hold your hand. Neither do Carrie or Suzette. You and Rani and Samantha are all out of the game. We've got twelve other women up at the Villa to focus on. Plus him." I gestured at Romeo-Dylan.

"I'll hold her hand," he said.

"Don't you fucking dare hold her hand," I snapped at him, annoyance finally getting the better of me. "We agreed on the story we're telling this season, Dylan. Epic romance. Fairy-tale shit. If the audience sees you running down here to hold her hand, it'll look like you're trying to find a wife while having a fuckbuddy on the side."

"I meant metaphorically," he replied. "I'm not an idiot, Murray. I know the story we're telling. I'm not interested in telling a different one. We're still on exactly the same page. I just want to add this little subplot."

I argued the point longer, out of a combination of principle and desperation, but that was the moment I gave up. This was going to create a lot of work, but if I got Romeo-Dylan off-side and he decided to be uncooperative, that would create even more.

Plus, I reflected, the evening breeze brushing my sweaty hair back as I sped up the hill on my golf cart, Cece really was a disaster on camera. My best bet was to let them try it, for Romeo-Dylan to see that she was in active agony, and for him to end it out of kindness. People always reacted better if you let them think they were doing things on their own terms.

I parked the golf cart back at the trailer village and hiked over towards the Villa. Suzette and Carrie and I had re-divvied up our evening duties when my unplanned detour had been added to the schedule. Suzette was doing the set-up for tomorrow's single date. Carrie was pinch-hitting for me and doing an interview with Juliet-Dylan. I'd taken over her job, supervising the shoot set-up for the Dylans' one-on-one intimacy time, which we were filming at the centre of the hedge maze beside the Villa.

It should have been easy. I'd set up a million intimacy time shoots over the years. It was hardly rocket science.

"What are you doing?" I barked at Tim and Tom.

They both froze. "Um . . . is this not right?" one of them asked.

"Have you never seen an episode of this show in your life?"

Marry Me, Juliet had an extremely maximalist aesthetic. We dripped with the visual language of romance: candles, roses, fairy lights, lush velvets and satins.

The convo couch that Tim and Tom had set up looked like the student dive bar I used to meet Julia at when she was doing her PhD. They hadn't scattered the cushions right, and some threadbare patches on the couch were showing. They'd strung one sad string of fairy lights on the trellis behind it. On the coffee table, two—two! only two!—tealights were flickering.

"We're not finished yet," the other one said.

"Have you started?"

They exchanged glances.

I pinched the bridge of my nose. "Go to the set dressing trailer. I want three blankets. Jewel tones: blue, green, magenta. More cushions to match. More fairy lights—"

"We've got fairy lights." One of them pointed to the green shopping bags sitting next to the coffee table.

"*More* fairy lights. One of the outdoor chandeliers. How many candles have you got?"

"There's a pack of fifty tealights in that one," the other one said, pointing to the bags again. "That one's cheese and shit."

"I want two hundred electric tealights," I said. "There's a breeze, the real ones might blow out. Any roses from last night that still look fresh."

"Do you really need so much stuff?"

I fixed him with one of my top-shelf glares.

"Sorry, Murray," the other one said. "We're going."

I let out a sigh when they left. That display was not going to earn me a World's Best Boss mug. Ruling with an iron fist just made people resent you—and, if they were motivated and Machiavellian enough, start plotting to overthrow you.

But the job had to get done. Properly.

I sighed again, took a long swig of water, and started the thankless task of untangling strings of fairy lights.

I ran through my to-do list as I wove the lights through the trellis. Set up the one-on-one time. Shoot it. Conduct the post-mortem interviews with both Dylans. Run through Romeo-Dylan's schedule for tomorrow with him. I should put the first of his little friend chats with Cece in the early morning. It'd mean a pre-dawn start for me, but if I could make the chats feel like a sleep-robbing chore to him, maybe I could persuade him to give up on them.

A quick war room meeting with Suzette and Carrie to go over tomorrow's plan. I'd hang back afterwards, go through some dailies. I could get one of them to do it, but I wanted to make sure I had a firm grasp on all the emerging storylines. Plus, I didn't trust anyone else not to miss things.

"You're missing the sunset, Murray."

I leaned my forehead against the trellis, exhaustion breaking over me like a wave.

"Look!" Lily said. "It's gorgeous. I know full night is traditional for intimacy time, but maybe you should consider shooting at golden hour."

I succumbed to temptation and turned around.

Lily was wearing the same long dark purple dress she'd worn pre- and post-costume on the group date, a deep eggplant colour that evoked Ursula from *The Little Mermaid* (a villainous enough colour palette that I'd made one of the other contestants, who'd been wearing a shirt in the same shade, change). She'd washed the hairspray out of her hair, and it was straight again, glossy black in the last rays of the sun. She had her hands on her hips, the way she usually stood when she was assessing the set-up for a shot, smiling at me.

"You shouldn't be here," I said.

"Why not?"

"Because I'm busy!"

I turned back to the trellis, gripping it with one hand as I tried to loop the fairy lights through the top railing. "The Dylans are going to be here soon, and I've got about an hour and a half's worth of set dressing to do."

"I didn't know this kind of menial labour was part of your job."

I shot her a look over my shoulder. "It isn't. But the network's cut our crew numbers to absolute shit this season. We've all got to help out. Which is why I don't have time to—don't touch that!"

She didn't stop unpacking the bag, laying cheese and quince paste and grapes on the coffee table. "If you need help, then I'll help."

"You don't know what you're doing."

She scoffed. "Murray, you know better than anyone that I can assemble a cheeseboard."

I ran out of things to say. Or maybe I had too many things to say. All I could manage was a glare and a choked growl.

"Don't try that with me," she said. "I'm not scared of you. What kind of cheeseboard do you want? Simple and clean, or a real cheese extravaganza?"

My knuckles were white as I clung to the trellis. The adrenaline and caffeine in my veins had evaporated. I wanted to melt into a puddle on the ground.

"Extravaganza," I said. "Dylan G's a frontrunner. We want this one-on-one to have a real cornucopia feel. Abundance. Overflow."

I looped the last of the fairy lights around the trellis and then stepped back, walking over to the green bag with the tealights. I licked my finger and held it up to the breeze.

105

"They'll blow out." Lily didn't look up from the cheese-board. "Have you got the electric ones?"

I started rearranging the cushions instead. "I sent the PAs to get them."

"Multiple PAs? To carry one box of tealights?"

"And some other things."

She didn't need to say anything. The quirk of her eyebrow, the twitch of her lips, said it all.

"They were underfoot," I said defensively.

"Tell me—" she cut a wedge out of some camembert, draping some purple grapes next to it, "—how many hours of sleep have you had in the last two days?"

I switched a red cushion with a blue one.

"And when was the last time you actually ate something off a plate?"

I stood back and regarded the trellis. I'd been right to make Tim and Tom get more fairy lights. There weren't enough.

"Murray!"

"It has to be right!"

"What has to be right? This date? Because if you're still on that girl-Dylan-is-going-to-win train . . ."

"Everything has to be right."

"Sit down."

"I don't have time."

"Sit down."

I sank down on the couch. My eye was going again. I jammed the heel of my hand into it.

Lily got up, her eggplant skirts swishing around her heels. "Head forward."

I obeyed. She came around behind me and dug her thumbs into my occipital muscles, the ones at the base of my skull.

"Head back."

I tipped my head back, closing my eyes and leaning into her thumbs, the way I'd done a thousand times before, ever since the *Desert Island Castaway* physio had taught us this trick a decade ago. She found the pressure points and pushed, hard.

Gradually, the twitch in my eye slowed. Slowed further. Stopped.

"Better?" she asked.

"Yes. Thank you."

"You know this is only a quick fix. You need to drink more water. Less coffee. Take magnesium. And you need to delegate."

"I do delegate."

"I don't care how few crew you have. There is no universe where the showrunner should be doing the PAs' job."

"They were fucking it up."

"I refuse to believe that you hired anyone for this season who wasn't experienced and competent." She dug one of her thumbs in harder to punctuate her point. "They would have figured it out."

"Of course everyone on the crew's competent. But they're not . . ."

Lily dug her thumb in again. "They're not what?"

I exhaled, twisting around on the couch to look at her. "They're all competent," I said, "but they're not you."

She blinked.

Once.

Twice.

Then, "I should get back to the Villa," she said. "The other Juliets are probably wondering where I am."

I couldn't begin to quantify how much work I had to do. I didn't have a single minute to spare.

But I sat there for several long moments after she walked away, missing her so badly it was like an iron band around my chest.

I finally got to bed just after midnight, collapsing onto the thin mattress of my trailer bed and doubling up the lumpy pillow under my head.

The one-on-one time with the Dylans hadn't been a disaster. They were two extremely likeable, telegenic people. Their conversation didn't have any awkward silences. They made each other laugh. And they both responded well to instruction. If I said "jump," they would both ask for specific details around how high and whether they should hold hands.

But Lily was right. The spark—that magical, ineffable chemistry—just wasn't there.

And no matter how many cheeseboards she put together for me . . . realistically, I had no one to help me fake it.

. . . and now I never would again.

I adjusted my pillow again and checked my phone. Yes, I had remembered to set my alarm for 5am for the Convent friend shoot. That gave me almost five uninterrupted hours to sleep.

I didn't, though. One eye open, one eye closed, I scrolled through my photos until I found the one I was looking for.

I never looked at the photos of my wedding anymore. Even though Julia and I had split amicably and she was still one of my closest friends, looking at pictures of our wedding seemed like an odd thing to do. They were full of the symbolic codes of love, the visual language of romance, and that wasn't who we were to each other anymore.

There was one photo, though, that I looked at all the time.

It was from before the ceremony, when I was getting ready. My groomsmen were in the background, boutonnieres pinned to their lapels. I was standing in the foreground, as my best man did my tie up for me.

There you go, Lily had said, smoothing my tie down and tucking it into my waistcoat. *Let's go get you married.*

She'd smiled up at me. In that moment, my feet had been very, very cold.

But I'd worn that same suit when she married Jeff, when I stood up at my best friend's wedding the way she'd stood up for me. It was a different tie this time—bright yellow, like a sunflower, so I could match Thuong and the other bridesmaids—but the picture her photographer had snapped was almost exactly the same: Lily, in her wedding dress, tying my tie and tucking it into my waistcoat.

Let's go get you married, it had taken everything in me to say to her.

Lily Ong was the love of my life. I had known that for a long, long time. I didn't know quite when it had started— long enough ago that it made me feel disloyal to Julia, certainly, although I hadn't realised just how deep my love for Lily went during our marriage—but now, it was a fundamental, unchangeable truth about myself. I had dark hair that was turning grey, I was addicted to coffee, and I was in love with Lily.

We were never going to be together. I'd known that for almost as long. She'd never felt like that about me, and we were probably too similar to be functional anyway.

But it didn't matter. I didn't need to live with her or sleep with her or share finances with her to love her. As long as she was beside me—as long as we were still a team—so what if part of me was always going to be pining for her? No one said that the love of your life had to be a romantic one.

I had missed her so much this past year. Respecting her desire to go no-contact while she grieved was one of the most difficult things I'd ever done. The longing for her to come back had been almost unbearable. It felt like someone had cracked open my skull and ripped out half my brain and forgotten to sew me back together again.

I had never anticipated that seeing her again would somehow be worse.

I traced the line of Lily's face in the photo with my finger. There were two familiar pangs in my heart.

One of pain.

One of guilt.

8

Lily

Ten years ago

"This," Murray said, rummaging in his utility belt for a bottle opener, "is an opportunity."

I snorted, taking the beer he offered me. "This is glorified babysitting. Have you ever seen any material from the Adjudication Station make an episode cut? Beyond like five seconds of interview shit?"

This was our fourth season of *Desert Island Castaway*, and the showrunner had made out like it was a big deal when he'd sent us here to look after the eliminated castaways who would return in the finale to vote for the winner ("Normally I wouldn't trust two such junior crew members with this level of responsibility, but you two show real promise").

And, like, it wasn't *not* a big deal. Murray and I would get to conduct exit interviews, which we'd only ever been allowed to assist with before. For career development, it was a step in the right direction.

But only a small one. Realistically, the biggest reason to be excited about this gig was that it was filmed in a motel rather than out in the wilderness, so we got to stay in an actual building.

Murray sat down on the couch next to me, stretching his legs out and putting his feet on the coffee table. "There's potential here, though, Lily," he insisted. "Think about it. Everyone's so focused on the stories happening in the game. But there have to be stories here too. This could absolutely be its own segment. Or a webshow or something."

I took a sip from my beer, thinking. My lipstick marked the rim of the bottle. "Okay," I said slowly.

The motel had no air-conditioning, and my hair was sticking to the back of my neck. I leaned over and put my beer on the coffee table so I could put it in a ponytail. "I hear you. The castaways were all scheming in the wilderness. Surely that didn't just stop when they got eliminated. They might be out of the game, but the final vote means they still have influence over it. There might still be schemes going on."

Murray didn't respond. His eyes were fixed on my neck.

. . . where I could feel a bead of sweat trickling down, down, before getting caught in the strap of my tank top.

Now wasn't *that* an interesting thing for Mr "Oh, We Still Haven't Set A Date Yet Because Julia's PhD Timeline Is So Intense, Definitely No Other Reason" to be noticing.

"Murray?" I said lightly. "Are you listening to me?"

"Yes, I'm listening."

Despite his distraction, I knew this was true. In all the time we'd known each other, he'd listened to every single word I'd said.

And *god* it was hot. It was so unbearably sexy that sometimes I couldn't stand it. It felt too big for my brain, too big for my body, a volcano of a feeling that made it feel like I was going to explode into a million little pieces.

"You're right," I said. "There's potential here. But we don't have a way to shoot anything. Cameras and sound only come over to film the exit interviews. And you've heard everyone going on about the budget. There's no way they're going to allocate us extra resources."

Murray shrugged. "We've got phones, don't we? We'll do it ourselves. At least for proof of concept."

I thought about it.

"Okay," I said. "I'm game. Let's do it."

He took a swig from his beer then set it down, grabbing the cheap phone message pad and motel-branded pen from the coffee table. "We can't just wander around, phones out 24/7, looking for drama. We need a strategy. Where do we think the stories are?"

He clicked the pen and scribbled on the pad to see if it was working. Some tendon in his forearm flexed. I wanted to bite it.

He glanced up at me. "What?"

"There's something about you with a pen in your hand," I said. "Or a whiteboard marker. Any kind of writing implement, really. This criminal mastermind vibe comes over you, like you're the guy in a heist movie explaining how you're going to steal the diamonds."

"Thank you? I think?"

In the humidity, his hair was curling more than usual. There were little ringlets forming just behind his ears.

If I didn't hook my finger in one of those curls, pull it straight, and watch it spring back into place, I might die.

"You should thank me," I said airily, leaning back and folding my fingers behind my head. "You know I don't like to compliment white men when I can possibly avoid it. What about Jonno and Harriet?"

"What about them?"

"They're about three seconds away from falling into bed. You've seen the way they look at each other over the breakfast buffet." It was the same way I'd be looking at Murray if I thought there was any chance he'd look back at me the same way.

Although . . .

Just because I liked and respected Julia—had become genuine friends with her, even—it didn't mean I had to blindly ship them together, no questions asked. Not if he was watching sweat roll down my neck.

Murray was scribbling on the notepad. "I like that. They were in different wilderness alliances. Jonno was teamed up with all those tradies; Harriet was in that girl gang. But if—"

"—if they start hooking up, they could potentially form their own little alliance here in Adjudication Station. Which could have a huge impact on the final vote."

"Exactly. It could completely upend the power dynamics."

"We'd have to give them a nudge, though."

I shifted position, crossing my legs under me and turning to face him on the couch. "What about something like this? We start tomorrow by doing a couple of casual little interviews with them, no big deal, nothing to see here, and we plant a few seeds. And then . . ."

Murray wrote as I talked, occasionally jumping in with some of his own suggestions or yes-and-ing mine, grin getting wider and wider.

"Well?" I asked, when we were done. "What do you think?"

"I think," he said, looking over at me, "that you're a fucking genius."

Something clicked into place inside me, a key turning in some hidden lock.

For the second time, I decided.

Sorry, Julia. This boy was going to be mine.

"Murray O'Connell," I purred, "I love it when you talk dirty to me."

Pulling the strings was so unbelievably thrilling.

Nothing had ever felt as good as adopting my friendliest, most girl-chatty tone to interview Harriet, to lean in and say, "Just between us, because I have to ask: you've seen the way that Jonno looks at you, right?," and to see her turn bright red. To meet Murray later, to watch the playback of his interview with Jonno, to see him say, "Be real with me, mate: what's the deal with you and Harriet?," and to see Jonno prevaricate in the most obvious, tell-tale ways.

To see their fingers brush at dinner in the bistro. To see them sit beside each other next to the kidney-shaped motel pool. To do a little more nudging, to press a tiny bit harder— and to see Jonno disappear into Harriet's motel room at night, their shadowy figures embracing through the thin curtains.

"Got them," Murray breathed.

The thrill was so strong that the only thing that kept me from pouncing on him was that he already had his phone out, filming. "Thank god we got everyone to sign releases," he breathed, leaning in so close to avoid the sound picking up that I could feel his stubble against my ear.

I had never wanted anyone or anything like I wanted him.

We made an announcement the next morning at breakfast. "We're having a dinner party tonight," Murray said. "We know there's a lot of disunity right now in the Adjudication Station, and we think it's best to get it all out in the open. Lily and I are going to leave a box at reception, and you have until two pm to put your anonymous questions in."

There was a disquieted murmur around the motel bistro. It was exactly the reaction we'd hoped for, and it made my whole body feel alight with excitement.

That afternoon, we reclaimed the box and sat down in my room to go through the questions. Murray laughed as he read the first one. "You were right, drama queen."

He turned the piece of paper around so I could read it. *WHAT DISUNITY?????*

I laughed too. "You'd think people playing a strategy game wouldn't be so easy to fool."

We left enough of the real questions in there that we'd have plausible deniability, but added some carefully worded ones of our own. "Is it true," one of the castaways read out, several questions deep into the dinner party, after everyone was well and truly destabilised, "that Jonno has betrayed the tradies' alliance?"

"No!" Jonno exclaimed. "I'm tradie strong!"

Surreptitiously, I hit a key on my laptop. The projector screen at the other end of the bistro flickered to life.

It had been a production to get the projector set up. My nicest, sweetest begging hadn't swayed the motel staff into letting us borrow it. Murray had had to go full bad cop to make it happen—and then getting the fucking thing to *work* had been another story. Who knew it was that difficult to find a HDMI cable?

It was worth it, though. It took about three seconds of the footage of Jonno and Harriet kissing for the room to explode.

It was intoxicating, that feeling of blowing everything up; I was drunk on it when Murray and I finally left the bistro, after a completely insincere apology to the manager about one of his tables mysteriously getting flipped.

I couldn't contain it. I wanted to tip back my head and howl at the moon. I wanted to run five marathons in a row. I wanted to lift a car over my head and hurl it a hundred metres, smashing it through the side of a building.

"I can't fucking *wait* to cut this together," Murray said. "This is going to be unbelievable TV. Unbelievable!"

I couldn't find the words to respond. Instead, I flung my arms wide to the night sky, spinning around and laughing like a madwoman.

"What did we just do, Lily?" He was laughing too, eyes and face alight with it. "What the fuck did we just *do*?"

"That," I said, "was magic."

"There's this part of my brain that's telling me 'you should feel bad, Murray, you should feel bad about pushing people's

buttons like that, normal people don't enjoy shit like that,'"
he said, "but you know what?"

"What?"

"I don't care."

I did not believe in fate, or destiny, or the universe. In that moment, standing there, looking at him, listening to him say that, I only believed in two things.

Myself.

And that this boy—this boy, with his pullable hair; this boy, who always paid attention; this boy, who had as few lines as I did—was my *person*.

"I don't care either," I said.

There was the briefest pause, and then we were both laughing again, wild, uncontrollable. I wrapped my arms around his neck, and he lifted me clean off the ground, spinning me around and around as we laughed, and I was so happy it felt like my heart was going to leap out of my chest.

Mine. Mine. *Mine.*

"God, Murray," I said, when we finally slowed, "I loved that so much."

He was still holding me off the ground. His chest was pressed against mine, and I could feel his breathing, shallow, rapid.

"Me too, Lily."

His face was very close to mine.

Should I lean in and kiss him? Or did I need to play this slower?

Julia was his first and only everything. Crossing that line would be a big deal. Did I need to coax him across it gently, or did I need to put a bomb under it and blow it up?

He set me down. I was disappointed, but it made my decision for me. Slow play it would be. And fair enough, really—Julia would still be *hurt*, of course, and there was a strong chance she would hate me forever, but it probably wouldn't be as bad if—

"I have something to ask you," he said.

. . . or maybe this wouldn't be a slow play. Maybe this would be very, very fast. Maybe I wouldn't need to make a play at all.

"Ask away." My heart was in my throat.

"I was wondering if you'd be my best man."

My soul left my body.

"We finally set a date. Julia wants to get married before she graduates, so she'll have her married name on her testamur. She's hyphenating—there's some other Julia Scott out there, and she says Scott-O'Connell will be better for recognisability on her research metrics."

"What a good reason to get married," I choked out.

He chuckled. He had the audacity to *chuckle*.

"I've been thinking about it," he said. "There are other friends I could ask—male friends—but . . . the whole idea behind a best man is that they're the person you trust the most. And you're my best friend, Lily. There's no one I trust more than you."

He smiled at me. He looked so happy it made me want to rip my eyes out.

Oh god. Oh *god*.

"Obviously I'll be your best man," I said, because what the fuck else was I supposed to do? What the fuck else was I supposed to say? "But I have conditions. Number one, I want to wear a suit."

9

Lily

Nine years ago

Weddings weren't my thing—so many *feelings*, ugh—but as far as weddings went, Murray and Julia's was lovely.

I leaned against the bar at the reception, watching Murray slow dance with the new almost-Dr Scott-O'Connell. He was holding her close, one hand pressed into the small of her back, one curled possessively against the nape of her neck, fingers playing in some loose tendrils of her hair.

He caught my eye over her shoulder and winked. I smiled back and saluted him with my almost-empty glass of wine.

It was all right. Really.

At the end of the day, nothing between us was going to change. We were even shifting jobs together. The forbidden love story of Jonno and Harriet had been such a TV sensation that we'd been headhunted by the Romeo and Juliet franchise. We'd be shooting our first season pretty much as soon as Murray and Julia got back from their honeymoon.

He was still my best friend. He was still my partner. A ring on his finger affected none of that. I had lost nothing.

It was a compelling story, but I hadn't quite managed to sell it to myself yet. I'd been trying to work on my innate territorialism—the fact that it had taken Thuong and Michael literal years to tell me they were in a relationship because they were worried I might think I was losing them to each other had led to my most sustained flirtation ever with therapy—but I was going to have to work harder, because the knowledge that Murray was going to peel that wedding dress off his bride later was like fingernails scraping across a blackboard in my mind.

I finished my glass of wine and turned around. "Can I get another of these, please?" I asked the bartender.

"Hey." Murray appeared beside me, a little breathless. "Come and dance with me."

"You know I don't dance," I said. "It's the only thing I'm worse at than cooking."

"Not even today? Not even with me?"

"I think there's a different woman you should be dancing with."

"She's dancing with her dad. Please?"

I sighed, gave in, and let him lead me to the dance floor.

It was a slow song, thank god. There was no way Murray ever would have lured me out there for a fast one. One hand settled on my waist—lightly, impersonally, like I was his sister—and he took one of my hands with his other one.

"So I think you've revolutionised the best man speech," he said. "That was awesome. Thank you."

I gave him one of my sunnier smiles. "Everyone will be getting hot girl best men soon. It'll be a whole thing."

"I was thinking about how we could incorporate it into the Romeo and Juliet shows. Their whole structure is based on romantic rituals, right? The best man speech is a classic, so—"

I let go of his hand and flicked him between the eyebrows. "Stop it, Murray. Stop thinking about work at your own wedding."

"I don't know how to." Murray looked a little sheepish. "Part of me is always thinking about it. Julia's the same. No matter what she's doing, at least twenty-five per cent of her mind is on her research."

Ugh. He just had to rub it in, his perfect happiness with a perfect woman who wasn't me.

"Of course," he added, "the other seventy-five per cent is focused on destroying Elias."

And he had to remind me that I actually fucking *liked her.*

"You really love her, don't you?"

I was horrified that the question had slipped out of my mouth, but all Murray did was smile. "For as long as I can remember."

I made a decision.

Inside my mind, there was a vault. It was the place I put things when they got too big, too overwhelming, too much; a place where I could keep them until I was calm and steady enough to unpack them properly, to draw lines around them and file them—or bury them completely.

I loved him so much.

But I couldn't have him.

So I opened the vault.

I took it all: all the feelings, all the emotions, all that volcanic attraction, all that bone-deep certainty that he was mine, mine, *mine*.

And I locked it away.

"I'm really happy for you, Murray," I said, patting him platonically on the shoulder. "Let's get another drink."

10

Murray

It was still dark when my alarm went off. My head felt heavy, like it was stuffed full of wool.

I drank my coffee strong at the best of times, but the one I made myself in the tiny kitchenette in my trailer was practically tar. I made it with lukewarm water, so I could slam it down. I boiled the kettle while I splashed water on my face, pulled on a clean black polo shirt and jeans, put my earpiece in, laced up my boots, and buckled on my utility belt. My second coffee—just as strong, but actually hot this time—came with me, in the world's largest travel mug.

"Morning, Murray," Frida said. "Petra and I are going to head down to the Convent now and get the cameras and mics set up. Do you want a ride?" She gestured at the golf cart they'd loaded up with equipment.

"Go on ahead. I'll be right behind you. I've just got to grab a few things first."

I'd come up with a plan, before I finally managed to doze off the night before. If Romeo-Dylan and Cece were determined to do these friend spots, then I needed to give them a different visual language to the rest of the show: something spartan and sexless, instead of spectacular and sexy. They could come across as comfortable, but the second that crossed over into intimate, it would step all over the romance plot.

Years of being a man with a female best friend had taught me how easy it was for people to assume that "friends" was just a transitional space you were passing through on the way to "lovers." I could make that work in my favour with the friendly dynamic between the Dylans, despite their lack of a romantic spark, but I was going to have to tread *extremely* carefully if I was going to prevent audiences reading Epic Romance into Romeo-Dylan and Cece, especially after he hero-carried her down the hill.

I arrived at the Convent with a bag full of blankets and cushions in the least-romance-coded colours I could find, and a selection of very ugly and shapeless cardigans for Cece. She wrapped a particularly hideous beige one around herself as Frida and Petra mounted cameras and hung mics, and I probed for the pressure point that would let me manipulate her.

It didn't take long to find. The pandemic had left her broke and unemployed, and so here Cece was, trying to become an influencer in order to make money, even though she froze up whenever people looked at her and, as anyone who'd taken even a brief glance at her Instagram could see, she didn't know anything about social media strategy.

It was a terrible plan, but that didn't matter. I could use it.

I spun a story for her. How if she played her cards right in these friend spots with Romeo-Dylan, there were more possibilities. A spot on *Juliet on the Beach*. Possibly even the lead on *Wherefore Art Thou Romeo?*. Underpinning them all, money, money, money.

Then after the possibilities, the demands. She had to keep her shit together on camera. She had to keep the conversations focused on Romeo-Dylan, not her. And most importantly, at every opportunity she got, she needed to make it painstakingly clear that she and he were not a match.

Later that morning, I scrubbed through the footage from the first friend spot, sitting in the war room with another enormous cup of coffee. Given Cece's disastrous performance on the first night, my expectations had not been high, but I found myself cautiously optimistic.

It wasn't perfect. Cece was trying, but she definitely wasn't comfortable with the cameras, and she was coming across stilted and awkward.

But that just allowed Romeo-Dylan to shine. Covering for her so she didn't have to talk, he delivered a golden monologue about the twelve Juliets left in the game, audio we could splice in whenever we needed a quick character introduction.

And there were other lines, too, which were going to be perfect sound bites. "Just because there's a spark with me and Dyl, and not with me and you, doesn't make her 'better' than you," he told Cece.

I could use that grab for so many things. I could emphasise that he and Cece were friends and that non-romantic friendships were important—but I could also isolate the phrase "there's a spark with me and Dyl" and drop it in any Double Dylan scene I wanted. Showing was a better narrative technique than telling, but sometimes if you told people something often enough, they'd believe it.

I made notes as I scrubbed through more footage from the first few days of filming, jotting down timecodes of particularly good moments. We wouldn't do the real work of editing until we had the whole season in the can, but I could assemble some rough cuts from what we had, good enough that even Fucking Greg would have to admit it.

"Was Jess K a bitch to wardrobe Tess?" Lily asked from the doorway. "That First Night Party dress was hideous."

I paused playback. "That door was locked."

She smiled and held up a bobby pin.

I wavered for a moment, then sighed. "Close it behind you. I don't want the other Juliets barging into the war room whenever they feel like it."

Lily obeyed, locking the door again from the inside. "Here." She set a plate down on the table in front of me. "This is for you."

I looked at it.

"This is smashed avocado."

"And poached eggs." She sat down across from me. "Don't forget those."

Perfectly poached too, if looks were anything to go by. The yolks were oozing out, a golden puddle slowly forming.

"Have you forced one of the other Juliets into being your personal chef?" I asked. "Because that's fast minion development, even for you."

"Given my culinary history, I can see why you would think that, but no. I made it myself."

It looked unbelievable. My stomach growled.

"I've had to learn a few new things," she said, "this last year."

It was a testament to how starving I was that my appetite didn't immediately vanish.

"My mother's still deeply ashamed of me, though," she said conversationally, like she hadn't just said something completely heartbreaking. "My Vietnamese cooking is still terrible. Not that I could make anything with what we stock in the Villa kitchen anyway. You should get someone to revise those grocery lists for next season, Murray. I didn't realise how white they were until I was on this side of them."

I picked up the knife and fork, but I didn't start eating. "Why are you feeding me?"

"Firstly, because you seem like you're at genuine risk of malnutrition. Secondly, avocados are hot property out there. If they start disappearing, people will start fighting, and that'll be good TV."

I considered all of this for a moment.

Eventually, though, my stomach won out. "Thanks," I said, and took a bite.

"Answer the question." Lily pointed at the image from the First Night Party frozen on the screen. "What did Jess K do to wardrobe Tess? Why did she put her in such an awful dress?"

"It's not that bad, is it?"

"Are you joking? That dress is a war crime."

I took another bite of toast. She'd whipped feta with the avocado, sprinkled pepitas on top, and cracked enough pepper over it that a normal person would be in a sneezing fit. It was one of the best things I'd ever eaten.

"Keep going." Lily gestured to the footage.

"You know I can't do that."

"Who's stopping you?"

"You know the rules. You shouldn't even be in here."

"That wasn't the question. Who's stopping you?"

I gave her a look.

"Suzette and Carrie are off producing Jess D and boy-Dylan's date, right? Well done for delegating, by the way. Nice to know you still listen to me sometimes."

I growled and took another bite of toast.

"So what do you think is going to happen? It's not like Fucking Greg is going to burst through the ceiling. Anyway, he's the one who sent me here to help you."

I drained the dregs of my coffee, weighing it up.

I should say no. If any of the other Juliets realised she was in here with me, it'd be disastrous.

But she was sitting across the table from me, right in the spot where she always sat, and some animal part of my brain had sagged in relief.

"Fine," I said. "On one condition. Make me another coffee."

"Deal."

I knew the second I tasted it that she'd made me decaf, but I didn't say anything.

I scrubbed through some footage from the First Night Party. Lily kicked her shoes off under the table and twisted her chair sideways, folding her feet up under her in a way that was so familiar it made something inside me ache. "Are you planning to develop anything around her?" she asked, as we went through Romeo-Dylan's first chat with Marija, footage on 2x speed. "They've got a nice vibe together. I noticed it during the photo shoot date. He likes her."

"Marija's definitely a wifey." I made some notes. "She's got a good backstory: cancer survivor, now a philanthropist. Matches up well to Dylan JM's whole charity deal. She'll be final four for sure."

"You should make sure Amanda gets cut before then."

I stopped typing and looked at her. "What?"

"Amanda and Marija look too similar. Think of the optics. You don't want to get to final four on the first ever diversely cast season and have half the top contenders be blonde white girls."

"Oh. Yes. Good."

"What did you think I was going to say?"

I considered it for a moment.

"This is strict cone of silence," I said at last.

"Of course."

"I mean it."

"So do I. Seriously, Murray, who do you think I'm going to tell?"

I ate the last bite of my toast and wiped my fingers on a serviette. "I don't always know what you're going to do anymore."

Lily sighed. "How long am I going to have to grovel?"

"Significantly longer than two days."

She didn't say anything.

I cracked first. "What?"

"Nothing," she said. "I'm just putting together a mental list of all your favourite foods so I can plan some apology meals. My skills definitely don't extend to osso bucco, but maybe if I do some strategic bullying of the right people, I can make it happen."

"I can't be bribed that easily."

"Yes you can. Tell me what you were going to tell me."

I exhaled. "Amanda's bi."

Lily snorted. "No shit, Sherlock."

I ignored her reaction. "She's not out on the show—didn't even come out to us in her application—but one of the reasons we cast her is because we were hoping to develop a little queer romance B-plot on the side. A feel-good one, not a Tony special."

"Okay."

"There are a few other bi women in the mix. Including Marija. I was hoping you would tell me they were vibing and that I should get Amanda cut if I wanted to make Marija believable as a potential winner."

Lily gave me a look. "Murray."

"I know, I know. You don't have to tell me."

"What are you going to do about it?"

"I haven't decided," I said. "I don't want to cut Amanda yet. She and the Romeo have a lovely, warm little dynamic. It wouldn't make narrative sense to lose her. Plus, if I can get a romance B-plot out of her, then . . ."

"Which you obviously can!" Lily said. "I know you're married to this idea of girl-Dylan winning for some reason, but come on. You've got the building blocks of something great there. Exactly the kind of B-plot you want. A backup love story, even—if boy-Dylan doesn't find someone he likes, you can make Amanda and girl-Dylan the A-plot."

"Look, yes, it's obvious that Amanda likes Dylan G. But there's no evidence to suggest that Dylan G likes her back. Or that she even likes women, full stop."

"You obviously haven't been through much of the day two footage, then. I went for Amanda's throat during the group date card reveal. The way girl-Dylan practically dove in front of her to take the bullet . . ." Lily made a heart sign with her fingers.

"I told you to back off Dylan G."

"I did! Until she came at me, anyway. Like I said, I went for Amanda. Girl-Dylan's the one who rode in on her white steed to save the damsel in distress."

"That doesn't mean she's into her. Friends do that kind of shit for each other all the time."

A micro-expression flitted across Lily's face so fast I couldn't register what it was. "Why are you so determined to shove the two Dylans together anyway? It doesn't make any sense."

I didn't reply.

"I know you're still furious with me, Murray, but surely all those years of being partners entitles me to an answer."

"I can't tell you."

"Because you don't have a reason?"

I stayed silent.

"You always have a reason."

She looked at me closely. "But you'd always tell me. No matter how pissed off at me you were, you'd tell me."

I kept everything—everything—off my face.

But there was no fooling Lily Ong.

"You signed an NDA," she said.

I finished my lukewarm decaf.

"A-ha," she said. "What can't you disclose?"

"I'm not going to tell you. That's the whole point of a non-disclosure agreement."

"Fine. I'll guess."

It took her—conservatively—a second and a half to put it together.

"You rigged it," she said, pointing her finger at me. "You rigged the season."

"Note that I have not disclosed one single thing to you. Do you want another coffee?"

She nudged her coffee cup across the table to me. "Yes or no. Have both Dylans also signed NDAs?"

I turned my back on her and flicked the kettle in the corner of the room on.

"They have! I'm right! You rigged it."

"Sorry there's only instant coffee in here," I said, spooning it from the jar into our mugs, adding an extra spoonful of coffee to mine and two sugars to hers.

"Murray, *why*? You're the best producer in the country. You don't need to rig a season to get people to do what you want."

I put the coffee down in front of her and sat back down.

"You've just made life a million times harder for yourself," she said. "You've taken all the flexibility out. You're stuck with a Romeo and a winner who don't have any chemistry, and you've closed off a bunch of other narrative possibilities. And boy-Dylan is exactly the type to fall head over heels for someone, and—"

"I have to get it right!"

"Get what right?"

"This season," I said. "If Fucking Greg is ever going to let us cast diversely again—if he's ever going to shut up about the heartland audience—I have to get this season right. I have to deliver the most dopamine and serotonin-filled feel-good hit you've ever seen. It's got to be a fairytale. And the only way I can guarantee a fairytale is to write it in advance."

"That's not true," Lily said. "Not with the way you can work people."

"I couldn't work Brett, when it came down to it," I said. "This season has stakes. This season matters. I can't risk it not going to plan. So yes, I rigged it."

There were three reasons the season mattered.

Firstly, there was the reason I'd told Fucking Greg. The reason Lily and I had both told Fucking Greg, over and over again. When you only told stories about white people falling in love, you were communicating that only white people deserved love. This story mattered.

I did not think of myself as a good person. I manipulated people for a living, after all, and I liked doing it.

But you didn't have to be a saint to believe in basic principles of social inclusion. If I could tell a genuinely heart-warming love story about two likeable and charming people of colour on a show as big as *Marry Me, Juliet*, that would be a thing I could point to that did something positive in the world. Maybe even *to* the world. It was probably a very white saviour thing of me to think (Lily had certainly laughed at me and called me that, more than once), but that was why I'd got into reality TV in the first place, thirteen years ago.

The size of the platform we had meant that the stories we told could have real reach, real impact.

Secondly, there was the reason Fucking Greg had given me. If I didn't deliver a ratings bonanza fairytale for the ages, I'd lose my job.

Then there was the third reason.

Lily.

It was always Lily, in the end.

We'd been working towards this for years. Not just this season—we'd been working towards systemic change in the franchise—but this was what I'd got fixated on, after Jeff had died.

If I could just do *one* perfect diversely cast season. If I could lay it at her feet and say *I made you this, I know you're in so much pain and you need space and I respect that, but this is for you, please remember how much I love you*, then it would . . .

I'd never been able to finish the thought. I was a pro at leaving a silence at the end of an unfinished sentence to make someone finish it, but I couldn't make that trick work on myself.

I just knew I had to make this season work. For her. I couldn't bring Jeff back, but I could give her this thing that she wanted, and then maybe she'd be on the way to being all right again.

Although I'd never anticipated that she'd be *here*.

And I still had no real idea, I reflected, standing next to the cameras and watching Lily terrorise an assortment of the other Juliets at the Episode Two Last Chance Party, why she was doing this.

I believed she wanted to help me. I believed she wanted to reinvent herself. I even believed, cautiously, that this wasn't some kind of extreme emotional reaction to Jeff's death, given she was clearly in firm and precise control of everything she was doing.

But you didn't do something like this—so big, so dramatic, so incredibly public and irreversibly life-altering—without a major fucking reason. You didn't take the nuclear option without deep, profound cause. Not if you were a Machiavellian twelve-dimension-chess-playing mastermind like Lily Ong.

And she wasn't the only problem I had to solve. Not even close.

We'd elected to send Juliet-Dylan on the Episode Three single date, in an effort to light a fire under her and Romeo-Dylan. I pulled a lot of tricks out of my bag to try and generate some sparks.

One of our tried-and-true date formats was the messy date. We used it whenever we needed to communicate that two people were sexually attracted to each other, because it was an excuse for them to touch each other. Sometimes we did it with paint, sometimes with massage oil, but this time, we did it with food: cookies, specifically, which had the added benefit of being coded very domestic and wholesome and couple-y.

We set the Dylans up in a makeshift kitchen in a tent by the lake. We laid out a bunch of ingredients and baking equipment, along with a laminated recipe, and I made it very, *very* clear to them that I expected it to descend into a playful food fight.

They did exactly what they were told. They smeared cookie batter all over each other, laughing good-naturedly.

It still wasn't working.

I regrouped. Our single dates had two halves: the activity and then the intimacy time, with a break between them for ITMs. I'd initially planned for the Dylans to sit down, still flour-smeared, and chat while they ate the cookies, but letting them talk more just seemed like it would make the problem worse.

I got wardrobe to put them in swimwear instead and sent them out into the lake. "You're not miked, so you can say whatever you like to each other," I told them. "But I need you to kiss."

"Is that okay with you, Dyl?" Romeo-Dylan asked. "We don't have to if you don't want to."

I bit back a sound of frustration. Me shouting *you both signed a contract saying you would kiss* would probably not produce great results.

"It's fine," Juliet-Dylan replied. "We've got to do it sometime, right? Might as well rip the band-aid off."

What romance.

I made them go out deep. Most people thought that close-ups were how you conveyed intimacy, but sometimes the best thing you could do was shoot from far away. It was innately voyeuristic: it made it feel like you were watching a stolen moment, something private that you weren't supposed to be seeing.

The Dylans kissed.

It was . . . fine.

"What the fuck are we going to do about this?" I murmured. "Any ideas?"

No one answered.

"Interesting choice," Lily said, "cutting Marija."

We hadn't wrapped up the Episode Three Last Chance Party and Necklace Ceremony shoot until almost 4am, but it had apparently made no difference to her determination to feed me. She slid another perfectly peppered plate of avocado toast across the table to me.

I caught it with one hand before it slid off the edge, pausing the dailies I was going through with the other. "Go—"

"—to bed, Lily," she finished, dropping her voice to mimic me. "I will. Soon. But I need two things first. One, tell me why you got boy-Dylan to cut Marija instead of Amanda. Two, promise me you'll also go to bed."

"One, you'd have to ask him that. That was all him. Two, don't have time."

"You have a crew, Murray."

"Not much of one. And this has to get done properly."

"One, the perfect is the enemy of the good; and two, you can share the load better than this." She gestured at the screens. "It is not humanly possible for you to actively produce the show, manage all the cast and crew, *and* go through every frame of dailies."

She was right—I was just keeping on top of the footage from our main shoots, but I was well behind on the Convent footage, and I hadn't touched the mounted camera Villa

B-roll at all—but I wasn't about to admit it. "Thank you for the toast."

She shook her head. "Sometimes you are unbelievably infuriating. Do you know that?"

"I'm infuriating? *I'm* infuriating?"

My tone would have made anyone else quake, but she didn't even blink.

"You want to talk about workload?" I demanded. "You want to talk about things that are robbing me of sleep? You want to talk about *infuriating*?"

Nothing. Absolutely nothing.

I closed my eyes for a second and took a deep breath through my nose. "It would make my life a million times easier, Lily," I said, "if you'd just tell me why you're here."

"I have told you. Several times."

"But it doesn't make any sense!" I exclaimed, the frustration getting the better of me again. "If you want to do something new and be someone else, then go and do something new! Be someone else! Don't come back here!"

Lily stood up. She was wearing a silky black dressing gown, and it fell around her in sinuous waves, fabric slithering against the leather of the conference room chair. "It doesn't have to make sense to you, Murray," she said. "It's not about you."

She crossed around to my side of the table and pressed her lips to my temple. "Get some sleep." Her fingers were cool against my jaw. "Please. I worry about you."

I finally made it back to my trailer in the grey pre-dawn. I went into the bathroom to grab a quick shower before I fell into bed for an hour, and caught sight of myself in the mirror.

There, smudged at my hairline, was *Blood of My Enemies.*

11

Lily

Seven years ago

"All right, assignments," Tony barked, at the end of our 7am production meeting. "Rookie, you're running point on the date card reveal. Can you handle that?"

Suzette nodded firmly, although she looked apprehensive. I wasn't surprised. She was a newbie subbing in for the most recent producer Tony had crushed under his heel. This would be the first segment shoot she'd run on her own.

"Sit Pete M and Harry next to each other," I told her. I'd noticed them posturing at each other during the previous evening's Last Chance Party, much more involved in defeating each other than they were in Melisa, the Juliet for this season of *Wherefore Art Thou Romeo?*. "They hate each other. You'll get good TV."

She smiled gratefully. "Thanks."

"O'Connell," Tony said, speaking over the top of Suzette, "you're running point on the group date shoot."

I glanced at Murray across the conference table. This was

the third major setpiece in a row Tony had outsourced to him. Was it a vote of confidence, or laziness? Or somewhere in between?

Murray didn't glance back. There were dark smears under his eyes, and he was looking at his hands, left thumb twisting his wedding ring around and around his finger.

"And you're on night shift," Tony said, looking at me. "Dailies duty."

Busywork.

Middle of the night busywork.

Again.

It had been like this for two years, ever since we'd moved to the Romeo and Juliet franchise. If there was busywork to be done, more times than not, I was the one to do it.

"Lily and I are going to swap," Murray said, not looking up.

It wasn't a question. It wasn't even a statement, really. It was somewhere closer to an order.

"Don't look a gift horse in the mouth, O'Connell," Tony said. "I gave you a prime assignment."

"I know," Murray said. "But Melisa's been complaining she feels isolated and she never gets to talk to any other women. We'll get more out of her in ITMs with a different approach."

Tony eyeballed me. "You get one shot at this," he said, a warning note in his voice. "If you fuck it up, there'll be consequences."

"Well, I better not fuck it up then," I said, in my brightest, cheeriest, least I-will-kill-you-in-your-sleep tone. "Thank you for the opportunity."

I glanced at Murray again, but he was still looking at his hands, twisting his wedding ring around and around.

"Hey," I said, once the meeting had broken up. "Can I buy you a coffee?"

"Sure, but you bought the coffee yesterday," Murray said. "It's my turn."

I sighed. "Don't be obtuse. It's not cute."

"No, Lily," he said tiredly. "You are not buying me coffee for getting a racist, sexist megalomaniac to take his thumb off the scale for a second."

He put the strap of his satchel over his shoulder. "If you want to grab coffee before you head out to set, though—on me, because it's my turn—that's a yes. I'll need the caffeine for the night shift."

We went down to the café on the ground floor of the network building. I got a cappuccino. Murray bought himself two coffees—one, an espresso shot he knocked back like tequila; and the other black, in the size the café labelled "bucket."

We talked shop. Things I would try and get out of Melisa when I was shooting the group date. Things he would look for in the dailies, potential bits of audio we might be able to Frankenbite together in service of the story. Things we could do to make sure Suzette wasn't the next person Tony ate for breakfast.

He spoke. He listened. He paid attention.

But there were those dark smears under his eyes. And he kept twisting his wedding ring around his finger, over and over again.

Group date shoots included the date itself and the one-on-one intimacy time afterwards with whichever contestant the lead had deigned to choose, so I didn't leave the *Wherefore* set until late. Then I had to make a stop, so it was after eleven by the time I pulled my car into the network building carpark. The corridors were deserted, and my footsteps echoed loudly. All the rooms were dark, apart from the dim light emanating through the glass door of the Romeo and Juliet production office.

Murray looked up, startled, when I swiped in. "Lily," he said, hitting pause on the dailies. "What are you doing here?"

"Bringing you this." I set the keep cup on the desk.

He looked at it for a long moment. "That's not . . ."

"I have temporarily lifted the ban," I said. "Fresh from my mother's kitchen, made especially for you."

The first time Murray ever had dinner with my family (around the time that Thuong and Michael finally came clean about their relationship—I'd brought him along to be my buffer and stop me killing both of them) he'd fallen head over heels in love with my mother's coffee. "I've had Vietnamese coffee before, but it's never been this good," he'd moaned.

"That's because she makes it strong enough to kill a horse," I'd replied. "Don't pour him another one, Má, no matter how much he begs."

He'd begged. She'd caved. Recognising the sign of another Ong woman falling head over heels for Murray O'Connell, I'd swiftly put measures into place to limit his access to her and thus her coffee, so that he didn't develop permanent caffeine jitters to go with his eye twitch.

Murray looked from me to the keep cup then back to me suspiciously. "I told you I didn't need a thank you."

"It's not a thank you. It's a trap."

"What?"

"I'm buttering you up," I said, taking my usual seat opposite him, "so you'll tell me what's wrong."

"Nothing's wrong."

"Don't bullshit me, Murray. I know you're not sleeping." I ran my thumbs under my eyes. "And that usually means you're brooding about something."

"Genuinely, nothing's wrong." He took a sip of coffee. "It's right, actually. Julia—"

My brain filled in the words *is pregnant*, and I had an out of body experience.

"—got a job."

I blinked. "That's great." Julia had told me about what a knife fight getting a permanent academic job was. "Did she beat that nemesis of hers? Elias?"

He cracked a smile. "Yeah, she did."

"Tell her I'm proud of her."

"I will."

Murray took another long sip of coffee. "I should be over the fucking moon. And I am. She's been working towards this for years. I'm thrilled for her."

"But . . .?"

"The job's on the other side of the country."

The crushing sadness started, of all places, in my toes. They turned to stone first. My feet followed, then my ankles, my calves, my knees, my thighs, until it was all the way over my head and I was drowning in it.

Murray was going to leave.

"I don't know what to do, Lily." He set the coffee down and looked over at me, eyes suddenly desperate. "I love her. This is all she's ever wanted. I would never, ever stand in her way."

Murray was going to leave *me*.

"But this is all I've ever wanted."

He gestured around us, at the empty production office. "Even when this job is shitty and menial and hard and stupid, I love it. I'm addicted to the adrenaline of it, the thrill of working out how to find the story, how to make it go. I try and imagine myself doing something else, and I can't. It's just a void. A wall of static. White noise."

"Oh, Murray," I said helplessly, because it was the only thing I could say, the only thing that wasn't falling at his feet and begging him *don't go, don't go, don't leave me*.

"She can't stay," he said, "and I can't go."

He buried his face in his hands for a moment. When he looked up again, his eyes were wet. It was the first time I had ever seen him cry.

"Julia and I have been together since we were fifteen," he said. "She's so important to me. I don't know how to be without her. But things have been rocky for a while now, and—"

His voice cracked.

I was up before I could even think about it, so fast I knocked the keep cup over. I wrapped my arms around him as tight as I could, anchoring him to me as he sat in his chair, as if I could keep him here forever if I just held on hard enough.

"What am I going to do, Lily?" he whispered into my belly, as my mother's coffee dripped onto the floor around us. "What if I love my job more than I love my wife?"

12

Murray

"If I were a different kind of wife," Julia said to me once, when things were still good, "I would have a lot of questions about how often you come home covered in another woman's lipstick."

"Sorry, darling." I scrubbed at the collar of my shirt in our laundry sink. "Lily's fucking lipstick is ridiculous. It gets on everything."

"She should find one with better hold."

"You try weaning her off *Blood of My Enemies*," I said absently. "Can't be done."

I glanced over at Julia. She was leaning against the laundry door, arms folded, not saying anything.

"I'm sorry, darling," I said again. "I know what it looks like. It's not like we're constantly mashing our faces together. But if she leans over to whisper something to me during filming, and she gets too close . . ."

Julia sighed. "You don't need to apologise. I'm not accusing you of anything. I know you and Lily are just friends. I like

146

that about you. I like that your best friend is this very cool, very smart woman who you're not trying to fuck or undermine. I'm just jealous."

"What are you jealous of? How much time we spend together?"

"No. I mean, yes, that's part of it, but no. It's the way you understand each other. The way you're on the exact same wavelength. The way it seems like you're telepathic sometimes."

She crossed the room and wrapped her arms around my waist. "This feels like such teenage girl bullshit," she said, her voice muffled in my shoulder, "but I hate the thought that she might know you better than I do."

I'd kissed my wife. Told her I loved her. I'd meant it.

She'd been right, though.

Julia and I had grown up together. We'd been each other's first everything. But we could have stayed married for a thousand years, and she still wouldn't have known me like Lily did.

And not being in sync with Lily now—not knowing what she was thinking, why she was really doing this—was driving me up the fucking wall.

She was in full Lily Fireball mode, terrorising everyone around her as we shot the preamble to the Episode Four group date. "I'm not wearing this!" she shrieked at wardrobe Tess, flinging the red and black checked satin jersey back in her face. "Not a chance in hell!"

"Please," Tess said. "Everyone has to wear them. They're going for a whole jockey look."

"I'm not everyone!"

147

Tess had been working with the eminently reasonable and personable Lily Ong for years. She was visibly shaken to be faced with Lily Fireball.

"For god's sake, just put it on," Juliet-Dylan said, stepping between Lily and Tess.

Lily looked her up and down.

"What?" Juliet-Dylan snapped.

"You just can't stop yourself, can you? You can't bear to let people stand up for themselves."

"Lily!" I barked. "Out here! Now!"

She glanced over at me. "Or what?"

"Don't," I snarled, "make me ask you again."

She rolled her eyes. "Fine, fine."

Lily followed me into the production tent. "You know I hate it when you use the daddy voice on me."

"That is not something you get to have an opinion about anymore," I said shortly. "My partner gets to have opinions like that. My contestants do not."

There was a glint in her eyes. "Is that how we're playing it now?"

"You're the only one who's playing. I'm just trying to do my job. And so is Tess. Don't speak to her like that."

"I'll apologise later. It's just for the cameras."

"And like I've told you a thousand times already, back off Dylan G."

She took a beat.

"I'll back off," she said coolly, "when you convince me it's the right thing to do."

People did not walk away from me on this set. I was the boss. The buck stopped with me.

Lily turned on her heel and swept away.

I should have followed her. I should have made her come back. I should have made her stand there and just fucking *talk to me.*

I didn't.

Instead, I sank down in a squat where I was, every last remaining ounce of energy leaving me.

My whole body ached. My calf, which had already cramped up twice that morning, was twinging ominously. My stomach was a roiling mess, and there was a hot, scratchy feeling behind my eyes, like someone was scrubbing at them with steel wool from inside my head.

It had been hard, when Julia and I split. It had been the right thing to do, but that hadn't made it easy. I'd missed her horribly. I'd been deeply, profoundly lonely.

But I'd had Lily. At every step, at every hurdle, at every setback, my best friend had had my back. I might have been lonely, but I'd never been alone.

"Murray!" Romeo-Dylan said from behind me. "Are you all right, mate?"

Do your job, do your job, do your job, I chanted to myself.

"Yeah, yeah, no worries," I said. "I just haven't had much sleep."

The Episode Four group date was a clusterfuck.

It was intended to be a clusterfuck—we'd pitted five active Juliets against the five eliminated ones in a nonsense sport called Love Jockey Hockey, with the express intention of starting a Villa vs Convent shitfight—but it swiftly turned into a different kind of clusterfuck when one of the Juliets, a blonde named Belinda, got hit in the face and lost most of a front tooth.

Because of the strict bubble our set was in, we couldn't take her to a dentist. I had a long, painful argument about it with Juliet-Dylan, who'd once again dived in to provide emergency first aid. Then, once I'd calmed her down, we'd had to spend another fifteen minutes trying to find Romeo-Dylan, who'd apparently found all the blood very confronting.

By the time the date wrapped, my brain was moving at about a third of its normal speed, my eye was twitching so badly I could barely keep it open, and everything hurt. I didn't even have the energy to care about the missed story opportunity. I'd intended to rig it so the Convent team won, with the promise that Romeo-Dylan could resurrect one of the eliminated women to full Juliet status. However, in all the chaos, the Villa team had run away with it . . . due in no small part to Lily playing incredibly viciously. Yet another way she was making my life harder.

After ITMs, we set Romeo-Dylan and the five Juliets up on a picnic blanket beside the lake. Instead of the usual champagne, we gave them some six-packs of beer. We normally would have set out food too, but given they were still filthy, I opted not to suggest that they were eating. I wanted to communicate a relaxed, pleasantly tired vibe, not disgust the audience.

"Belinda," Romeo-Dylan said, reaching over and taking her hand, "can I steal you for a second? Let's go and have a chat."

One by one, we had Romeo-Dylan lead the women to the second picnic blanket Tim and Tom had set up in a grove of trees (which, I grudgingly had to admit, they'd done a good job on—it was giving off the *Midsummer Night's Dream*-esque fairy bower ambiance that I wanted).

"I wanted a few moments with you alone," Romeo-Dylan said. "Today was a tough one. How are you doing?"

He used the exact same opening line with all five of them, but it didn't matter. It would make it easier to edit together.

At least one thing was going right. Romeo-Dylan had recovered from his disappearing act and was in peak Prince Charming mode, pitching his conversations beautifully. He comforted Belinda, reassured her that she was still beautiful, tooth or no tooth. He laughed with Jess K; redesigned the rules of Love Jockey Hockey with Naya; and even gave me some not-terrible business with Juliet-Dylan. "Chin up, all right?" he said to her, gently hooking a finger under her chin and lifting her face to his, after she'd talked for several minutes about how powerless she felt not being able to help Belinda. "The situation we're in right now is really weird and strange, but it's not going to be like this forever."

"I hate feeling helpless," Juliet-Dylan whispered.

"Dyl," he told her, looking into her eyes, "I've never met a person less helpless than you in my entire life."

I had to clear my throat and hold my phone up, the word *KISS* emblazoned across it, and then spend about twenty minutes coaching them through it, to get the money shot I wanted, and even then, it wasn't exactly great—but it was something.

"I wanted a few moments with you alone," Romeo-Dylan said. "Today was a tough one. How are you doing?"

"Tough?" Lily said. "Really? I didn't think so."

Romeo-Dylan opened his mouth. Closed it. Opened it again.

"Physically tough, at least, right?" he said at last. "There are Olympic sports less hardcore than Love Jockey Hockey."

"Oh, I broke a sweat." That irritating Lily Fireball smirk crossed her face. "But I don't mind working hard for the things I want."

"That's a very admirable quality," Romeo-Dylan said, rallying valiantly. "I, uh, I really like that you're a fighter, Lily."

She reached out and traced a line from the crook of his elbow, down his arm, and then up and down his index finger, stroking gently back and forth across the length of his hand. "I know you don't always like my methods," she said, modulating her tone down a notch. "You're a nice person, Dylan. I'm not."

"I'm sure that's not true."

"Oh, it is. I'm fierce, and protective, and tough as hell, but I'm not nice. That's why . . ."

Lily let her eyes drift down. Her eyelashes fluttered. She stopped stroking his hand and instead let her fingers fall, curling gently around his thumb. You couldn't have visually constructed "vulnerability" more perfectly if you tried.

Romeo-Dylan fell directly into her trap. "That's why what?"

"That's why I need someone like you," she whispered. "Someone nice."

She raised her gaze to meet his. "I'm all hard edges. I need someone soft, to balance me out. I'm fiery, so I need someone calm. I'm—"

"Cut," I bit out.

They both looked over at me. "Did I do something wrong?" Romeo-Dylan asked.

"You're fine. You're doing a great job. It's—"

"It's what?" Lily said icily.

I looked at her. She looked at me.

My stomach clenched. I could taste bile in the back of my throat.

"It's the lighting," I lied. "It's too harsh. Indigo, can you bring it down a little?"

He kissed her.

I made him kiss her.

Or maybe she made him kiss her. Even now, even here, even after everything, it was hard to tell where my mind ended and hers began.

I had to turn away and pretend there was something wrong with my earpiece when she whispered against his lips that she had hard edges. For a few moments, I was genuinely worried I was going to vomit.

As soon as we were done, I made up some story about a network fire I needed to put out, and fled. I grabbed some food from craft services, locked myself away in the war room, and threw myself into work.

This, I knew how to do. This wasn't the least bit confusing. This, I could exert all the control in the world over.

The date might have been a clusterfuck, but putting together the story of the date was simple. Even an untrained eye would have been able to pick out the pieces of the narrative puzzle. The desire of the Convent women to get back in the game. The determination of the Villa women to stop them.

The danger that the feud between Juliet-Dylan and Lily might sabotage them. I isolated a grab from Rani, one of the Convent women. "We can all see that Lily Fireball and girl-Dylan hate each other, right?" she said to their team huddle. "That's our opening. If we can turn them against each other and make them fight among themselves, we've got this."

I tapped my fingers against the table. Lily obviously wasn't going to back off Juliet-Dylan, no matter what I said, so in story terms, my best bet was to steer into the skid. If I couldn't get the classic, pristine, rising-above-the-drama winner edit I'd originally wanted, then I'd have to lean into positioning Juliet-Dylan as a hero figure. I could keep feeding contestants to Lily the way I'd fed Cece to her on the first night, but Juliet-Dylan would be the one person she couldn't destroy.

Of course, to do that, to make Juliet-Dylan a hero, I'd have to lean even harder into Lily as the villain. She couldn't just be a mean girl. I'd have to edit her as a monster for the ages, one that audiences would remember for *years*.

Just like she wanted me to.

I was an extremely good, extremely convincing liar, but there was no way I could pretend to myself that the white-hot nausea gripping my entire body was only coming from the deeply unhealthy amount of coffee I'd been drinking.

I let my head fall to the table. My mind felt like it was circling a drain.

Why? Why was she doing this? She wasn't just doing this to herself. She wasn't just burning her own life down. She was doing it to me too.

I'm all hard edges. I need someone soft, to balance me out.

She couldn't say those words without knowing what they would mean to me, how they would hurt me. She just couldn't.

I should have gone back to my trailer after our production meeting, or assigned some of the dailies to Suzette or Carrie, but I sent them away and lingered in the war room, scrolling through footage of Dylan JM and Cece. If I stopped working, I'd start thinking, and old wounds I'd worked incredibly hard to close would start gushing blood.

The door of the war room rattled. I glanced over at it. I'd put a chair underneath the handle after Carrie and Suzette had left.

". . . they fell in love super quickly," Romeo-Dylan was saying on the monitor, midway through telling Cece the story of how his parents got together. "Not quite love at first sight, but fast. Weeks, not years."

"Murray?" Lily called through the door.

"Go away."

She knocked.

I didn't answer.

She kept knocking.

"He told me that falling in love was simple," Romeo-Dylan said, "but that isn't what love really is."

"Murray, please."

I paused playback. "What?"

"Will you let me in?"

"Why should I?"

A moment of silence.

"Can we talk?" she said.

"About what?"

More silence.

"I've tried to talk to you," I said. "It's got me nowhere. What's the point of talking when you won't tell me the truth?"

I curled my fingers around the edge of the table, knuckles turning white. "And then today, you had the audacity to—"

I couldn't bring myself to finish the sentence.

She didn't fill the silence. She couldn't do that one little thing for me.

"Go to bed, Lily. I've got work to do."

There was no answer.

I cracked after five minutes of silence and opened the door. She was gone.

Fine. That was fine.

I made myself another coffee, sat back down, and pressed play.

"Love was choosing her," Romeo-Dylan said to Cece. "Always. Even when it was hard."

There was a note on my pillow when I finally went back to my trailer in the early hours of the morning. *M* was scrawled on the front, in Lily's distinctive spiky handwriting.

I paused. Set the note down on the table. Cracked open the bottle of whiskey Fucking Greg had sent me. Poured a splash into my last clean mug.

Sat down. Took a deep breath. Braced myself.

But then, when I finally opened the letter, all it said was, *Put Naya and Heather together on the next group date. They hate each other. You'll get drama. L. x*

I crushed the letter into a tight ball and hurled it across the trailer. It bounced off the lid of the bin, ricocheted off the wall, and landed right back at my feet.

I sighed, knocked back the whiskey, picked the note up, and uncrumpled it. Carefully, I smoothed it out as best I could, then tucked it inside one of the romance novels I kept a stack of for inspiration.

A long-forgotten bookmark fell out.

It was a strip of photobooth photos from some network party several years ago. Me and Julia, smiling, laughing, kissing, touching noses. Classic happy couple nonsense, easy and intimate. The perfect visual representation of a romance, even though things had already started falling apart.

I put it back in the book, behind Lily's note.

Then I lay on my bed and stared at the ceiling for four hours, until it was time to get up again.

I was in a storm-cloud mood as I presided over Amanda and Romeo-Dylan's single date. "Murray, I can cover this," Suzette murmured, as the two of them took off in the Lamborghini we'd been loaned as product placement, headed on a short drive from the front door of the Villa down to the lake. "Go get some sleep. You're barking orders like a dictator."

"Amanda's my contestant. This date is my responsibility."

"You can share the load. You always have before. It's okay."

"No," I said shortly.

Past Suzette's shoulder, I could see Lily. She was looking directly at me, one eyebrow raised. She was wearing the Ursula dress again, dark purple skirts twisting around her ankles in the breeze.

"Monitor the lipstick cameras," I said to Suzette. "Keep me apprised of the position of the Lambo and their ETA. I'm headed down to the bottom of the hill."

I turned and walked away.

Do your job, Murray. Just do your fucking job.

I didn't have to try very hard to get Amanda to wax lyrical about the car—she was a mechanic, after all, there was a reason we'd picked her for the fast car date. "God, she's such a beautiful girl," she gushed in our ITM. "I've never seen such a beautiful girl in all my life."

It was an easy opportunity, so I took it. "You've used that phrase a few times. Beautiful girl."

Amanda froze.

"That's just how we talk about cars in the industry," she managed, after a long pause. "I bet Dylan JM talks the same way about boats. Don't you call boats she?"

I let the silence hang.

It took about five seconds for her to break. "I'm not doing it. I'm not saying it. I know what you want, but—no."

I sent the crew away so I could have the discussion I wanted with her, get her where I needed her to go. "If you don't want to come out, I'm not going to make you do it," I reassured her.

I had my mouth open to say *but*, but, to my surprise, Amanda cut me off. "But you'll have someone do it for me, right? How long is it going to be before your little plant stands up and announces 'guess what, Amanda likes girls!' to everyone?"

Keeping my feelings off my face was usually an instinct, but I really had to put in effort to keep my expression neutral. "What do you mean, my little plant?"

Every line of Amanda's body was tense. "I know about Lily."

"What do you think you know about Lily?"

The rhetorical question gambit worked. The doubt crossed her face immediately. "I know—I know . . ."

"Lily's not a plant."

I could not put a percentage value on how true or how false that was. I wasn't sure that was even measurable on the truth/lie spectrum.

The image of Lily with Romeo-Dylan rose up in my mind again. *I'm all hard edges. I need someone soft, to balance me out.*

The admission that slipped out of me next was completely uncharacteristic. "Trust me, if I was going to plant someone, I'd pick someone I could actually control."

Thankfully, Amanda was too wrapped up in her own problems to realise that I'd just exposed a pressure point to her, one that she could dig her thumbs into if she wanted to.

I dug my thumbs into her pressure points instead. I wasn't going to out her, make someone else out her, or make her out herself (all true: I wanted to court our queer audience, not alienate them). "I need you to give me a story," I told her. "If it's not going to be the 'I also date women, are you cool with that?' story, that's fine, but I need something."

I got her agreement.

Then I used it as leverage. "Stop making heart eyes at Dylan."

"Isn't the whole point of this show that I make heart eyes at Dylan? I'm on a date with him. A date where he let me drive one of the most beautiful cars in the world. How do you expect me *not* to make heart eyes at him?"

I fixed her with one of my best intimidating stares. "Amanda, you know perfectly well which Dylan I mean."

It had the desired effect. She visibly paled.

And then she gave me exactly what I wanted. Open, vulnerable admissions during her wine-and-cheese picnic with Romeo-Dylan, perfect character moments that would let me build her up as a major contender, slotting her into that potential runner-up spot Marija had vacated. Enough eye contact that I could edit it as connection. A kiss that, if it wasn't exactly fireworks, at least had something of a warm glow.

The visual codes of attraction. The performance of romance. The TV version of a photobooth photo strip. The puzzle pieces of a potential love story, edges and corners, that I could put together. Another potential path for Romeo-Dylan, an obstacle for him and Juliet-Dylan to overcome, providing enough jeopardy to make their happy ending feel earned.

"Good job," I told her afterwards. "It's good to know one of you can actually take instruction."

Amanda didn't answer. It didn't take an expert to read her face, the feelings of disquiet bubbling away behind her eyes.

You've taken all the flexibility out, I heard Lily say in my mind. *You've closed off a bunch of other narrative possibilities.*

What kind of story could we have told about Amanda, if Jeff hadn't died and Lily hadn't left me to manage everything alone? What other relationships had I inadvertently torpedoed by trying to exert such rigid control?

I'd wanted so badly for this season to be perfect. I'd told myself over and over that if I could get this right—if I could give her this—maybe everything else would magically be all right. She would be all right. We would be all right.

Everything was fucked.

I spent another long evening alone in the war room. I hadn't put a chair under the door handle this time, but the doorknob didn't rattle.

I didn't go back to the footage of Lily and Romeo-Dylan. I didn't make myself watch it again.

But it played on a loop in my mind, just the same. *I'm all hard edges. I need someone soft, to balance me out.*

Her lipstick, all over his face.

The jagged pieces of her, falling apart in my arms, no matter how badly I tried to hold her together.

Her lipstick, all over my throat.

The twin pangs that had lived inside me every day since.

The pain, that the most precious thing in her life had been ripped away from her.

And the guilt, because of the tiny, hopeful flame that loss had rekindled in my heart, after all these years.

13

Lily

Six years ago

". . . I'm sorry?" I said. "I don't think I caught that. Can you say it again?"

"Sure, honey."

Denton leaned back in his chair in front of the green screen and repeated one of the single most racist things I'd ever heard in my life.

"I'm not sure I understand." I smiled at him, batting my eyelashes. "Can you explain it to me?"

"Okay."

With a lack of self-awareness so astonishingly low it belonged in the Guinness Book of World Records, the Season Five *Marry Me, Juliet* Romeo unpacked what he'd said in excruciating, wildly offensive detail. "I'm surprised you haven't heard that before," he told me. "Given you're, you know, the same as her."

Jeanette, the woman he was talking about, was Singaporean, not Vietnamese, but there was no point trying to

162

explain that. There was no way a man like this would be able to fathom the fact that not all Asians were "the same." "Thanks for your time," I said, keeping my tone so friendly I sounded to my own ear like I was talking to a pre-schooler. "That's our interview done for today."

"Do you know who I'm taking on the next single date?"

"I don't, I'm sorry. Tony makes those calls, not me."

"How about I take you?" He waggled his eyebrows at me. "You're as much of a smokeshow as any of the other girls."

I forced myself to laugh. "You're very kind, but I belong on this side of the camera."

After Denton left, I let my head fall back against the wall, took a breath, and gave myself ten seconds.

Ten seconds to be angry. Ten seconds to be absolutely fucking furious with Tony's piece of shit investment banker nephew that he'd somehow talked the network into casting as the Romeo.

And then I started to scheme.

Murray was on dailies duty that night. He'd been volunteering for it a lot lately, ever since he and Julia had separated. He said it was because he wasn't sleeping well, so he might as well work nights, but I strongly suspected at least part of the reason was making sure Suzette and I had our fair share of the opportunities.

"Hey," he said, pausing playback and sniffing the air as I swiped into the production office. "Is that Thai food?"

"Yes." I dumped the takeaway bag on the table. "We've got work to do."

"Not that I'm ever going to say no to free food, but I've got this, Lily."

I grabbed a couple of paper plates and plastic forks from the stash I kept in my desk drawer. "I take it you haven't seen it yet."

"Seen what yet?"

The screen was frozen on a shot from the group date. Denton was hollering as five women splashed through a muddy obstacle course (which I was fairly sure was a reused challenge set from *Desert Island Castaway*) in an effort to win some one-on-one time with him.

One of the women was Jeanette.

This man. This *fucking* man.

"Lily?"

"Give me the remote."

He did. I scrolled through until I found Denton's interview.

I watched Murray watch it. He folded his arms. His eyes narrowed. His jaw turned to granite.

"Are you all right?" he asked, when it was over.

"I'm fine. So—"

"Lily," he said, twisting around to face me, "are you all right?"

"Yes," I replied, looking him in the eye. "I'm fine. Because we're going to ruin him."

"Okay. What's the plan?"

An unexpected well of emotion rose up in my chest.

There was simply nothing I could say to this man that would shock him. Nothing I could do that would make him look at me any different. *We're going to push Denton off a bridge,* I might say, and Murray would think for a moment, and then he'd say something like, *We're going to need something heavy to weigh him down. What if we steal that photocopier Tony won't replace?*

"We're going to get the women to unionise," I said. "Now let's figure out how to do it."

It was a three-pronged strategy.

We worked through the night, putting together our first prong, a video package of Denton's worst moments (affectionately dubbed "the shithead reel"). The interview I'd done with Denton that afternoon was the centrepiece, but we weren't lacking for material. "This could be three hours long and we'd still be leaving shit on the cutting room floor," Murray said, through a mouthful of green curry.

Keeping it from Tony was the biggest challenge. Given Denton was his nephew, there was zero chance he was going to be on board with our plan to ruin him. However, he was also profoundly lazy, so when Murray volunteered to run point on the Last Chance Party and the Necklace Ceremony, he went for it. "You splitting up with your wife is the best thing that's ever happened to me," he guffawed. "You two girls should look at this guy's work ethic. This is the kind of thing you should be emulating."

"Actually, I thought Lily and I could run point together," Murray said mildly. "I don't have as much experience as you, Tony. I might miss things on my own. That all right with you, Lily?"

"Of course," I said. "After all, I need to step up my game."

"Whatever." Tony waved a hand dismissively. "I'll be looking closely at the footage tomorrow. Don't fuck it up, or there'll be trouble."

"We won't," I promised, fantasising about the day I was going to put a stiletto heel through his throat.

We headed out to the Villa early. "Fingers crossed we can actually figure out how to make this thing work," Murray said, heaving the screen we'd stolen from the equipment room into the boot of his car.

"It'll be fine," I said, shoving the projector in next to it. "If we can't work it out, we'll get Saurav or someone to help us. We're not the only people that hate Denton."

We managed to do it on our own, though, setting up the screen in the makeup room and balancing the projector on top of the mirrors. "Got it," I said, flicking the projector on as I stood on one of the tables. "Can you pass me some more gaffa tape? I don't want this to come tumbling down."

Murray did, and then his hands settled on my hips. "I don't want you to come tumbling down," he said, when I raised an inquisitive eyebrow at him.

As I secured the projector, I made a mental note to re-download Bumble the next time I had a night off. Murray might be separated from Julia, but he was still a) technically married and b) definitely not over her, and despite the air-tight seal of the vault, I liked the feeling of his hands on me a little too much.

He helped me down from the table. "I'm going to go call Cooper Pryce and see what it would take to get him out to set," he told me. Cooper, who had been on track to be the Romeo before Tony overruled everyone, was our second prong. "You got this?"

"I've got this. Now get out. No boys in the makeup room."

Murray grinned. "Hey, Lily?"

"What?"

"I know I make fun of you for being a drama queen sometimes," he said, "but don't listen to me. Your instincts are fucking flawless."

Once I did some emergency repairs to the vault, I was *definitely* going to have to spend some time swiping on Bumble.

"I know," I said airily.

We'd set up the screen in the makeup room for Tony-proofing reasons—there were no cameras in there, so, on the off-chance he actually decided to do his job, there was no chance of him getting wind of what we were doing before it was done—but it meant I had to resort to our old *Adjudication Station* filming methods to capture the Juliets' reactions to the shithead reel.

And there were a *lot* of reactions. Too many, really, for me to properly get on my phone, although I did my best. Gasping. Crying. Protestations of "I can't believe this," "What the hell?" and "This is a joke, right?."

Jeanette looked at me. "Why are you showing us this?"

"Because you deserve to know the truth about what this man is really like," I said. "And because you have an opportunity to take the power back."

"How?"

"I'm glad you asked. I'd suggest that every single one of you listens, because the only way you'll pull this off is together."

I waited a beat to let that sink in before I pulled out the third prong. "And if you do pull it off," I said, "there is every chance this becomes the highest-rated episode of *Marry Me,*

Juliet of all time. The spon-con opportunities it could open up for you are endless."

It was irritating that it was that, rather than the fact that their Romeo was a racist misogynist shithead, that *really* made the seven white women in the cast listen to me—maybe if I'd tapped Murray in to use his daddy voice and his white privilege they would have just done what he said—but a big part of doing this job was using the tools at your disposal.

And we used them to create something magical.

"Jeanette?"

I wanted to isolate that nervous quaver in Denton's voice as he called her name at the Necklace Ceremony. I wanted to pin it to a piece of cardboard, like a lepidopterist with a butterfly, and frame it. I wanted to hang it above my front door, an "Abandon all hope ye who enter here" to anyone who dared try to fuck with me.

"Jeanette, I want to know if your heart is the other half of mine." Sweat was beading on Denton's forehead. "Will you take this necklace and commit to finding out with me?"

Jeanette laughed in his face. "Absolutely not."

The other Juliets cheered. The seven of them had all refused their necklaces too, and they were standing arm in arm, the picture of solidarity.

Murray's elbow brushed mine, before his fingers found mine and squeezed, hard. *You did it.*

I squeezed back. *We did it.*

"This is an unprecedented situation," Z said. "This has never happened before in *Marry Me, Juliet* history."

The women cheered again. Jeanette had rejoined them, linking her arm with another Juliet, an unbroken chain. I was so fucking delighted that it was the only woman of colour in the cast who'd put the nail in this piece of shit's coffin.

"Denton, every single Juliet has refused your necklace." We'd only given Z the script five minutes before the Necklace Ceremony, but he was delivering it perfectly. "And that can only mean one thing."

Denton was shaking his head. I had never seen a man look so utterly crushed.

"This is the end of your journey."

The cheering from the women was so loud the sound designers were going to have to lower it in the mix, but I could barely hear it above my own heartbeat.

Murray was still holding my hand.

"Tony's going to murder us," I whispered to him.

"I don't care. Want to make a bet on who can make Denton cry first in his exit interview? Loser buys drinks next time we go out."

This man. This fucking *man*.

"You're on."

Murray won the bet, although it hardly seemed fair. "That was a technicality," I complained. "He started crying the second he opened his mouth! You only won because you asked the first question."

"I'm sorry," he said loftily, "but the ancient rule of 'you snooze, you lose' comes into effect here."

I jabbed him in the ribs with my elbow. He laughed and draped his arm around my shoulders. "Let's go watch him leave."

We stood at the front window of the Villa, watching the limo with Denton in it pull away. We'd sent Suzette along for the ride so a) we could milk his elimination for all it was worth, and b) she could get a slice of the credit too.

The Villa was quiet. The crew had finished breaking down the Necklace Ceremony set while we were interviewing Denton. The Juliets had gone to bed, the adrenaline crash knocking them all out. We'd have to come back early tomorrow and shoot pickup ITMs, but it'd be worth it. We couldn't avoid Tony's inevitable wrath, but maybe it wouldn't be *quite* so bad if we gave him time to cool down.

I laughed.

"What?" Murray asked.

"You snooze, you lose," I said. "Do you think we might have accidentally forced Tony to develop a work ethic?"

He chuckled. "If we have, then we deserve some kind of industry award."

I laughed again, and he laughed too, and then we were both laughing, uncontrollably, hysterical, bent over, clutching at each other to stay upright. "Did you see Denton's *face*?" I gasped.

"Which one?" Murray wheezed. "After the first rejection? the second? or the eighth?"

"Eight!" I howled. "We just got this man dumped eight fucking times in a row!"

"Oh no," he said, imitating Denton's voice. "I never thought there'd be *consequences* for my actions."

"No, no, no, you have to do the face too," I was almost crying with how hard I was laughing. "The way he sort of pulls his eyebrows together like he's trying to suck the tears back up into his eyes."

"Like this?"

"No, no—like this." I cupped his face in my hands so I could use my thumbs to manipulate his eyebrows. "You've got to draw them in *this* way, and . . ."

My voice trailed off.

Murray wasn't laughing any more. Neither was I. Around us, everything was dark and still and quiet.

"Lily," he said.

I stroked his cheekbones with my thumbs. Let my fingertips brush gently against his hairline, his ears, the well-past-five-o'clock shadow on his jaw.

"Say it again," I whispered. "Say my name again. Like that."

"Lily," he growled.

My breath caught.

"Are you sure?" he asked.

There was only one possible answer.

"Yes," I said.

And then we were kissing.

There were mounted cameras all through the downstairs living area. He picked me up, and with my arms around his neck and my legs around his waist, we stumbled into the Villa laundry, pressed so tightly together you couldn't tell where I stopped and he began. "What if one of the Juliets wakes up and comes down here?" I asked breathlessly as he kicked the door closed and sat me on top of the washing machine.

Murray yanked his shirt off and threw it to the floor. "Then they're going to get a fucking show," he said, and hiked my skirt up.

I would never forget how it felt when he dropped to his knees and put his mouth on me, one hand firm on my thigh, holding me open. I would never forget the sounds he made when he was inside me, the heat of his breath against my throat, the way his hair felt tangled in my hands as I pulled him closer, his teeth sinking into my collarbone as I came apart, as he came apart.

Never, as long as I lived, would I forget a single second of it. I would preserve it, piece by piece, moment by moment, frame by frame.

"Oh god," he gasped into my shoulder afterwards. "Oh fuck."

I tightened my fingers in his hair. He made a growling sound in the back of his throat, and—oh god. Oh god. Oh fuck.

Murray kissed his way up my neck to my face, our noses sliding together, foreheads slipping sweatily against each other. "Hi."

I smiled. "Hi."

He smiled back, then leaned in and kissed me, just once, on the lips.

Everything up until that point had been quick and fast and hot—passionate, aggressive, almost violent. I'd have bruises where his fingers had dug into me. My nails had drawn blood, scraping down his back.

This kiss wasn't like that. It was tender. Sweet. Gentle.

White-hot panic closed a fist around my heart.

I pulled away, scrambling back as far as I could on the washing machine. "Hey, hey, Lily, hey!" Murray said, blinking, surprised. "What's wrong?"

"Nothing!" I said. "Nothing, nothing!"

"It's obviously not nothing! Shit, did I hurt you? I'm so sorry. I'm—"

"No, no, no, no, you didn't, you didn't, don't worry. Nothing's wrong. It's just—oh shit, my lipstick's all over you." I tried unsuccessfully to wipe it off his face.

"I don't care."

He caught my hand in his, and fuck fuck *fuck* he still had a tan line where his wedding ring had been, what was I doing what was I doing *what was I doing*?

"Lily, please! Tell me what's wrong. You're scaring me."

The words came out of me in a rush. "You know we can never do this again, right?"

I hadn't thought about it, not at all, but I knew it was true, felt instinctively deep in my bones it was true, because this was too big, too overwhelming, too much, and I was going to burn up, I was going to explode, I was going to die.

"This was great," I said desperately. "This was so great, Murray. Just in case Julia didn't tell you enough, you are fucking great at sex. Congratulations. But we can't do it again. Never, ever, ever."

"Slow down, Lily." He took my face in his hands. "Take a breath. Talk to me. Tell me what you mean."

I wrapped my fingers around his wrists, anchoring him to me and holding him away all at once. "I care about you, Murray. I don't care about most people, but I care about you."

I was about to cry. Shit, I was about to cry. I *never* cried.

"We can't ruin this." I dug my nails into the tendons in his forearms. "What we have—we can't ruin it with sex."

"So let's not ruin it!" he said. "I care about you too, Lily. So much. What about this felt like we were ruining anything?"

I closed my eyes and leaned into him, pressing my forehead to his. I couldn't look at him. It was too much, too much, too much.

"We had to do this once," I whispered. "We had to get it out of our systems. But if we tried to do this for real, we'd wreck each other. We'd burn each other out."

"You don't know that's true."

"Yes, it is. We're too similar. That's why we get each other the way we do. We think the same."

"Why is that bad?"

I was going to break apart. I was going to ignite, like a firework, and burn this whole Villa down.

"We both have hard edges." I dug my fingernails harder into his forearms. "When they rub against each other, they make a spark. But they also wear each other down. Erode each other. Destroy each other."

I took a long, shaking breath. "What we have—this thing of ours—this friendship—this partnership—it's so important. It means so much to me. And if we destroyed it—if I lost it—"

"Hey, hey, don't cry!"

Murray put his arms around me, but this was the hug of a friend, not a lover, hand pressed to the back of my head. "Whatever you want, Lily," he said, voice muffled as he spoke into my hair. "If you don't want to do this again, that's fine. Of course that's fine. This doesn't have to change anything."

"You understand what I'm saying, right?"

"Of course I understand."

I didn't need to see his face to know he was lying. How could he understand, when I didn't understand it myself?

14

Murray

"What?" Suzette said.

"Trust me."

"Do *you* trust you, Murray? Because this is the exact opposite of what you said two weeks ago."

"I've changed my mind."

I gestured at the whiteboard with my marker. On the Episode Five group date, we were going to split the nine Juliets into three teams. I'd written my proposed groupings on the board. Kumiko, Parisa and Jess D would be one team (level-headed serious contenders). Naya, Heather and Belinda would be the second team (less level-headed, less serious contenders).

Neither of these were controversial, but it left Amanda, Juliet-Dylan and Lily as the third team—ie. the three women we'd been working our hardest to keep separate.

"I know it sounds counter-intuitive," I said, "but let me explain."

I started drawing a diagram. "I put the fear of god into Amanda on her single date." I drew a love heart beside her name and then crossed it out. "Her crush on Dylan G isn't going to be a problem anymore. But—"

I drew an arrow from Amanda to Lily. "—she's so damn sweet that Lily will definitely run a villain play on her, which will—" I drew an arrow from Juliet-Dylan's name, intersecting the Amanda/Lily line, "—trigger Dylan G's hero instinct."

"But then it becomes Dylan G versus Lily," Carrie said. "Which is exactly what we don't want."

"Winners focus on the romance with the Romeo," Suzette said. "They don't focus on the drama with the other Juliets."

"Yes, that's always been our approach," I said. "But the rivalry between Dylan G and Lily is too pronounced for us to try and edit around it now. We've got to lean into what we've got, not force what we've . . . not. Don't. You know what I mean."

Suzette didn't look convinced, raising her eyebrows at my grammatical tangle, but Carrie looked thoughtful. "It's a different kind of season. It makes sense to try a different approach."

"Exactly. Let's mix it up. Let's make it more interesting."

"Isn't this just going to play into our girl-crush problem, though?" Suzette said. "Dylan G's protecting Amanda. Amanda'll get all stars-in-her-eyes about it."

"No, she won't. Like I said, fear of god. And if we centre our narrative on Dylan G versus Lily—a hero versus villain story—rather than on Dylan G and Amanda—a hero protects damsel story—then we can gloss over any potential girl-crush content and—"

"Look at the diagram you've just drawn, Murray," Suzette said.

My scribbles were an incomprehensible tangle of lines.

"The very first thing you taught me when I started working with you was that reality TV is a broad-strokes medium. 'Subtext is for cowards,' I believe your exact words were."

Suzette gestured at the whiteboard. "How do you expect the audience to understand any of this? I don't."

"Easy," I said, stamping firmly on the voice in my brain that was unhelpfully chanting *Lily would understand*. "We're going to use Cece."

Carrie blinked. "Cece?"

"This is going to be a surveillance date," I said. "You know how we'd normally get a sibling or a friend to secretly watch the Juliets and then sit down with the Romeo to discuss who they like and who they don't? We'll use Cece instead."

"But she can barely string a sentence together," Carrie said.

"She's improved a lot. You haven't seen her friend spots with Dylan JM."

"Because you won't let anyone else watch the dailies," Suzette muttered.

I ignored her, scribbling Cece's name on the board and then an arrow, connecting her to my messy mind-map. "We usually try and keep all the plotlines relatively separate. But let's lean on the fact that this season is unusual. Let's do some really interesting storytelling. Let's use this friendship as a narrative lever rather than just as a tool for exposition and as Dylan JM's security blanket. Let's—"

"Murray, slow down!" Suzette said.

"It makes sense!"

"But it's so fucking complicated! You know that GIF of the conspiracy theory guy from *It's Always Sunny in Philadelphia*? That's you."

"All right, fine. What's your alternative?"

"Here's a pitch," Carrie said. "I like what you're saying about Dylan G and Lily, and how we can lean into that to make Dylan G seem like a hero. But what if we switch out Amanda for someone else? Naya, maybe?"

I shook my head. "It's got to be Amanda. She's the only one who will trigger that mama bear protective thing in Dylan G. Besides, Naya and Heather hate each other. I want to keep them together. That could be good secondary drama."

Carrie blinked. "Since when do Naya and Heather hate each other?"

"You haven't noticed?" I kept my tone deliberately casual.

"Here's what I've noticed," Suzette said. "You're wearing the same clothes as yesterday."

"Your point?"

"My point is that you're not sleeping, you're barely eating, and you're coming up with plans that need a serial killer board to explain."

"I'm doing my job."

"You're doing everyone's job!" she said. "I know you don't want to talk about Lily, and—you know what? Fine. Feel your feelings on your own time. They're none of my business. But this isn't about your feelings, Murray. It's about the show. We've still got four weeks of the shoot to go. You've got to let us help you."

I finished the cold dregs of my coffee. "You can help me by getting this group date set up. This way." I stabbed at the whiteboard with my marker. "I'm going to the Convent to get Cece."

Suzette was right about one thing. I wasn't sleeping. Even when I managed to slip away to my trailer at night, my mind wouldn't turn off. I was lucky to catch anything more than a few hours of uneasy dozing.

But this wasn't my first rodeo with insomnia, and I'd been trying to use it to my advantage. If my brain wouldn't let me sleep, I'd use the extra time to work.

I set Cece up with Saurav in the monitor room to observe, then went down to run point on the group date. The little smirk that crossed Lily's face when Z announced the composition of the three teams was so enraging it made my teeth hurt.

I hated that I'd listened to her. Hated that I'd done exactly what she told me in that carefully uncrumpled note, tucked behind the photo-strip of me and Julia. *Put Naya and Heather together on the next group date. They hate each other. You'll get drama. L. x*

But I just didn't have it in me, when it came down to it. It wasn't in me not to trust the dramatic instincts of Lily Ong.

Even when I shouldn't.

I realised what she'd done about thirty seconds after I sat down to film an ITM with Heather.

I was running on autopilot. I'd already decided what the A-plot of the group date was going to be: unsurprisingly, I'd been right about the hero/damsel/villain dynamic that putting Juliet-Dylan, Amanda and Lily together would trigger. They'd drawn the bulk of my focus during the shoot, but Lily had (also unsurprisingly) been right too. I could have been fifty kilometres away and still heard Naya and Heather screaming at each other.

"Talk to me about how today went," I said to Heather, hoping for a few grabs about the fight that I could use for a B-plot.

"Today went fine," Heather said, "but it would have gone so much faster if Naya didn't make so much trouble."

Bingo. "Why don't you get along with Naya?"

"Naya's an uppity bitch. It's disgusting that someone like her talks the way she does to someone like me."

Heather tossed her long blonde hair over her shoulder. "She's always trying to bully me."

The pieces clicked into place. My stomach lurched, like the ground had just suddenly fallen away beneath me.

"It's like she thinks she's on my level," she said, "but she's not."

"All right, thanks, Heather," I said swiftly. "That's all for today."

None of that would be going in the episode.

"Damn it, Lily," I murmured to myself, as Heather tossed her hair over her shoulder again and walked away.

When Romeo-Dylan had signed the contract for this season, there were a few conditions he'd made crystal clear. One was that he didn't want to do any kind of Very Special Episode about racism. "I'm not interested in putting myself or any of the women of colour in the Villa in harm's way," he'd told me. "Or putting the POC audience in harm's way, for that matter. We all experience enough racist bullshit as it is. So if you're deliberately planning to cast some All Lives Matter types to create drama: I'm out."

"No problem, mate," I'd said. "We're completely on the same page."

I'd meant it. I wanted to make a feel-good season, and there would be nothing feel-good about that. I'd taken care when we were casting. I'd dotted the I's. I'd crossed the T's. I'd double-checked all the research on the potential Juliets that my team had done. We'd delved deep into their social media profiles, the ones they'd told us about and the ones they hadn't, combing through all the things they'd posted and reposted and liked for the last five years.

We must have missed something. I'd fucked up.

There was no way I could put a white woman like Heather on television, talking like that about a Black woman, and not have it turn into an entire episode about racism. The shithead unmasked/shithead humiliated one-two narrative punch was a Lily Ong special—but I couldn't use it.

What must Heather have said to Lily for her to set her up like this?

I set that question aside. That was one for later, repercussions to dole out when I had brain space to come up with something really vicious.

I had a more immediate problem. If Romeo-Dylan found out one of the Juliets was making overtly racist comments, he'd immediately assume I'd cast her to kick off the very conflict he'd told me he didn't want to engage in.

I'd lose his trust.

I couldn't make this show—couldn't do my job—if that happened.

So I needed to figure out a different way to convince him

to cut Heather. That way, I could bury this so completely that neither he nor anyone in the audience would have any idea it had ever happened.

Thankfully, Romeo-Dylan had never seemed particularly attached to Heather. When he sat down with me for his ITM, I started nudging him where I wanted him to go, asking pointed questions about which women he was feeling a connection with—

Then Cece came down the stairs.

In a few quick sentences, she told him what she'd seen on the monitors.

Romeo-Dylan's jaw tightened. "Show me."

My brain started whirring as I followed them up to the monitor room. Fuck. How the fuck was I going to fix this? Fuck. *Fuck.*

His jaw tightened even further as he watched the footage from Heather's ITM. He crossed his arms over his chest, the muscles in his shoulders turning to stone.

"I'm really sorry, Dylan," Cece said.

He didn't move, but his body language softened as he looked at her. "You don't need to apologise. You did the right thing, telling me. It's not your fault."

I tried to take advantage of the softening. "I'm so sorry about this, mate. That interview I did with her today was the first time I've heard this kind of language from her. I genuinely had no idea—"

"Save it."

You didn't need to be a genius to see that he didn't believe me.

"I want her out," he said. "Right now."

"Done. We can film a snap Necklace Ceremony. Give us twenty minutes to get Z and the Juliets in place, and we can shoot right away."

He nodded, just once, sharply.

"Dylan, I'm so sorry," I said again. "Once we're done with the Necklace Ceremony, we can cancel the rest of today's filming, if you like. Push your intimacy time with the winners until tomorrow, and—"

"No."

"No?"

He fixed me with the most penetrating stare he'd ever given me. "Can you edit around this?"

"Around why you're cutting Heather?"

"Yes. This is not the story I want to tell."

And you knew that, I heard, in the way he bit out the words.

"Of course. If that's what you want. We can suggest some other reason as to why you cut her."

I had no idea what footage I had, or what reason I'd use, but I'd figure it out. Use some clips out of context. Frankenbite some audio. Invent something out of nothing.

"That's what I want," Romeo-Dylan said.

"Then that's what we'll do."

There was a slight unknotting in his posture. I didn't have his trust back, not all the way, but maybe twenty per cent of him believed me.

"Good," he said. "Then we'll film tonight like we planned. Business as usual. I don't want this to be a thing."

"We can do that," I promised.

The longing to have Lily back was an undercurrent

through my thoughts all the time, but it rose up and crashed over me again like a wave. Being a white man at the helm of this season was already dicey, but now . . . fuck, I'd fucked this up so badly.

I forced myself to focus. Action. That was the way forward, not spin. The only way I'd get him back on side was if I did everything in my power to correct it.

I briefed Z before the snap Necklace Ceremony and got him to keep his language deliberately vague, so I could edit in a reason for Heather's elimination later. "Dylan JM's friend was the one responsible for picking the winning team today," Z told the assembled contestants. "But because they're his friend, they were also looking for red flags—for women who might not be right for our Romeo. And I'm sorry to say, they spotted one."

Lily started smirking.

I pressed two fingers into my eye before it started twitching.

"Heather, your heart isn't the other half of mine," Romeo-Dylan said. "We're on very different pages, and I don't think it's right that you continue on this journey."

Lily's smirk didn't change, but something about her posture did, the slight tilt of her head. *That's not how this play works,* it said. *Have you forgotten how to make people bleed?*

My teeth were clenched so tightly my ears started aching.

One problem at a time, I told myself, as Heather started loudly declaring that her elimination was bullshit. Fix this situation. Get Romeo-Dylan's trust back.

I did my job.

185

"I know I've said this several times already," I told Romeo-Dylan, as he sat down in front of the green screen later for an interview, "but I'm so sorry about Heather."

"I don't want to talk about it anymore."

His body language suggested that I had maybe forty per cent of his trust back, so I risked pushing it. "Can you talk about it a little? In very generic terms? Something about how seeing Heather through Cece's eyes made you realise that you're not compatible? It doesn't need to be specific. The less specific the better, really. That'll help me edit around it."

He considered it.

"Yes," he said. "I can do that."

"Thank you. Okay. Tell me about the group date today. What were you looking for? What was Cece helping you look for?"

Romeo-Dylan launched into a monologue about cooperation, and how being in a relationship was like being on a team. It was beautiful and eloquent. It had paragraphs, packed with Prince Charming shit.

"It's interesting to see how people work at something," he said. "Even if it's something completely ridiculous. A relationship should be a partnership, and that takes work. Collaborative work."

Partnership.

Lily was going to be so furious I'd undercut her play.

"Murray, you've got to come now!"

"For fuck's sake, Tim!" I snapped. "We're in the middle of an interview."

"I'm sorry, but I was in the monitor room, and—" Tim/

Tom stopped, hands on his thighs as he bent over and took a gulping breath of air "—and I looked over at the Convent feed, and—Heather's beating the shit out of Cece."

Romeo-Dylan bolted out of the room so fast it was barely perceptible to the human eye.

"Pack it up and follow him," I barked at the startled crew. "Now!"

It was instinct, my mouth skipping ahead of my brain, but I would have done the same thing even if I'd had more time. If something dramatic was happening, then we needed to get it on camera.

We caught up to Romeo-Dylan just as he reached the Convent, our golf carts barely a match for his dead sprint. "Are you okay?" he was asking Cece when we pulled up, her chin in his fingers as he examined her face for injuries. "Did she hurt you?"

"I'm okay," Cece said.

Romeo-Dylan pulled her to him. "I'm so sorry. I should never have put you in this situation. I'm so sorry."

Cece wound her arms around his neck. One of his hands came up to cup the back of her head, pressing her face into his throat—and I made a mental note to comb through the Convent footage in more detail, because this was starting to smell like a very inconvenient development.

"What are you doing here?" Cece asked him. "How did you know that she . . .?"

"We were filming an interview when one of the PAs came rushing in to tell us that she'd seen Heather beating the shit out of you on the monitor," I interrupted, before they could declare passionate undying love to each other.

I couldn't see any blood or bruises, so it seemed like Tim/Tom had been exaggerating (thankfully, for both our insurance premiums and my relationship with Romeo-Dylan), but I needed to check. "Did she? Beat the shit out of you?"

"No," Cece said. "She just slapped me. It's not that big a deal."

"Not that big a deal?" Romeo-Dylan exclaimed. "She hit you!"

He let go of Cece and started up the stairs of the Convent—and I did a lot of calculations very, very fast.

"Dylan, wait!"

"No!" He wheeled back to face me. "This can't stand. Absolutely the fuck not."

"I'm not saying it will stand. Just wait a minute."

I prayed, to any higher power that might be listening, that he trusted me enough to listen to me.

"One minute." Romeo-Dylan folded his arms. "That's it."

"We need to think about this from a production standpoint."

There wasn't going to be a way to edit around this now. You could cover a lot of sins in editing, but someone getting slapped?

You couldn't stop that kind of chatter among the contestants. Inevitably, it would spread. An argument could be forgotten. A physical fight could not.

I could do what Romeo-Dylan wanted. I could cut it out of the episode. I could make it seem like Heather getting eliminated, and her slapping Cece, was about something else entirely.

But I'd been getting constant updates from the monitor

room through my earpiece as we rocketed down the hill on the golf cart. Cece might have managed to step outside and remove herself from the situation, but inside the Convent, the women were having a knock-down drag-out screaming match about Heather's racist behaviour.

I could keep that off the show, but the odds of keeping it off social media afterwards were miniscule. Even if I could convince Fucking Greg to give me a hush money budget, at least one of the women would talk. *THE SECRET RACISM SCANDAL THAT* MARRY ME, JULIET *TRIED TO COVER UP!!* would become the story. All the audience goodwill that we needed—all that fairytale romance energy—would be lost.

So if we didn't want it to consume the entire season narrative, we had to deal with it now. On the show. No matter what Romeo-Dylan wanted, we had to do a Very Special Episode— one single, contained episode—so we could move on.

"What's it going to look like if you go storming in there now to scream at Heather?" I asked. "We can do a lot in editing, but we're not magicians. If you go in there now, with a full head of steam, and start yelling at a crying blonde woman, you're going to come off as a bully."

"If I don't go in there, I'm going to look like an arsehole who lets his best friend get clocked in the face and does nothing about it."

Romeo-Dylan wasn't wrong. Above all else, we needed to preserve his heroic image.

"Not if you didn't know about it," I said.

"What?"

"That's the play here. In narrative terms."

The story flowchart started assembling itself in my mind. "We make it clear you don't know about the slap. Then we can sidestep this whole issue."

There was a waver in Romeo-Dylan's body language. His eyes slid inexorably to Cece.

It told me a lot, the way he looked at her. That combination of desperation and frustration. That obvious desire to protect her, to put his arms around her and keep her safe.

It was going to be a problem.

It was also a pressure point.

"We film a quick little interview with Cece about how she decided not to tell you about getting slapped because she didn't want to distract you from your journey," I said. "She comes off looking like a hero, you don't have to get involved, and it'll be clear as crystal to the audience who the villain is."

The word *villain* triggered another set of calculations, but I clamped down firmly on them. One problem at a time.

I dug my thumbs into another one of Romeo-Dylan's pressure points. "We've got to tread carefully. The show doesn't carry nuance well. It's got to be broad strokes. Racist girl: bad. You: good."

"I know that," Romeo-Dylan forced out from between his teeth. "But what am I supposed to do? Let Heather smack her around and get away with it?"

"Heather's not going to get away with it. She's going to get crucified on social media."

"That's not what I want either!"

Even when he was furious, this man was too kind for his own good.

190

"We talked about this," he said. "I told you I didn't want to do a Very Special Episode about racism."

"I know. And I'm sorry."

I was going to sit him down tomorrow and go over this until he believed me. "Normally we can pick up these kinds of views when we go through prospective contestants' social media. We missed it. That's on us."

"Did you?"

"Yes. That's the truth. I promise. I know the show's record on diversity is terrible, but it's like we talked about," I said, trying to guide the conversation back from the shaky ground to the familiar. "This season represents a new commitment to diversity from us, and to representing it respectfully and responsibly. I've done some shady things as a producer, but I wouldn't stunt-cast a racist, Dylan. I wouldn't do that to you."

He didn't believe me.

But I'd dug my thumbs in hard enough in the right places. It worked anyway.

I got what I wanted from Cece. A little speech about how it was better for Dylan not to know about the "ugliness" between her and Heather—better for him to keep his head in the game.

Romeo-Dylan was standing just behind me as Cece spoke. I could feel his gaze. Tender when he looked at Cece. Glowering when he looked at me.

Tomorrow, I promised myself. Tomorrow, I was going to cancel the whole day of filming. It would have been the Episode Five Last Chance Party and Necklace Ceremony, and with Heather's elimination, we didn't need to do those anymore. I was going to cancel everything, and I was going to sit down with Romeo-Dylan, and I was going to do whatever it took to get him back on side.

I was a master of detachment. It was hard to play chess when you cared about the pieces. I needed him to trust me. I didn't need him to like me.

That didn't help the sick feeling in my belly.

Romeo-Dylan insisted on staying to sit with Cece while I went into the Convent to shoot interviews. I let him. Any concession I could make—anything that would help him feel like I was on his team—I would do it.

I did my job with ruthless, clinical precision. I interviewed each of the women in the Convent about the fight. I got some grabs that would make this Very Special Episode one of the most talked-about pieces of television of the year. I got content that would make Fucking Greg cream his jeans.

I took Heather aside. She was crying, shoulders shaking, big blue eyes red with tears. "You have to help me," she hiccupped, clutching at my sleeve like a lifeline. "Please. They're all bullying me."

I fixed my gaze on her fingers on my arm and went completely, aggressively silent.

It took her a moment to catch up.

Then her breath caught in her throat. A stillness came over her, one I'd seen many times before: a stillness born of total, abject fear.

Slowly, she let go.

"You should count yourself lucky," I said.

"What—what do you mean?"

"You thought tonight was bad, dealing with all the women down here." I didn't have to dig deep to find my most terrifying, threatening, dangerous voice. "But I want you to think about how that would have gone if Lily Fireball was in the room."

Heather paled, but she balled a hand into a fist. "I'm not scared of her."

"Then you're not very smart."

Her lip started quivering again.

"Crying isn't going to work on me," I said. "It's not going to work on her either. She might not be down here yet, but she will be, sooner or later. Maybe even in the same bedroom as you. Do you know what it's like to sleep with one eye open, Heather?"

Tears were pouring down her cheeks. "I didn't do anything wrong."

"This place is full of cameras and microphones. Anything you say, I'm going to hear. And if I hear one thing I don't like—not even one thing, half a thing, or the mere suggestion of a thing—you're going to be sleeping in the same bunk as Lily Fireball."

I leaned in closer. "Maybe we'll even have a movie night, when Lily gets here. I've got plenty of footage of you from the Villa. I could put together a supercut of your greatest hits. Set up a screen out on the lawn, perhaps. Make some popcorn. Really make an event out of it."

Heather buried her face in her hands, shoulders shaking.

"You know what that sounds like to me?" I said. "Great television. Everyone would see. Your friends. Your family.

Your co-workers. Sharing a bunk bed in here with Lily might seem like a relaxing holiday, after what you'll face out there."

"Why?" she sobbed. "Why are you being so mean to me?"

"Because I want you to understand, Heather," I said. "I want it to be very clear. We have a zero-tolerance policy for racism on this show. If you put a single toe out of line in here, I'm going to know about it—and there will be consequences."

Romeo-Dylan and Cece were still on the verandah when I left the Convent. They were sitting on the steps, the slightest of distances between them.

They were holding hands.

They looked at each other before they looked at me. In that glance, that silent, subconscious communication between them, all my suspicions were confirmed.

"It's late," I said. "Go home."

Romeo-Dylan went.

I went too. "That was fucked, what happened today, Murray," Frida said, as I helped her unload equipment from the golf cart. "Do you need to talk about it?"

"Thanks, but no," I said. "I just want to get some sleep."

Craft services was closed, so I dug around in my kitchenette cupboard and ate three muesli bars in quick succession, each in two bites, not registering the flavour. I knocked back a shot of Fucking Greg's whiskey. I took a couple of ibuprofen, even though I knew the throbbing in my head wasn't something they could fix.

I hiked back over to the Villa and let myself into the war room.

I found the footage from the mounted cameras, the B-roll I'd been putting off scrubbing through for two weeks now. I scrolled through hours and hours of it on 8x speed until I found what I was looking for.

Heather and Lily, alone in the kitchen.

Heather opening her mouth.

That slight tightening in Lily's shoulders. "What was that you said, Heather? I don't think I understood what you meant."

Heather explaining.

One side of Lily's mouth quirking. "What an interesting opinion."

That glint in her eye.

I'd missed it. All the signs had been there—all the evidence I needed—and I'd missed it, until it was too late.

I'd fucked up. Inadvertently or not, I'd violated my agreement with Romeo-Dylan. I'd put him and Naya and every person of colour in the cast in harm's way. Including Lily.

She was perfectly capable of defending herself. I'd known that long before today.

She wouldn't have had to, though, if I hadn't fucked up in the first place.

I had to fix this. I wasn't sure how I was going to do it, but I had to find a way to fix this.

I got up. I made myself two cups of coffee.

And I got to work.

15

Lily

Six years ago

The morning after the night before, Murray and I met at the Villa to film pickup ITMs. We talked in great detail about our strategy for getting the best soundbites out of the eight women who had so dramatically ditched Denton—and not at all about what happened in the laundry. I had to resist the urge to swing by my parents' place before work so I could bring Murray some of my mother's Viet coffee as an apology. He had clear lines around when I did and did not owe him things, and I didn't think a "Sorry I fucked you and then freaked out" peace offering would be accepted particularly . . . well, peacefully.

Instead, we did our jobs. We interviewed the eight Juliets, used the various tools in our toolbelts to nudge them into giving us the gloating, gleeful grabs over Denton's elimination that we needed, and Did Not Talk About It.

"Will you wait for me before you go into the building, once we get back?" Murray asked, as we walked to our respective cars to head back to the office.

Oh god. He was going to make me sit down and talk about it. "If you want."

The dread must have shown in my voice. "I don't want you facing Tony on your own." He gestured at my phone, where fourteen missed call notifications showed on the screen. "We both know who he's going to blame, and I'm not going to let him."

"He's not wrong," I said. "It was my idea."

"Then maybe I want some of the credit." Murray opened the driver's side door of his car. "Wait for me, Lily."

I usually rolled my eyes and told him not to when he used the daddy voice on me, but I didn't say anything.

I waited. We walked into the network building together. I swiped in. Murray held the office door open for me.

Suzette looked up from her desk. "Lily, get out of here!" she hissed. "You're in so much—"

"You!" Tony snarled, pointing a finger at me. "My office. Now."

Well, this was going to be fun.

Murray followed me in. "Get out, O'Connell," Tony said tersely.

"Oh, I'm not getting cut out of the glory for this." He was completely ignoring Tony's vibe, using the jovial, blokey tone he used with the male contestants on *Wherefore*. "What a twist, hey? They're going to be talking about it for a—"

Tony slapped the wall so hard one of the awards on his shelf fell to the floor and smashed. "You fucking *broke the show*!"

"No, we didn't," Murray said calmly. "We've got it all sorted out. Cooper Pryce will be here—"

197

"*You.*"

Tony jabbed his finger at me. "I know this was you, you little bitch," he snarled, flecks of spit landing on my face. "You think I can't tell when your fingerprints are all over something? You think I don't know you think you're smarter than everyone else? You think I—"

"Get that finger out of her face," Murray said, voice suddenly low, dangerous, threatening, "right now."

"O'Connell, I advise you to get the fuck out of here if you know what's good for you."

"And leave her alone with you? Not a chance."

Murray took a step forward, positioning himself between me and Tony. "You can fire her if you want. You're the boss. But if you fire her, you'll have to fire me too, because this was a joint effort—something I would, of course, be only too glad to communicate in a wrongful dismissal lawsuit."

Tony folded his arms. "So this is why you left your wife," he said. "She suck your dick that good, huh?"

I grabbed the back of Murray's shirt with one hand, holding him back in case he did anything stupid, and took my phone out with the other.

Tony's eyes flickered to me. "What the fuck do you think you're doing?"

"I just think it'd be helpful to have a record of this conversation," I said. "To show my lawyers in that wrongful dismissal lawsuit. Proof of hostile work environment, you know? Probably also sexual harassment—although I'm not sure if that's technically harassment of me or you, Murray. What do you think?"

"You could make a case for both."

"Plus, it's always useful to have things on camera. We got a ton of footage last night. A lot of it on this very phone, in fact. And wouldn't you know, it shows exactly who pulled off this incredible, innovative, game-changing stunt. I thought I might email some of it to Greg McDonagh. I'm sure he'd like to know who's responsible for the spike in his ratings."

"I'm sure he'd also like to know that you weren't there," Murray said.

"Oh, good point. It'll look great for you, Tony, the fact that two of your producers pulled this off without you having the faintest clue."

Tony's nostrils flared.

"Or," I said, "you can rest on your laurels, as showrunner of a season with one of the greatest twists of all time, and thank your lucky stars we removed your racist, misogynist piece of shit nephew from the equation before he made himself look even worse."

"You *humiliated* him!" Tony slapped the wall again.

Murray tensed.

"Yes, I did," I said coolly. "And I'd do it again."

"I'm really sorry," Murray said to me, as we left work later that evening.

"What for?"

"The way Tony spoke to you. It was awful. Disgusting. If he does it again, there are going to be some serious fucking consequences."

He ran his hand through his hair, tugging at the ends. "I'm just . . . sorry."

I didn't need the pregnant pause to tell me that he wasn't talking about Tony anymore.

"Do you want to get a drink?" I asked abruptly.

"What?"

"I owe you one. You won the bet. You made Denton cry first."

"Lily . . ."

"Please."

He thought about it for a moment, then nodded.

"I saw a sign out the front of our old fave the other day," I said. "It's under new management. Meet you there?"

"All right."

I got there before him. The bar still looked pretty much the same as it had seven years ago, when I'd first surveilled Murray at his birthday drinks, but they'd updated a lot of the drink options (including, sadly, taking away our beloved, terrible, cheap *Desert Island Castaway* beer). "Two of . . . I don't know, whatever you have on tap that you recommend," I told the bartender, a tall, broad-shouldered man with a man-bun and a row of little silver rings lining one ear. "And fries."

"Sure thing."

"Can you split that into two bowls? Same amount of fries, but in two different dishes? And can you cover one in pepper? Like, an amount of pepper that might potentially kill someone?"

The bartender grinned at me. "Whatever you want, love. Sit down and I'll bring it out to you."

It was a quiet night, and the food and drink arrived at the same time Murray did. "Before you start complaining about it, I've done the calculations," I said, as he slid into the booth and the bartender set the dishes down. "It is definitely my turn to buy the bar snacks. You bought them last week. So shut up."

Murray didn't say anything. The bartender visibly swallowed a laugh. I glared at him until he went away.

I held my beer up. "Cheers."

"Lily."

"I know. I know we have to talk about it. But can we just . . ."

I bit my lip.

"We pulled off something amazing," I said at last. "I don't want that to get lost. We made an awful man look like a complete dipshit, and we made sure there isn't anything Tony can do about it. That deserves to be celebrated."

Murray paused, then he clinked his beer against mine. "Cheers."

We drank.

Then we just looked at each other, for a long time.

"I'm sorry," I whispered.

"You don't need to apologise."

"I want to, though."

I closed my eyes. How the fuck was I going to put this? I was good with words, but how could anyone possibly explain the swirling mess of my thoughts?

I loved him.

I'd wanted him for years.

I *loved him*.

But he loved Julia. It had always been Julia, when it came down to it—and he was technically still married to her, even if it was only a matter of time until their divorce was finalised.

He loved her, but they'd split up anyway.

I loved him, but I'd spent years drawing lines around him, lines that separated me from him. If I crossed them—if I opened the vault and let him all the way in—if I did that, and we split up anyway . . .

If we crossed the Rubicon, I might drown in it.

"It's all right."

I opened my eyes at the brush of Murray's fingers against mine. "It's all right," he repeated. "I heard you last night. I get it."

"Really?"

"Really."

He took his hand away and leaned back, eating a couple of his pepper-covered fries. "You're right," he said. "We both have hard edges, and our partnership is too important to risk. The thought of fucking that up makes me feel sick."

"Me too."

"Did I have a good time last night? Of course," he said. "But you're my best friend before you're anything else. That will always be true. That—us—is the most important thing."

I should throw myself at this man. I should wrap my arms around his neck and my legs around his waist and press his hard edges into mine and never, ever let go.

"So we're good?" I asked instead.

Murray gave me a look. "You can't scare me off that easily, Lily. I'm not a fucking amateur."

God, I loved him so much.

I ate a couple of my fries, trying to give myself a chance to swallow down all the inconvenient feelings lodged in my throat. "At least one good thing came out of it," I said lightly.

"What's that?"

"You definitely won the breakup. You think Julia is pulling something as good as this?" I gestured up and down my body.

Murray grunted and drank some of his beer.

"Oh no," I said. "What?"

"You know her nemesis? Elias?"

"She didn't."

"She did."

"Shut up. When did this happen? Why didn't you tell me?"

"A while ago, and because it's embarrassing." He drank some more of his beer. "I'm supposed to be some big genius at reading people. My wife hooking up with the guy she told me definitely not to worry about because she hated him more than anyone else on the planet doesn't exactly help my reputation."

"One, we just went on and on about how we're best friends, you could have told me. Two, this is embarrassing *for her*! I've been helping her ruin that man's life. This is like if I turned around and fucked Denton."

Murray choked. "Please don't put that image into my head."

His phone rang a little while later. "I should probably get this," he said, glancing at it. "It's Cooper Pryce. The logistics of getting him in are going to be hell, and—"

"—it's not like you can kick the work to Tony," I said. "Take it."

He stood. I stood too, and, before I had a chance to think about it, I wrapped my arms around his waist. "I love you," I said, voice muffled in his shoulder.

Murray pressed his lips to my hair. "I love you too."

He pulled back. My lipstick was all over his collar. "See you at work tomorrow, okay?"

I nodded.

He answered the phone. "Cooper! Sorry about that—couldn't work out which one of my pockets my phone was in. How's things?"

His voice trailed off as he left, the bar door swinging shut behind him. I watched him go, wondering if I'd just made the best decision of my life, or the absolute worst.

I needed another drink.

I left our table and went to the bar instead, sitting on one of the barstools and hooking my ankles around the crossbar. The bartender set down the glass he was polishing. "What can I get you, love?"

"Alcohol."

"I think I can make that happen."

He had a slight burr to his voice—Irish, maybe, or Scottish. "Breakup?" he asked, taking a bottle of whiskey down from the top shelf.

"No. Kind of the opposite."

He put the glass down in front of me. "That's not what it looked like."

I raised an eyebrow.

He looked back, undaunted.

"That was my best friend," I said. "He absolutely railed me last night on top of a washing machine."

"Interesting choice. The washing machine, that is. High degree of difficulty."

I snorted.

"The man a high degree of difficulty too?"

"No. It's just . . ." I sighed, looking down at my drink. "He's just getting out of a very long, very serious relationship. And I'm . . ."

"What?" he said, after I'd let the silence hang too long. "Too stunningly beautiful for the likes of him?"

"Now *this* is a high degree of difficulty. You hitting on me right now."

The bartender flashed me a smile. "You've not touched your drink."

"I'm not much of a whiskey drinker."

"Well, then, you should have been more specific when you ordered then, shouldn't you? But give it a try. You might like it."

I hesitated.

"Come on then," he said. "Are you ready to be brave?"

I took a sip. It burned going down.

"I'm stealing that line," I said. "I'm a reality TV producer. I can make a lot of people do a lot of things by asking them a question like that."

"Now that's an interesting career." He spread his hands wide on the bar. "Tell me more about that."

I started laughing.

"What?"

"Nothing," I replied. "I'm Lily."

He held out his hand. "Jeff."

16

Murray

My trailer smelled like bacon and bad coffee.

I rubbed at my eyes. The sun had been rising when I finally collapsed on my bed. I must have fallen asleep at a terrible angle, because the crick in my neck was worse than usual.

"Oh hey, you're awake," Lily said. "Sit up. I got you breakfast."

I rubbed at my eyes again. I felt strangely lightheaded, like I'd had too much champagne and too few canapes at a network party.

The bacon smell was coming from a cardboard container on my bedside table, *B+E XXX pepper* scrawled on the top. Beside it, Lily set down a cup of coffee, wisps of steam curling off the top. "I washed all your mugs," she said, gesturing to the kitchenette.

I pushed myself up on my elbows. "Is that decaf?"

"Against my better judgement, no."

She sat down on the end of my bed. "I figured I owed you an apology. I would have got you Viet coffee if there was any way to magically transport my mother into the bubble."

"What?" I couldn't seem to make my thoughts go in the right order.

"I had a conversation with Suzette last night, after my ITM. I wanted to know why you didn't follow through on my humiliation play."

Things started to swim into focus. Heather tossing her hair. Romeo-Dylan's jaw, tight with anger. His arms, even tighter around Cece. Heather weeping.

That glint in Lily's eye.

"Suzette told me about the promise you made to boy-Dylan when he signed on," she said. "How upset he was about how things with Heather went down, and . . . I'm sorry, Murray. Genuinely."

I sat up and took a long sip of coffee. It was much too hot, burning the inside of my mouth, but I needed to make sure my brain was online again before I responded.

"How is it," I said, after several long moments, "that of all the things for you to apologise to me about, you picked the only one you don't need to be sorry for?"

"Murray, if I looked like you do—" Lily ran her thumbs under her eyes, where I had dark smears of tiredness, "—and someone did that to my show, I'd be livid."

"I went back last night and pulled the tapes. I heard what Heather said to you."

I took another long swallow of my coffee. I didn't know what she'd put in it, but now I'd fully transitioned from sleep to wakefulness, my brain felt like it was working better than it had in weeks.

"I should be apologising to you," I said. "If I'd seen that footage earlier—if I'd done my job properly—"

"If you finish that sentence, I'm going to throw something at you."

"Lily—"

"I went behind your back, and it made a huge mess," she said. "I wanted to help, but I'm so used to pulling the strings that it didn't even occur to me that there might be information I didn't have."

She stood, pacing the length of the trailer. "I did the same thing with girl-Dylan. I decided on what the best move was, and then I went barrelling ahead without any context. Kept doing it, too, when I did have the context, even though you asked me not to. These—" she ran both her thumbs under her eyes again, "—these are my fault."

I wanted to put my coffee down. I wanted to reach out and close my fingers around her wrist and pull her to me. *It's all right,* I wanted to say. *Stop being such a drama queen about it.*

I wanted to hug my best friend.

But there was a part of my brain that was always scheming, always calculating, always looking for vulnerabilities I could exploit.

And she'd just exposed her throat.

"Yes," I said, tone cool. "They are."

I sipped my coffee again, locking down my expression. The second she saw how fast the wheels in my brain were turning, I'd lose my advantage.

I'd played a lot of people in my time. Usually, it wasn't very difficult. They assumed you would have qualms about playing on their weaknesses, because they would have qualms. They never saw you coming. Most of the time, they didn't even realise they'd been played.

Lily was different. She knew all my tricks. She knew I didn't have qualms, because she didn't either. She knew exactly how my mind worked, because usually, we were playing people together.

I had tried to play her exactly once. Six years ago. I had sat opposite her in our favourite bar and tried to call her bluff. *Yes, you* are *right that we'd never work romantically,* I'd told her, hoping to provoke her into disagreement, convinced that if I gave her time and space to think about it, she'd come around, that she'd realise she felt about me the way I had slowly been realising I felt about her.

To say it hadn't worked was an understatement, given it had ended with her marrying the bartender.

So I was going to have to tread very, very carefully. If I told her everything was all right and assuaged her guilt, I'd lose my way in. But if I just snapped my teeth at her throat, the way I'd been doing for the past few weeks, she'd withdraw, and we'd be right back where we started.

This would require finesse. Patience. Strategy.

"I appreciate the coffee, Lily," I said. "And I don't want or need your apology over the Heather thing. She deserved what she got."

I drained my mug. I could, in theory, make a play now. Lily's apology, combined with all the late-night meals she'd been bullying me into eating, showed that my wellbeing was a weakness for her. I could take an impassioned route. Fall to my knees at her feet and tell her I was drowning without her.

It would be true.

But she could already see I was drowning. And I'd tried impassioned sincerity, all those times I'd practically begged her to tell me why she was here. All it had got me was hand-waves and half-truths.

I'd showed her how much I cared, and it hadn't done a fucking thing.

So, "But I need you to leave," I said.

"Not before you eat."

I was starving. The bacon smell was delicious. I wanted to fall on it like a wolf on a carcass.

"I'll eat on the way down the hill," I said instead.

I got up, pulling last night's shirt over my head with one hand and throwing it in the vague direction of my laundry pile. "I don't blame you for last night, but I don't have time to discuss it either," I said, grabbing a clean shirt. "I've got to go and fix it. Fuck knows how I'm going to do it, but I'll figure that out on the way. Where's my radio?"

"I hid it."

I turned slowly to face her, shirt clutched in my fist. "You what?"

"I hid it. And I'm not going to tell you where it is until you eat something, have a shower, and drink at least two litres of water."

I was right. This was it. My way in.

That small victory was swept away, though, in a tornado of frustration and panic. "On what fucking planet do you think I have time for that?!"

I grabbed my phone, and nearly had an aneurysm when I saw that it was 3pm. I'd slept for almost ten hours!

"Lily," I said, "if you don't give me my radio right now—"

"What? You'll use the daddy voice on me some more? Oh no."

I threw my shirt to the floor and started rummaging through drawers.

"Please," she said. "As if I'd hide it somewhere you could find it."

"Are you trying to ruin my life?"

"What would I get out of doing that?"

"I don't know. You tell me. Because it sure fucking feels like that's what you're trying to do." I pointed to my eyes. "This isn't just overwork, Lily," I said. "This is you. This is what you being here has done to me."

I'd hoped for a bigger reaction, but she didn't give me anything. "Then let me help you," was all she said.

I folded my arms across my bare chest. "You can help me by giving me my radio back and getting out of my way."

"I caused the problem. Let me solve it."

"How do you propose doing that from the Villa, Lily Fireball?"

There was venom in my tone, but she ignored it. "I've already started. I talked to Suzette and Carrie. Filming's cancelled for today. You obviously don't need to film a Last Chance Party or a Necklace Ceremony, given Heather's been cut, and it's in everyone's best interests to cool off and take a breath. And a nap."

The look she gave me on those last three words was pointed. I refused to acknowledge it.

211

"The key to getting boy-Dylan back on side is to remind him why he's here," she went on. "So I got Suzette to set up a private no-cameras chat with girl-Dylan."

"Great. They can talk about how they have no chemistry and fuck up my plans even more."

"That's a risk, I admit, but it's not the most likely outcome."

I raised my eyebrows.

"Talking with girl-Dylan should trigger some thought processes for boy-Dylan," she said. "It'll make him remember why he agreed to do the show in the first place."

Lily poked me in the chest with one perfectly manicured fingernail. "And it'll remind him how far you specifically were prepared to go to make sure he had control over his story."

I clenched my jaw. Almost against my will, my mind was connecting the dots.

"Then tonight," she said, "once you've had some more sleep, and something to eat, and you look more like a human than a troll who lives under a bridge, you're going to sit down with him. You'll offer him the most heartfelt apology in the history of time."

"He doesn't want an apology. He wants it not to have happened."

"But it did happen, and you can't even edit it out, because just about everyone fucking hates Heather now—and if we don't put it in the show, then someone'll start talking about how we did a big racism coverup to protect her, and it'll be a thousand times worse. I know."

We.

She'd said *we.*

If Lily had realised her semantic slip, she didn't give it away. "I'm confident boy-Dylan will understand that too, now he's had time to calm down," she said. "But just in case he doesn't, you're going to send me on the next single date."

I was so stuck on *we* it took me a moment to process that suggestion. "Absolutely not," I said. "He's actively afraid of you."

"Look, you know him better than me. This whole situation is proof of that, so if that's what you think, then fine. Send someone else. But hear me out first."

"What the fuck do you think I'm doing?"

She ignored my tone again. "Boy-Dylan's a tenderheart. Too nice for his own good. He might be scared of me, but he's much more scared of people getting hurt because of him."

The image of him and Cece flashed involuntarily in front of my eyes. How fast he'd run down the hill when he thought she was in danger. How tightly he'd held her to him. Their fingers interlaced on the Convent verandah.

"I'm telling you, I'm the right choice," Lily said. "At least while he's in this frame of mind. I'll put the least pressure on him, because he knows he can't hurt my feelings."

"Does anything hurt your feelings?"

She stopped. For a few seconds, she was perfectly still.

"What kind of a question is that?" she asked.

A calculated one, was the truth. She worried about my wellbeing. She felt guilty about how overworked I was as an *I* instead of a *we*; felt guiltier when she felt like she'd made it worse. Those feelings—those Lily Ong feelings—were the

213

levers I could wedge in the cracks of the Lily Fireball mask and use to break it, use to find my best friend beneath it so she could tell me why she was really here, why she was really doing this to herself.

"A serious one," I said instead.

That was also the truth.

"I don't understand how you can ask me that," she said. "You of all people should know—should know that—"

"Should know what?"

"Should know that I feel things," she said. "I don't want to, a lot of the time. Sometimes I wish I could just cut that part of myself out. But I feel things."

"You could have fooled me."

"Murray—"

"*I'm all hard edges*," I snarled. "*I need someone soft, to balance me out.*"

She paused for a long moment. "You remember."

"Of course I fucking remember! You think those words haven't been seared into my brain for the last six years?!"

She closed her eyes.

"I know you don't have a lot of lines, Lily. But I never thought you'd cross that one."

"Murray—"

"Save it."

I walked over to the door of my trailer. It was calculated, pushing her away like this, a manoeuvre, a stratagem.

It didn't make the feelings behind it any less real.

"I'll consider your suggestions," I said. "Now get out."

My first instinct was to not to use Lily's plan.

The apology to Romeo-Dylan part was, of course, a given. There was no world in which I didn't spend the better part of an hour sincerely apologising to him for the series of fuck-ups that had led to the Heather debacle; and for the fact that, to ensure the scandal didn't overwhelm the whole season, we were going to have to make a Very Special Episode.

He accepted the apology, but his jaw was clenched the whole time. Romeo-Dylan had retreated behind his own mask.

The only time the mask fell away was when I commented, with deliberate casualness, how well Cece was going to come out of the whole affair. "The Instagram deals she's going to get will be massive, especially once we slingshot her onto another show," I told him. "You were right about the friend spots, Dylan. I was wrong. And beyond that—you've done exactly what you wanted. You've helped her. Immeasurably."

"Good," Romeo-Dylan said faintly. "That's good."

I wondered, afterwards, while I was scrubbing through mounted cam footage in the war room, whether I should have brought Cece up at all. Making it clear that he'd set her up for a bright future without him in it was a good way of refocusing him on the story with Juliet-Dylan, but if I became this looming villainous figure in his mind tearing him and his beloved apart it was hardly going to be good for our working relationship.

Maybe I should offer him an out from our agreement. It would be a huge pain for me to recalibrate all my narrative plans—not to mention getting him and Juliet-Dylan out of their contracts—but it might be worth it.

The war room door handle rattled. I'd put a chair under it again. "Murray?"

"Go away, Lily."

"You don't have to talk to me. Not if you don't want to. I'll be in and out. But I brought you something to eat."

God, that sounded good.

"Eat it yourself," I said tersely. "I'm busy."

No, I decided. I would not be offering Romeo-Dylan an out. Lily would be delighted that I'd conceded, and I was not giving her any more ground.

Especially because I had, in the end, decided to go with her plan, and was sending her on the Episode Six single date. Her dramatic instincts were, as usual, flawless. The show needed a tonal reset after the Heather incident. Lily Fireball was many things—including my personal tormentor—but she was, above all, fun.

That didn't mean I was going to let *her* have fun, though. I'd co-written the book on malicious compliance a long time ago.

"What?!" Lily exclaimed. "Is this a joke?"

". . . no?" Romeo-Dylan said.

"Who told him?" she demanded, looking around at Z and all the assembled crew. "Who told him I can't dance?"

Her gaze passed over me. *I'm going to kill you, Murray.*

I shifted position, adjusting my earpiece.

"Which one of you was it?!"

Her gaze whipped back the other way, passing over me again. *I mean it. I'm going to murder you in your sleep.*

"No one told me anything," Romeo-Dylan said. "Look at me, okay, Lily? Breathe. It's going to be all right. It's going to be fun. I can't dance either. We can look like idiots together."

"I don't make a habit of looking like an idiot."

"Are you telling me that someone who's named herself Lily Fireball takes herself seriously *all* the time?"

Lily looked down, eyelashes fluttering.

"Are you?"

"No." She infused her voice with just the right level of vulnerability to offset the tantrum. "But this is different. I'm a hard bitch. Who's going to believe that when they see me falling over my own feet?"

This was a play on one of our classic single date formats: the commitment date, where the lead and the contestant had to totally commit to some ridiculous task as a way of symbolically demonstrating their capacity to commit to each other. It was a great way of making it seem like two people were compatible when they weren't, so I'd been intending to send the Dylans on a commitment date in Episode Eight or Nine. However, if you made the task absurd enough, it could also be very funny—and as I wanted to infuse Episode Six with lighthearted hijinks after the serious drama of Episode Five, I'd decided to use it here.

We'd set up a game called Pash Mash Smash, which was somewhere between Dance Dance Revolution and Twister. Romeo-Dylan and Lily would have to learn a dance routine that involved mashing some coloured light-up buttons with their hands and smashing some with their feet. As they went along, the buttons would light up faster and faster.

If they won the game, it would send electricity along a fuse and start a fire, AKA the strongest visual code there was for passion.

The fuse wasn't connected. I had the button that would turn on the firepit in my utility belt. If and when it ignited was completely in my control.

Lily wasn't lying. She couldn't dance. I still had the scar on my left foot from going clubbing with her and her friends on her twenty-fourth birthday, when she'd slipped and somehow managed to pierce my shoe and several layers of my skin with her heel.

"We'll start slow," Romeo-Dylan said, urging her onto the Pash Mash Smash mat.

Over his shoulder, she caught my eye. *I know I asked for this,* her pained gaze said. *But please don't let this go on too long.*

I found my stoniest, most implacable expression. I'd spent the last few weeks trying to get things out of her and getting nothing back. She needed to know what that felt like.

I took mercy on her after two hours.

"Oh thank god," she said, flopping flat on her back as the firepit ignited, chest rising and falling rapidly as she sucked in huge gasps of air.

Romeo-Dylan flopped down next to her. "Screw the Olympic flame. This is the only flame I care about now."

It was a warm day. They had discarded various layers of clothing. He was shirtless, rippling six-pack on display. Lily was down to a tank top, sweat glistening on her collarbone.

It was archetypical thirst trap stuff. Fucking Greg was going to be delighted. *Look at her,* I could practically hear him saying, leering at her. *She really is a spicy meatball, isn't she?*

"I hope you know," Lily said, turning her head to look at Romeo-Dylan, "that if you ever tell anyone how bad I was at this, I will hunt you down and seek revenge on you and everyone you love."

"Lily, this is a TV show. I suspect a few people might see."

"They'll know I was bad at this, sure. But they won't be able to show more than a quick montage. You're the only person who'll know how genuinely awful I was."

Romeo-Dylan chuckled. "I promise you that if anyone ever calls me up one day and asks for a reference because you've applied to be a Pash Mash Smash professional, I'll lie through my teeth."

The corners of his eyes crinkled as he smiled at her. Lily smiled back.

It wasn't a Lily Fireball smile. It was Lily Ong, sitting opposite me at our desk as we worked late. *Oh hey, babe,* she'd say, something in her softening as she looked past me at Jeff. *You brought us dinner? You're so sweet.*

"Shall we go sit by our fire and have a glass of wine?" Romeo-Dylan asked.

"I hope by glass you mean bottle. Bottles, ideally. Plural."

"Look, as a professional athlete, I can tell you that we really should be hydrating first." He got to his feet and offered her his hand. "But as someone that just played eight hundred hours of Pash Mash Smash—bottles plural sounds great."

Lily took his hand. Romeo-Dylan pulled her up.

There was no part of me that believed that she was attracted to him, or that he was attracted to her. It would be difficult to find two people as wildly mismatched as Lily Ong and Dylan Jayasinghe Mellor.

But I'd done my job too well. Just for a moment, as his fingers wrapped around her wrist, I could see it, and it took everything in me to stamp on that toxic cocktail of feelings and bury it deep.

There was a healthy distance between them as they sat next to the firepit, but it was comfortable, friendly, not coloured with the fear and tension of their previous inter-actions. Romeo-Dylan held his glass up. "Cheers."

Lily clinked hers against his. "Cheers."

They both drank. "Sorry for putting you through that," Romeo-Dylan said. "But I hope you had fun."

She examined him shrewdly. "Is it exhausting?"

"Is what exhausting? Pash Mash Smash?"

"No," she said. "Caring about what other people think as much as you do."

"I could ask you the same question," he replied. "Is it exhausting constantly having to come up with ways to put people off-balance?"

"Oh, no," Lily said brightly. "That's not hard at all. You just have to know where to apply pressure. Where the start of the domino line is, so when you shove one person in the shoulder, another one ends up in the pool."

Romeo-Dylan opened his mouth. Closed it again.

Lily took a sip of her wine. "For instance," she said, gesturing with her glass, "sometimes you whisper the right words in the right ears, and the house racist gets humiliated on national television."

If Romeo-Dylan had been drinking, he would have done a spit-take.

If I'd been drinking, so would I. My mind started racing, connecting the dots.

"It was easy, really." Lily leaned back on one hand and swirled her glass. "All I had to do was mention to my producer that Heather and Naya didn't like each other. I didn't even have to tell him why. He ate it right up. Heather and Naya got put together on the group date, Heather couldn't resist being *Heather*, and—bam." She mimed a flicking motion with her fingers. "Over go my dominoes."

Romeo-Dylan paused.

Paused a moment longer.

Gulped down half his wine glass in one go.

"It was *you*?" he said. "You're the one who—who . . . ?"

"Don't get me wrong, I felt bad about putting Naya in the firing line," Lily said. "But she was already in the firing line with Heather in the Villa anyway, so . . ."

She shrugged, in that entirely studied, deliberate way of hers.

Romeo-Dylan gulped down the other half of his wine.

"I did think about trying to get Heather paired with me instead," she went on, as calmly as if she were discussing what she'd watched on TV the night before. "But I'm a stone-cold bitch, so if I did that, people might take Heather's side. And I didn't want that."

"No," Romeo-Dylan said faintly. "You wouldn't."

"But I have a fatal flaw. I'm like one of those serial killers that gets caught because they can't resist taking credit."

Lily turned and looked directly down the barrel of the camera. "So Heather," she purred, "when you watch this one day—I want you to know it was me."

She paused for a second and put on a thoughtful expression. "Well, actually, no," she said. "It was you. You did this to yourself. All those little comments you made when you didn't think anyone else was listening? That was you. But the fact you got caught? That was me, baby. All me."

"Is it true?" Romeo-Dylan asked me afterwards, as we sat down to shoot his ITM. "What Lily said? She orchestrated that whole thing?"

Not you? was implicit, but I heard it loud and clear.

I glanced over, checking that Saurav already had the camera rolling.

"Yeah, mate," I replied. "It's true."

Romeo-Dylan exhaled, shoulders unknotted in a way they hadn't been in any of our conversations since the Heather incident. "That woman is terrifying."

"Yes," I agreed. "She is."

Later, in the war room, I isolated the first two sentences of our ITM conversation, noting down the timecodes to go into the Episode Six rough cut. "Is it true? What Lily said? She orchestrated that whole thing?" Romeo-Dylan asked on screen.

"Yeah, mate," my disembodied voice replied. "It's true."

I didn't typically like being part of the on-screen narrative. The more audiences saw of how the sausage got made, the more cynical they got about how real the romances were.

In this case, though, it was unavoidable. And it was going to be *incredible* TV.

I skipped over to the footage from Lily's ITM. I'd conducted Romeo-Dylan's interview, so Carrie had been in charge of Lily's. "That was quite a revelation," she said.

Lily batted her eyelashes. "How does it feel?" she cooed. "That I can do your job better than you can?"

I paused the replay, scribbling down the timecode. That would be a perfect intercut to go after the grab from Romeo-Dylan's interview.

She was such a drama queen. Such an incredible, perfect, flawless drama queen.

The screen was frozen on Lily's face. One corner of her mouth was curved upwards, halfway to a smirk. Her chin was raised, the long line of her neck exposed. The glint in her eye couldn't be described as anything other than predatory.

She was entirely in character. She was fully Lily Fireball.

But it was her too. Right there on the screen in front of me. My Lily, the woman I'd loved for years.

If Fucking Greg wanted her to be the kind of archvillain that people threw fruit at in the streets, he was going to be very disappointed. Heather, yes. Lily, not a chance.

They'll love to hate me, Lily had said to me, three weeks ago, when I'd been trying to convince her not to get out of the limo.

Jodi McAlister

She'd been wrong. If getting people invested in hating her had been a key part of her secret master plan, she'd made a major misstep.

She wasn't a villain. She was an anti-hero. People might hate how much they loved her, but god, they were going to *love* her . . . and she loved this.

That was it. That was the key. That was the other lever I'd use to break her.

She was addicted to pulling the strings. She couldn't help herself. Give her a problem she had no business solving—repairing my relationship with Romeo-Dylan, for example—and she'd find a way to do it.

This would have to be a two-pronged approach. I'd have to play on her guilt about how overworked and exhausted I was—and exploit her love of puppet-mastering, make her see there was no way she could give this up.

Then I'd crack that fucking mask of hers. I'd pull Lily Ong out from behind Lily Fireball. And I'd finally get her to *talk to me*, to tell me why on earth she'd cut me off for a full year, only to reappear like this, flamethrower in hand as she burned everything we'd built down.

I hit play again.

"You think you're so smart," the Lily on the screen said. "But I'm smarter."

224

17

Lily

Five years ago

"I can't believe he's so fucking stupid," I grumbled, taking another handful of peanuts from the bowl I'd stolen from behind the bar.

"It's more complicated than that, I think," Murray said.

"Hello, yes, Asian woman living in the world, I know it's more complicated than that. But it's also just so fucking *stupid*."

Jeff came by the table, setting a glass of white wine down in front of me and a beer in front of Murray. "You looked like you needed these," he said, leaning down and kissing the top of my head. "It didn't go well, love?"

I shook my head. "It was a perfect pitch, too. We knew the social justice angle wouldn't play, so we barely touched on it. We went for a ratings angle instead—talked about how casting more diversely would let us tell new, exciting kinds of stories, and open up new markets."

"But all Greg heard was the word 'diverse,'" Murray said. "He started yelling *go woke, go broke* so loud they probably heard it at the other end of the building."

"He didn't even let us finish," I said mournfully.

That was what had really got to me. Murray and I had worked so hard—and avoided so many Tony-shaped landmines—to get this meeting with the executive vice-president of unscripted programming. We'd spent weeks preparing, doing exhaustive, laborious research. And he hadn't even let us *finish*.

"Ah, shit, I'm sorry," Jeff said. "Anything I can do?"

"Bring us dinner?" I tangled my fingers in his and pressed a hopeful kiss to his wrist.

"I think I can make that happen." He smiled fondly at me.

"Not for me, thanks, mate," Murray said. "I think that's my date." He nodded at a brunette in bright red lipstick who'd just walked in.

"Then let me donate a drink for the lady to the cause." Jeff slid my untouched glass of wine across the table to him. "Come with me to the bar, love. I'll get you another one."

I perched on my favourite barstool on the end. "Don't you want to sit on the other side tonight?" Jeff asked, taking a fresh wineglass down. "So you can spy on him?"

"No," I said. "I can watch you work better from this angle. Can I have red instead of white, please?"

"You're ruining his plan." Jeff closed the wine fridge with his foot and took a bottle of red wine from the counter instead.

"What plan?"

"Do you think he parades all his dates through my bar because he wants my opinion on them?" He poured the wine into my glass. "He's trying to make you jealous."

I snorted. "No, he's not."

Jeff gave me a look.

I shifted slightly on my barstool. One of my only frustrations with our otherwise excellent relationship was that he thought exactly the same thing that Thuong and all my other friends thought: that Murray was in love with me. And Jeff had more ammunition, because he was the only person in the world—besides Murray and me—who knew about the washing machine incident.

I'd tried to explain what it meant to put something in the vault to Jeff once before. He hadn't got it, hadn't been able to grasp how you could just draw lines around something, set it aside, and close the door on it. If he didn't understand my vault, he sure as hell wouldn't understand that Murray had one too, and that the washing machine incident was locked away in there.

So I sighed and chose a different one of the many truths. "Babe, we have been coming to this bar since long before you bought it," I said. "Meeting a new person is inherently frightening, but doing it in a familiar environment makes it easier. That's part of why we make the experience on the shows so weird for the contestants. Unsettled people make good drama."

I took a sip of my wine. "And Murray doesn't exactly have a ton of dating experience under his belt. He's never been on the apps before. He was with Julia since they were basically children. Entering his slut era at age thirty is already scary as hell, especially for a control freak like him. At least here he can control the environment."

Jeff sighed. "Come here."

I leaned across the bar so he could kiss me.

"Sometimes, love," he said against my lips, before kissing me again, "I think you might be too clever for your own good."

18

Murray

It was delicate, setting this trap for Lily. Playing a player was never easy—and I couldn't let her realise I was doing it until my teeth were in her throat.

That meant everything I did had to not just be plausibly deniable, but likely. This woman understood me better than anyone on the planet. She wasn't going to suspend her disbelief if I acted out of character. I needed to take my existing patterns—and weaponise them.

The next group date card reveal was early the next morning. These generally didn't have a lot of overarching narrative implications, so I usually delegated them to Suzette and Carrie; but I dragged myself out of bed for this one, glancing in the mirror before I left my trailer to make sure the circles under my eyes were good and dark.

Five of the eight remaining Juliets were going on the Episode Six group date. Lily, having been on the single date, already knew she wasn't one of them, and I could feel her

229

gaze on me as I stood up the back of the shoot, arms folded, leaning against the wall.

I took a muesli bar out of my utility belt. I waited for a break, so the crinkle of the wrapper wouldn't ruin a take, and ate it.

"All right, that's a wrap!" Carrie announced. "Naya, Parisa, you're first in hair and makeup."

I pushed myself off the wall. "You two are in charge of date setup," I told Carrie and Suzette, making sure Lily was in earshot. "Give me a fifteen-minute warning before the shoot. I'll be in the war room until then."

"Murray, we don't need you supervising," Suzette said. "We've got this."

"I said," I bit out, "give me a fifteen-minute warning."

Suzette rolled her eyes. Carrie shook her head. I made a mental note to buy them both very nice thank you/I'm sorry gifts once the season was over.

I shut myself in the war room. I put a chair under the door handle. I made myself two coffees, one with lukewarm water, one with hot. I put them down on the conference table, flicked on some of yesterday's mounted cam footage, and waited.

I'd only just finished my first coffee when the door handle rattled. I allowed myself a smile before I locked my expression down.

"What?" I barked.

"Let me in, Murray."

I didn't respond.

She started knocking.

I gave it a good ten seconds before I got up, kicked the

chair out of the way, and reefed the door open. "I don't have time for this, Lily."

I'd braced my arm against the doorjamb, but she ducked under it, exactly the same way she'd ducked under it a million times before, and slammed a plate of toast down on the table. "You're going to eat something if I have to force it down your throat."

I folded my arms. "Is that all?"

"Yes."

Well, shit.

"Although I was wondering if you'd like me to tell you when your crew start plotting an uprising against you, or if you'd like it to be a surprise," she said coolly. "*Tony*."

Got her.

"Don't compare me to Tony."

"I'm sorry." She didn't sound sorry at all. "You're right. You're a reverse Tony. He never worked. You won't stop."

"You think I like micromanaging? I don't. But I'm working with limited resources—and you saw what happens when I'm not across every single thing that happens on this set. I can't risk another Heather situation."

Conveniently, for once, my eye started twitching. I jammed the heel of my hand against it. "Can you please leave? I've got work to do."

Lily paused. I had to resist holding my breath.

"Let me help," she said.

I sat back down, stabbing a little too viciously at my tablet as I entered the pin. "Thank you for the toast. Go away."

The door closed. I didn't let myself look up to see which side of it she was on.

The press of her thumbs into my occipitals nearly made me moan.

"Head back."

I didn't move.

She fisted her left hand in my hair and pulled my head back, digging her right thumb so hard into the muscle at the base of my skull it would probably bruise. "Let me help you, Murray."

"Lily," I said, "let go."

She pulled my hair harder, pressing her thumb in deeper— and god, it felt good, it felt so fucking good that I couldn't let myself process it, not if I wanted to keep my concentration. "The daddy voice doesn't work on me. You're going to let me help you."

I pretended to consider it.

"If I give you a task, will you leave me alone so I can work?"

"We can come to some sort of arrangement."

I pretended to consider it again—then gestured to the seat across the conference table.

She let go of my hair, but she didn't move. "I have a condition."

"For fuck's sake, Lily."

"Eat."

I exhaled, pulled the plate towards me, picked up a piece of toast, and took a bite. "Happy?"

"Yes. Thank you."

She sat down, lacing her hands together demurely in front of her. "What do you want me to do?"

I rubbed my left thumb across the base of my ring finger,

an old thinking tic of mine from when I wore a wedding ring that I knew she'd recognise. "I need Belinda gone."

"All right," Lily said. "Too many blondes?"

"And she's not very dynamic television. But getting Dylan JM to eliminate her after she had her tooth knocked out is going to be tough, so if you can take that off my plate, I would appreciate it."

"Take that off your plate—" she gestured at the toast, "—and we have a deal."

I waited a beat, then took another bite.

The smile that spread across her face was pure Lily Ong. "That wasn't so hard, was it?"

"Don't push it."

Her smile only deepened. "What else?"

I let the silence hang for a long moment.

Then I exhaled, as if in surrender. "Have you got any ideas on how to make the Dylans come across like they're actually into each other?"

Something sparked behind her eyes. "Are you finally admitting I'm right about that?"

"Forget it. I'll figure it out myself."

"No, no, no, I'm sorry, I'm sorry," she said. "That was cheap. I will make the Dylans work for you, Murray, if it's the last thing I do."

My plan was working.

I didn't know quite how Lily had done it, given she hadn't even been on the group date, but she started a fight.

233

That night, in the Villa kitchen, all the women turned on Juliet-Dylan for clearly and obviously being Romeo-Dylan's favourite.

Juliet-Dylan protested.

Lily hung back, waited, and picked her moment.

"How about we ask your little sidekick?" she said sweetly. "Amanda, do you think it's obvious that Dylan is the Romeo's favourite?"

Everyone looked at Amanda. Her eyes were wide as she tried to disappear into the floor.

"Well?" Lily said.

"Yes," Amanda said, her voice barely audible. "Yes, I think he likes her better than anyone else."

It was a perfect moment of reality TV, because it did several things at once. It established that the Dylans had a special kind of bond ("oh," your typical audience member might say, "I can't see it, but if the other women can, they must really have something"). It set up conflict between Juliet-Dylan and the other women in the Villa, so the progression towards the Double Dylan happy ending had interesting obstacles to overcome. It also set up great tension between Amanda and Juliet-Dylan, a pressure point that could be exploited down the track.

And, as a bonus, it continued what had emerged in the single date, the thing that was going to make audiences fall in love with Lily. She was a delicious, delightful diva—a shit-starter who knew exactly what she was doing.

There was no producer in the world who could have engineered it any better.

Then, at the Last Chance Party the next day, Belinda—apparently out of nowhere—decided to leave. "It was her decision," Romeo-Dylan told the assembled women. "It was her choice."

The smirk on Lily's face was very Lily Fireball—but it was Lily Ong too.

My plan was working. I had this brilliant, frustrating woman right where I wanted her: and she hadn't even noticed.

I pretended to be annoyed when she snuck into the war room again after the Episode Six Necklace Ceremony, but I was so thrilled that I almost forgot to resist the plate she put down in front of me. "Lily, go to bed before people realise you're gone," I growled at her, clenching my hands into fists under the table to keep them off the food, two liberally peppered poached eggs on top of a stack of toast.

"No one will miss me for a while. They're too busy fighting over bathroom space. How did I do tonight?"

I gave in and pulled the plate towards me. "Fine."

"Fine?! I went above and beyond. I got Belinda out of your hair—and I used Amanda to wedge the Dylans. That was better than fine."

"Stop taking credit for things you didn't do. *I* used Amanda to wedge the Dylans."

"Excuse me, do you think girl-Dylan would have walked in on that Amanda/boy-Dylan kiss at the Last Chance Party if it wasn't for me?" Lily looked outraged.

"Do you think Amanda and boy-Dylan would have even been kissing if it wasn't for me?" I replied calmly, refusing to match her level of energy. "There's no punchline without the set-up."

It had been such a good punchline, though. The kiss I'd coaxed Romeo-Dylan and Amanda into hadn't even been close to convincing until Juliet-Dylan had interrupted it, jealousy written all over her face. Once I edited it together, the audience would have no clue she was jealous over the wrong person.

I expected Lily to push back harder, but she just leaned back in her chair. "I set you up the building blocks for a fight there," she said. "Do you want me to knock them over? The more you let girl-Dylan and Amanda stay in each other's orbits, the more obvious it's going to be that they're obsessed with each other."

I thought about it—genuinely, this time. She had a point.

"Hold off for now." I dipped my toast into the runny egg yolk. "We've still got six episodes left to shoot. If we're going to blow their relationship up, we need to get the timing right."

"Or, here's an idea." A wicked smile spread across her face. "The contract is for the Dylans to get together, right? But surely it doesn't say *just* the Dylans. They both like Amanda, and you've got her earmarked to be runner-up anyway, so: throuple."

I nearly choked. "God, can you imagine how loud Fucking Greg would yell if we tried to sell him on that?"

"He'd be stupid to say no, though. The audience would go wild for a throuple. Especially those three. They're the perfect combination of hot and wholesome. Can you imagine what it would do to the ratings?"

"I'd consider pitching it and seeing what happened—" I swallowed, "—but Dylan JM would never go for it. I don't think he could cope with another deviation from the plan."

The image of him and Cece holding hands on the Convent verandah drifted across my mind again.

"What?" Lily said.

"Hmmm?"

"You stopped chewing. And you got those two lines, right here." She tapped the space between her eyebrows. "You're not telling me something. What is it?"

"Maybe nothing," I said. "Just a problem I might have worked out how to solve, that's all."

I ran it past Romeo-Dylan, so I could keep him on side. "I want to use Cece on the Episode Seven group date. But given how the last group date she was on went, I wanted to make sure you were okay with it first."

"The more screentime she gets," he said slowly, "the better for her, right?"

"Absolutely. Cece's really standing out to the network. She's a serious contender to be the lead on the next *Wherefore Art Thou Romeo?*"

This was actually true. The notes Fucking Greg had been sending back on my rough cuts were very pro-Cece.

"We need to reveal your friendship with Cece to the Juliets at some point," I told Romeo-Dylan. "The women still in the game don't know she was the one observing the Episode Five group date. They have no idea you've built this platonic relationship with her. There's a danger you might come across dishonest if we don't come clean—and that'll make selling the happy ending that much harder."

"I don't want them to direct their anger at her, though. She's been through enough."

"I'll level with you," I said. "Can I promise you that none of the Juliets will be angry with her? No. But will it only get worse for both of you the longer you leave it? Yes."

He exhaled. "All right. Let's do it."

The group date I'd planned was a trivia game. All the questions were about Romeo-Dylan, things that the women should know if they'd been paying attention. Each correct answer would win them a point, and whoever had the most points at the end would win the Episode Seven single date.

All seven of the Juliets left in the game were competing— but so was Cece, which should, if everything went like I intended, set off a cascading series of events.

No matter who won the group date, Romeo-Dylan would be forced to confront his feelings about Cece and take action, either inviting her back to the Villa or ending their friend spots.

He and Cece were falling for each other. That was obvious to me, even if neither of them had realised it yet.

I could, in theory, let them continue with the friend spots. Whether or not they articulated their feelings to themselves, I didn't think they would articulate them to each other. They both had too much to lose.

But letting them continue would be bad for both of them— and, more importantly to me, bad for the show. I knew perfectly well how miserable pining for someone could make you. And if said pining showed up on screen (which it inevitably would) I'd have Brett and CJ vs Brett and Mary-Ellen all over again: the Romeo with the woman he did pick, instead of the one he clearly had something with.

So we had to make a move. We either had to end it now,

and nip it firmly in the bud; or we had to bring Cece back into the game, let them explore it, and *then* nip it in the bud.

It went the way I intended. Much to the chagrin of the other Juliets, Cece won the trivia game, and thus the single date.

I got Suzette to run point on their date shoot. "They both think of me as the man who pulls the strings," I said. "They'll feel freer to make big moves if I'm not front and centre."

"Look at you," Suzette said. "Relinquishing control to someone else. Does it hurt?"

I didn't dignify that with a response. "I'll be in your earpiece."

Just like I planned, Romeo-Dylan and Cece's date built to a perfect crisis point. "Are you sick of me?" he asked her softly, his affection for her evident in every line of his body.

"Of course I'm not sick of you, Dylan," Cece replied, equally softly, the fact that she was head over heels for him written all over her face in the twinkling fairy lights.

Then she swallowed, and in a move I recognised very clearly, shoved all her emotions down.

"But I don't think we should spend time together any-more," she said, the words running into each other as she tried to get them out.

So it was Cece, in the end, who took decisive action, who made the narrative move we needed, the woman who once couldn't string a single sentence together on camera giving us a reality TV moment for the ages. "I don't want you to think our friendship isn't important, because it is," she said to Romeo-Dylan, voice wavering. "It's so important to me. I couldn't even start to tell you how important it is to me."

"To me too," he said. "It's—you're—you're my lifeline."

"But I'm not what you came here to find. You didn't come here for friendship. You came here for love."

Despite the language they'd used, it was going to be very difficult to edit this together in a way that didn't suggest they were star-crossed lovers. I was going to have to make some very pointed music choices. Maybe do some work in post so no one noticed the tears in their eyes.

Just for a moment, guilt crept in.

I pushed it back down. If me engineering their separation was enough to keep them apart forever, then they never really had anything in the first place.

But, "Let them go," I told Suzette, when she asked if she should insist on the two of them staying to film ITMs. "We'll do pickups tomorrow. Let Dylan walk her home. Let them say goodbye."

Cece was red-eyed and withdrawn when I filmed her ITM the next day. I had to push hard to get more than a few sentences, and what I did get came through tears.

Romeo-Dylan wasn't much better. He didn't cry, but he'd sunk deep into himself, and drawing him out took more work than usual. "It was tough, saying goodbye to Cece," he said, looking past me instead of at me, voice distant. "It was really, really . . . tough."

Once I had what I needed, I waved at Frida to turn the camera off. "I'm sorry, mate. I know how much that friendship meant to you."

"I'm sure Cece and I will be friends on the outside." Romeo-Dylan still sounded very far away. "But it was nice. Having someone to talk to."

I glanced at his hands. His fingers weren't tapping, but his fists were clenched.

"It's hard," I said. "When friends suddenly disappear out of your life."

"Very."

Romeo-Dylan's shoulders were slumped when he left. It wasn't subtle body language. He might as well have a sign saying *I HAVE REGRETS* pinned to the back of his shirt.

I wondered how he and Cece had left it, when he walked her home. How long he'd hugged her. How tight he'd held her. How hard it was to let go.

I shook my head, trying to clear it. I'd had five whole hours of sleep last night. I should be more in control of my thoughts than this.

And I had a plan to focus on.

I shut myself in the war room for the afternoon, getting prepared for that evening's shoot. Technically, it was work I could outsource—"Take a fucking break while you have the chance, Murray!" Suzette snapped at me—but I gave the majority of the crew the afternoon off instead. This stunt required precision.

"Oh, Murray, no," Lily breathed.

I hadn't put a chair under the door handle this time, and she'd snuck in almost silently. The grin spreading across her face was fifty per cent delighted, fifty per cent wicked, one hundred per cent *her*. "Not the Adjudication Station special."

I put the notecard I'd just finished writing into the box. I didn't say anything, but I let my eyes flicker briefly up to hers.

"You are a bad man." She sat down at the table opposite me. "Murray O'Connell, you are a bad, bad man."

"You shouldn't be in here."

"I couldn't resist."

Blood in the water. I was so close.

"I had to ask you about the whole friend thing with the Romeo and the fainter," she continued. "I can't believe you were running a whole plotline on the side and you didn't tell me."

Her tone was mostly still delighted, but it was the accusatory edge in there which thrilled me. That hatred of not knowing what was happening, that very specific type of FOMO—*that* was how I was going to break her.

"You didn't need to know," I said mildly. "Lily Fireball isn't involved in the Convent plot."

"I will be. Or have you lost count of the episodes? We're in Episode Seven. Fucking Greg is only making boy-Dylan keep me for eight."

I had not lost count. There was a reason I was pulling this stunt—a version of the first stunt that Lily and I had ever pulled together—now.

Manipulation was about two things: knowing people's pressure points, and knowing when to exploit them. In an ideal world, I would have set a longer, more gradual fuse on this play, to let Lily's worry over my exhaustion and her addiction to string-pulling build and build and build.

But with her elimination on the horizon, I didn't have

that kind of time. Once she was in the Convent, her access to both me and the game would be significantly limited, simply due to the geography of the set.

So instead of setting a longer fuse, I had to add more fireworks. I couldn't wait for the pot to boil. I had to turn up the heat.

"Of course I haven't lost count." I kept my voice even.

"I'll make sure I focus some serious attention on her when I get down there." Lily laced her fingers together and stretched her arms over her head. "The fainter, that is."

"Don't go too hard on Cece. She's had a hell of a time. I don't want you to ruin her life."

"I will go the appropriate amount of hard."

I made a noise in the back of my throat, but I didn't argue. There wasn't any point. Anyway, it might generate some good content that would help me continue Cece's storyline, in preparation for slingshotting her onto *Wherefore Art Thou Romeo?* or *Juliet on the Beach.* That kind of pre-existing audience investment in a character was golden when it came to getting eyeballs on a season.

"Besides," Lily said, "I have to continue the legend of Lily Fireball somehow."

Cece wasn't the only one with her eyes on future seasons.

I thought about it before I pulled the trigger. Did an entire cost/benefit analysis in one and a half seconds. Was it too soon to apply pressure on my levers?

But Lily looked so much like *herself,* sitting there across from me, leaning back in her conference room chair.

And I missed her so, so badly.

"Do you?" I asked.

She didn't freeze, exactly, but she went still; the way an antelope goes still when it's been wounded and can no longer move.

"Do you really need to set Lily Fireball up for something long-term? Is that actually what you want?"

"Murray," she said, "we've talked about this."

"And I listened to you. But are you listening to yourself?" I gestured to the room. "You're in here with me. Again. Backseat producing. Doesn't that tell you something?"

"I know what I'm doing."

"Yes, you do." I forced myself to keep my voice calm. "Because you're a producer, Lily."

She didn't say anything.

"I know Lily Fireball is fun. And I get that you wanted to be someone else for a while, I really do. But there's a reason you decided to be someone else *here*." I tapped the table. "This is who you are. This is what you're good at. You're a fucking genius at this."

There was the barest flutter of something across her face, so swift I didn't know what it was, so slight I wasn't sure if I had imagined it.

But it was something, so I risked pressing more. "I don't know how we get you back from that side of the camera to this one, but we can figure it out, if we just put our heads together. We can do fucking anything, if we do it together."

I wasn't imagining it. That was definitely a waver.

I pressed harder. "I need you, Lily." I thumbed the dark circle under one of my eyes. "I need you so badly. I don't know how to do this without you."

Lily rose to her feet.

"I'm looking forward to this." She waved her hand at my box of questions. "Adjudication Station was always fun."

She left.

It was my turn to go still for a few moments, the way a lion goes still when it's about to ambush its prey.

She was on the run.

I was close.

"Since none of you are going on a single date this episode, we need to do something else with you," I told the seven Juliets, arrayed around the Villa dining table. "So we're going to have a dinner party."

The first time Lily and I had used the question box gambit, ten years ago in the Adjudication Station, we'd been trying to expose cracks in *Desert Island Castaway* voting alliances so we could shift the power balance. However, as we'd gone on to discover, it was a startlingly versatile stunt. You could use it for a whole variety of narrative purposes.

This time, I'd filled the box with romantic compatibility questions. In the narrative of the show, I was going to make this dinner party read like a punishment. We were going to put pressure on the Juliets for knowing less about Romeo-Dylan than an eliminated contestant did. This part of the episode was going to be driven by one question: were any of these women actually compatible with him?

It didn't matter how any of the women actually answered the questions from the box. I hadn't even posed them to Romeo-Dylan. Juliet-Dylan was going to win this dinner party.

And that would be the framing I used for the Dylans' relationship going forward. I couldn't rely on chemistry to carry it, so I'd use compatibility instead, emphasising repeatedly that these two people just *fit* together.

Amanda was gazing at Juliet-Dylan over the dinner table, a complex cocktail of emotions bubbling behind her eyes. Juliet-Dylan hadn't noticed, but Lily had. "Are you open to changing the seating arrangements at all?" she asked me, in her trademark Lily Fireball purr.

"No."

"Shame. I could have done a much better job."

I looked at her. *Come back to work and show me, then.*

She looked away.

Ha. Point O'Connell.

Kumiko reached into the box of questions. "Name one thing you and Dylan JM have in common."

"Subtle," Lily said dryly. "I'll start. Dylan JM and I have nothing in common."

"Then why are you here?" Parisa asked.

"Because opposites attract, obviously." Lily waved her hand dismissively. "Who's next?"

We're too similar, Murray. We both have hard edges.

I dug my knuckles into the meat of my thigh. No. I was not going to let her get in my head. Not now, not when I finally had an advantage.

"We're both very clear about what we want," Juliet-Dylan said.

A good answer. I had some ITM footage from last week of Romeo-Dylan saying something similar. It would cut together beautifully.

Jess D took the next question out of the box. "What's the worst thing a romantic partner could do to you?"

"Clearly a man wrote that question," Kumiko said. "How many kinds of abuse do you want us to list?"

Lily shifted slightly in her seat.

From her, that was practically ants-in-her-pants fidgeting. *I could have done it better,* she was trying not to let me read.

I had her. After all this time, I finally fucking had her.

I'd got her off-balance. If I just pushed a little more, dug my thumbs in a little harder, the thing she wasn't saying would spill out. She'd give me the final piece of the puzzle.

And once I had all the pieces, I could put it—could put her, could put *us*—back together.

"Lie," Amanda said. "You can't be in a relationship with someone you can't trust."

"I agree with Amanda," Naya said. "That goes for lying by omission as well."

"Yes." I was still paying enough attention to note the tension in Amanda's shoulders, the way her knuckles were white around her fork. "Absolutely."

"Making you feel small," Juliet-Dylan said. "Making you feel worthless. Making you feel like you're nothing and no one without them."

Another good answer. No one could accuse Romeo-Dylan of doing that.

"I can't believe none of you have mentioned the most obvious one," Lily said.

"And what is the obvious one, Lily?" Kumiko asked.

"Die."

There was nothing heavy in her tone. It was cheerful, almost; upbeat, as casual as if she were telling everyone what was for dinner.

It brought my entire brain to a stuttering halt.

"I'll ask the next one, shall I?" Lily reached into the box, tone unchanged. Smiling. She was *smiling*. "All right, here we go. What's the sexiest quality a person can have?"

"Lily," I said.

She ignored me. "Far be it from me to state the obvious, but the sexiest quality a person can have is to be good at sex. No one can be sexy if they're bad at it."

"Lily," I tried to say again, but her name wouldn't come out around the lump in my throat.

"I don't think that's true," Naya said. "There's plenty of men I find sexy, and I have no idea if they're good in bed."

"Dylan JM, for instance," Parisa said. "Sexy as hell! That smile! Those hands! The way he rolls up his shirt sleeves and gets his forearms out! I have no idea what he's like in bed, but that doesn't mean he's not sexy."

"He's got to be good in bed," Jess D said. "He's so considerate. He'd be generous."

"But what if you found out he was bad in bed?" Lily said. She leaned back in her chair, gesturing expansively, lips curled in a half-smile, serving perfect reality TV shit-stirrer. "Would he be sexy then?"

My heart was pounding in my chest. Blood was rushing in my ears. Cold sweat was beading in my hairline. My brain was ricocheting wildly between different images, different memories, trying to compute exactly what the fuck she was doing.

Die.

What the fuck was *I* doing?

I'd spent all this time and effort and energy on cracking the Lily Fireball mask. I'd been so desperate to get my best friend back—so desperate to get her to finally fucking *talk to me*—that I'd forgotten that I already knew what was under it.

Her sobbing into my neck. Her screaming Jeff's name, my name, Jeff's name again. The shattered pieces of her, even as I tried so desperately to hold her together.

Her lipstick, all over my shirt.

"Lily, if you don't think Dylan JM is sexy, no one's forcing you to be here," Kumiko said.

"That wasn't the question, though. It was 'What is the sexiest quality a person can have?' The answer's in the question, people."

"Competence," Juliet-Dylan said.

The rushing in my ears was turning into a ringing, so loud I wasn't sure if it was my brain or whether my earpiece was malfunctioning.

Lily didn't lie. *You knew me, Murray,* she'd told me, all those weeks ago in the limo, but I hadn't heard what she was really saying.

There was no going back. There was no getting my Lily back. She didn't exist anymore. She'd broken apart when Jeff died.

She wasn't having a nervous breakdown now, but she'd had one then.

And this was how she had put herself back together.

"You know when people are really good at something?" Juliet-Dylan was saying. "It doesn't matter what it is. It could be, I don't know, flower-arranging. Singing. Dog-grooming."

"Sailing?" Kumiko asked.

"Sure, sailing, whatever. Like I said, it doesn't matter what it is. It could be simple. Tiny. When you see someone absolutely killing it at something they're great at, that's the sexiest thing in the world."

Another good answer. Something else I could use to make it look like the Dylans were a perfect match.

Do your job, I tried to tell myself.

But I'd lost control. It was like someone had come in and narrowed the focus on the camera, making the close-up more and more extreme.

All I could see was Lily.

She was tapping her fingers on the table again, fingernails *Blood of My Enemies* red. Her eyes were darting between Juliet-Dylan and Amanda, assessing what was happening.

It felt like I was looking at a ghost.

Amanda smashed her fork down on her plate so hard that it broke, the cracking sound like a gunshot. "Excuse me," she snapped, and stormed out of the room.

"Mandie!" Juliet-Dylan exclaimed.

The cameras swarmed, immediately tracking Juliet-Dylan as she followed Amanda, the other women hot on their heels. "Amanda's on the staircase," Suzette said in my earpiece. "She's either headed to the bedroom or the bathroom."

"Follow her," I said. "You're running point."

"What do you—"

I yanked my earpiece out and grabbed Lily by the wrist.

"It wasn't me," she protested. I jerked her back past the crew members as they chased the other women upstairs and kicked the door closed behind them. "I know I've played fast and loose with your rules around girl-Dylan, but whatever drama is happening between her and Amanda has nothing to do with—mmph!"

I pulled her to me so hard that it almost knocked the wind out of me, and buried my face in her hair.

Her arms came around me, fingers smoothing gently over my shoulder blades. "Murray, hey, hey," she said softly. "What happened?"

What happened?!

What happened?!

I drew back, and—there she was.

Lily Ong was looking at me, face full of concern. "Talk to me." She reached up and cupped my face in her hands, stroking her thumbs along my cheekbones. "Is everything okay? Did something to happen to your parents, or Julia, or—"

I shoved myself away from her, stumbling back like we were standing at the edge of a cliff.

She blinked. "Murray, I'm confused. What—"

"You're confused? *You're* fucking confused?"

"You just crushed my ribs and then ran away from me like I was radioactive, so yes, I'm pretty fucking confused."

"You are *ruining* me, Lily!"

She just looked at me.

"You are absolutely destroying me," I said, fighting to control my tone. "Every time I see you it's a different kind of heart attack."

Her lips were parted slightly. One of her earrings was caught in her hair, but she didn't make a move to free it.

"One minute, it's like it always was," I said. "Like we're partners again. Like you've got my back. Like I've got *you* back. And then the next minute—"

I dug my fingers into my temples.

"When you weren't here, I missed you," I said, "but at least I could trust that you were still out there. That you still *existed*, god. But now I look at you and I don't have a fucking clue who I'm looking at."

I pointed my finger at her. "Every time I think I have a handle on what you're doing you rip the carpet out from under me. I'm angry with you all the time. I'm worried about you all the time. I miss you all the time."

The barest flicker of something across her face. God, couldn't she give me more than that?

"I need you to explain it to me, Lily," I said. "I am losing my mind over this, so if you give a shit about me at all, you're going to tell me why you really came here. Why you're doing this to yourself. Why you're doing this to *me*. And you're going to tell me the truth this time."

She hesitated.

For a long, agonising moment, I thought she wasn't going to say anything at all. That she was going to let the silence hang there, unfilled, forever.

"Everything I've told you has been the truth, Murray."

My fingers curled around the top of one of the dining chairs, wood digging painfully into my palm.

"I was lonely, and sad, and bored," she said, "and I knew you needed me."

She crossed the room, heels clicking against the floorboards, and stopped just short of me, not quite close enough to touch. "Once I heard that Greg was letting you do this season, I *knew* you needed me. So . . ."

I didn't finish the sentence for her. I was not going to break first, not this time.

"So that's why I came. Just like I told you. But . . ."

I dug my fingers even tighter into the top of the chair.

Her voice was so soft it was almost inaudible. "I needed you too."

"I didn't go anywhere. Any time you needed me, you could have called me, and I would have been there. Straight away. No questions asked."

"I know. I know. But—fuck!"

The word exploded out of her, sudden, a whipcrack. She clawed at her chest, fingernails leaving angry red scratches on her skin.

I caught her hand. "But *what*, Lily?"

"Don't use that voice on me!"

"But," I said, biting out the T, "what?"

"I couldn't call you! I couldn't be around you, not unless I turned myself into someone else first! Otherwise— otherwise—"

"Otherwise what?"

"I loved him!"

She clenched her fists. Her wrist was tense as a steel cable in my fingers.

"I loved Jeff," she said, after a long moment, modulating her voice down to a more normal volume. "I'm not good at loving people, but I loved him. After he died—god, I wanted to cut that love out of me, because it hurt so badly, but I still loved him."

She looked up at the roof, taking a long breath through her nose.

"I wasn't lying," she said. "Dying is the worst thing that man ever did to me. That stupid, patient, gentle man, who deserved so much better than me."

"Lily, no." I shifted my grip from her wrist to her hand. "Jeff adored you. It was all over his face, every time he looked at you. He didn't want anyone else."

"I know." Tears were beading in the corners of her eyes. "He only wanted me. He could have lived for a thousand years, and he would have been perfectly content being married to me every single one of them."

She took a shaking breath. "But do you know what I thought, the night of the funeral? Just a few hours after we buried my husband, who thought I hung the moon?"

"You were grieving. Everyone has terrible thoughts in high stress situations like that. Don't beat yourself—"

"Shut up."

I shut up.

"I was crying. You were holding me together. And I looked up at you, and I thought, *Thank god it wasn't Murray. Thank god I didn't lose Murray. I couldn't survive losing Murray.*"

Oh.

Oh.

"So I drew a line," she said. "A line between me and that woman, because I couldn't be her. I couldn't be the woman who had that thought on the day she buried that beautiful man."

She'd drawn a line, and she'd cut me out.

And she'd become Lily Fireball.

A person everyone was supposed to hate.

"And I tried and I tried and I tried," she said, the first tear falling. "I thought if I just drew the lines clear enough—if I came back different—I could do this. I could be here. I could help you."

My heart was pounding. My mind was racing. The picture was finally coming into focus.

"But I can't help it," she whispered. "No matter how hard I try, I'm still that woman."

It happened sharply. Suddenly. As if she were a marionette and a puppetmaster had just abruptly yanked her strings.

Lily reached up with her free hand and pulled my face to hers.

The kiss was so brief I barely had a chance to react. Her lips pressed so hard against mine I could feel her teeth behind them. Her fingers dug into my cheek, index and middle fingers pressed into the twitching muscle beside my eye.

She drew back.

For a long moment, we just looked at each other.

And she pulled her hand from my grasp and walked away.

19

Lily

Four years ago

"There," Thuong said, adjusting the last bit of beading on the dress. "You look spectacular."

I looked at myself in the mirror. I wanted to say something—anything—but the words were stuck in my throat.

"Don't tell me I've done such a good job I've rendered the great Lily Ong speechless," Thuong said, grinning at my reflection. "Not the hardest bitch I know, overwhelmed by one of my designs?"

I managed a weak laugh. Better she think that. Better she think I was just overwhelmed by the wedding dress she'd made for me than by . . . than by . . .

"Here," Murray said, pressing a glass of water into my hand.

"Don't spill it," Thuong instructed. "And don't forget to fix your lipstick after you drink, either. You know how that shit smudges."

I nodded.

"I'm going to go and check if they're ready to start," Thuong said. "You've got everything you need? Feeling good in your dress? Anything itching? Scratching? Sticking into you?"

I shook my head.

Thuong grinned at me again. "Jeff's the luckiest guy in the world, to be marrying you," she said. "I love you, okay?"

"I love you too," I managed to croak out, as she left.

My fingers were shaky around the glass of water. Murray whisked it out of my hands before it spilled. "Do you need to sit down?" he asked me.

"No," I said. "No, no, no. It's—it's just—"

"Overwhelming?"

"Your tie's crooked," I said, so I wouldn't have to tell him the truth.

I started fiddling with it, smoothing it down and tucking it into his waistcoat. "I love you, Murray," I said, moving on to his boutonniere. "You know that, right?"

"Of course I know that." Murray caught my wrist, pulling it gently away from his lapel. "I love you too, Lily. Do you think I'd wear a tie this colour for just anyone?"

A nervous laugh escaped me. "I don't know why I'm freaking out."

"Everyone freaks out on their wedding day." He was using the voice he used to console crying contestants after they got eliminated. "I did."

"No, you didn't."

"Yes, I did."

"I was there. No, you didn't."

"I was also present at my own wedding," Murray said dryly, "and I can assure you that yes, I did."

I looked up at him.

What would happen if I just turned and ran into the night, and dragged him along with me?

"It's going to be all right, Lily." He let go of my wrist, putting his hands on my shoulders instead. "You love Jeff. Jeff loves you."

I swallowed. "I know. I know."

Murray leaned in and pressed a kiss to my temple, just above my hairline, where it wouldn't ruin my makeup. "Come on. Let's go get you married."

20

Murray

I was the kind of person who always had a plan. I was decisive. I weighed my options, calmly and collectedly, and moved forward from there.

It was a trait which had served me well professionally, of course, but I'd run my personal life like that too, ever since I'd been old enough to have one. My relationship with Julia was the perfect example. Every decision—from getting together to moving in to getting engaged and married and separated and divorced—had been laden with emotion, but I'd always been able to step back from it, make a cool assessment about what was best.

It had even been like that with Lily. When she had told me, sitting on top of a washing machine with her legs around my waist, that we'd never work as a proper couple, that our hard edges would wear each other down, I'd let her go, confident in the knowledge that one day, when she was ready, she'd decide she felt the same way I did and come back to me.

Then, when she met Jeff and I realised that wasn't going to happen, that I'd just have to live with hopelessly pining for her—I considered my options. I loved her too much to walk away, so I locked my feelings up, accepted my new normal, and got on with my life.

But she did feel like I did. Maybe my unrequited love had been requited, all this time.

And I didn't have a fucking clue what to do.

I handed the reins of the Episode Seven Last Chance Party over to Suzette and Carrie. I hid in the studio, doing long, in-depth interviews with Amanda and Juliet-Dylan, trying to use their turmoil to distract me from my own.

"Do you want to film an ITM with Lily before we head into the Necklace Ceremony, Murray?" Carrie asked in my earpiece, after I'd sent Juliet-Dylan back to the party. "She's picking fights with everyone in sight."

"No," I said, too quickly. "That's all right."

I stood up the back at the Necklace Ceremony, as deep in the shadows as I could possibly conceal myself. "I'm sorry, Naya," Romeo-Dylan said, "but your heart isn't the other half of mine."

Lily was in silver tonight, a long dress with a fringed hem that swished around her ankles. Rhinestone pins held back her hair, dotted all over her head like little stars. Her lips were curled in that cat-that-got-the-cream Lily Fireball smirk.

It hurt, looking at her. Every single part of me ached.

I'd spent the past three and a half weeks trying to reconcile two different versions of Lily, trying to make Lily Fireball make sense in the context of Lily Ong. It all made sense now, in its own strange way—but it only made things worse.

And there were still two Lilys.

There was the Lily I'd always known. The Lily who was just like me. The Lily I would trust with my life, the one who was in total control, playing twelve-dimensional chess.

Then there was the Lily who was lost. The Lily who *had* lost. The Lily who had let the stray thought *Thank god it wasn't Murray, thank god I didn't lose Murray, I couldn't survive losing Murray* slip through her defences. The Lily who had been panicking ever since.

The Lily who loved me, and had decided to burn everything down as a result.

It was a dream. It was a nightmare.

I loved her too. Unbearably. Enormously.

But if I took her up on this—on this thing that I wasn't even sure she was offering!—then I would go from morally grey to the worst man alive. Nothing about any of this indicated she was in her right mind, let alone in a position to commit to the serious romantic relationship she'd been so adamant in refusing six years ago.

I tramped across the grass towards the trailer village in the grey light of pre-dawn after a long night in the war room, icy dew soaking the bottom of my pants. Once the initial shock wore off and my brain started working again, I was going to have to make a plan. I dug in my utility belt, finding three pens and an emergency-horny-contestant condom before I finally closed my fingers around my keys, my mind somehow both blank and racing, trying to figure out where I would even start.

The light in my trailer snapped on. Lily was sitting at the table, Greg's bottle of whiskey open in front of her.

"If you ever look at me again the way you looked at me tonight," she said coolly, "I'll fucking kill you, Murray."

I paused, hand poised above the kitchenette counter, about to drop my keys.

"Don't think I didn't see you, hiding up the back of the Necklace Ceremony," she snarled. "Don't think I didn't see you, looking at me like some poor broken toy."

"Lily—"

"Shut up."

She took a swig of whiskey. "Just because I've been going through some shit doesn't mean I'm suddenly some fragile little porcelain dolly who needs to be babied. I told you I wasn't having a nervous breakdown, and I meant it. Don't you dare look at me like that ever again."

I put my keys down, harder than necessary. "Do you really expect me not to be worried about you?"

"You can worry all you want. But I'm a grown woman in control of her own mind and her own actions. I am not a problem for you to solve."

She rose to her feet. "Yes, I've spent most of the last year being very, very sad. Yes, I've been experiencing more complicated emotions than I am comfortable with. Yes, my coping mechanisms have been a bit left of centre. But I am still an adult, and I am still competent and capable and in control."

"I never said you weren't."

"You didn't have to. Your face did."

She crossed the trailer, three steps bringing her directly in front of me. She looked dead into my eyes. For a moment, I thought she was going to kiss me again.

"Move," she said. "This is a big episode for me. I'm getting eliminated. I need my beauty sleep."

I moved.

After she left, I collapsed into the chair she'd been sitting in. Jesus fucking Christ.

I took a swig of my own from the whiskey bottle. The level hadn't changed much since the last time I'd drunk some. Clearly Lily had been using it mostly for dramatic effect, rather than liquid courage.

Made sense. She'd never liked whiskey.

How long had she been sitting in the dark, waiting for me? God, that was classic Lily Ong, setting up a cinematic moment like that.

I took another swig from the whiskey bottle.

Classic Lily. Drama queen Lily. My Lily. She was still in there. She was still *her*, underneath the Lily Fireball façade.

What the fuck was I supposed to do?

"It's Episode Eight," Romeo-Dylan said in our ITM the next morning. "I can cut Lily Fireball now, right?"

I sipped my coffee to give myself time to clamp down on any traitor emotional responses. "If that's what you want."

"Yes. It is."

At least one of us wasn't confused.

"Okay," I said. "I'll keep that in mind as we figure out the dates for this episode."

Romeo-Dylan gestured at my coffee. "Is there any more of that? I didn't sleep well."

We sent him on a single date with Parisa, the last Juliet who hadn't been on one. It was an easy, uncontroversial choice, but compared with the high drama we'd been getting, it was fairly uninteresting. "We need to keep up the tempo," Carrie said in our production meeting. "If we're cutting Lily, we need to send her out with a bang."

"Absolutely," Suzette said. "It's got to be a Thunderdome date. Lily versus Dylan G."

The Thunderdome date was a format we used when two contestants had formed a clear rivalry. We sent them together on a date with the lead. One would receive a necklace. One would be eliminated on the spot.

Wifeys like Juliet-Dylan didn't feature often on Thunderdome dates, but villains did. If Lily had been a garden-variety villain, in a garden-variety not-here-for-the-right-reasons edit, this would be where we revealed her true colours.

But that wouldn't work here. There were many phrases you could use to describe Lily Fireball, but "garden variety" was not one of them.

I spent a lot of time standing in front of my whiteboard trying to figure out how to shape the date before I abandoned it. I couldn't control what Lily was going to do.

I threw myself into preparing Juliet-Dylan for the date instead. "We have to walk a careful line here," I told her. "You need to come out of this looking like a hero, not someone who's spent more time and energy disliking Lily than she has falling in love."

"I get it. You don't want me to look like a petty bitch."

"Not the words I would use, but yes. Do your best not

to let Lily get a rise out of you. Nothing else matters now. Only the Romeo."

"Nothing else matters," Juliet-Dylan repeated firmly. "Only the Romeo."

I recognised the body language of compartmentalisation immediately, but I didn't say anything. If her bust-up with Amanda was going to be a problem, I'd deal with it later.

I just needed to get through tonight.

A lot of our date formats had bells and whistles attached: activities to do, rules to learn, games to play. The Thunderdome date wasn't like that. We didn't need an activity to illuminate interpersonal tension, because the tension was already there. It was the purest form of subtext-is-for-cowards: in the Thunderdome date, all the subtextual tension became text.

We'd set up a romantic dinner in the middle of the hedge maze. Every fairy light we had was strung up. Our most ostentatious outdoor chandelier was hanging from the tree. Around the table, three hundred candles were flickering.

Pure maximalism. Pure excess. Pure romance.

Wardrobe had got the memo. Romeo-Dylan was in a classic tux. Juliet-Dylan was in a dark green sheath dress, accessorised with statement gold jewellery.

Lily was wearing the most spectacular dress I had ever seen.

It was dark red, the colour of wine. The skirt was long and full, almost conservative, matching her severe updo; but the neckline was daringly low, a V cut almost to her navel, leaving her collarbone bare. It was covered in sequins, reflecting the twinkle of the fairy lights, the shimmer of the chandelier, the flickering flames of the candles.

I wanted to cry, looking at her in that dress. I wanted to drop to my knees, put my head in my hands, and weep.

She'd kissed me.

She was in the middle of a huge, destructive personal crisis.

But, *I'm a grown woman in control of her own mind and her own actions*, she'd snarled.

And she'd *kissed me*.

What the fuck was I supposed to do?

"You look beautiful," Romeo-Dylan said to both the women.

"Thank you," Juliet-Dylan said.

"I know," Lily said.

Both Dylans blinked.

"Really?" Lily said. "You want me to be modest? You want me to lie?"

She waved a hand at Juliet-Dylan. "Did you even try?"

"Murray, should we cut?" Carrie said in my earpiece. "If Lily goads Dylan G too much . . ."

My job. That was what I was supposed to do. My fucking *job*.

I forced my brain into gear. If Lily sank her teeth in too deeply, Juliet-Dylan might crack. Having a rivalry behind the closed doors of the Villa was one thing, but a full-scale fight in front of Romeo-Dylan would be very difficult to walk back.

Which Lily knew.

She'd been opposed to the Double Dylan endgame since she'd worked out I rigged the season. If she wanted to, she could completely sabotage them here. She could destroy everything I'd built, make telling a romance story about them utterly impossible.

That was not something Lily Ong would do. My partner would not cut me off at the knees like that.

But the woman who didn't want to be Lily Ong anymore might.

A fireball, I remembered her saying on that first night, stroking a finger along Romeo-Dylan's jaw, *can burn it all down.*

"I'm not doing this high school mean girl thing with you, Lily," Juliet-Dylan was saying evenly. "I didn't come here to spend my night arguing about who's prettier."

"And it's not a competition," Romeo-Dylan said, holding up his hands placatingly.

Lily burst out laughing. "*It's not a competition?* Oh, darling, did you even read the rules when you signed your contract?"

"Murray?" Carrie said again in my earpiece.

Lily flicked her fingers at me—a small movement, one that the camera wouldn't pick up—but I understood it immediately. *I've got this.*

I hesitated.

She flicked her fingers again. *Trust me.*

"Don't cut," I told Carrie. "Not yet."

"If this is a competition, that makes me the prize, and I don't like to think about it like that," Romeo-Dylan was explaining gently. "Just because I choose someone doesn't make them automatically better than everyone else. It just means that we have a connection."

Lily rolled her eyes. "You keep telling yourself that, Prince Charming."

Juliet-Dylan took a step between them. "Back off, Lily."

"It's all right," Romeo-Dylan said.

"No, it's not."

"Murray?" Carrie said in my earpiece.

"It's okay," I said. "Dylan G's protecting him. The mama bear shit is good."

Juliet-Dylan turned to look at Romeo-Dylan. "You've done nothing but be kind to everyone here. You don't deserve to be treated like this."

"Dyl." Romeo-Dylan reached out and touched her hand, just lightly, one finger brushing her knuckles. "It's okay."

Juliet-Dylan bit her lip, hard—and I saw it.

I saw what Lily was doing. The careful way she was playing this, digging her thumbs into the pressure points, to give us exactly what we needed. To give *me* exactly what I wanted, even though she thought it was the wrong call.

I will make the Dylans work for you, Murray, she had told me, *if it's the last thing I do.*

I flicked my radio to the all-crew channel. "Whatever you do, don't cut the scene," I said. "The Dylans finally look like they're into each other."

As if she'd heard me, Lily's lips curled in a predatory smile. "How long are you two going to keep lying?"

Both Dylans' heads swivelled to look at her. Their fingers were still touching, shoulders almost brushing. It was a flawless hero couple shot, the type that directors of scripted shows would spend forever trying to choreograph.

I was only dimly aware that it was happening. The idea of taking my eyes off Lily was unthinkable.

"No one's lying to you, Lily." Romeo-Dylan's tone was gentle, kind, calm—all the things which would work beautifully on TV but would never, ever, not even for one second, work on Lily.

"Why would I bother lying to you?" Juliet-Dylan said. "I'm not going to waste that kind of energy on you. I know where my focus is."

Lily regarded them both for a long moment. She had one hand on her hip, her head cocked slightly to the side, and that look in her eye from that first day I'd spoken to her at the crew briefing for *Desert Island Castaway*, the look that said *this woman is trouble.*

"Did I say you were lying to *me*?" she said sweetly.

Yes, my coping mechanisms have been a bit left of centre. But I am still an adult, and I am still competent and capable and in control.

She was more than that. She was a fucking genius.

She knew *exactly* what she was doing.

And she was doing it for me.

A drop of water was trickling its way down Romeo-Dylan's cheek. For a moment, I thought he was crying, but then another drop hit, and another, leaving spots on his white shirt. It was starting to rain.

"You're lying to each other," Lily said. "And you're lying to yourselves."

She gestured between them. Juliet-Dylan laced her fingers defensively through Romeo-Dylan's.

There was a roll of thunder in the distance, as perfectly as if Lily had cued it. God, god, god, she was *so* fucking good.

"Don't think I have noticed what's going on here," Lily said. "Don't think I haven't noticed that you've already made your decision, Romeo."

"I—" Romeo-Dylan started, but Lily held up a finger.

"If you finish that sentence," she said, "then you will be lying to me."

A brilliant flash of lighting lit up the sky. "And if you pick her in the end," Lily said, alight for an instant as the sequins of her dress refracted the light, "you'll be making a huge mistake."

The rain started to get harder, going from drizzle to a steady shower. "Should we stop this and wait for the weather to pass?" Carrie asked in my earpiece.

"Don't you fucking dare," I replied.

The thunder rumbled. The three of them were framed perfectly, clothes clinging to their bodies in the rain.

The two Dylans, together.

Lily, alone.

Prince Charming and Cinderella, hands locked together, each of them desperate to protect the other, a pair of star-crossed lovers.

The evil queen, that wicked glint in her eye, bent only on chaos.

She was spectacular.

Romeo-Dylan held up his free hand reassuringly. "I haven't made any decisions yet."

"Oh really?" Lily said. "Not even who you're cutting?"

A pained expression came across Romeo-Dylan's face.

Lily smirked. "I'll save you the trouble. Dylan Jayasinghe Mellor, your heart is not the other half of mine."

Juliet-Dylan snorted. "No shit."

"Don't cut," I said into my headset, before anyone could stop them and make them reshoot for swearing.

"And your heart isn't the other half of his either," Lily said, raising her chin, rain cascading over her as she looked Juliet-Dylan in the eye. "You can tell yourself he's the person for you as much as you want, but he isn't—and you know that."

"You don't know a thing about me, Lily," Juliet-Dylan replied coolly, meeting her gaze. "Not one single thing."

Another perfect moment of television. Two women, equally matched. Two rivals. Two sides of the same coin.

The heroine, the one everyone would love. And the anti-heroine, the one everyone would love to hate and hate to love all at once, driving the hero and the heroine together as she went out in a blaze of glory.

My heart was beating so fast.

"You keep thinking that." Lily didn't give an inch as Juliet-Dylan glared at her. "You can add it to all the other lies you tell yourself."

"All right, that's enough," Romeo-Dylan said firmly.

He positioned himself in front of Juliet-Dylan, Prince Charming standing up for his princess. "Lily, you've made the right decision. Your heart is not the other half of mine. I hope you find what you're looking for, but it isn't me."

"Now there's something she and I can agree on." Lily waved her hand at Juliet-Dylan. "No shit."

Then she drew herself up. There was no softness in her, no vulnerability—only hard, jagged edges, so sharp the merest touch would make you bleed.

"I hope you find what you're looking for too," she said to Romeo-Dylan. "You're a nice man. A bit of a wet blanket, but you're nice."

She was magnificent.

"But it's not her," Lily said. "The person you're looking for—it isn't her."

Afterwards, I would watch the footage of what happened next. Of how, after Lily walked away, the Dylans turned to each other.

She's wrong, Juliet-Dylan said. *She doesn't know you. She doesn't know me. She doesn't know anything. And the way I feel about you is . . .*

Dyl, Romeo-Dylan replied, even as Juliet-Dylan choked on the lies she could not bring herself to tell. *I'm so grateful for you.*

I'd watch Juliet-Dylan clutch at his lapels. Watch him raise his hand to her cheek, stroke the backs of his fingers down her face. Watch them lean their foreheads together in the rain, water pouring over them, another flicker of lightning illuminating them. Watch them kiss, once, twice, three times. Watch them wrap their arms around each other and embrace like their knees might give way if they let go.

Afterwards, I'd watch that perfect piece of reality television, the one that would finally make people believe that the Dylans were the real deal.

But now, there was only one thing I cared about.

"Carrie, you're running point," I said into my headset. "Call Suzette if you need backup."

"You're leaving?!"

"Lily set you up a slam dunk. She made the Dylans interesting. All you have to do is follow through."

"Murray—"

"Just do your job," I snarled, and yanked my earpiece out.

One of the PAs had accompanied Lily off the date set. I caught up with them at the entrance to the hedge maze. "Thanks, Tim. I'll take it from here."

"That's Tom," Lily said.

"Tom, I'd like you to organise the transfer of Lily's things down to the Convent." I fastened my fingers around her wrist. "Can you do that?"

He nodded. "I'll load her bags onto the golf cart. Once you're finished filming your ITM, I'll take Lily down there too."

"Just take her things. I'll get Lily where she needs to go."

"Copy that," said Tom. Then he just stood there, gaping at us.

"Well?" I asked. "Are you waiting for something?"

"Oh. Um. Bye."

He glanced back over his shoulder before he disappeared down the path to the Villa, a thousand questions in his eyes.

"You really should learn his name," Lily said. "If you don't want him to try and overthrow you."

"Lily," I said, "we are not talking about the fucking PAs right now."

She looked up at me. The rain was falling down around us in sheets, but she didn't blink.

"You have a choice," I told her.

"What are my options?"

Her voice was calm and even, her gaze steady; but I still had my fingers around her wrist, and her pulse was jumping.

"We can go back to the Villa. You can dry off. We can film your ITM, and then I'll take you down to the Convent."

"Or?"

"Or you can come back to my trailer, and I can take that dress off you with my teeth."

Her intake of breath was swift. Colour rushed to her cheeks.

"I have loved you for years," I said. "I will love you forever. That will be true no matter which option you pick. That, you don't get a choice in. You are my best friend and I love you and you can never change that, no matter how hard you try."

"I love you too." Her voice was barely audible.

"I know."

I took a calculated risk and dropped her wrist. We were still standing close together, but we weren't touching now.

"If you don't want this—if you don't want me—if you don't feel like I do—that's fine," I said. "If it's still too soon—if you're not ready—that's fine too. But no more playing, Lily. No more half-truths. No more hiding. No more running away. Tell me what you want."

She paused.

I lived a thousand lives in that pause. I died a thousand deaths. I married her and fought with her and made up with her and started an empire with her. I lost her and found her and married someone else and watched her marry someone else and made brilliant TV with her anyway.

In every second and minute and hour and year and century of that pause, I loved her.

"I already told you what I want," she said.

"Then you're going to have to tell me again, because I didn't hear you."

"On the first day. In the hotel. I did my own interview, and I asked myself, *Why did you come on* Marry Me, Juliet?"

Lily put her hands on my chest. She went up on her tiptoes, leaned in, and bit my bottom lip, hard.

"I said," she whispered, so close her lips were touching mine, the taste of her mixing with the salt of the rain, "I came here to get my man."

We didn't make it back to my trailer.

We stumbled down the hill, half-running, half-kissing. She shoved me into the hedge and jumped on me, so violently that if we'd been caught on camera it would have looked like she was attacking me.

The sharp sticks of the hedge pierced my clothing, drawing blood, and her arms were locked so tight around me that I could barely breathe, but I didn't care. I couldn't get close enough to her. I pushed the sleeves of that wine-red dress off her shoulders and buried my face in her breasts, relishing the feeling of her fingers twined tight in my hair as she cried out.

We slid to the ground, her knees on either side of my lap, skirt of her dress riding up to her waist. "I need you," she whispered urgently in my ear. "Murray, I need you."

"Whatever you need," I told her, as her fingers fumbled with my belt buckle. "Whatever you need, Lily, always."

"Your belt. Your belt. Help me with your belt."

I found the buckle of my utility belt and cast it aside, rummaging in one of the pouches as she got my actual belt undone. "Here," I said, only just stopping my eyes from rolling back in my head as she unzipped my fly.

She took the condom from me. "Oh fuck, I'm shaking," she said, trying and failing to open it.

"We don't have to do this if you're not—"

"Shut up and help me."

I always listened to Lily Ong.

The rain was pouring down as she sank onto me, the sound of the storm swallowing her cries, keeping them secret from everyone except me. I snaked my fingers through her hair, bobby pins flying, and pulled her head back, burying my face in the curve of her neck, pressing my open mouth to her throat, sinking my teeth into that exposed clavicle.

"Harder," she breathed. "I need you closer."

I tipped her backwards, pressing her into the grass, wet and slippery and cold. She gasped as I thrust hard into her. "Like that?"

"Yes, god, yes, like that," she said breathlessly, wrapping her legs around me. "I need you, I need you, I need you. Don't stop."

"Never," I growled into her ear, and meant it.

21

Lily

Four years ago

"Thanks, babe," I said, as Jeff put the two bowls of fries down on the table, one catered to human tastebuds, one to Murray's broken palate.

"No problem." Jeff sat down beside me and slung his arm across my shoulders. "Do you need more? Is the lovely Naomi joining you?"

"No thanks." Murray cracked even more pepper on his fries. "I don't think we're going to be seeing the lovely Naomi again."

I blinked. "What?"

"You broke up?" Jeff asked.

"A while ago."

"A while ago?!" I exclaimed.

Murray's slut era had been short-lived. He and Naomi had been together for about a year. She'd been his date to my wedding six months ago. He hadn't exactly been on the verge of marrying her or anything, but they'd seemed . . . I don't know, fine.

"How long a while ago?" I demanded. "Days? Weeks? Months? Why didn't you tell me?"

"A few weeks," Murray said. "And it never came up."

"It never came up?!" I gaped. What sort of fucking answer was that?

"This seems like a conversation that needs alcohol." Jeff kissed my cheek, then got up and disappeared behind the bar.

Murray shrugged. "I didn't tell you because it wasn't important."

I stared.

"Not that Naomi wasn't important," he said. "She was. Is. But it was never going to be her. There was no point sitting around waiting for it to somehow magically be her."

I let out a breath. "God, Murray, why didn't you tell me?"

"It wouldn't have changed anything."

"We could have talked about it."

"That wouldn't have changed anything either," he said. "It just . . . wasn't her."

"Please tell me your breakup speech wasn't 'It's not me, it's you.'"

He chuckled. "It was slightly more eloquent than that."

"I could have helped you write a speech! You know how good I am at breakup speeches." I had written a few for Romeos who were too chickenshit to find their own words to break up with the runner-up.

"That is not something I am ever going to need help with." Murray pointed one of his horrible fries at me. "I can break up with women on my own, thank you very much. I'm not a coward."

I couldn't put my finger on why, but something about that stung.

"I can't believe you didn't tell me," I grumbled.

"Believe it or not, Lily," he said, as Jeff returned with drinks, "sometimes I don't tell you everything."

22

Murray

As Lily Fireball's producer, part of my job the next day was to shoot pick-up ITMs with her, interview moments we could splice into the edit of the Thunderdome date. As I parked my golf cart out the front of the Convent, five hours after I'd left her there, my heart was in my throat.

I'm sorry, I was terrified she was going to say. *I'm still fucked up with grief, and you were there, and I made a mistake. I love you, Murray, but not like that.*

"Finally," she snapped, when I came in. "I've been waiting for ages."

She was perched on the arm of the couch, on which three other eliminated Juliets were sitting. Her hair was pulled back severely, exactly as it had been the previous night. Her makeup was perfect, *Blood of My Enemies* expertly applied. She was wearing the red dress again, but it was miraculously, pristinely clean, as though I'd only dreamed shoving it off her shoulders and hiking it up around her hips in the mud and the rain.

"I'm busy, Lily," I snapped back. "Believe it or not, my entire job does not revolve around you. Come on. Pick-ups. Move it."

"Later, ladies," she said airily to the other Juliets. "Don't wait up."

We were silent as we walked out to the golf cart. Cece was sitting on the verandah, red-eyed, hands wrapped around a mug of coffee. On the lawn, two of the other women were doing yoga.

"Between you and me," Lily murmured, "I'm having trouble walking straight."

Her fingers brushed mine, once, twice, deliberately. In that moment, I was the happiest I had ever been in my entire life.

"Lucky I'm driving, then," I murmured back, working hard to keep the smile off my face, "and not making you hike up the hill."

"Very." She slid into the passenger side. The full skirt of her dress spilled across my lap, and beneath it, her hand settled proprietorially on my thigh. "Especially because I seem to have forgotten to put on any underwear."

If life followed the logic of narrative, my head would have spun around three hundred and sixty degrees and then exploded.

I could still taste her on my lips as I sat in my chair in the studio. I'd pulled the golf cart over halfway up the hill, yanked my earpiece out, put her knees over my shoulders and flipped her skirt over her head.

"All right, Lily Fireball," I said, as Indigo finished adjusting the lights. "You told Dylan that his heart wasn't the other half of yours. Talk to me about how you came to that decision."

Lily was perfectly composed again, as if she hadn't been crying my name fifteen minutes earlier and nearly ripping my hair out. She crossed her ankles, hooked them around the crossbar of the stool, lifted her chin and looked me right in the eye.

"I decided to cut him loose," she purred, "because there is no way a man like him could ever satisfy me."

I hadn't had to work this hard to keep my face expressionless in years.

When we were finished, I took her back to my trailer, sneaking her into the crew village when no one was watching. "Are you sure?" I asked her, as she rifled through my first aid kit, finding a strip of condoms and throwing them at me. "If you can't walk straight . . ."

Lily shoved me down on my lumpy trailer bed. "Stop trying to look after me, Murray."

She knelt over me, straddling me, hands braced on either side of my head. "Everyone's spent the last year trying to look after me, and I hate it. I don't want that from you. I don't want you to second guess me, or worry about me, or handle me with care."

An image of her the night of the funeral, sobbing into my shoulder, flashed across my eyes. I blinked.

She kissed me, long and lingering. "Just shut up and do what you promised," she whispered. "Take this dress off me. With your teeth."

That proved to be a more difficult task than I had anticipated. It had two hidden zips and a set of hook and eye
closures. Solving that problem drove any other thoughts
entirely out of my mind.

We had a light shooting schedule that day, and I'd delegated the bulk of it to Suzette and Carrie, but even still,
I eventually had to get back to work. "What's on the agenda
for tonight?" Lily asked me, holding her hair up as I refastened
the dress for her. "I assume it's not a nutritious dinner and a
good night's sleep."

I gave her a look, but my heart wasn't really in it. "Another
night in the war room. The Episode Nine dates don't start
until tomorrow, but I need to get the Episode Eight rough cut
ready to send to Fucking Greg."

She handed me her compact to hold so she could fix her
lipstick. "Have you looked at any of the footage from last night?"

"Not yet. Thankfully, though, someone—" I snapped the
compact shut and handed it back to her, leaning in to press
my lips to her temple "—made my job very easy. I know it'll
be good."

"Not that footage."

Lily's tone was light, her body language casual as she sat
down on my bed to do up her shoes, but something gave me
pause.

"What footage?"

She looked up. I raised my eyebrows.

She exhaled. "You didn't tell me you had mounted
cameras in the Convent."

"You knew I was filming down there. How do you think I got all the friend shit with Dylan and Cece?"

"I had it in my head you were sending a camera and a soundie down there whenever you wanted to film. Then you inconsiderately fucked my brains out, so when I finally went into the Convent last night, it took me a while to realise I was on camera."

I wanted to fold my arms across the pit of disquiet in my belly. "What am I going to see?"

"You're not going to like it."

"Then tell me now, so I can prepare myself."

I reached for my utility belt and buckled it around my hips, trying to shove away the familiar sensation of frustration.

I didn't want to be frustrated with her. I'd just spent four weeks being frustrated with her. I wanted to stay here in this precious, golden bubble, the one I'd spent so many years not letting myself dream of; the one where it was just her and me, two puzzle pieces that fit perfectly together.

I wanted not to have to strategise. I wanted not to have to think. I wanted to peel that dress off her again and take her to bed and bury my face in the crook of her neck and *sleep* and not have to worry about what she was doing and which version of her I'd be confronted with when I woke up.

"It's nothing bad." She held up her hands placatingly.

"How bad?"

"Not bad. Well, maybe a little bad. Medium? Medium, maximum."

"Lily, what did you do?"

"I might have let slip to Cece that the show is rigged."

"What?!"

"Only Cece, no one else! She was the only one still up when I arrived. And it's not like she's going to tell anyone. She's got no friends down there. They all hate her because she got so much extra facetime with boy-Dylan."

I pinched the bridge of my nose. It was only going to be a matter of moments before my eye started twitching. "How did you just let it slip to her? That's not the kind of thing that just comes up in casual conversation."

"Would you believe I was trying to be nice?"

I took my hand away from my face and gave her a look.

"Because I was," she said. "The place Cece occupies in the story: it's so interesting. What you've done with her, Murray, it's so interesting. She's clearly miserable, so I was just trying to tell her how well she's set up to slingshot onto another show, and it just kind of—don't glare at me like that, I didn't sign a fucking NDA."

"I did! And if Cece talks, of course they'll trace it back to me!"

"She won't talk. Who's she going to tell?"

"How about one of the eight thousand media outlets who cover this show?"

"Does she really strike you as the type?"

"No," I said, "but she's surprised me more times during this shoot than I care to admit."

"Look, it'll be all right. I know how to fix it."

Hours. We had been together in my trailer for literally *hours*. How was she only just telling me this now?

"Firstly," Lily said, ticking it off on her fingers, "just don't put it in the edit. As soon as I realised the cameras were rolling,

285

I went back out and staged another entrance—full Fireball mode—so you're not going to have any story gaps."

The first twitch happened. I pressed the heel of my hand into my eye.

"Secondly, we give Cece what she wants."

"A shot on another show, so she can make more money?" I said. "She's already got that sewn up. That won't work as leverage."

"You know she's head-over-heels for boy-Dylan, right?"

"Do I look like a fucking amateur?"

"She wants—she needs—some closure. So we give it to her. Let them meet up one more time. She'll ask him about the rigging. He'll tell her why he agreed to it. She'll get a full personal understanding of the stakes, and—"

"And she won't talk," I said. "Because she cares about him."

I pressed my hand harder into my eye. The flowchart was unfolding in my mind.

"Dylan cares about Cece too," I said. "A lot. A *lot*. If we give them alone time without cameras, there's a strong chance it turns romantic."

"So? Just say they smooched. Hell, say they fell into bed. He's got a lot of skin in the game, telling the story you've rigged for him. Do you really think he'd blow everything up?"

I thought about it. Romeo-Dylan clearly cared deeply about Cece—but did it really outweigh how much he cared about telling the fairytale we'd set up for him? Would it cancel out all the anxiety he felt about how he came across?

"No," I said at last. "But it's still a risk."

"The cost/benefit is pretty clear, though," Lily said. "And honestly, it might give him closure too. Help him get it out of his system."

We had to do this once. We had to get it out of our systems. But if we tried to do this for real, we'd wreck each other. We'd burn out.

"Besides," she added, "if he did blow everything up, it would probably be a better story."

"For fuck's sake, Lily," I groaned.

"Think about it, though! Forbidden love! Literal Romeo and Juliet shit! It'd be an unbelievable story."

"Do you know why I rigged the show?" I said abruptly.

"You told me. Fucking Greg's up your arse and you didn't trust you could deliver a perfect fairytale without writing it in advance."

"I wanted to make something perfect," I said, "for you."

She stilled.

"But I knew I couldn't make it perfect," I went on, "without you."

I pressed harder at my twitching eye with one hand and hooked my earpiece in with the other. "You're the other half of my brain, Lily. You've always been there before to bounce things off, to "yes, and" things, to make them better. It's always been both of us, working together. And the only thing I could think of that would help—that would make up for not having you there—was to impose some structure. To give myself some certainty. A way to *know* that it would all turn out all right in the end."

I held up a finger before she could say anything. "I know it looks like mashing a Barbie and Ken together whenever the

Dylans are on screen," I said. "I *know* that, in a perfect world, there are other stories we'd chase. But I'm on my own now, and we are too far down this path to change it. Too many people have signed off on too many things. And you put the last nail in the coffin yourself. There's no way Fucking Greg will let me change the plan after he sees the footage from the Thunderdome date."

"You're not on your own," Lily said softly.

I looked at her.

"I know it's not like it used to be," she said, "but you have me, Murray."

She pushed gently at my shoulders until I sat down at the kitchen table. "Head forward."

I obeyed. She dug her thumbs into my occipital muscles, then tugged gently at my hair until I tilted my head back, leaning into her.

"I hear you," she said. "And I'm going to help."

Part of me—the part that had pined for her for years—wanted to pull her into my lap and wrap my arms around her and not let go, even if the show started blowing up in my earpiece.

Another part of me—the part that was always thinking—couldn't help remembering that she'd said that to me before.

Later that night, I watched Lily's conversation with Cece eight times.

I told myself I was doing due diligence. That even though Lily had done what she'd told me, and staged a second—extremely Lily Fireball—entrance into the Convent, there might be a few grabs I could use from her first conversation with Cece. "Don't you dare air this footage," she snarled, right at the end, once she'd realised there were mounted cameras, staring directly into one of the lenses. "Don't you fucking dare. If you do, I will rip off all your extremities and feed them to you, starting with your balls and ending with your dick. I mean it."

Part of me wanted to be petty. To call her bluff.

I knew, though, after I watched their conversation the first time, that there was nothing here I could use.

I watched it again anyway. And again. And again.

"After this show," the Lily on the screen said, sitting on the floor, in front of the Convent coffee table, "the world is going to be my oyster."

She stretched her arms over her head. I could see the shadow of a bruise on her collarbone, where I'd sunk my teeth into her skin.

"So this was all for Instagram?" Cece asked her. She was sitting behind Lily, pulling leaves and bobby pins out of her hair.

"Of course it was."

If only she hadn't elaborated.

"Not just Instagram, obviously. I've got a whole five-year plan worked out. It all starts here with becoming an iconic TV villain. That's going to let me grow my brand as a hard-as-nails bitch. Then I'll go on *Juliet on the Beach*, have a redemption romance, get tragically dumped, gain more followers and sponsors, do *Wherefore Art Thou Romeo?*, find my true love, stay with him until the revenue starts to fall and then have another tragic break-up so the whole cycle starts again."

What did you want her to say? I demanded of myself. *"Oh, my plan is to be a producer again?" Did you really think one night with you would change everything for her?*

God, I wished the sex had made me stupid. Hell, I wished it had made me an amnesiac, so I could forget all the things that were making this pit in my belly grow; so I could pretend it was just all the coffee I was drinking on an empty stomach now that Lily wasn't in the Villa to force-feed me.

But if Lily Fireball had been some other contestant—just Fucking Greg's spicy meatball, not the love of my life—and she'd come to me for advice on how she could leverage her newfound fame, this was exactly the five-year plan I would lay out for her. I'd bring her into the war room, scribble out a flowchart on the whiteboard, laying out the narrative steps between points A and B and C.

That doesn't mean this actually is her plan, I told myself.

She didn't lie, though.

On the screen, Cece was crying. "I'm so glad I'm not a feelings person," Lily told her. "Love looks like an absolute fucking nightmare."

That was bravado. I knew she loved me. After all, why would the thought *Thank god it wasn't Murray, thank god I didn't lose Murray, I couldn't survive losing Murray* have crossed her mind otherwise?

The thought that had made her cut me out for a full year. That had made her give up the career and the life that she loved.

I could ignore it as much as I wanted. I could listen to her when she told me that she was an adult and she was in control and she knew exactly what she was doing. I didn't doubt that she was, that she did. I trusted her.

But the woman I loved knew how to destroy someone—and no matter how much I didn't want it to be true, she was doing it to herself.

23

Lily

Three years ago

"What did you just say?!"

"I said this is a terrible idea," I replied. "Casting women in pairs—making them compete with their friends and their cousins and their sisters for the same man—it's an awful idea."

"Lily's right," Murray said. "This is taking the worst, most misogynistic elements of the show, and turning them up to eleven."

"Think of our most iconic moments, the ones that have really captured the cultural imagination," I said. "Like the episode Denton got booted in Season Five, that image of all the women arm-in-arm. This is the opposite of that. This is aggressively and deliberately turning our contestants against the women who are closest to them."

The vein in Tony's forehead bulged. "I swear to god, woman, if I ever hear you mention Denton again, you're fired. Am I clear?"

"I'm not trying to put one over on you here, Tony. I'm thinking about what's best for the show. And—"

"*Am I clear?!*"

I held my hands up and said nothing.

I fell into step beside Murray as we left the meeting. He was brooding, the muscle above his eyebrow jumping.

I opened my mouth to speak, but he got in first. "Come around to my place tonight. We'll order in. We've got work to do, and it's not the kind of shit we can do at the bar."

"It's a date," I replied. "It's going to take a hell of a lot of work to save Season Eight."

"We're not going to save it."

Murray looked around, checking there was no one listening, before bending his head towards mine. "We're going to tank it."

It took me a few moments to put together what he meant. "You want to gun for Tony?"

"I told you that there would be consequences if he spoke to you like that again," he said, "and I meant it."

On the surface, Murray and I had never been such model employees.

Marry Me, Juliet production meetings had never been so short, because we agreed with everything Tony said. We still made suggestions, of course—it would have been a dead giveaway that something was up if we didn't—but they were all "yes, ands," taking Tony's worst impulses and making them bigger, broader, more spectacular—and much, much worse.

"Can I ask you a question?" Suzette asked me, catching me alone in the women's bathroom.

"Of course," I said, fixing my lipstick.

She bit her lip.

I raised an eyebrow at her in the mirror.

"This season is going to be a trainwreck, right?" she said eventually. "Like an absolute, complete, total and utter trainwreck."

"Yes." I capped *Blood of My Enemies* and put it back in my bag.

The words came out of her so fast it was like an explosion. "Then why are you and Murray going along with it?"

She put her hand on the paper towel dispenser and leaned on it heavily, as if her knees were about to buckle. "You pitch for more socially responsible storytelling all the time. You fought Tony on this idea. And now you're—what, just leaning into it?"

I did not particularly want to gaslight Suzette. She was a promising producer with real talent. Tony hadn't picked up on how strange it was that Murray and I were suddenly on board with all of his worst ideas, but she had. And I was not a liar.

But the more people knew about our strategy of extremely malicious compliance, the more likely it was that it would blow up in our faces.

So I said, "You know what people do to trainwrecks, Suzette? They watch them."

"We're going to get destroyed. Everyone will be talking about what a regressive, misogynist, problematic show this is. We're going to get more complaints than any other show in the history of time."

Exactly. And the network was going to need a scapegoat.

"Hate-watching is still watching," I said. "And if people are talking about us, at least we're in the conversation."

Murray and I reconvened at his place later that night. "That was a good line to run," he said, when I told him what had happened. "I don't like keeping Suzette in the dark either—or her thinking that we both suddenly love hating women—but we can't give the game away now. Loose lips sink ships."

"That's what I thought. We can sit her down later and explain why we did this, but if she slipped and it got back to Tony . . ."

"It's kind of ironic, isn't it?" Murray said. "How furious he would be if he found out our master plan to bring him down was to . . . agree with him?"

I snorted. He grinned.

"Come on." He opened the whiteboard app on his tablet. "Let's work out how we can plus him up some more in the next episode."

We took a quick break a couple of hours later for dinner. "What's the likelihood, do you think," I asked, scraping half the container of pad thai onto my plate and then swapping with him for the green curry, "that what I said to Suzette actually turns out to be true?"

"Which bit?" Murray took some roti out of the bag then passed it to me. "About how people love trainwrecks?"

"There's a chance Tony gets rewarded for this, not fired. You know Fucking Greg already leans conservative. He might look at the ratings and say fuck the outrage."

"He might. That was always a risk."

"If that happens, where do we draw the line? Sacrificing one season's worth of women to Tony's misogyny is one thing. If Greg loves this, and demands more, more, more . . ."

"Then we'll re-evaluate."

Murray reached across the table and touched the back of my hand lightly, with just one finger. "We got headhunted off the back of *Adjudication Station*. If this awful season turns into some enormous success, we can find new jobs. We've got good reputations. Someone will want us."

"Both of us?"

"Yes," he said firmly. "We're a package deal, Lily. I'm not going anywhere without you."

His finger was still touching my hand, resting gently on one of my knuckles.

I should pull my hand away. I should definitely pull my hand away.

He tapped that finger gently. "But even if it takes forever, and even if we have to do it from afar, and even if we have to sacrifice thousands of contestants," he said, "we're taking down Tony."

Vault. Jeff. *Jeff.*

I pulled back, wrapping my fingers around my fork instead. "Let's grind his bones to make our bread."

"Let's use his blood," Murray said, "to make your lipstick."

24

Murray

"You're angry with me," Lily said.

She was standing in front of my golf cart, arms folded. I'd been heading back up the hill from shooting the Episode Nine single date (the Dylans again, building on the strengths of the Thunderdome date), and she'd stridden out of the trees, directly into my path. How long had she been waiting there to stage such a perfect entrance?

I turned the engine off. "Hello to you too."

"You're angry with me. Or you would have found a way to sneak me out of the Convent again by now. It's been forty-eight hours. Why? Which bit did it?"

It was the first time I genuinely understood what Lily had meant that day in the laundry when she said we were too similar. It was inconvenient, really, that she thought in flow-charts too.

She climbed into the golf cart beside me and took my hand, lacing her fingers through mine. "I don't want it to be like this, Murray. I didn't finally cross the fucking Rubicon just for you to try and throw me back over to the other side. Tell me what upset you so I can fix it."

I looked at our joined hands for a long time.

I should let go.

A better man would let go. A better man would never have let it get this far. A better man would never have slept with his widowed best friend, no matter how actively she wanted it and how long he'd been pining for her. A better man would have found a way to keep her off the show in the first place, would have wrapped her in cotton wool and looked after her, rather than sinking his teeth into her vulnerabilities until she cracked.

But I wasn't that man. I was a man with a fundamentally broken moral compass. I was a man who loved her infinitely beyond any kind of better judgement. I was a man who didn't know how to be without her.

And I was a man who always listened to what she said.

She had told me to trust her. That I wasn't on my own anymore. That I had her.

Did I, though?

I had turned it all over in my head over the last couple of days, staring at the ceiling in my trailer, trying to use my work brain to think through things, to set the emotion aside and find the story.

Lily becoming Lily Fireball was destructive. There was no way around that. She was actively throwing Lily Ong's life away.

But where did I fit into the puzzle?

I wanted to believe that being with me was ... helping, somehow. That the admission of what she'd thought on the night of Jeff's funeral was an opening of the floodgates. That us being together was actually constructive, allowing her to reconcile the two halves of herself that she'd drawn such a stark line between.

I was deathly afraid, though, that this was just wishful thinking. That sleeping with me was just another way for her to throw away Lily Ong, the Lily who had been married to Jeff. That once she was done, she would throw me away too, like she was throwing away everything else we'd built together.

"Hey." She nudged me with her elbow. "Look at me."

She didn't wait for me to obey, reaching over with her free hand and cupping my jaw, turning my face towards hers. "Stop brooding. Start talking."

A rush of anger pulsed through me. Didn't she understand how momentous this was? How much this meant to me? What was she going to do, stick a band-aid on the fact that she was committed to being a different person and then go on her merry way?

"We're a team, Murray. Please talk to me."

"Are we?" My voice came out harsh, snappish.

Hers was steady, though. "Yes. Always."

I forced myself to take a breath. If she couldn't give me a satisfactory answer to this question, I told myself, I would let go.

"Then tell me about this five-year plan of yours."

"Oh!" She sounded genuinely surprised. "Is that all?"

"What do you mean, *is that all*? You've got five years of Lily Fireball all planned out! Five years—minimum!—of being an entirely different person! Five years—"

299

"—of working with *you*, Murray."

She brought my hand to her lips and kissed my knuckles. "I know it's not the same as it used to be. I'm not the same as I used to be."

So I drew a line. A line between me and that woman, because I couldn't be her.

"But look at all the shit we can do with an inside man," she said. "The ways we can shape the story. The delicious messes we can create."

"You do realise," I said, teeth gritted, "that in all your plans, you're publicly dating other people?"

"And I'm sure those relationships would be incredibly real and deeply sincere. Just like the Dylans."

"Don't joke. Not about this."

"I'm sorry."

I wanted to believe—so badly—that she meant it.

"But come on, Murray. Do you really think there's a world where I would throw you away for some waxed-chest man-child on *Juliet on the Beach*? If I was some ordinary contestant, you'd be rubbing your hands with glee about the potential of Lily Fireball."

"Yes," I said, "but you're not."

"No, I'm not. Because I'm better."

She tangled her fingers in my hair, pulling my head back so she could press her lips behind my ear. "We'd be stupid to throw Lily Fireball away. She's too good a storytelling tool. And even if we wanted to, we can't. She's going to be too famous. We've both done our jobs too well."

She bit my earlobe. "So we use her. You and me. Together."

I pulled back, so I could look her in the eye. "Together?"

"Together."

It was such a compelling story. That word—*together*—made me ache with wanting.

"Imagine what it'll be like," she whispered. "I'll be terrorising all the little waxed-chest boys by day. You'll be standing there, watching, playing them, pressing all their buttons. They'll have no idea that we're in on it together. That they never had a chance. That when it's late at night and it's just you and me, you're yanking my dress up and bending me over and—"

I kissed her, hard, swallowing the rest of her story. If I let her finish, I might never have another clear thought again.

"We have to set some ground rules, though," I growled, when my mind was organised enough for me to get the words out, fingers curled around the nape of her neck.

"Okay—" she kissed the tip of my nose, "Daddy."

"Number one: don't call me 'Daddy.' You're my partner, not my subordinate."

I desperately wanted her to agree with me—*yes, Murray, I am your partner, just like I've always been*—but she just smirked. "It's hard, when you do the voice," she said, "but fine."

"I don't want it to be like our first weeks here," I said, trying to focus as her fingers stroked down my neck, playing with the chest hair that peeked out from the open collar of my shirt. "No working around me. No holding things back."

She shifted, swinging a leg over me so she was straddling me. "That goes for you too. No withholding information from me. I'm in on all the plans."

"No undermining them."

"No more rigging."

301

The sound I made was half laugh, half strangled gasp, as she ground herself into me.

"If we're going to be partners again, Lily," I said, before my brain entirely clouded over, "then it's in everything, and it's for good."

She leaned in and kissed me, a long, deep kiss that left lipstick streaked everywhere. "On one condition."

In that moment, I would have given her anything. The world. The universe. My neck, so she could step on it.

"Fuck me right now," she whispered, "before I lose my mind."

I was still thinking about it as we filmed the Episode Nine group date. My ability to compartmentalise—to think at all—had been significantly impacted by the remembrance of what it had felt like, my partner's body, pressed against mine.

Together. God, that word was a drug.

But I wasn't the only one who was distracted. Romeo-Dylan turned in his worst performance of the season on the group date, clearly running on autopilot. When we sat down to do our ITM, it took him ten minutes to get one satisfactory sentence out.

I needed to get his head back in the game, by whatever means necessary, so I took a calculated risk. "Are you thinking about Cece?"

The shock on his face told me I was on target.

"Would it help to have another chat with her? No cameras. No mics. Just the two of you?" Lily, being Lily, was probably right about the two of them needing closure, and if we were really partners again, I should use some of her plays.

Romeo-Dylan's thumb and middle finger started tapping. "Only if Cece wants that," he said. "What I want doesn't matter."

God, he was such a fucking *good person*.

I arranged for Romeo-Dylan to take Cece over to his boat for a private chat after the Episode Nine Necklace Ceremony. It was going to take some manoeuvring to pull off without anyone noticing, so I took over a task I usually delegated and went down to the Convent to get the women ready to welcome their new arrival.

In the hubbub of all the women trying to squeeze onto the sofa, I caught Lily's hand. "Find an excuse to come outside with me," I murmured.

She nodded. "Move!" she ordered one of the other women. "I want to sit there."

I had gruffly answered a few questions about the ongoing pandemic restrictions when Lily saw her opportunity. "What kind of attitude is that?" she demanded, rising to her feet and putting her hands on her hips.

"It's the attitude of someone who hasn't slept for weeks and is sick of dealing with your shit, Lily. Now sit down."

"We've had this conversation, Murray. You don't talk to me like that."

"You all know the drill." I deliberately addressed the other women instead of her. "Actually wait for the person who's been cut to get in if you want any screen time. I'm out of here."

I strode towards the doors. "Murray!" Lily screeched. "Don't you dare walk out of here like that!"

I kept going. She followed me. "You don't fucking speak to me like that!" she exclaimed.

The glass in the French doors rattled as she slammed them shut behind us. "Good?" she whispered.

"Perfect."

She smiled wickedly, putting her hand on my chest and backing me up against the wall. "See how hot playing pretend is?"

I curled my fingers in her hair, holding her back. "Wait, wait, wait."

"What? Worried that someone will come out here and catch us?"

"Worried that you'll distract me before I tell you what I need. Can you make sure Cece stays down in the living room tonight? By herself?"

"Sure. You're going to let her talk to boy-Dylan?"

"Against my better judgement, yes."

"I'm telling you—" she nuzzled her face into my neck, kissing my pulse point and making her way up, "it's the right move. Even if they end up boning, they can get each other out of their systems."

I bit down gently on her bottom lip. "That day in the laundry didn't get you out of my system."

Lily stilled. "Really?"

"Of course it didn't."

"But you put me away, right?" She traced her fingers along my jawline. "There were other women after me. Naomi. That redhead with the weird laugh."

"Her name was Dee, and of course there were other women. You made it clear that you weren't an option. What was I going to do, become a monk?"

"If the last few days have taught me anything—" she licked the shell of my ear, "it's that your talents would be profoundly wasted in a monastery."

It was hard not to feel smug at that.

"But boy-Dylan is in the same position," Lily said. "Cece's not an option for him, not right now, and he knows that. Giving them tonight, no matter what happens—it might be the push he needs to put her away for a while."

She was right.

I didn't need forever from the Dylans. I only needed enough time after the show aired that it looked like they'd fallen in love, and then hadn't quite been able to make it work in the real world. And if Romeo-Dylan and Cece circled back around to each other afterwards . . . that was their business.

"Trust me," Lily whispered, nose sliding against mine.

I stroked her hair out of her eyes. "I trust you."

She smiled and kissed me. "How long do you think this little fight of ours should last?"

"Well," I said, trying to think straight even though she was unbuckling my belt, "producer Murray is an arsehole, and—"

"—Lily Fireball is a bitch, so it's probably going to take a minute for either of them to give ground."

She unzipped my fly. "The real question is," she said, going to her knees in front of me, "how quiet can you be?"

It was lucky I didn't need to go back into the Convent. I'd sunk my teeth so deeply into my hand in an effort to keep silent that I'd drawn blood.

"Well," I heard Lily say cheerfully to the other women,

closing the French doors behind her, "that's put him in his place."

I was addicted to her. I was addicted to this. I was addicted to *us*, to having her back again, and finally being able to hold her as close as I wanted.

So whenever the pain and the guilt and the worry came creeping back, I shoved them down, locking them away in the darkness.

I tried, at least.

"What are these?" Lily asked a few days later, rubbing her thumbs along the dark smears under my eyes. We had a couple of hours' gap in our shooting schedule between two of the Friends and Family date shoots we always did in Episode Ten, so I'd smuggled her out of the Convent and up to my trailer. We were sitting on my bed, her knees on either side of my lap.

"I don't know if you've noticed," I said, pressing a kiss to the hollow at the base of her throat, "but I have a fairly demanding job."

"You shouldn't still be pulling all-nighters at this stage of the season. Not with only four contestants left."

"I know, I know."

There was no way I was going to tell her why I wasn't sleeping. That it wasn't workload—overwhelming as it still was—as much as worry that she might have made me into just another one of her weapons of self-destruction. That no matter how often she whispered *Trust me*, all of this might be a mirage. That she might realise she couldn't fuck the pain away after all and break my heart again.

Instead, I gently redirected the subject from cause to effect. "I almost fell asleep in an ITM with Amanda today."

"Murray!"

Lily smacked me in the shoulder and then clambered off my lap. "No sex for you. You need a nap."

I caught her hand. "Will you stay?"

I didn't know if it was the desperation in my voice or something else that caused it, but she smiled, the lines of her body softening. "Of course I'll stay."

She sat back down on the bed, grabbing my pillow and putting it on her lap. "Come here."

I lay down, head on the pillow. She started threading her fingers through my hair, over and over again.

I closed my eyes. Her fingernails scratched gently against my scalp.

"So how did Amanda react when you fell asleep in her interview?" she said.

"Asked me if I was all right."

"Of course she did."

"Then I asked her about Dylan G and she clammed up. I had to push hard to get much out of her after that."

"They're still mad at each other?"

"Yes. Any idea why that is? You just spent a month sharing a bedroom with them."

"Genuinely no idea. I mean, they're obviously attracted to each other, and something clearly went down around that dinner party, but I have no idea what the specifics are."

"Mmm . . . okay." Her fingers were turning my bones to liquid. "Reason doesn't really matter. Easier to build a feud in the edit off a blank slate. And now you're gone, that's basically the only conflict I have left in the Villa, so . . ."

"Shhhh." Lily's thumb brushed over my temple. "Turn your brain off for a while, Murray. Get some rest."

It was too easy, really, to do what she said and turn my brain off. I'd spent too many years compartmentalising, and now I was too good at it.

And how could I not put the inconvenient things away, when the woman I loved was right in front of me? When I finally had my best friend back—and I had her right where I'd always wanted her?

". . . wait, so Amanda and girl-Dylan are fucking now?" Lily asked me a few days later, the next time I managed to sneak her out of the Convent.

We certainly had been. We were both naked, and she was sitting between my legs on my bed, leaning back against my chest. I'd just given her the second half of my show update. The first half had happened during foreplay—we were both very good at multitasking—but she'd made me wait until after to tell her the rest, on the grounds that she wasn't doing her job properly if I could think about anything but her while we were actually having sex.

"Something's happened, that's for sure," I replied, resting my chin on her shoulder. "They told me this morning that they'd made up and they wanted to film a reconciliation scene. I've never seen two people do a worse job of hiding their feelings. Their heart eyes are going to jump off the fucking screen."

"So now both Dylans might blow up your terrible plan."

"Can you lay off the plan? I don't need your criticism. I need your help."

"My criticism *is* helpful." She elbowed me in the ribs as she nestled deeper into me. "But fine. Let's figure this out. What are you thinking?"

"Two options," I said. "I've got to separate them—so I can either break them up, or get Dylan JM to eliminate Amanda an episode earlier than I planned."

"Or let it play out."

"Lily."

"I'm serious." She twisted her head around to look at me. "Girl-Dylan and Amanda are into each other. Boy-Dylan and Cece are into each other. Just let them all be together. Let them find a genuine happy ending. Problem solved."

"Problem absolutely not solved. Firstly, the network just offered Cece the lead on the next series of *Wherefore*. I don't care how much she likes Dylan JM, she's not turning down that sign-on fee. Secondly, Dylan G is just as money-motivated. She's not risking her fee either, even if she's fallen for Amanda. Thirdly, Dylan JM won't risk the story; and fourthly, even if none of these were concerns, we're too far gone. I've put too much time and effort into the Double Dylan plotline. I don't have the building blocks for anything else."

"You're resourceful."

"Yes, but I'm not magic. The amount of work it would take to re-shape the narrative is sickening."

Especially without you, I wanted to say, but didn't. If the only version of partnership she could offer me was one where she dated other men on television and snuck around with me, then I would take it.

It was a truth the last week had made me face. Lily had ruined me for anyone else. I didn't *like* it—hated it, in fact— but there was no escaping it. I would break myself in half if it meant my jagged edges would fit like puzzle pieces with hers.

"I don't know," she said lightly. "That thing you did with your tongue before was pretty magic."

I hooked a finger under her chin so I could kiss her. "Stop trying to distract me by stroking my ego."

"Would you rather I stroke something else?"

"Once you give me a minute to recover, absolutely. But I want what's in here first." I tapped her temple. "Tell me how to fix my problem."

"Hmmmm."

God, I loved that little half-smile of hers she had when she was plotting something. That wicked glint in her eye.

I would do just about anything for this woman— compromise on just about anything—if it meant I could keep her.

"You need to trigger a breakdown in Amanda," Lily said, after a few moments. "Then you can either have boy-Dylan cut her out of kindness, or have her eliminate herself."

I thought about it, playing with her fingers. "Self-elimination would be better. It's the penultimate episode. It'd be a strong promo hook."

"Obviously it wouldn't be as iconic as *my* self-elimination—" Lily pressed her lips to my knuckles, "but it'd give you a good plotline going into the finale. A bunch of contestants have taken themselves out, which gives you a whole dark-night-of-the-soul story for boy-Dylan. You can ask a "If all these women keep leaving me, is the right person for me really here?" question."

"And then answer it. Yes. She is. Dylan G."

"Of course," Lily said, craning her head around to look at me, "it'd be an even *better* story if at the last minute both the Dylans announced they were in love with other people. No one would see that coming."

I groaned, letting my forehead fall onto her shoulder. "How many times do we have to have this conversation?"

"If you want my genius brain, you have to take my genius criticism."

"I rigged the season because I didn't *have* your genius brain," I said. "The wheels are in motion. This is what we're doing. If your genius brain gives a shit about my genius brain not liquefying from stress, you'll help me figure out how I get Amanda worked up enough to eliminate herself without doing any permanent emotional damage."

The plan was, to say the least, morally grey.

It wasn't like I hadn't done some extremely morally grey things in the name of story before. I lived in the grey shades. Season Eight—the season of malicious compliance—had seen some of those grey shades turn perilously close to black.

This wasn't quite as dark as that. However, it was easily the closest I'd skated to the line since.

"Think of it this way," Lily said. "We went along with all of Tony's nasty shit in Season Eight for the greater good, right? This is the same."

She wasn't wrong. The principle was the same. Sometimes you had to sacrifice pawns to win the game—and Amanda was only one pawn, as opposed to the twenty Juliets we'd sacrificed then.

Still.

"I hoped, when we took over," I said, "that we could do better than this. Be better than this."

I expected her to flash me a Lily Fireball grin and shoot off some snarky quip about how none of this would have happened if I hadn't rigged the season, but instead, she just caressed my cheek with the back of her fingers. "I know, Murray," she said. "I know."

The plan we'd come up with was to centre the Episode Eleven dates on the women's exes. We'd keep our three remaining contestants separate, so they wouldn't have a chance to warn each other what they were about to be faced with. In Dylan G and Kumiko's case, that wasn't going to be more than mildly unpleasant memories. Amanda's most recent ex, though, a) sounded like a piece of shit, and b) was a woman—a fact I'd promised her weeks ago I wouldn't reveal.

And I wasn't going to. We'd be Zooming with an earlier ex-boyfriend instead of her ex-girlfriend.

"But if Amanda *thinks* you're going to blow up her spot," Lily said, as we flow-charted it out, "she'll be fundamentally destabilised, and you can trigger fight or flight."

"What if she fights?"

"Then you'll probably have footage of her having a screaming meltdown, and you can get boy-Dylan to mercy-cut her. But—" she snuggled back into me, head resting in the crook of my shoulder, "trust me, she'll run."

Lily was right. Amanda ran. But the whole thing went completely sideways, and it made me feel like the worst piece of shit on earth.

The plan was complicated by the fact that at some point, unbeknownst to me, Amanda had come out to Romeo-Dylan. "Are you really going to do this to her?" he demanded of me, when we shot pick-up ITMs the morning after his date with Kumiko and her ex. "Are you going to out Amanda on national television without any warning?"

I couldn't tell him what I was actually planning—somehow, I didn't think "Don't worry, I'm just trying to psychologically destabilise her because I think she's sleeping with your soon-to-be fake girlfriend and I don't want the fact they're obsessed with each other to show up on screen" would go over particularly well—so I had to hedge, and it didn't really work.

I fingered my radio. The urge to send out an SOS on what had once been mine and Lily's private comms channel was intense. As the good cop in our partnership, she would have been much better equipped to calm Romeo-Dylan down.

But I could radio all I liked. She was in the Convent, and she wouldn't hear me. I had to figure it out on my own.

It took a lot of work on the date shoot—and a lot of shouting—to prevent Romeo-Dylan warning Amanda about what was to come, but I managed it. I got my money shot, when Z announced that they would be Zooming with her ex and all the blood drained out of Amanda's face. I got the destabilisation, too—the whiplash of the shock and the fear and then the relief when it *wasn't* her ex-girlfriend, the pressure applied in just the right place, the one that would make her do what I wanted.

But afterwards, when she burst into loud, noisy tears, a pang of guilt snuck through my defences, sharp as a stiletto.

"Do you care about anything?" Romeo-Dylan demanded, glaring at me. He was holding Amanda to him, one hand on the back of her head, pressing her protectively into his shoulder.

That question hit me right in the gut, a much more brutal blow than I had ever thought this innately good, kind man could land.

"I care," I said tightly, "about making good TV."

At that, at least, I was good.

After I tightened the thumbscrews by telling a few strategic lies in our ITM, Amanda did exactly what I wanted. During the intimacy portion of the date, she gracefully, graciously eliminated herself from the show. "We both know it's not me," she told Romeo-Dylan. "I don't want to hang around in the background, being some side character in your love story."

A perfect line.

It would cut together beautifully with the footage we got at what would have been the Necklace Ceremony, when we revealed to Dylan G and Kumiko that they were the last two women standing. "Mandie's gone?" Juliet-Dylan said, white-lipped.

"I'm sorry, Dyl," Romeo-Dylan said. "I know you two were close."

I'd stitch Amanda's line about being a side character over the top of the Dylans hugging, I decided, writing down the timecodes and making a note. That way, I could frame her self-elimination as a heroic sacrifice, stepping aside so her best friend could have the love story she wanted.

Amanda would come out of the show looking golden. She'd get more Instagram spon-con offers than she could ever possibly manage. That was the best way I could make this up to her.

I'd paused the footage so I could make my notes. It was frozen on Juliet-Dylan's stricken face, as Romeo-Dylan tried to comfort her.

Spiders went skittering in my stomach.

I had taken nothing from them, I told myself. Neither couple, not Juliet-Dylan and Amanda, not Romeo-Dylan and Cece.

If what they had was real, they would find their way back to each other. If their love was worth shit, then some minor psychological violence and a fake relationship would not be ruinous. If Lily and I could survive marrying other people— could survive divorce—could survive death—could survive *Lily Fireball,* for fuck's sake!—then they could survive this, if they really had something.

That was love stories 101. Happy endings had to be earned. If these two couples ended up together in the long run, they would probably be stronger for what I had done to them.

The spiders were still skittering.

It was never supposed to be like this.

"You were right," I murmured to myself, thinking of Lily. "I shouldn't have rigged it."

But I was alone, working late in the war room, without her there to rub it in.

25

Lily

Two years ago

We weren't in the meeting when Tony got fired, but it didn't matter. The shouting was so loud we could hear it through the walls.

I wanted to stand and watch as he left the building for the last time, really revel in the gloating, but Murray wouldn't let me. "Tony doesn't have anything left to lose now. I don't want him anywhere near you."

We watched from the window instead. Watching him go—and knowing we'd caused it—was absolutely, utterly, completely delicious.

A few days later, Fucking Greg formally offered us the role of co-showrunners for the Romeo and Juliet franchise. "I offered it to this guy first—" he said to me, jerking his thumb at Murray, "—but he said he wouldn't do it without you. Even took a pay cut so we could afford it."

Caught perfectly between wanting to ask *Greg, why would*

you tell me that? and *Murray, why didn't you tell me that?*, all I could do was smile politely.

I wheeled on Murray the second we were a safe distance away from Greg's office, but he held up a warning finger. "No," he said. "Everything we've ever done, we've done together. All the success we've earned, we've earned together. So don't you dare—"

I threw my arms around him.

"—fucking thank me," he said, voice muffled in my hair. "I could never do this without you."

We took each other out to dinner to celebrate, and stumbled into the bar afterwards. "Champagne!" I said expansively, leaning over the bar to kiss Jeff. "Showrunners deserve champagne!"

"All right," Jeff said. "Give me a minute. I've got customers."

Murray nudged me. "He okay?"

I looked at Jeff. The lines of his shoulders were tight as he served some people on the other side of the bar. "Maybe he's had a rough night. It seems busy."

"How about I go find us a table, and you bring the drinks over when you're ready?"

I nodded. Murray disappeared.

It took Jeff almost ten minutes to make his way back to me. "Champagne," he said. "Any preferences?"

"Do you have the one we serve on the show?" Jeff's favourite hobby, when we watched the episodes, was trying to ID the alcohol.

He bent down to pull a bottle out of the wine fridge. "It's cheap piss," he warned.

"That's all right. We started our careers drinking cheap piss in this bar. What's wrong?"

"Nothing."

"Jeff, I know you. What's wrong?"

He braced his hands on the bar, the same way he had on the first night we met, and looked at me.

"I don't like his influence on you." He nodded over at Murray.

I stared.

"Look at what you're celebrating, Lily."

"A huge promotion."

"Which you got by knifing someone."

"He deserved it."

"What about all those women? The ones who went on the show with their friends and their sisters and their cousins and whose relationships you systematically destroyed? Did they deserve it?"

"No one forced them to come on the show," I said tightly. "They were there of their own free will. And if a boring white man and a little manipulation could destroy their relationships, they weren't very strong to begin with."

"He encourages you." Jeff jerked his head towards Murray again. "I know he's your best friend, but he's not good for you. He brings out your worst impulses. He drags you down into the dirt with him."

"Excuse me?!"

Blood was roaring in my ears. I couldn't remember the last time I had been this angry.

"Is that what you think of me, Jeff?" I spat out. "That I'm so easily led? That I just do whatever he says? Is that who you think I am? His puppet?"

Jeff opened his mouth, but I wasn't finished. "If that's what you think, then you have no idea who I am. If you think you married some girl who really is nice deep down but who keeps getting egged on by a bad man, then I'm sorry, but you married a different person. I haven't been dragged into the dirt. I am the fucking dirt."

Jeff apologised a few days later. "I'm sorry, love," he said, combing his fingers through my hair as we lay in bed. "It's just . . . hard for me, sometimes."

"What is?"

"Seeing you with him."

"I'm not going to stop." I propped myself up on my elbows. "Ever."

There was a sharp note in my voice. The makeup sex had been good, but this was not something on which I would ever, ever give ground. It was my sharpest, hardest edge.

"I'm not asking you to." Jeff splayed a hand on my belly. "I just . . . I want you to understand where I'm coming from."

He leaned over and kissed the apple of my cheek, next to my nose. "I love you so much, Lily. And sometimes . . ."

I braced myself. I loved him too—loved him more than I had ever thought myself capable of—but if he said anything else about Murray being a bad influence on me, I was going to throw myself out the window, run naked down the street, and never return.

But, "Sometimes I get jealous," was all Jeff said. "There's this whole world you two live in that I don't understand, and I never will."

26

Murray

I tried to apologise to Amanda a couple of days later, on the morning of our final day of shooting. I'd gone down to the Convent to talk to Cece about the arrangements for *Wherefore Art Thou Romeo?*, and when we were finished, I sent Lily to fetch Amanda for me.

But she returned empty-handed. "I did my best," she said, "but Amanda's still pretty upset with you."

I sighed. "That's all right. She doesn't have to talk to me if she doesn't want to."

"I can work on her for you."

I shook my head. "She's entitled to her feelings."

My radio squawked, and a burst of static came through my earpiece before the line settled. "Status update," Suzette said. "Kumiko and Dylan G are both in hair and makeup. Dylan JM's ready. We've put him in one of the spare rooms in the Villa to chill before shooting."

"Copy that."

Lily's fingers brushed mine. It was gentle, subtle, so that if anyone was watching they would have no idea it meant anything, but I understood.

"Do you need to get back to the Villa now," she asked, "or do you have time for a walk?"

"I wish I did," I replied, brushing her fingers back, "but I've got to go help with finale set up."

I glanced around. There were a few women doing yoga on the lawn, but they weren't looking our way.

"I have something to ask you," I murmured, bending my head closer to hers than was strictly professional.

That glint I loved so much came into her eyes. "Do you need me to wreak some havoc down here? Create some backup content, in case the big break up and the big hook up don't hit the spot?"

"No. Feel free, but no."

She smiled. "What do you need?"

"It's more . . . what I want."

I took a breath. "I'm staying here once the shoot wraps. There's only a month before we start shooting *Wherefore.* Cece's formally signed on, but she obviously needs intensive camera training, so I'm going to stay here and work with her. And I was wondering . . ."

Lily raised her eyebrows, but she didn't fill the silence. Of course she was going to make me spit it out.

"Do you want to stay?" I asked. "Here? With me?"

She paused. Every millisecond of that pause felt like an hour.

"I'm not coming back to work."

"All right. I understand. I just—"

"But I'll stay," she said. "With you."

321

I glanced over at the yoga women again. They were all facing the other way.

So I took the risk, cupped her face in my hand, and kissed her. "I love you."

"I love you too."

Then Lily swiped her thumb across my lips. "Make sure you wash your face before anyone on set sees you. You are *covered* in my lipstick."

I kissed her again. "Copy that."

"Still on schedule?" I asked into my headset a little while later, parking the golf cart outside the Villa.

"Affirmative," Suzette replied. "Ready to shoot in forty-five."

"Copy that. Carrie, do we have the government all-clear to send the Convent women home today?"

"Yes, all clear. The first limo will arrive in two hours."

"Copy that. I'm going in now to shoot the final ITM with Dylan JM."

The Romeo-Dylan that sat down across from me in front of the green screen was listless. "Just tell me what you want me to say," he said tiredly. "I'll say it."

He pulled it together enough to do a creditable job for the final breakup. "Kumiko, I so value and treasure the time we've had together," he said earnestly, holding her hands and looking into her eyes. "You're a wonderful person. But I'm so sorry. Your heart is not the other half of mine."

Kumiko cried. Romeo-Dylan held her. "There's someone out there for you," he whispered into her hair. "I have no doubt about that whatsoever."

We were waiting until full night to shoot the Dylans' declaration of love, which gave me a couple of hours' grace. I sat in the war room by myself, just me and my coffee, mindlessly scrubbing through some B-roll, occasionally making some notes, and let myself fantasise.

She'd said yes. She was going to stay with me.

We still had a lot of things to work through. I had no illusions about that. Just because I'd been ruthlessly shoving things down didn't mean they'd gone away. The future I wanted and the one Lily had set a course for were completely different. We had rough seas ahead.

But tomorrow?

Tomorrow, this long, painful season would be over. Tomorrow, this terrible plan of mine would finally be fully executed. Tomorrow, maybe I—and Lily, because she wouldn't be able to help herself—could start making some better plans for Cece's season of *Wherefore*, ones that didn't involve rigging it.

In the afternoon, anyway. Because tomorrow, we could fucking *sleep in*.

"Sun's almost down," Suzette said in my earpiece. "We're good to start shooting in thirty."

"Copy that."

It was a clear night, so we were staging the final declaration of love outside, in the rose garden. Every single fairy light we had was strung up. Candles were flickering between the rose bushes. The ground was strewn with petals, mirroring the sky, which was strewn with stars.

"How are you feeling?" I asked Romeo-Dylan. "You ready to declare your love?"

Jodi McAlister

His fingers were tapping, thumb into middle finger, over and over again. "Can you give me an earpiece?"

I blinked. After the First Night Party, when I'd fed him the words that would allow him to keep Lily Fireball, he'd steadfastly refused one.

"I'm worried I won't say the right thing," he said. "I don't—I can't—I know how important it is to get the ending right."

"Of course you can have an earpiece, mate. I've got you covered."

We had Juliet-Dylan waiting around the corner, out of sight. I went to check on her. "How are you feeling? Are you ready?"

She had the same white lips as when she'd found out Amanda was gone, but she nodded. "I'm fine. Can we just get this over with?"

How romantic.

"All right," I said to her. "Let's do this."

We shot her walking up to Romeo-Dylan four times so we could capture different angles, resetting the rose petals and touching up her makeup between each shot. "Go slower," I instructed her. "You're marching at him right now. We want this to come across a little more bridal."

Juliet-Dylan nodded, jaw set.

After the fourth try, we had what we needed. "All right, mate," I said, flicking my radio to the channel Romeo-Dylan's earpiece was on. "Take her hands."

He did. "Hi, Dyl," he said softly.

That drew the slightest smile from her, a minute unclenching of her jaw. "Hi yourself."

324

They were holding onto each other so tight it was practically a death-grip. "Loosen up a little," I said into my headset. "You look like you're about to arm-wrestle her."

"How are you feeling?" he asked her.

"Nervous. You?"

"Nervous too."

He'd taken my note, but they were both still holding so tight their knuckles were white.

Oh well. We'd probably have to shoot this a couple of times. They'd relax into it after they'd done it once.

"All right," I said. "Here goes."

"Dylan Gilchrist, I have loved every single second of getting to know you," Romeo-Dylan obediently repeated. "You are one of the most remarkable women I've ever met. You're brave. You're strong. You stand up for people. You care about people. I'm completely in awe of you."

"Now pause," I whispered.

This was the moment where everything teetered on the precipice. In a breakup speech, like the one we'd shot with Kumiko this afternoon, the next word would be *but*.

Romeo-Dylan took a breath. "Dyl—"

"Not yet," I said. "Longer."

He closed his eyes and took another breath. Juliet-Dylan swallowed.

"Open your eyes," I told him.

He did.

"Now take one more breath," I instructed, "then say, *Everything changed the first day I met you.*"

His nostrils flared as he breathed in. Juliet-Dylan's chest rose. They looked each other in the eye.

Then—

"No," they both said.

❤

"What the fuck do you mean, no?" I exclaimed.

❤

"No," Romeo-Dylan said. "No, I can't do this. I'm sorry, Dyl—I'm sorry, Murray—but I can't."

"It's okay," Juliet-Dylan said. "Fuck, Dylan, it's okay; I can't do it either."

They threw their arms around each other. Both of them were shaking, pressed hard together as they held each other up.

"What the fuck?" I exclaimed again. "What the fuck do you mean, no?!"

❤

It was chaos.

"You signed a contract!" I bellowed. "We agreed on a story! This fucking story!"

"I know!" Romeo-Dylan said. "I know, but—I can't! I *can't!*"

"And you waited until now? The last possible second?!"

"I'm sorry! But I didn't know at the start—I didn't feel— I didn't—"

He clawed at his chest, fingernails scraping over his lapel mike. One of the soundies winced, tripped, knocked over several candles, and set a rosebush on fire.

Somewhere in the tumult, as people scrambled to put out the fire, Juliet-Dylan disappeared. The part of my brain that wasn't just endless screaming filed that away to deal with later. "I've got to go to her," Romeo-Dylan was saying, eyes wide, desperate. "Cece. I need her. I love her."

Through the screaming, I did the calculations.

All Suzette and Carrie's contestants had already left. The limos had taken them away. But my contestants were still on set.

So Cece was still in the Convent.

And so was Lily.

It'd be an even better *story if at the last minute both the Dylans announced they were in love with other people,* she'd said.

Lily would know how to play this.

"Wait. You're not going alone."

"I have to go now!"

"If you're going to do this," I snarled, "you're doing it on fucking camera, Dylan."

So it was a convoy of golf carts heading down the hill, loaded up with crew, all going as fast as they possibly could.

My mind was racing even faster. My grand plan was shot to pieces. How the fuck was I going to make this make sense on television?

I got the most romantic declaration of love scene I could have ever hoped for, so melodramatic it was like something out of a soap opera. Romeo-Dylan burst through the Convent doors and confessed his love to Cece. "I love you," he told her, "I love you, I love you, I love you, Cece."

Cece was so overwhelmed she fainted. Romeo-Dylan caught her in his arms like a princess, perfectly mirroring the first episode.

In the background, Amanda was sobbing. Lily caught my eye. Her whole face was alight.

"Nnngh," Cece groaned. She was stirring.

"Let me take her somewhere quiet," Romeo-Dylan said. "She needs a minute."

"Fine, fine, whatever." I needed a minute too.

"Where should we go?"

I stared at him. My brain was in overdrive. I didn't have space to figure out a single other thing.

"Down the hall," Lily said, gesturing. "It's quiet."

Romeo-Dylan nodded and disappeared, Cece in his arms.

God, I wanted to do the same with Lily. I wanted to pull her into some still, silent room so we could whiteboard our way through this. *You were right*, I would say. *I was wrong. I shouldn't have rigged the season, and now it's blown up in my face. You can gloat later. Right now, I need you to help me figure this out.*

But I didn't have that luxury. The Convent was filled with crew, all of whom needed my direction. The most I could manage was a quick whisper. "I need to get Dylan and Cece to stay on set to shoot pickups, if I'm going to turn this cluster-fuck into a watchable season of television," I murmured to Lily, curling my fingers around her wrist and jerking her into the kitchen when everyone was distracted. "And I need to find the money to do it."

"Copy that," she whispered back. "I'll help you get them there."

I loved her so much. She was going to be unbearably smug about this later, but I loved her so fucking much.

I gave Romeo-Dylan and Cece one more minute while the crew finished setting up, and then I practically beat down the door of the room he'd taken her to. It was a laundry, and Cece was sitting on top of the washing machine, arms and legs wrapped around Romeo-Dylan as she sobbed into his shoulder.

I almost laughed. Of course they were having some major emotional moment in their relationship in a laundry.

"For fuck's sake!" I exclaimed. "I don't have time for you two to fuck on the washing machine! Get out of there, both of you. Now. You've really fucked me over, and we have to work out how to fix it."

It wasn't hard to find my angriest, most terror-inducing producer voice. It required absolutely no pretence to let the fury and the frustration out instead of compartmentalising it away. Romeo-Dylan and Cece might actually have the fairytale love story I'd set out to create with the Dylans, but telling it was going to be an absolute mountain of work.

Despite my best efforts, I'd ended up exactly where I had with Brett and CJ and Mary-Ellen last year. I had to burn down everything I'd built and start again. I might get a great story, but it was going to be exhausting. *Exhausting.*

I would not be getting that sleep-in tomorrow.

"How long has this been going on?" I demanded.

I was pacing back and forward in front of the fireplace. Romeo-Dylan and Cece were sitting so close to each other on the couch they were practically in each other's laps, holding hands like one of them was about to fall off a cliff. Amanda and Heather were in armchairs, awkwardly third-wheeling,

329

while Lily perched on the arm of another one, third-wheeling much more elegantly.

"Um . . ." Cece said.

"Let me put it another way. When did you start fucking?"

"Don't yell at her," Romeo-Dylan said. "Yell at me all you want, but don't yell at her."

"I'm going to yell at both of you as much as I damn well please. Answer me. When did this start?"

I knew the answer perfectly well, but that didn't matter.

They needed to understand how angry I was—just how disastrous their choice was, for me and for the show—because the pressure point I was going to sink my thumbs into was guilt. The guiltier I could make them feel, the more I could make them do.

"Surely you can work that one out for yourself, Murray," Lily said, examining her fingernails. "Why do you think Cece snuck out that night? So they could go and play bridge?"

It was the perfect interjection. She'd figured out my ploy immediately. Reminding them of the huge favour I'd done them by letting them have their one night together would only compound their guilt at screwing me over.

I shoved away the impulse to fall at her feet. I'd do that later. "And it was that mind-blowingly good it made you break your contract?" I barked at Romeo-Dylan and Cece.

They both looked at the floor, saying nothing.

Then they looked at each other. One single, stolen glance.

It took a second. Maybe second and a half, as my brain cross-referenced that glance with the way Romeo-Dylan had behaved over the last couple of weeks, his increasing distraction and detachment, that ultimate decision to say *no*.

Then it added in the intimacy of the way they were sitting together now, hands clasped tight, physical intimacy communicating emotional intimacy.

Everything came into focus.

"It wasn't just once, was it," I said tightly.

"No," Romeo-Dylan admitted.

I pinched the bridge of my nose, hard.

How the hell had they pulled this off? This room was wired with cameras. I'd been through a lot of the footage personally, and someone had at least glanced at all of it. Explaining away the one night that I'd let Romeo-Dylan come here and take Cece away had been difficult. Someone absolutely would have told me if it had been going on every—

Oh.

Oh hell.

"Fuck me," I groaned.

There was only one person who could have masterminded this. One person who had *extensive* experience sneaking out of the Convent for sex purposes.

"Did you know about this?" I asked Lily.

In that moment, if a genie had appeared and given me one wish, it would have been for her to say no.

If it had given me another, it would have been for her to say no in a way I actually believed.

If it had given me a third, it would be to turn back time.

I would sacrifice sleeping with her. I would sacrifice ever having any kind of romantic relationship with her. If she wanted to marry fifty other Jeffs, I would be the best man at every one of her weddings, if it meant I could have Lily Ong back—the best friend who would never lie to me, the woman

I could trust implicitly, the partner who had my back the way I had hers.

The genie didn't appear. There was only Lily Fireball, perched on the arm of an ugly armchair, batting her eyelashes.

"You knew these two were undermining the whole show," I said, "and you didn't say a word to me?"

"I'm not your servant, Murray. You know that very well."

All those times she'd been in bed with me. All those times she'd helped me with my plans. All those times she'd elbowed me jokingly in the ribs and told me rigging the show was a bad idea.

All that time, *she'd known.*

"They didn't undermine the show."

"What?" I snapped.

It had been Amanda who'd spoken. "They didn't undermine the show. It's supposed to be about falling in love, isn't it? They fell in love."

I love you too, Lily had said to me, just this morning.

I had rigged this season in the first place because I wanted to make something perfect for her. My heart, laid on her doorstep.

And I had rigged it because I didn't know how to make something perfect without her, the other half of my brain.

She knew all of this. How high the stakes were. How hard I had flung myself into a wall of work, trying to make it come together.

She'd undercut me anyway.

I was willing to break myself into a million pieces for her. Go along with her awful, *awful* plan to turn herself into Lily Fireball. Have half a life with her, stolen moments in the dark, late at night. I loved her so much I would do anything—become anything—compromise on anything—if it meant keeping her.

She had told me she loved me, and then she'd *done this anyway.*

"That's not actually correct," I said tightly. "This show isn't about falling in love. It's about telling a love story the audience can believe."

"And who would believe he could fall in love with me, right?" Cece muttered.

"Shut up, Cece. I don't have time for you to get in your feelings about this."

"That's what you're saying, though! That I've ruined your perfect love story because no one would believe someone like Dylan would fall in love with someone like me?"

"That's not what I'm saying at all!"

I slapped my hand against the mantel. "I can tell a Cinderella story! That's the easiest story in the world to tell. People fucking love an underdog! But I don't have the right pieces!"

And I had told Lily that. More than once. Every time she told me it would be a better story to let the two couples that had fallen in love just be in love, I had told her why that wouldn't work.

She'd sat in bed with me, naked, whiteboarding out ways to get to my endgame, the endgame I'd broken myself in half trying to achieve—and all the while she'd been working against me.

"I'm not committing to Dyl." Romeo-Dylan's body was tense, like he might dive in front of Cece to take a bullet.

"She's great, don't get me wrong, but you can't make me shoot that scene, Murray. I won't do it."

"You are not in a position to tell me what you will and won't do right now." I only just resisted the urge to slap the mantel again. The sharp sting was overwhelmingly preferable to the crawling mass in my stomach. "You've broken your contract. You're going to be paying back a shit-ton of money."

"Don't yell at him!" Cece protested. "You think he made this decision lightly?"

"And you!" I snarled, furious that she'd clearly take a bullet for him too, that they'd known each other for six weeks and they'd already fucking figured everything out. "Don't get me started on you! 'Oh yes, Murray, I'll be your next Juliet, whatever you say, Murray!'"

"I'm sorry."

"Sorry doesn't help me, Cece!" I gave in to the urge and slapped the mantel again, sending a vase rattling dangerously close to the edge. "Your love might be pure and true and eternal or whatever the fuck you've been whispering to each other behind my back, but it doesn't give me a love story you can tell on TV!"

"So film one, dipshit," Lily said.

I glared at her.

"Don't pull that face, Murray, it doesn't work on me," she said. "There's no point in getting angry and hitting things when you could be finding a solution. If you don't have what you need to tell a love story between these two saps, then work out what you do need and film it."

I just kept glaring. If I spoke—if I said anything at all to her—I would never stop shouting.

"We all know the story is engineered anyway. Why not do a little more engineering? You two—" she waved a hand at Romeo-Dylan and Cece, "when did you first kiss?"

"After that date I accidentally won," Cece said. "Dylan walked me home, and . . ."

"That's easy enough." Lily didn't make her finish the sentence. "You could film that tonight, if you wanted. Just send them out on the verandah."

Lily Fireball had fallen away. This was Lily Ong, standing in front of a whiteboard.

It only made it worse.

"It wasn't on the verandah," Cece said. "It was up the hill a bit. Near the hedges."

"More *in* the hedges," Romeo-Dylan said, pressing his lips to her temple.

Lily blinked. She paused for a second longer than she normally would when she was in full flight, and her cheeks turned red. "Either way, very filmable."

The Murray of yesterday would have teased her mercilessly about that. Lily Ong was not a blusher. It took a lot to make her turn that colour.

That Murray felt very far away now.

"One kiss isn't enough," I forced out from between my teeth, because even now, even with everything, I still had to do my fucking job. "That was, what, episode seven? I've got to keep the plot alive for five more episodes."

"I'm sure you've got plenty of footage of Cece sitting

around here looking like a sad sack," Lily said. "Get some drone footage of her sneaking onto his boat. Some shaky-cam stuff of them kissing on the deck. Some audio of them moaning. I hope you two are loud lovers."

She was looking at me. *I'm sorry*, I could see in her eyes. *But—*

I looked away.

"Won't that make Dylan look like an absolute dick?" Cece was saying. "Dating all these other women while being with me?"

"That's exactly what he was doing, so if he comes across as a dick, that's fair," Lily said. "But if you cut that together with some soppy confessionals of you two going on about how perfect and wonderful your love is, and how you're being torn apart like a real-life Romeo and Juliet, the audience will eat that shit up. Am I right, or am I right, Murray?"

The most I could summon was a growl.

"I'm right," she said. "As usual."

Her tone was cheerful, but it was totally at odds with the pleading look in her eyes. *I'm sorry, Murray. But let me explain.*

I summoned every ounce of skill I had and closed my expression down. I wasn't going to give her the satisfaction of getting a single thing from me.

"You're both making my life extremely difficult," I said to Romeo-Dylan and Cece instead, turning my back on her. "I hope you know that."

27

Lily

Two years ago

"All right." Murray added in our last agenda item, then handed me his tablet. "Does this look good to you?"

I scanned the list quickly as our crew for Season Nine of *Marry Me, Juliet* began to file in for our pre-season briefing. "We should probably add a reminder about NDAs. I don't want us to kick off our first season as showrunners with a bunch of leaks to the press."

"Good idea." He took the tablet back. "Do you want to speak to it, or do you want me to?"

"You do it. We need to scare them. Use the daddy voice."

Murray gave me a withering look, but he didn't say anything.

Instead, he set the tablet down on our lectern and looked out at the room. "Do you remember our first one of these?"

"I'm amazed you do." I poked him in the shoulder. "You were so hungover the feedback screech from the microphone nearly made you throw up."

He chuckled. "That hangover was so bad it nearly made me give up drinking."

"I'm not surprised. Imagine being so drunk you couldn't remember meeting *me*."

Murray didn't say anything.

"What?"

"I might," he said, "have been a little less than truthful about that."

I blinked.

"Not that I was lying, exactly," he said. "I don't remember speaking to you that night. But I remember seeing you, sitting there on the other side of the bar. Noticing you."

In the grand scale of revelations, this wasn't much of one. *Can you embellish?* I would ask a Romeo who had just revealed he'd once noticed a Juliet across a bar. *That's too subtle, as a storytelling beat.*

It absolutely floored me.

He'd been in that bar—the bar that was now Jeff's—eleven years ago. He'd been sitting there with his friends—with his *fiancée*, god, Julia had been there!—talking and laughing and listening and drinking: and he'd noticed me.

And he'd never mentioned it. For more than a decade, he'd kept this from me.

Of course he hadn't mentioned it. What was Murray of Murray-and-Julia going to do, mention to his new female friend he remembered noticing her across a bar, and make things weird before they even began? And what was Murray-after-Julia going to do, casually tell me out of nowhere—a Lily who was now half of Lily-and-Jeff!—that he'd actually clocked me a full twelve hours earlier than I'd thought?

What difference would it have made?

"Of course you noticed me," I said, before the silence turned into a question. "I know how you feel about red lipstick."

Murray rolled his eyes. "Oh, shut up."

The room was almost full now, the last few stragglers making their way in. "Should we get started?" I asked, jamming my thumb hard into the diamond of my engagement ring, grinding it against my wedding band

"Sure." He stabbed at the tablet so the screen didn't fall asleep, and then stepped away from the lectern. "After you."

Later that night, I did one last walkthrough of the Villa, doing final checks before filming started tomorrow.

There wasn't much to check. We'd filmed in this particular Villa for several years now, so all the problematic edges had long since been smoothed away. "I know everything is fine," I'd told Murray. "But now that we're in charge, I just want to make extra sure."

"Do you want me to stay? Do it with you?"

I shook my head. "Go get some sleep. I've got this."

My footsteps echoed on the floorboards as I walked through. I straightened a few blankets on a few bunk beds. I checked the bathroom cupboards, made sure there were some emergency toiletries for the women who forgot things. I made sure the kitchen had the basics, that the grocery order list was on the bench. I straightened some cushions in the living room, bringing forward the most romantic-coded colours.

I went into the laundry.

There was nothing exciting about it. Nothing at all. The cupboards were stocked with detergent and fabric softener. There were some spare towels, for when some inevitably got ruined by makeup. All was well.

Our washing machine was still in the same place. Unchanged. Immovable.

I folded my fingers around its edges, gripping it so tightly my knuckles turned white, my engagement and wedding rings pressing uncomfortably into my finger.

I loved Jeff. I was happy with him. The thought of being without him was unspeakable.

And Murray was happy too. He was dating someone again, a redhead whose name I kept forgetting because I got distracted by her laugh. I was sure part of him still missed Julia, but he was happy.

But if I'd listened to him that day—*I care about you too, Lily. So much. What about this felt like we were ruining anything?*—if I hadn't been so scared and overwhelmed by how *much* it all was—if I hadn't been so petrified that I'd lose him, so terrified that I'd fuck up something which had proved over and over again to be unfuckuppable . . .

Murray O'Connell might have loved me forever.

28

Murray

Hours later, I sat alone on the Convent steps, staring out into the night sky.

Maybe one day I'd be able to look back on this day and think of it as a success. A clusterfuck, but a success.

I was going to produce the most talked-about season in the history of the Romeo and Juliet franchise. The star-crossed surprise twist of Romeo-Dylan falling in love with the woman he friendzoned in Episode One was going to be jaw-dropping television.

On top of that, Juliet-Dylan had turned up at the Convent a while later and declared her love to Amanda. I was going to get two incredibly romantic, wholesome, marketable couples out of this. Two beautiful love stories, unlike anything the show had ever done before.

And I had the time and money I needed to actually tell them. I'd had a long conversation with Fucking Greg and the network lawyers and got it worked out. Because Romeo-Dylan had broken his contract, he had to pay back his appearance fee. I was going to keep him, Cece, Juliet-Dylan and Amanda here for a couple of weeks, and use the money from his fee to pay some select crew members to do reshoots.

"Can you make sure Dyl still gets paid, though?" Romeo-Dylan had asked me anxiously. "I don't need the money. She does. I'll pay it out of my own pocket if I have to."

"Fine, fine," I'd replied.

His fee was large enough that his pocket was safe, though. There was even a little money left over, which I earmarked as a bonus for Amanda. She'd earned it, after what I'd done to her.

The four of them were in bed now. Romeo-Dylan and Cece had gone back to his boat. Juliet-Dylan and Amanda had gone back to the Villa. "Reshoots will start early tomorrow," I'd told them tersely. "I can only afford to keep one makeup artist here, so no fucking all night and ending up with eyebags. Get some sleep."

I should go to bed too. I had more long days and long nights ahead of me, with little respite.

But there was no point. There wasn't much difference between staring at the stars and staring at the ceiling.

"Hi," Lily said softly.

She sat down on the step beside me, skirt brushing my leg. "Quite a night."

I didn't reply.

"Do you remember when we first started out? On *Desert Island Castaway*? When we'd do those night shoots, and we'd sit together like this?"

I didn't say anything.

"I know you're angry with me, Murray. But don't shut me out. Please."

"Why not?" I said. "You did it to me."

She paused before she spoke again. Less a hesitation, more an absorption of a blow.

"I deserve that."

"Yes. You do."

Another pause.

"I should have told you, when Cece asked me to help her sneak out to see Dylan again," she said. "I nearly did. Several times. But you were so caught up in your vision for the show that I knew you'd find a way to stop her."

"And what a tragedy that would have been. Two young, attractive people, who might have had to wait a while to hook up. Disaster."

"Do you know what one of the biggest regrets of my life is?"

I cracked. I looked at her.

"Running away from you, that day in the laundry," she said. "It—you—made me feel so much. It was so big. So overwhelming. I got scared. I bundled it all up and I locked it away, because it was so . . . much."

She sighed. "Then there was Cece. Doing the opposite. Running towards something, even though it was probably going to end in disaster, and I just thought—what was the point? What was the point of everything I've ever done, every mistake I've ever made, if I couldn't help someone be braver than I was?"

I didn't respond.

"Plus, judging by everything you said about how committed everyone was to the plan, I thought I was just helping them get a headstart on a secret relationship." She smiled weakly. "And if it did blow up, well . . . better story, right?"

On cue, my eye started twitching.

"Sorry. I'm not trying to one-up you or anything. Even though I *am* right."

"Lily."

"Sorry."

I stood up. I needed space from her if I was going to be able to think clearly.

"When you walked into that hotel room six weeks ago," I said, "and you were wearing that ridiculous yellow dress, I just about had a heart attack."

"I know. I'm sorry."

"I heard you before I saw you. I was looking at my tablet, and I said something to the PA. I got his name wrong, and you told me off."

"I can apologise for that too, if you want."

"Lily, do you know the first thing I thought when I heard your voice? Before anything else sank in?"

I looked down at her. She shook her head.

"I thought, *oh thank god.*"

I took a few steps and then turned around to face her again. "It was relief," I said. "Before everything else, it was relief, because I thought I had you back again."

She stood up too. "You do."

"No, I don't."

She fell silent.

"I always listen to you," I said. "I might not always agree with you, but I listen. You have had my absolute trust, the whole time we've known each other."

Tears were beading at the corner of her eyes. She knew me well enough to know what I was going to say next.

"But you don't give it back." I did my best to keep my voice steady, but it wasn't working. "It isn't just this. It isn't just that you undermined my plan for the show. It's everything. Everything that you've been doing to me, over and over again, since you came back. You don't listen to me. You keep things from me. You—you lie to me."

The first tear fell down her cheek.

"I thought you were my partner," I said. "I would have done anything for that to be true. *Anything*. Even go along with you turning yourself into Lily Fireball, even though I hate it more than anything else in the fucking world. I would have filed down every one of my hard edges for you. Every single one."

The words made a visible impact on her. The worst parts of me were viciously glad of it. Let her feel it. Let her feel even a little bit of what she'd made me feel.

"But you couldn't do this one thing for me," I said. "There was only one thing I asked of you, Lily. Let me do my job. Even if you refused to help me do it—just don't stand in my way. Don't make my life any harder. And you couldn't even do that."

I ran a hand through my hair, tugging at the ends. "I've been so worried that I've been helping you burn your life down," I said. "But you just cavalierly burned down everything I was trying to build here without a second fucking thought."

"Please." She choked on the word. "Just—let me fix it, Murray. We've got a couple of weeks here. Let me help you put it back together."

I shook my head. "The limo's coming back in the morning. You're leaving."

More tears spilled down her cheeks. "Murray, please."

"I love you," I said. "But I need you to listen to me this time. I need you to do things on my terms for once. I need you to trust me when I tell you I need time and space to figure this out."

29

Lily

One year ago

After Jeff died, I did nothing. I just sat, and felt.

It went against every instinct I had. Everything in me was screaming at me that I should pack those feelings away like I was packing away all of Jeff's things, close them up in a box and relegate them to the darkest, dustiest corner of the vault, one where I would never have to think about them ever again.

But I didn't. I sat on the couch, hugging the cushion he'd had made for me as a joke gift for our first anniversary, the one that had *Are you ready to be brave?* embroidered on it, and I made myself feel it all.

I made myself feel the grief. I made myself feel the pain. I made myself feel the aching absence in my heart and in my life where he had been, the void of a future without him in it.

I made myself feel the guilt.

Thank god it wasn't Murray. Thank god I didn't lose Murray. I couldn't survive losing Murray.

"Are you familiar with the five stages of grief?" asked a therapist Thuong had bullied me into going to see. "One of those stages is bargaining."

"I know," I said, annoyed by her condescending tone. "But this is not the direction you're supposed to bargain in. I should have been offering to trade Murray for Jeff, not the other way around."

"Sometimes our minds work in strange ways. What if this is one of your brain's defence mechanisms?"

"Like, my subconscious is trying to protect me by convincing me that things could actually be a lot worse?"

"Just a thought," she said gently.

I didn't go back. She was wildly misreading what I was telling her, wildly misreading me.

I didn't want solace. I didn't want comfort. I didn't want to *feel better*.

I needed to suffer.

I'd married a man I loved—but I'd known perfectly well there was someone else I loved more. And now Jeff was dead, and there was no way I could ever make it up to him.

"Is there anyone else you could talk to who's been through the loss of a spouse?" another therapist asked me. "Someone else who's been widowed? Or even divorced?"

I started laughing.

"Tell me why that's funny, Lily."

"Murray," I said. "Murray's divorced."

"Let's talk about Murray some more. Depriving yourself of what sounds like a key person in your support system at a time like this isn't a great idea. So tell me why you can't contact him."

"Because I owe him that."

"Murray?"

"No. Jeff."

I didn't go back to that therapist either. At Thuong's urging, I tried a couple more, but eventually I gave up. What was I hoping to get out of this anyway? An official diagnosis that I was a bad person? I knew that already.

I first heard about what Murray had pulled off via one of the industry newsletters I was still subscribed to. *Season Eleven to be first ever season of* Marry Me, Juliet *to feature diverse lead,* was the headline (disappointingly but unsurprisingly, they still hadn't figured out that one individual person couldn't be "diverse"). Most of the article was focused on the casting, but there was one little line buried in the penultimate paragraph: *Murray O'Connell to serve as showrunner.*

It was the first time I'd ever seen his name in an industry publication without mine. They were always together: *Ong and O'Connell move to the Romeo and Juliet franchise*; *Ong and O'Connell promoted to senior producers*; *Ong and O'Connell replace Tony Spitieri at helm of Romeo and Juliet shows.*

It made something inside me ache.

And then it started to itch.

I hugged Jeff's stupid *Are you ready to be brave?* cushion tighter and tighter to me, but it itched and it itched and it itched.

We'd worked so hard to get this season off the ground. The thought of not having a hand in it—not being able to help Murray with all that heavy lifting . . .

Was there a way I could manage it? If I drew some very clear lines—maintained some very aggressive boundaries—could I go back? Even if it was just for one last ride?

The plan came together when I was going through some invoices for the bar. Jeff's brother Nathan and I had each inherited half, and while he had taken over the day-to-day, I still had to sign off on a lot of things.

One of them was an invoice for Fireball whiskey, and for the first time in a long time, a memory of Jeff made me smile. He'd spent so long trying to get me to like whiskey, and he'd been disgusted that Fireball was the only one I would drink. "You're not a whiskey-drinker if you only drink this," he'd grumbled.

Then the words on the invoice blurred as some switch flipped in my brain.

If I could drink Fireball and not be a whiskey-drinker—could I still somehow help produce Season Eleven and not be a producer?

The flowchart unfolded.

Murray was going to hate it.

That was okay, though. It was better that he hated it. That would help me keep the lines clear. The Rubicon was not to be crossed. I owed Jeff that much.

I scrolled through my phone and found Fucking Greg's number. "Hi Greg!" I said, using my brightest, smiliest, most sunshine-y tone, the one that he was always vulnerable to. "It's Lily Ong here. I've got a proposition for you."

30

Lily
After

After Murray sent me away, I made myself keep busy. If I stopped for even a single second, I would crumble.

The first couple of months were the hardest, before Season Eleven went to air and performing Lily Fireball every time I was in public became a full-time job. I was the same amount of single I had been the previous year—no Jeff, no Murray—but now it felt crushing, like the walls of the world were closing in.

I took a more active interest in the behind-the-scenes running of the bar and our new door-to-door alcohol delivery service (much to the chagrin of Nathan, who I suspected was eventually hoping to buy me out). I finally finished cleaning out the house. When lockdown restrictions allowed, I visited Thuong and my brother and my baby niece. I finally let my mother attempt to teach me how to cook. I developed Lily Fireball's social media, so it was there as a launchpad once the season premiered, and helped Cece with hers on the side.

Nathan wanted me to host *Marry Me, Juliet* viewing parties at the bar—"If you're going to be famous, Lily, we might as well leverage it, get us back on the map now we can have customers again"—but I said no. I needed to watch it alone.

It was obvious to me, after I watched the first episode, curled up on my couch with the *Are you ready to be brave?* cushion hugged to my chest, that Murray had created a masterpiece.

I already knew it would be good. I'd been there, after all, antagonising girl-Dylan and shoving Cece into the pool. But what he'd put together was . . . well, it was a clear indication that Murray O'Connell was a fucking genius.

The way he'd drawn out boy-Dylan, emphasising his kindness and his emotional literacy. The way he'd drawn out the women, too, ensuring they came across as people rather than caricatures. The seeds he'd planted for the love stories that I knew were to come: the stolen looks between Amanda and girl-Dylan, boy-Dylan hero-carrying Cece down the hill.

There wasn't much in the first episode that jumped out to me as a pickup he'd filmed after the fact—one ITM with Amanda where she said she was bisexual, that was about it—but they became more obvious as the season went on, especially after the hurdle of the Heather episodes (something which coincided with a substantial amount of the abuse in Lily Fireball's DMs turning into messages of support, although the general levels of racism stayed about the same). He'd shot little conversations here and there between Amanda and girl-Dylan that slowly turned into pleas from Amanda that girl-Dylan leave the show with her.

Then there was boy-Dylan and Cece, hugging a little too long, having trouble letting go. Murray had utilised the security-camera feel of the mounted cams perfectly. I might know that the two couples were perfectly aware they were being filmed—but no one else would have a clue.

And then, in Episode Nine, one episode after Lily Fireball departed, declaring to the Dylans that they weren't right for each other, Murray dropped the hammer. He shot a conversation between boy-Dylan and girl-Dylan through trees, to give the feeling of a spy-cam, where they revealed that they'd both signed contracts, and the show was rigged.

It was breathtaking, game-changing television. He'd cast aside the usual question we asked—"Who will the Romeo fall in love with?"—and replaced it with the much more interesting "How can these two couples ever be together?." All our usual obstacles (time, distance, other people) were replaced with the whole commercial enterprise of reality TV itself, trying to force the Dylans together: and keep the real lovers apart.

I got a call from Fucking Greg the day after Episode Ten aired. "I'm going to say the same thing to you that you said to me," he announced, sounding very satisfied with himself. "I've got a proposition for you."

"All right," I said. "I'm listening."

"Two propositions for you, actually. One, we want you to co-host one of our big finale parties. The Romeo and his girlfriend will be doing one, and we want you to do the other one, with the Japanese Juliet and the lesbians."

I rolled my eyes—*Fucking Greg*—and then did the calculations. Given boy-Dylan was the star of the season, they'd almost certainly send Murray with him and Cece, so I'd still be keeping my promise to give him time and space. "Okay."

"And then the second . . ."

My heart started beating faster as he told me. And faster. And faster.

I should say no. It was the opposite of giving Murray time and space. The opposite of doing things on his terms.

But then my eyes fell on that stupid cushion. *Are you ready to be brave?*

No more hiding, Murray had told me, that day in the rain when he'd given me a choice between filming my ITM or him taking my dress off with his teeth. *No more kissing me and running away. Tell me what you want.*

I'd been brave then, but it was an outlier. Every other time when things had become too intense, I'd run.

But that one time I'd been brave? When I'd finally cracked and crossed the Rubicon?

It had paid off. I might have sabotaged it swiftly afterwards, but it had *worked*.

I could be brave again. Instead of fleeing, I could stand. I could fight.

"I love that idea," I purred at Greg.

31

Murray

I didn't see Lily for five months.

I spent the first two and a half months on set—first, doing reshoots with my two sets of star-crossed lovers so we could patch the story holes; and then shooting a new season of *Wherefore Art Thou Romeo?*, starring Kumiko.

The pandemic protocols weren't as strict as they had been for Romeo-Dylan's season, but they weren't exactly loose either, so we were still operating in a bubble with vastly reduced crew numbers. Consequently, my workload was enormous, but I didn't mind. The more I had to work, the less time I had to stare at the ceiling.

The premiere of Romeo-Dylan's season aired about a month after we'd wrapped shooting on Kumiko's. It rated through the fucking roof.

Typically, in a season of a Romeo and Juliet show, ratings went down after the premiere, as viewers fell away or got bored.

Our ratings went up.

We'd moved beyond being a ratings success story. We'd moved beyond high social media engagement. We started getting coverage in major media outlets. We'd become a cultural phenomenon.

In finale week, Fucking Greg called me into his office. "O'Connell!" he roared, ignoring the elbow I'd offered him to bump and practically yanking my shoulder out of its socket in his ferocious desire to shake my hand. "The man of the moment!"

I extricated myself as politely as possible. "Hi, Greg."

"Just watched the second draft of the *Wherefore* finale you sent through. I didn't think you'd be able to top the *MMJ* twist, but mate—you're damn close. Close the door, would you?"

I did.

"I've got two things I want to run by you." He leaned back in his office chair. "But before I do: well done, O'Connell. What you've pulled off here is pretty fucking incredible."

"Thank you."

"So let's talk future plans. Thing number one: we've been having some chats around here about *Juliet on the Beach*. The pandemic means we can't fly the contestants out to the island like we normally would. We could shoot local, of course, but everyone's been trapped in their fucking houses. They don't want local."

"I've actually got a plan for that." I opened the folder I'd brought with me. "I was thinking—"

"Trust me, I've got a better plan. Check this out."

He turned his computer monitor around to face me. I had to stamp down very, *very* hard to keep my expression in check.

It was a *Wherefore Art Thou Romeo?* concept poster. *Love is an inferno* was the tagline at the top, emblazoned above a picture of Lily, lips curved in that infuriating Lily Fireball half-smile.

"Instead of *Juliet on the Beach,* we double up on *Wherefore* this year," Greg said. "And we capitalise on the momentum of this season of *MMJ.*"

My mouth had gone completely dry.

"Didn't I tell you this spicy meatball would make things happen for us?" He waved at the picture of Lily. "She's already signed on. It's going to be fantastic."

She'd already signed on? She'd already *fucking signed on*?!

"The work you've done has been stellar, O'Connell. That leads me to the second thing I want to run by you."

He slid a stack of paperwork across the desk to me.

I scanned the top sheet quickly, and blinked. "A development deal?"

"The Romeo and Juliet shows are the jewel in the crown of our unscripted programming," Greg said. "But we need more jewels. We need that whole crown to be really fucking shiny. That's where you come in."

He tapped the contract. "You've proven that you've got what it takes to make a show a hit. So how would you feel about moving out of the Romeo and Juliet world and developing some new shows from the ground up?"

I could barely believe what I was hearing.

It was everything Lily and I had never even dared to dream of. A season of TV like Romeo-Dylan's could change a conversation, but it was still only one season.

A deal like this? Developing whole new formats?

That could change the whole fucking *game*.

"I need to read the terms, of course," I said, "but I'm interested."

"Great!" Greg said. "We'll have you film this one last season of *Wherefore* so you can get Suzette prepped to take over from you, and—"

"No."

"No?" He raised his eyebrows.

"Suzette doesn't need any training. A lot of the great shit that happened on Kumiko's season was her, not me. And besides . . ."

My mouth was dry again. I swallowed reflexively.

"Besides," I repeated, "Lily knows what she's doing."

For the finale, the network threw huge viewing parties in two major cities. One was hosted by Romeo-Dylan, Ceçe, and Z. The other was hosted by Juliet-Dylan, Amanda, Kumiko—and Lily.

I tried desperately to get Suzette to swap supervising duties with me, but geographically, it didn't make sense. Her mother was sick, and she was in hospital right near the venue for Romeo-Dylan and Cece's party. Given Suzette would soon be locked away in the bubble shooting the next season of *Wherefore*, even I wasn't heartless enough to begrudge her the opportunity to spend time with her mother.

So I laced up my boots, buckled on my utility belt, slid my earpiece in, and sucked it up to supervise the other party. The show was so popular that the four women would probably be mobbed by fans. If I was careful, I'd barely have to interact with Lily at all.

The first thing I saw when I entered the venue was her. There were cardboard cut-outs of the four women hosting the event right near the doorway, and hers was first in line.

She was wearing the red dress. The one I'd taken off her with my teeth.

What would happen if I turned on my heel and just walked back out again?

My radio squawked. "Murray, Amanda and Dylan G have arrived, but there's press at all the entrances," someone said in my earpiece. "How should we proceed?"

"They came together?!" I said, grateful for the distraction. "Fucking hell. We can't let the paps get a shot of them before the finale airs. Make Amanda get out of the car and come in, then get the limo to head back to the depot. Get them to change cars before they bring Dylan G back."

"Copy that."

I threw myself hard into keeping Amanda and Juliet-Dylan apart. If I focused on that, I didn't have to think about anything else. "We *cannot* let the ending be spoiled before the episode airs," I growled at both of them, once they were safely inside the building and ensconced in the private VIP area. "You two will be on your best behaviour. Do I make myself clear?"

"Yes," Amanda said.

"Could you settle down about it, though?" Juliet-Dylan said. "Not to rain on your parade, but I think the audience have figured out that we're kind of into each other."

"Only kind of?" Amanda said, playfully nudging Juliet-Dylan with her shoulder.

Juliet-Dylan grinned and pecked her on the lips. "Love you, babe."

"This is the kind of shit I'm talking about!" I exploded. "You've been here two seconds and you're already wearing each other's lipstick! I want you on opposite sides of the room at all times until the episode is over."

I managed to avoid Lily for the first two hours of the event, when the women were doing meet-and-greets with fans. "I'll look after Amanda and Kumiko," I told the PAs. "Tim, you're with Dylan G; Tom, you're with Lily."

I knew she was there. I could feel her. You could put me blindfolded into a crowd of a million people and I would be able to tell you where Lily Ong was.

But I didn't speak to her until five minutes before the beginning of the finale.

The four women were going to introduce and then do a New Year's-style countdown to the start of the episode. I'd got Tim and Tom to run point on getting them sorted, figuring that lining up a few intelligent women in front of some charity banners was not exactly a task that required my expertise.

I was wrong.

"Tim, split Amanda and Dylan G up," I said into my headset, watching them from across the room. "Put them on opposite ends of the line. Their couple vibes are too strong."

He didn't reply.

"Tim!"

Nothing.

"Tom!"

Nothing again.

People were starting to filter from the meet-and-greet space into the viewing space. Shit.

I was in motion before my brain had really caught up with me. "For fuck's sake," I barked, glaring at Amanda and Juliet-Dylan. "You two can't stand together! It'll give away the ending. Kumiko, Lily, you're in the middle."

"So you're speaking to me now?"

Involuntarily, I met Lily's eyes.

She was wearing white tonight, a spangly, sparkly confection the colour of moonlight that it had been incredibly hard not to stare at from the other side of the room. It was backless, and her hair was loose, a long silky curtain slipping down her bare skin.

I wanted to wrap my hand in that hair and pull her to me and never let go.

I wanted to turn on my heel and run out of the room and never stop running.

She looked away first, muttering something under her breath that I didn't catch. My heart felt like a stone in my chest.

What the fuck was I supposed to do?

It wasn't the first time I'd asked myself that question over the past five months. Or the hundredth. Or the thousandth. I'd gone over it, again and again and again. But there wasn't a whiteboard on earth that would help me flowchart my way out of this one.

I loved her. I would never stop loving her. That was a fact. Nothing would, or could, ever change it.

But I couldn't trust her.

Her dramatic instincts had been better than mine. The story we'd ended up telling, about our two pairs of lovers fighting the reality TV juggernaut to be together, was much better than the one I'd planned about the Dylans. And, as a bonus, it had created two couples who were probably going to go the distance.

That she'd been right about the story, I could admit. And maybe, in the time and space I'd asked from her, I could have forgiven the fact that she'd kept things from me. That she'd undermined my plan.

What was I supposed to do, though, with the fact that she'd signed on to *Wherefore Art Thou Romeo?*? Without even consulting me?

I knew exactly what she'd say, if I confronted her about it. *I consulted you,* she'd say. *We talked about my five-year plan, remember?*

There, though, was precisely the problem.

She talked.

I listened.

It wasn't a consultation. It wasn't a relationship. It wasn't a partnership, not anymore, not like the one we'd had.

I'd spent a lot of time shoving things down and pretending it wasn't true, but that partnership had died when Lily Fireball was born.

Lily Fireball did whatever the fuck she wanted. And the only choice I had left was whether I was willing to be walked all over.

She found me later. Of course she did. Lily Ong was the queen of avoidance, but she never let anyone else get away with it.

"I brought you something," she said.

I was sitting at one of the tables in the private VIP area we'd sectioned off for the four women to escape to if the fans got too intense. I had my eyes closed, leaning my head back against the wall, but I opened them in time to see Lily set down a silver tray.

"I made a bespoke Murray O'Connell canape tray," she said. "I've been chasing the waiters around for the last half an hour, trying to get all the ones I thought you'd like."

It was an impressive effort. She'd collected nine different kinds.

"I know you probably haven't eaten all day." She nudged the tray towards me. "So even if you won't talk to me— please eat."

I picked up an arancini ball. "Thank you."

"You're welcome."

It was lukewarm, but delicious. The tiny taste made me ravenous. It was hard to resist the urge to grab canapes by the fistful and stuff them down my throat.

"The show turned out brilliantly," Lily said. "Congratulations."

I picked up a baby asparagus spear wrapped in prosciutto. "It was a team effort."

"I heard you pulled off a huge twist in Kumiko's season too."

I took a bite, mostly to give myself an excuse not to say anything.

"Please talk to me," she said quietly. "Please."

I swallowed, wiping my fingers on a napkin. "What do you want me to say?"

"Anything!" she said. "I've been giving you time, and I've been giving you space, and—I know I made you wait twice as long when I asked for the same thing from you, but it's fucking killing me, Murray."

"It doesn't show. You look beautiful."

She made a sound that was at the intersection of laugh, sob, and scoff. "That is the worst compliment you've ever given me."

I didn't reply.

There was a cheer from outside. "I love you," I could hear Dylan JM saying on the screen. "I love you, I love you, I love you, Cece."

"You should get back out there," I said. "Your official *Wherefore* reveal segment is right after this ad break."

She stood. "All right. If you're not ready to talk to me yet, that's fine. I love you. Take your time."

"Thank you for the canapes."

She closed her eyes for a moment and took a deep breath. I could see her pulling Lily Fireball on like a suit of armour.

When she opened them again, the glint was back. "Besides," she said airily, "good luck avoiding me when we're locked away on set for another six weeks. I'll crack you, Murray O'Connell. Just you wait."

"I won't be there."

She went completely still.

It wasn't the same way she normally went still, like a lioness before it pounced on a gazelle. She froze completely in place, as if she'd suddenly been turned into a statue.

"What?" she said faintly.

"I won't be there. Suzette is the new showrunner. I'm moving on."

"To where?"

"Your segment's about to start."

"To where, Murray?!"

"This is what you wanted, Lily," I said, as the return-from-ad music began to play. "Go and do your fucking job."

Two weeks after the finale aired, we shot a live reunion special. We hadn't done one for years—not since the very early seasons of the show, before I'd even joined it—but Fucking Greg was determined to milk the success for all it was worth. "This has been a groundbreaking season of television," he told me. "We've got to really hang a lampshade on that."

This, from the same man who'd said *Go woke, go broke* to me on at least eighteen separate occasions.

The reunion show also marked my last day working on the Romeo and Juliet shows before I transitioned fully to my new role. "All right," I said, standing backstage, studiously not looking at Lily as I addressed my six key characters. "We're going to begin with Z talking with all our bit players, before we bring Dylan JM out. I'm sure there'll be a few curly questions in there for you, Dylan—especially about the rigging—but it shouldn't be anything that you can't handle."

"That's fine," Romeo-Dylan said. "As long as you didn't invite Heather."

"Of course not. But you might get questions about it, so make sure you're prepared for that."

"No problems."

"Then we'll bring Cece out, and have Z interview you two," I went on, "before we swap you out for Amanda and Dylan G. Same deal, we'll have him interview you two, and then we'll bring Cece and Dylan JM back out and have Z talk to all four of you together. All good?"

"All good," Juliet-Dylan said.

"In storytelling terms, we need to do two things. We need to reinforce the happy ending, and we need to tease some new information. So I want you to talk about how happy you are—"

"Won't be hard," Amanda said, pecking Juliet-Dylan on the cheek.

"—but also reveal a new milestone. Cece, you can talk about how you and your friends have moved in with Dylan JM. Amanda, maybe talk about meeting Dylan G's kid."

They both nodded.

"Then we'll wrap this segment by talking about your new show." I gestured to the Dylans. "We've got a thirty-second teaser trailer ready to play."

The Dylans' show was the first piece of programming I'd developed in my new role. It was a six-part limited reality series on health and wellness, with vaguely the same sort of feel-good format and vibe as Queer Eye. Juliet-Dylan was focusing on physical health, and Romeo-Dylan on mental health, with an overall emphasis on connection and finding community in the wake of the pandemic. "Looks like we get to work together after all," Juliet-Dylan had said when we signed the contracts. Romeo-Dylan had laughed and said, "And we finally get to tell that story about how people can be friends without falling in love."

"After the trailer, you four are done, we'll move on to focus on teasing *Wherefore*," I said. "Kumiko, I know it's going to be hard, but I want you to talk to Z about how there's a huge twist in your season without giving even the slightest hint of what it is. Can you do that?"

"Yes," Kumiko said. "I'm a lawyer, remember? I can mince my words."

"Can you tell *us* what the twist is, though?" Juliet-Dylan said. "I feel completely out of the loop."

"No, she can't," I said. "I'm trusting that as a lawyer, Kumiko, you'll know better than everyone else here how dangerous it is to play fast and loose with your NDA."

Kumiko gave me a mock salute. Juliet-Dylan rolled her eyes.

"Then we'll finish the show by teasing Lily's season. All good?"

"Wait," Lily said. "What do you want me to say?" There was a look in her eyes I would have read as vulnerability if I didn't know her better.

"That," I said, "you can go over with Suzette. Any other questions?"

There weren't any.

"Good. Then my work is done."

That statement was about eighty per cent true. I still had my earpiece in, so technically, I was still on the clock.

However, the show was live, so Z was driving the bus, not me. Unless something went horribly wrong, all I had to do was sit back and watch.

Nothing went horribly wrong.

As predicted, the women asked a few hard questions of Romeo-Dylan ("How could you lead us on like that?"

Parisa asked, "given you already knew who was going to win?"), but he navigated them adeptly, mostly by apologising. The audience cooed delightedly at him and Cece together, even more delightedly at Amanda and Juliet-Dylan together, and reached a fever pitch of delightedness at the four of them together.

"The four of us are very close friends," Romeo-Dylan said, one hand holding Cece's, the other patting Juliet-Dylan affectionately on the shoulder. "There aren't many people out there who could possibly understand what we went through. Now that we can finally be seen together in public, we'll probably double date a lot."

That reveal made the audience *scream*. The trailer for the Dylans' new show was just the icing on the cake.

Kumiko was as good as her word, and was tight-lipped about the events of her season. "Oh come on, you have to give us *something*," Z said playfully. "Please. I'm begging you."

"You're a smart man, Mr Zelig. You've worked on these shows a long time. You know what would happen to me if I spoiled the ending."

He leaned in closer, conspiratorially. "It wasn't . . . rigged, was it?"

Kumiko laughed. "Here's something I can tell you: if there's one thing that the ending of my season will make abundantly clear, it's that it wasn't rigged."

"Tell Kumiko I said good job," I murmured into my headset, when we cut away to ads. "She nailed it."

"Copy that," Suzette said.

I meant it. Kumiko might have become the lead of *Wherefore* by default, after Cece and Amanda and Juliet-Dylan all so firmly took themselves off the board, but she had been incredible to work with: all the ease and charm and warmth of Romeo-Dylan with only a tenth of his need for reassurance. People were going to go wild for her season. After all the years I'd spent working on this franchise, I was glad to be leaving on a high note.

There was a flicker in my peripheral vision. Lily had moved to her mark on the side of the stage, ready to enter after the ad break. She was looking at the floor, a slight furrow between her eyebrows.

I loved her so much.

I couldn't be with her. I knew that. I wanted a partner—professionally and personally—but when Jeff had died and she'd drawn that line between us, she'd made that impossible.

For those glorious few weeks on set, I'd fooled myself into thinking we could fit our hard, jagged edges together. That we could click into place like puzzle pieces, find our old dynamic again somehow, even if it didn't look quite the same, but . . . well. Here we were.

Or rather, here I was, on this side of the camera; and there she was, on that one.

She was only a few steps away. Steps I could not make.

I still loved her so fucking much.

"Ten seconds until we're back," came through my earpiece.

"Copy that."

It wasn't something I really needed to acknowledge, but this was my last ever segment as the working showrunner. It shouldn't pass without recognition.

"It was the surprise announcement that took the nation by storm," Z said, looking down the barrel of the camera.

"When we first met her, we thought she was a villain, but she soon revealed she was so much more than that. She's the diva that stole all our hearts, and very soon, she'll be walking into the Villa as the Juliet on her very own season of *Wherefore Art Thou Romeo?*—please give your firiest warm welcome to Lily Fireball!"

The cheer from the audience was so loud I almost laughed. They might love her almost as much as I did.

"Hello, Z," Lily said, arranging her long skirts elegantly around her on the chair opposite his. "It's been a while."

"And yet it only feels like five minutes."

"Really? It's felt like ages to me."

Classic Lily, getting someone off balance right at the beginning of a conversation.

But Z was a pro, and he recovered quickly. "I'm sure it's been a massive change for you, this new level of fame and recognition. Tell us what's that been like."

"Well, I was prepared," Lily said. "After so many years working behind the scenes on the Romeo and Juliet shows, I knew what I was getting myself into."

My heart flipped over in my chest.

So, apparently, had Z's. The initial jolt had done nothing, but now he was staring at Lily in shock.

"I know you usually ask the questions, but how about I ask one?" Lily said pleasantly. "You and I have known each other for—what, nearly a decade, Z? How did *you* feel, when I walked onto the set pretending to be twenty-five and calling myself Lily Fireball?"

There was a burst of chatter in my earpiece. I ripped it out.

"I—I, uh, was definitely surprised," Z said.

"How about I introduce myself?" Lily said, tone completely even and calm.

Z just nodded. His finger crept up to his earpiece.

I put mine back in. "Don't anyone dare interrupt this," I growled, then ripped it out again.

"My name is Lily Ong," Lily said. "I turn thirty-six next week, and I've been working in reality TV for almost fourteen years."

Shocked murmurs and gasps came from the audience.

"This has been a season of twists and turns," Z said. "I suppose we should have expected one last twist."

He touched his earpiece again—a rookie mistake from him, I noted in the one part of my brain still functioning, he was normally much too professional to alert the audience to its presence. "We all know the scandals that have arisen this season around rigging," he said. "It's not surprising that the show had an inside woman. But you got away with it, Lily! Why are you coming clean now?"

"I wasn't an inside woman."

"So a producer ended up on a rigged season of *Marry Me, Juliet* by accident?"

"Oh, no. It definitely wasn't an accident. And the network *thought* they had an inside woman. But if we're being honest, I was more of a saboteur."

She looked directly down the lens. "The show wanted the Dylans to get together," she said. "But who do you think was the fairy godmother helping Cece sneak out of the Convent?"

She winked. The audience cheered. It was a hesitant cheer, but a cheer nonetheless.

"Part of me stands by what I did," she said. "I was horrible to all four of them at various points on the show, but I'm genuinely very happy for Dylan JM and Cece and for Dylan G and Amanda. I know what it feels like to lose someone you love. I'm glad that's something they don't have to go through."

My heart was racing. My palms were sweating. I felt like I'd swallowed a stone, and it had got caught halfway down my throat.

"But part of me—a bigger part—regrets it," she said. "Because I'm a very selfish person, and the price I paid was far too high."

The audience murmured in disquiet.

"Tell us more about that," Z said.

"Like I said, I know what it feels like to lose someone you love," Lily said. "Eighteen months ago, I lost my husband in a car accident."

"I remember. I'm so sorry, Lily."

"It was so sudden. One day he was there, and the next he was gone, and there were so many things I never got to say to him. It was like reading a book and then finding the last three chapters were torn out, and there was no way you could ever finish the story."

It was so hard to breathe around the rock in my throat.

"It was awful," she went on, "but at least it wasn't my fault."

"Of course it wasn't," Z said, injecting some warmth into his tone. "And you've got the opportunity for a fresh start now. To find a new love for this next chapter in your life. What a way to kick off your *Wherefore Art Thou Romeo?* journey with a clear conscience. What an amazing, brave, strong heroine you're going to be."

Lily started laughing.

It wasn't just a chuckle. It was completely, utterly uncontrollable.

"You seriously think I'm going to do *Wherefore*?" she choked out, mascara beginning to run. "Really?"

Z looked the most stricken I'd ever seen him. "I—"

"Losing my husband wasn't my fault," Lily said. "But doing this show cost me the fucking love of my life, and that *was* my fault. I'm not making that mistake again."

Later, I would realise what chaos the swearing must have caused backstage. You absolutely couldn't swear on prime-time TV.

In that moment, though, I didn't even notice. There wasn't room in my brain for a single thought.

There was only her.

"I could make you a brilliant season of television." Mascara tears were streaming down her cheeks. "You could serve me up twenty handsome men, and I'd eat them for breakfast. I might even like one or two of them. Stranger things have happened."

My hands were balled into fists, the material of my pants pulled tight around my thighs as I clutched at it.

"But that's not what you want in a season of *Wherefore*." She was addressing the audience now. "You want what those four people backstage have got. Real love. And I—" she struck herself in the chest, hard, "—I've already found my person. I self-sabotaged so hard that I sabotaged him too, and I lost him, but I'm going to do whatever it takes to get him back. I'll fight. I'll grovel. Hell, I'll *beg*. I am not someone who begs, but I'll beg if I have to, and—and—and—"

She buried her face in her hands. Her shoulders shook convulsively as she sobbed.

It wasn't instinct that drew me to my feet.

I took a second and a half, and I did the calculations.

I made myself wait.

I made myself think.

I made myself choose.

And then I was running to her.

Something in my left hip crunched as I slid to my knees in front of her, but I ignored it. "Lily," I said. "Lily, Lily, Lily, hey, I'm here."

I cupped her face in my hands, my palms against her mascara-stained cheeks, stroking her cheekbones with my thumbs. "Lily."

"Murray, no," she said, voice hoarse. "I didn't—you don't—you don't—"

"Shut up," I told her, pressing one hand to the back of her head and pulling her into me.

Her arms snaked around my neck, tight, so tight, as if she could hold us together if she just held on tight enough. "I love you," she sobbed into my throat. "Don't let me go."

"I won't," I promised. "Never."

"I didn't mean for it to happen like that," Lily said later.

We were in my hotel room. It was two in the morning—given all the chaos, we hadn't been able to leave the studio until much later than planned—and we were sitting side by side on my bed, leaning back against the pillows.

It would have been so easy to fall into that bed, to kiss her and peel her clothes off and let the pillows swallow us, but we hadn't. We were both still fully dressed, me in my producer blacks, her in her designer gown. The only things we'd taken off were our shoes, and the only place we were touching were our hands, fingers brushing lightly against each other on the covers.

"I want to be clear about that," she said. "That wasn't intended to be some stunt to manipulate you into feeling sorry for me and taking me back out of pity."

"I know," I said. "If it had been, it wouldn't have worked. I'm not a fucking amateur."

That drew a smile. "No. You're not."

Her thumb brushed over my knuckles. "Thank god," she added.

I chuckled.

"I don't want to watch it back," she said. "Ever. I don't think I can stand to watch myself have that many feelings in front of that many people. How embarrassing."

"You know," I said, "you're actually very romantic, deep down."

"Take that back."

"It's true."

"I've changed my mind." She pushed herself up out of the pillows. "This was all a terrible mistake. Bye."

I grabbed her wrist and pulled her back. "You," I growled, "are not going anywhere."

"Fine, fine."

I put my arm around her. She nestled into me, resting her head on my shoulder. I rested mine on top of hers.

It was comfortable. Easy. We fit together perfectly.

"I'm right, though," I said.

"Shut up."

"I am. Only someone who's *extremely* sappy would have said the shit you did about being a fairy godmother for Dylan and Cece."

She made a disgusted noise, but she snuggled deeper into me. "I promised grovelling—" she turned her head so she could press her lips to my collarbone, "—so I'll let you have this one."

I stroked her hair. "We have to talk about that."

"About what? The grovelling?"

"No. The point-scoring."

She looked up at me.

"I don't want to compete with you, Lily," I said. "We never competed when we were partners, not really. And if we're going to be . . ."

"Partners?" She raised her eyebrows suggestively.

"—then I don't want it to be like that either. If you and I are going to work, we need to work with each other, not against each other. We need to be a team."

She leaned up and kissed me gently on the lips. "I can agree to that."

"And we're going to couple's therapy." I threaded my fingers through her hair. "I want to be with you. I'm terrible at being without you. But we clearly have some work to do on being together, if we're not going to cut ourselves to pieces on each other."

She sighed. "I'm going to hate it."

"So am I. But that probably means we need it even more."

"I know." She ran a hand over her eyes. "Ugh. Thuong's going to be so fucking smug about this."

Then she sighed again. "I wish I was as brave as you, Murray. You knew when to end things with Julia. I'm going to be carrying around this guilt about Jeff for the rest of my life. I loved him, but not like I love you. I was always going to cross the Rubicon eventually, but I owed him an ending, and I ran out of time to give it to him."

I kissed her temple. "Sometimes things are just really fucking unfair."

"Our therapist is going to have a field day with us."

She looked up at me suddenly. "We're not going to anyone we've ever had on the show. Promise me that."

"Are you kidding? Of course we're not going to anyone we've ever had on the show. We're going to a real therapist, not an Instagram therapist."

"Good. If I have to talk about my feelings, I want it to actually achieve something."

I rested my forehead against hers and closed my eyes. We still had so much farther to go, so many more things to work out, but just sitting with her, just being with her, felt so fucking *right*.

"Coming back to the thing about competing with each other, though," she said, "I'd like to propose a caveat."

I opened one eye. "Hmmm?"

"Could we, perhaps," she said, fingers tangling in the patch of chest hair above the open neck of my polo shirt, "occasionally compete in bed? Because I don't know about you, but I thought some of our little battles there were pretty hot."

"Oh, did you now?"

Gently, I pulled her hair, drawing her head back so I could press my open mouth into her neck. "I'll win."

"You keep telling yourself that." Her fingers traced a line down my shirt to my zipper.

The score was about even when we were interrupted by my stomach growling. "God damn it, Murray," Lily said, shoving me in the shoulder to push me off. "When was the last time you ate something?"

"Hey, I did all right today. I had breakfast. But then I had a bunch of meetings, and . . ."

She shook her head. "Where's the room service menu?"

I found it on the bedside table and handed it to her. "Now that you're a fancy development exec, what's your per diem like?" she asked. "Because if the network's paying, I'm going to order one of everything."

"Maybe temper that ambition a little. I'm not *that* fancy an exec."

"Fine, fine. I'll just order half, then."

"Can I ask you something?"

"Of course."

"Why are you so obsessed with feeding me?"

"Because I'm trying to fucking keep you *alive*, dipshit," she said, slapping me in the shoulder. "Do you have any idea what it would do to me if you suddenly dropped dead?"

I stared.

"Lily," I managed to say. "Lily, I—"

"No." She held a finger up. "We've had enough big

emotions for tonight. I've reached my limit. Move over. I'm going to call room service."

It didn't take long to arrive. She pulled her shoulder straps back up and I rezipped my fly and we moved over to the table to eat. "This is a new level of luxury," she said, three fries in hand. "A hotel room with a dining table in it. You really have hit the big time."

"You, however, just very publicly quit your job." I nudged her foot under the table. "Are you in the market for a new one?"

She pointed the fries at me. "No. No charity."

"It isn't charity. You know how this business works, Lily. You might not be doing *Wherefore* anymore, but if anything, what happened tonight is just going to make you a bigger star. You're going to get more offers than you'll ever be able to even look at. If you wanted to, you could make a living off spon-con alone."

She laughed. "I could, couldn't I? What a thought."

"You should take your time. You should consider your options. But I want to put one on the table. Consult for me."

She leaned back in her chair. "I'm listening."

"I'm building six shows from the ground up. With more to come. I need someone who'll tell me when I'm doing something stupid."

"Like rigging a season?"

"Precisely. Plus, consultants get to work their own hours, so if you wanted to do other things, you could. And they get paid through the fucking nose."

"Now that interests me." Lily picked up another fry.

"Because my partner is this big fancy exec, and I don't want to be his kept woman."

I rolled my eyes. She smiled and ate her fry. "Can I think about it?"

"Absolutely. Take as much time as you want."

"And can I ask you something? Something that's really been eating me up?"

"Of course."

The words came out of her in a rush. "What happened on Kumiko's season? I've been driving myself insane trying to figure out what the twist could possibly be."

"Oh!"

I told her.

Her eyebrows shot into her hairline. "No way," she breathed. "Kumiko and *Z*?"

I nodded, my mouth full of hamburger.

"Z? Our Z? Tom Zelig Z?"

I swallowed. "The very same."

"Fuck me," Lily said. "How the hell did you pull that off?"

Epilogue

Lily

Three years later

"Wait," the cashier asked me, as she put the magazine in a paper bag and handed it to me. "Aren't you Lily Fireball?"

I laughed.

My number one line of defence against getting recognised was huge dark sunglasses, but wearing them inside the airport would have been a neon sign saying I AM VAGUELY FAMOUS. Luckily, my second line of defence—just laughing at people—was usually equally effective. All it took for most people to doubt their own eyes was the suggestion that they might be being ridiculous.

I went up the escalator to the business class lounge, found a couple of quiet chairs near the window, flipped the magazine open, and started reading.

Murray joined me about half an hour later. "Hey," he said, leaning down and kissing the top of my head.

"Hey yourself." I smiled at him as he sat down opposite me, stretching his legs out in front of him. "How's Julia?"

"She's fine. She says hi." By coincidence, Julia was flying out of the same airport as us to go to a conference, so she and Murray had grabbed a quick coffee before her flight. "Is that it?"

"It sure is." I held up the magazine.

"Is it bad?"

"What do you mean, *is it bad*? It's a 40 Under 40 article. They're not exactly in the business of writing slam pieces."

"I know, but—"

Murray sighed and ran a hand through his hair. The grey streak at his temple was very pronounced these days. Every time he touched his hair it made a new, fascinating shape that I wanted to trace, fingernails scratching into his scalp.

"We've worked so hard putting this deal together," he said. "I don't want anything to jeopardise it."

"It's fine." I beckoned him with the magazine. "Look."

He came around to my side of the table and knelt beside me so we could read the article together.

#11: Lily Ong (38) and Murray O'Connell (38)

These two might not be household names—but once you see Ong's face, you'll remember who they are.

Ong is better known as Lily Fireball, the diva contestant who became a cult favourite three years ago on Dylan Jayasinghe Mellor's (#26 on this year's 40 Under 40 list) season of Marry Me, Juliet. *She then caused an enormous scandal in the reunion show, revealing that she'd been planted by the network, backing out of her contracted appearance on* Wherefore Art Thou Romeo? *and declaring her love for one of the producers.*

Since then, she and that producer—O'Connell, now her husband—have gone from strength to strength behind the scenes, developing new reality TV programming. If you've found yourself addicted to a reality TV show in the last few years, chances are Ong and O'Connell were the masterminds behind it. Ong started out consulting for O'Connell directly after Marry Me, Juliet, *but within a year had signed on as an equal partner in his development deal.*

Soon, Ong and O'Connell will be jetting off overseas to ink lucrative international franchising deals on three of their original co-developed formats. Taken individually, either would be a worthy inclusion on the 40 Under 40 list—but together, this power couple is taking over the world.

Murray sketched his fingers along my face in the photo. "You look beautiful."

"I do, don't I?" The stylists for the magazine shoot had done a great job on us. Murray was sitting at one end of a leather couch, wearing all black (designer menswear, though, rather than his old producer blacks). I was draped across both the couch and him, wearing that same spectacular yellow dress I'd walked into the Villa in, the one Thuong had designed. Neither of us were smiling, and we were both looking directly into the camera, borderline confrontationally.

I tangled my fingers in his hair so I could pull his face to mine. "You do too, though," I said loyally, pecking him on the lips.

He grinned and kissed me back, harder. "If I'm going to walk onto this flight covered in *Blood of My Enemies*," he said, kissing me again, "I'd rather commit."

I loved him so much.

I brushed my nose against his, tugging his hair a little harder. He made a growling sound in the back of his throat.

"Challenge accepted," I said.

Acknowledgments

This book nearly broke me.

I've never really thought of myself as a particularly break-able person. Physically, sure; but not mentally. This is an arrogance characteristic of a lot of workaholics, in a capital-ist culture where productivity is viewed as king. When your response to stress is not to flee or hide but to do things, do more things, do all the things, you start to assume that there is no amount of labour your metaphorical shoulders cannot bear.

I've always known I was a workaholic, but I started to realise that it might be a capital-P Problem when some edito-rial feedback on an early draft of *Not Here To Make Friends* asked some questions about the depiction of Murray's stress levels. Specifically, they asked if he had a brain tumour.

And I was mystified, because . . . that was just what working that hard felt like???

(There are, I'm sure, many inaccuracies in *Not Here To Make Friends*. I've taken many liberties with, for example,

385

reality TV production. The depiction of overwork and what it feels like, though, is entirely true to life—my life, anyway.)

This was a minor feedback point, buried in what was ultimately a larger revision: turning a draft of a book written in a single point of view (Murray's) into one with a dual point of view.

It was absolutely the right call, editorially. I can't imagine *Not Here To Make Friends* without Lily's voice in it now.

It is a difficult thing, though, switching perspectives like that. It is an even more difficult thing when a large part of the narrative hinges on the reader not knowing what this new perspective character is thinking. It is more difficult again when that perspective character is someone as slippery and evasive and clever and complicated as Lily. And when you are as overworked and exhausted as I was . . . it felt almost impossible.

Many of you reading this will know that I have a demanding full-time job on top of my writing. I'm an academic. While I study things that a lot of people consider frivolous, I'm a very serious scholar. I've taken the phrase *publish or perish* to heart throughout my career. I work *a lot*, and have done so for a very long time.

Many of you reading this will also know that the pandemic was, to put it in blunt terms, absolutely shit for people working in higher education. The government changed the rules of their funding schemes several times to specifically exclude universities. University management responded by making wave after wave of cuts. Not only did we have to shift all of our teaching and learning online; not only did we have to deal with the same stresses of the pandemic that everyone did; we were constantly, *constantly* in fear that we would be the next people cut and that we would have to battle our own colleagues in the gladiatorial ritual of the spill-and-fill (a complete affront, I might note, to the dearly held scholarly value of collegiality). I will never forget the Zoom town hall my institution had where our Vice-Chancellor announced the next wave of cuts, and then we all had to log on to a website immediately afterwards (which promptly crashed) and search for our names in the org chart to see if our jobs were safe.

My name was in the org chart. I did not have to enter the arena. I got off so much lighter than so many of my colleagues. I tricked myself into thinking I was fine. I wasn't, though. And as the work piled up higher and higher (turns out when people are cut, their work doesn't magically go away?), and then as I found out just what a difficult revision I needed to do to this book . . . I just about snapped in half.

So it's not exactly Murray and Lily's fault that writing their book nearly broke me—but also, these two experts at psychological warfare definitely did some psychological warfare on me.

Also like many other workaholics, I pride myself on being professional and shutting up and getting on with it. However, I'm confident I was an absolute *nightmare* to deal with during the process of bringing *Not Here To Make Friends* to life. Acknowledgements are traditionally thank-yous, but for this book, these are also apologies.

First and foremost, to everyone at Simon & Schuster. Cassandra di Bello talked me down from about a hundred different panic spirals and off a thousand different ledges.

I did not even remotely deserve the patience she showed me when I stubbornly dug my heels in at various points in the editorial process. Anthea Bariamis picked up right where she left off, guiding me through a very tricky period with a quickly ticking clock, with wonderful and enthusiastic support from Lizzie King. Likewise, my publicist Gabby Oberman never once stopped looking after me and looking out for me. My frustration with my own inability to get this book right must have made me wildly frustrating to work with, and I appreciate you all, more than I can ever say.

Secondly, to my brilliant agent Alex Adsett, without whom I simply would not have an authorial career. Thank you so much for everything, and I'm sorry I didn't let you know I was struggling earlier.

Sincere thank-yous also go to the other two agents at Alex Adsett Literary, Abigail Nathan and Rochelle Fernandez, who both—entirely coincidentally!—did editorial passes of this book. Your advice was invaluable and useful (especially, as it turned out, that throwaway note about Murray reading like he might have a brain tumour, without which I might not have realised what a profound hole of overwork I'd fallen into). I'd also really like to thank Lucia Nguyen, whose cultural read of the manuscript was enormously helpful in bringing Lily to life.

Thirdly, to my friends, who have known for years that I work too much, and to whom I have stubbornly refused to listen (sorry). Steph, Kate, Adele, Anna, Claire, Katie, Meg, Mel, Sonya, Rashmi, Mabel, Hannah, Monique, Maria, Amy, Jess, all of you—I love and treasure you all, and I would have snapped in half a long time ago without your love and support. I'd also like to give a shout-out to my myotherapist Natalie Holmes, who physically has been holding me together for many years, and who taught me the trick that Lily uses to help Murray with his eye-twitch.

And lastly, if you are reading this—thank you.

Every book is a labour of love. Sometimes, though, we gloss over the weight of the word *labour*.

I worked extremely hard to write this book. The beauty of being an author is that there is a clear point when the work is finally done: when there is something tangible that we can hold, a thing that did not exist before that we have created.

But it doesn't exist—and all that work means nothing—if a book isn't read. So thank you so, so much for reading *Not Here To Make Friends*, for going on this ride with Murray and Lily, and for making my work mean something.

About the Author

Jodi McAlister PhD is an author and academic from Kiama, Australia. Her academic work focuses on the history of love, sex, women and girls, popular culture, and fiction. It means that reading romance novels and watching *The Bachelor* are technically work for her. She is currently a Senior Lecturer in Writing, Literature and Culture at Deakin University in Melbourne. For more, visit jodimcalister.com.au.